EXILES FROM

A TORN PROVINCE

Exiles from a Torn Province

Copyright 2016 Barry Lees.

Cover design by Simon East.

I wish to express my gratitude and appreciation to the English and Creative Writing Department at the University of Cumbria and to Wendy for her generous help with the research for this work.   BL.

For my wife.

Also by Barry Lees and available on Kindle Books:

This City of Lies

The Governor's Man

By Sword and Feather

Wasps Among the Ivy

Track and Eliminate

The Blue, the Green and the Dead

CHAPTER ONE

On a country lane in North Yorkshire on a Monday afternoon in March, an Irishman watched another Irishman planting out onion bulbs. The man doing the planting was unaware that he was being watched although he usually felt that he was. That day, his watcher was in the driver's seat of an old, brown, Leyland van, parked in a lay-by on an elevated stretch of road. A radio, turned down low, played the number one tune in the country at the time. It was a Whitney Houston number, 'One Moment in Time,' which he found appropriate.

Across a field of thistle and dandelion and edged with low hawthorn, he observed, through binoculars, the man he had come to find. An hour earlier, when he had arrived and taken up his position, there had been four men, all of them working on the cultivation of vegetables. He had spotted the man he wanted and had waited until the other three had left and only his quarry remained. Once he was satisfied that nobody could see either of them, he reached into the back of the van and took a rifle out of an already opened case. A sound-suppressor was fitted to the rifle. The other Irishman worked busily with a trowel, only another ten bulbs to plant before he could return to the storage building and put everything away for the day. The sights on the rifle were adjusted as the gun was raised

5

and pointed out of the open window. The planting of bulbs was paused as he stood upright to stretch his back. The bullet passed through the top of his ear and continued through his skull and into his brain causing instant paralysis, and death soon after.

The rifle went back into the case and the engine of the van started up. The driver steered it along the lane to a junction notable only for the red telephone box which had not been used for some time. He turned right and accelerated past the entrance to the open prison which was to have one less prisoner to feed that evening.

CHAPTER TWO

Ten years earlier.

"There'll be girls, James, real ones with lips and eyelashes and everything."

"The way you talk, you'd think there was a race of females that has developed without the standard features of a human face, so you would. What's wrong with the girls round here? Some of them have lips."

He was by no means an expert but compared to Pedro he was a modern day Casanova.

"They might have lips but that doesn't mean they're going to let me at them. It's alright for you and your 'eyes like pools' but the rest of us have to work bloody hard to get a look in."

Pedro, real name Pete Robertson, was referring to an episode at school when he and James had been fifteen. During a rain-affected lunch break in the assembly hall, a huddle of giggling girls had written, with all of the intimacy of a committee set a task without purpose or limit, a note intended as a Valentine's Day secret message. Its content rambled on in at least six different writing styles and colours, some adorned with circles over the 'I's and in one case, a tiny heart. The only memorable line in its largely inane text was; your eyes are like moonlit pools. Much mirth had been derived from that description and although diluted by post-school life, it remained in the vocabulary of James's former school friends.

Although a few girls found the young James Coleman appealing, most of their attention was lost on him. He was driven by his studies, basketball and more studying. Being top of the class should have made James a pin up for the clever girls but he wasn't interested. The red hair and pale complexion were far from the looks of a matinee idol, but he had a slim and handsome face, usually garnished with an expression of seriousness and intensity. As most teenagers did, James Coleman found a look and accompanying identity that he felt comfortable with, although he was past his teens when it happened.

The University had played host to many well-known musical stars. It was considered to be daring and edgy for a pop group to cross the water to perform in Belfast. If that decision was made, concert promoters usually took the relatively safe option of the Student's Union bar where a less confrontational clientele could be found. There would be students from other parts of the world and most of them could be relied upon to conduct themselves in a reasonably restrained manner. Having insufficient money to buy much alcoholic drink, the events were loud yet well conducted. Expression was restricted to a show of approval, or disapproval, of the entertainment talents of the performer or performers. The Student's Union decision makers had the job of booking acts and did so by committee, based on the intellectual, cultural, and less importantly, musical appeal of the acts.

It was rarely a roaring success. Many of the turns were out of date or out of touch for an audience mainly comprising educated people aged between eighteen and twenty-two. Faded glam rockers, struggling to fit into their extravagant stage costumes, could find themselves playing to a half-empty house whilst some exponents of regional folk music could expect even lower attendances. Soft and melodic soul singers, who appealed unashamedly to female audiences, generated good business. The young women who favoured that style of music, could predictably be pursued by equal numbers of young men. They were only there to meet girls and paid little notice of the music. Comedians were, all too frequently, miss and greater miss. Some of the old-fashioned, bow-tie wearing, sexist, racist, or both, comics managed to sell tickets in reasonable numbers, largely to students who had been exposed to their humour by the T.V. and radio preferences of their parents. Some felt an affinity to them as a result. Jokes about Irishmen in pubs were adapted to be about Scotsmen, Frenchmen or even Englishmen in pubs and the effect was usually accomplished by appealing to the more tribal elements of the province. Divisions within were taboo subjects for such places.

All that changed when the Punk revolution swept the pop music world. It gave young people a credible and exciting musical and cultural alternative to the cheesy, stage-managed, well-groomed performers of the sixties and early seventies. It had a raw energy, high volume, political undertones and, more importantly for the generation most acutely affected, it appealed to young men as well as young women.

Unsophisticated yet energetic leaping around to music became known as pogoing and could be done in large numbers at concerts in relative safety, although it may have appeared to an onlooker as a mass attempt to undermine the foundations of the building. The angry yet anti-violence brand of socialism that Punk professed, struck a chord with the disaffected urban youth, as it was supposed to do. It also appealed to the more culturally aware, the young intellectuals who had been looking for a banner to wave to express their dissatisfaction with how old and middle-aged people had been running things. Astute musicianship could be forfeited in favour of some basic three chord riffs, boosted by a turned-up bass and poured forth at breakneck speed to an easily satisfied audience. Student's Union bars were ideal venues for Punk bands to perform in. The music was made by the young for the young and the older generation didn't like that at all. A clear recipe for success.

It was at one such concert in the S.U. bar at Belfast University that the twenty-one-year-old undergraduate James Coleman found what he had been missing. A four piece group, no older than himself, took to the painted, black stack of packing crates that served as a stage in the corner of the concert room of the S. U. They let rip with a largely lyricless barrage of noise to a highly appreciative audience of students, all bouncing in time to the relentless drum beat and floor-shaking bass guitar. The lead vocalist was six feet two and weighed no more than ten stones. He wore torn and dirty blue jeans with a string vest under a motorcycle jacket that was several sizes too big for him. His face was white with greasepaint and his hair was jet black and teased up into spikes, giving him a look that resembled a cartoon hedgehog. His voice was a rasping rejection of all that had taken place before. His habit of letting go of his guitar so that he could grab the microphone stand as though strangling it, served to demonstrate that his playing of the instrument was entirely unnecessary. The crowd did not care at all.

James and his friends had missed the introduction. They had entered when they felt it was fashionably appropriate to do so, after all, it had long been considered uncool to arrive anywhere too early. The opening set had whipped up an energetic reaction from the assembly who cheered and appealed for more when the band departed the stage. They were replaced by an equally thin, yet slightly older man in a loose-fitting suit jacket and tight-fitting black jeans. He too sported a white face and black spiked hair but his defining visual statement was a pair of sunglasses of the Roy Orbison mould. He adopted a stance of undiluted, snarling arrogance that said, 'You are lucky to have me here.'

He spoke in a harsh, guttural manner with an urban Northern England dialect. His lips touched the microphone as he embarked on a verbal exercise in comic poetry that took in heavy satire and disillusionment with the contemporary establishment. With shrewd metric skill, he pointed out some of the illogical follies of modern life and after some initial protests against this non-musical interloping, he commanded the attention of the house and brought forth roars of laughter and approval throughout. The students had found a new form of live comedy that carried the same post-modernist rejections as the music had done. This was comedy for their age and it was cleverly packaged as poetry which made it intellectually acceptable too. James soaked it up and decided that night that his life had to move on.

The next day he had acquired all he needed to transform himself. Black hair dye, Vaseline (also for the hair) an ancient and dank smelling black leather jacket, that did not fit him, from a charity shop and the rebirth of a pair of sunglasses that had been the property of a lodger who had vacated the Coleman house two years before, leaving the outdated and previously unstylish sunglasses behind. His own deathly pale complexion alleviated the need for greasepaint on his face. The stark contrast of black and white was achieved by the hair dye alone.

His friends and neighbours mocked, laughed and stared for a few days but that was to be expected of people who were constrained by outdated and restrictive dogma, he thought. What did surprise him was the increased circle of friends he was gathering at the University. He had previously kept to a small yet like-minded set but, he was joined at break times and in the library and bar by others who shared his appreciation of all things Punk.

Pedro liked some of the music but not enough to buy any of the records. Poetry was lost on him, even that which was aimed at his age group and contained daring humour. He remained unaware of the notable aficionados of the movement which came to light when he innocently asked James.

"Why are they calling you Sid? Have you been telling people your name's Sid?"

James laughed aloud.

"I don't get it," continued Pedro, "what's so funny?"

"I didn't know anybody was calling me that but it sounds cool, don't you think? To be named after somebody."

Pedro tried to work it out for himself because asking James was not getting him anywhere. He suggested the only well-known Sid he could think of.

"Sid James?"

James stopped laughing and looked incredulously at him.

"Sid James? Sid bloody James? What kind of eejit are you? Why would anybody liken me to Sid James?"

Pedro tried to salvage some dignity with his own brand of logic.

"Your name is James, right? and people are calling you Sid. It's a perfectly logical thing to assume."

"Logical to you and you alone, maybe. If I'm being called Sid, then it must be to do with Sid Vicious of the Sex Pistols."

Pedro had the expression of a man who had spun a two-headed coin only to hear somebody else call heads.

"Oh!" he said, accepting his mistake and confirming to himself how out of touch he was with such matters.

CHAPTER THREE

Lizzie was restless. Life as a college student was not as full as it had been when she was studying for her O levels at school. The pace of study was more sedate, which did not suit her. She wanted more to do and the college tutor was not setting enough of a challenge. Instead she tried to initiate her own programme of reading. Staying in her bedroom for days on end, she was unaware that her parents and friends were worried about her.

"Come on Lizzie," said her father with light-hearted concern, "you can have too much of a good thing, you know."

"What do you mean Daddy?" she said, genuinely mystified as to his message.

"I mean that all work and no play makes Elizabeth Mary Cullen pale and unhealthy."

"Are you saying I'm pale and unhealthy?" she said, offended.

"I'm saying that you will be if you don't get some fresh air and exercise. I admire your commitment to your studies but there's more to life, my girl. There's a balance to achieve and you're not managing it."

"I can hardly go jogging round the city now can I?" she appealed.

"If I was younger and fitter I'd come with you Lizzie."

"I know you would Daddy. I'll get out and breathe a bit more if it will make you happy."

"It will." He leaned forward and kissed her on the top of her head.

As she heard his footsteps descending the stairs, she tried to read, but her heart was no longer in it. Lizzie put down her book on the dressing table and instead flicked through the edition of Look In magazine that she had not found time to read that week. Amid the plethora of carefully-posed pop stars and teenager-centred journals she spotted an article on Souxsie and the Banshees. It was adorned with several glossy photographs. The punk queen posed in black attire, part wicked witch and part vampiress, with a volcanic eruption of dyed black hair, alabaster skin and extravagant black eye make-up, intended, and succeeding, to shock all who saw her. A declaration of non-conformism reserved for the young and troubling for everyone else.

This was not the first time she had noticed that the new strain of empowered female pop stars had awoken something in her. A memorable performance on television by Toyah had found a place in Lizzie's imagination too. No longer at school and having nearly completed college, Lizzie was unfettered by previously compulsory codes relating to the acceptability of the appearance of those in education. Awaiting her results, she had shown potential for progression to University, where free self-expression was the norm. It was time she tried out this new found freedom. She took a small pot of black mascara, an eyebrow pencil, eye-shadow and a narrow make-up brush and perched in front of her dressing-table mirror.

15

"Pale and unhealthy is it Daddy?" she said aloud but to herself. "We'll see about that."

She set to work on her facial transformation. Black swathes swept across her eye sockets and curved upwards to a point above her temples. Eyelashes and eyebrows were treated to excessive amounts of what was intended to have been used sparingly. After thirty minutes of artistic application, she went down the stairs to the lounge to show her parents the result of her experiment.

"What on earth have you done to yourself Lizzie?" said Jennifer peering over her knitting and her spectacles.

"Thanks for that Mammy. What do you think Daddy?"

Arnie put down his newspaper and gave his daughter a long stare.

"I think Ming the Merciless has been in a fight and lost. I take it you still have two eyes in there somewhere and you can see out with them?"

"Well I think I look pretty cool," she declared. "I'm going out like this tomorrow."

"Surely not," said her mother.

"You'd better take something with your name on it, girl. Nobody will believe it's you by just looking."

"I'm doing it and that's that," she said and she swept out of the lounge and back up to her room.

Arnie and Jennifer looked at each other.

"She can't leave the house looking like that Arnie, surely not."

16

"Ah, she's a young woman now love, she's just doing things her own way. It's only a bit of face paint anyway. She'll grow out of it I expect."

Lizzie pulled the elastic tie from her long, light brown hair, shaking that dense mane loose and went to the window to peer out into the dusk. The street beyond the neatly trimmed privet hedge was devoid of animated life until a small, grey van chugged along slowly. It slowed almost to a stop as it passed the Cullen home. There were two figures in the front seats but she couldn't see their faces. The van changed gear and revved itself away to the end of the street. She wondered what was so interesting about her house.

Her family had lived there for six years, ever since Arnie Cullen had been promoted to the rank of Superintendent in the Royal Ulster Constabulary. Living in a house the family did not own, nor had any rights on, was a normal aspect of life for a policeman and his family. A new posting meant a new home, a new neighbourhood and for Elizabeth a new school and the forging of new relationships. This house was bigger, as should befit the elevated status of a senior officer. But for Lizzie, the only child of Arnold and Jennifer Cullen, it had meant a slightly smaller bedroom and a disproportionate mountain of adjustment to undertake.

CHAPTER FOUR

Arnold Worsley Cullen was born in Lurgan in 1922. He had been a robust and energetic kid who played football and cricket in all weathers. Sometimes after the sun had set. He believed that Northern Ireland was merely the platform from which to launch his plan to travel the world. He wanted to play football against people from every country mentioned in his father's atlas.

The influence of the movies dictated that the United States was, for young Arnie, the true land of opportunity. His ticket to ride was presented to him by the War Office, following his application to volunteer to serve. The British Army became his travel agent and America was not on the itinerary.

Posted to North Africa with the Eighth Army, Cullen suffered with heatstroke within a week of arriving there. Sick and immobile for the first time in his life, he experienced embarrassment and frustration at his condition. Once recovered and accustomed to the harsh desert environment, he knuckled down and tried hard to make up for the poor first impression he had made with his battalion. Volunteering to do more than he had to resulted in him being given more to do and the young Cullen rose to each challenge. Battlefield casualties resulted in some promotions in the field and Corporal Cullen began to cultivate a career in uniform. The success of the Africa campaign was followed by a more frustrating and uncelebrated

18

campaign through Italy. By V.E. Day, Cullen was a Sergeant and entrusted to lead a platoon of soldiers in their revised purpose of overseeing the transition of war into peace in Europe.

Cullen was demobbed in 1948. He went to Manchester where he found work in a factory making parts for bicycles but although he felt that the Salford area was a home from home for an Ulsterman, he found the work monotonous and unrewarding.

At a dance at the Masonic Hall, he met Jennifer Poole. He fancied her instantly as she did him, but she was smart enough to play hard to get, which made him fancy her more. Several dances and afternoon walks on riverbanks later, they spent every available evening together, usually culminating with kissing on her parents' doorstep and the long, yet justified, walk back to the digs for Arnie. They were married in Ordsall Parish Church on a cloudy but warm morning in September 1949.

Although he held no rosy view of the horrors of war, he did miss the comradeship of being a part of a uniformed body of men with a combined purpose. He joined the Royal Ulster Constabulary and patrolled a beat near to the docks. Being a policeman in the 1950s was initially nothing like being a soldier. The public knew their constables by name and reputations were earned by integrity, compassion, fairness, vigilance, doggedness and above all, fear. Any police officer who failed to instil the required degree of physicality into their methods of control in the neighbourhoods they policed did not last very long. The added difficulty of a police force that was predominantly Protestant trying to impartially keep order in a fiercely divided country, made the job even harder. Only the hardest of men could be relied upon to do it.

Parenthood made him rationalise how best to provide for his family. Seeking to better himself, he studied for and passed promotion exams and after twelve years he was promoted to Sergeant. He took responsibility for a team of constables patrolling the Falls Road. Burning missiles, mass rioting and sectarian beatings and killings required Cullen's wartime experiences to be revisited in the guise of a civilian force. The hierarchy of the Constabulary looked to those in their ranks who were prepared to fight fire with fire in order to contain the sporadic outbreaks of sectarian violence. Cullen was an Inspector for only eighteen months then he was made Chief Inspector, one week before the deployment of British soldiers on the streets of Northern Ireland.

On Cullen's fiftieth birthday he was promoted to Superintendent. The role of a police officer in Belfast had changed during his tenure. He carried out a dual role of commanding a police sub-division and liaising with the officers of the British Army. Neither party could operate without the support of the other. It was not how Arnie Cullen had perceived his role to be and from 1972 onwards he had harboured secret desires to retire and put it all behind him. When his clever daughter went off to University, he and his wife could drive across America in a VW Dormobile. He didn't do anything to prepare for it, but he thought about it a lot, particularly when he felt that his job had become impossible.

*

The brake lights on the rear of the van came on momentarily then went off again as it turned onto Mount Avenue and out of sight. The passenger switched on the interior light and took out a small, buff notebook with a narrow pencil in its spine. He opened it to a page that already said;

Cullen. 21, Pine Avenue, Lodale.

He touched the tip of the pencil on his tongue and wrote;

Brown Morris Marina THZ 6777. Metal gate left open. 4 foot hedges front and sides.

"Did you get what you wanted?" said the driver without appearing to take his eyes off the road.

The passenger put the pencil in the notebook and the notebook into his inner pocket before answering.

"I have, for the moment."

"Well switch off the light. We don't want to draw attention to ourselves. There's a time and a place, don't you know?"

"I know," said the passenger leaning forward to put out the light, "and we'll be ready when that time comes."

The van headed to the lock-up where it was kept when not needed. The two occupants locked it and applied two padlocks to the garage door before walking across the untendered grass bank and into the tenement block. Concrete and paint-peeled metal held together the neighbourhood in the sky, as the planners had intended it. Neglect, decay and underfunding had altered the plan.

Negotiating the rancid-smelling stairwell to the first floor, they lingered on the open landing to look for prying eyes. Certain that they had not been followed, they carried on to the third floor and across to the stairwell at the opposite end of the building before ascending another floor to their appointed rendezvous.

Once past the agreed identification ritual of a musical knock, a pause then a cough. The door was unbolted and the two were ushered inside, along the corridor and into what had been a bedroom but was no longer put to that use. A single angle-lamp lit the room from a small table in a corner. It left the ceiling and upper walls in darkness but allowed sufficient light for those seated to see each other. A man in his mid-50s sat in an armchair smoking a cigarette. His ruddy, weathered face bore no expression, giving away nothing of his thoughts. Three men stood against the wall behind the armchair, only their trouser legs could be seen. A two-seater settee of indeterminate age was in the centre of the room. The two visitors stepped forward and sat only when the man in the armchair nodded his invitation for them to do so.

"Well?" he snapped.

The man who had been the passenger in the van took out his notebook and started talking.

"Cullen's house at Lodale, semi-detached, three bedrooms – "

"I'm not fucking buying it, get to the point. Is it easy to approach? Who else lives there?"

The young man swallowed his embarrassment and pressed on nervously.

"There are four-foot high fences surrounding it. The double gate is closed but not locked. His wife and teenage daughter live there. The kid goes to the sixth form college. She has school friends round sometimes. The neighbours, women, call to see his Missus sometimes too, mainly at the weekends. There are two possible methods. One is from a vehicle, a high-sided vehicle, parked across the street. The other

would be on a knock, riskier 'cause it's right up close
but its less likely to miss."

CHAPTER FIVE

For Darry McTandlyn, compassion and compromise were for the weak and anyone who showed either characteristic became his prey. Even when he smiled or laughed it was inevitably going to end aggressively toward somebody. As a boy he had fought with anyone, taking little account of how much bigger they may have been. When the inevitable beatings came he seemed unaware of the harm he could sustain. True happiness for him appeared, to his neighbourhood, to be allowing larger boys to pummel him near to and sometimes beyond the line of unconsciousness. Expelled from school and frequently placed in local authority care, he had lived an almost feral existence, answering to nobody and making his life up as it went along.

A spell of borstal training imposed by Belfast City Magistrates Juvenile Court gave McTandlyn a formal structure that he had no choice but to adhere to. Not the routine prescribed by the prison service of slopping out, meal, cell, work detail, cell, meal, cell search, visit, meal, association and finally, lights out. The structure that gave purpose to McTandlyn's life was the pecking order among the young convicts. The inmates who held unwritten power over the rest called the shots on every issue. This hierarchy was underpinned with violence, or the threat of violence, and for a kid who willingly involved himself in violence every day of his life, it was like reaching the promised land. After enduring a kicking, resulting in damaged ribs and a hairline fracture of the skull and inflicted simply to demonstrate who was the boss, he was recruited as an enforcer for those at the top of that food chain. He could be trusted to inflict whatever degree of violence his leaders had decided upon and further relied upon to keep his mouth shut when the inevitable staff enquiries were carried out.

That institution was segregated, keeping the Catholics and Protestants apart within the same walls. When the young McTandlyn was restored to the community, he sought out the pecking order he had lived by whilst inside and he became aware that there was a similar structure, built on acrimony between political and religious communities. Again he found his place in that sectarian divide. Low level correction of Protestant trespassers, who had caused offence by their presence in a Catholic area, was administered by the young foot-soldiers and in that role McTandlyn excelled, although he did require some corrective action from his own side in order to help him remember who was in charge.

During the parade season he was tasked with marshalling the chaos and ensuring that sufficient missiles were discreetly positioned. He developed a skill of intelligence gathering, the results of which were passed up the chain of seniority and digested by those who held more ambitious ideas. By the time he was twenty years old he was fully enlisted in the covert and illegal organisation that was the Irish Republican Army.

CHAPTER SIX

At the age of twenty-three, Ken Hoggard experienced something of an epiphany. It was not his first. He had known since he was thirteen that he was somewhat different from his peers. They had realised before he did. This difference manifested itself in several ways. There was the high team-ethic but lack of competitive edge in sports, the generosity of spirit that made him show kindness to everyone regardless of whether they had done anything to deserve it and an appreciation of all things beautiful. Even if the world thought something to be ugly, it was beautiful in Ken's eyes. It was not until he turned eighteen that he gave that difference a name. He was gay.

The absence of a steady girlfriend throughout his University years was explained away by his family and friends as a side-effect of the high level of dedication and commitment he had displayed in his studies and extra-curricular good deeds. He was not the only celibate in his peer group. Repeatedly referred to, and with increasing irony by his school and college tutors, as a 'Straight A' student, Ken had volunteered as a porter at a cancer hospital, single-handedly produced a newsletter to aid the disadvantaged of his home city of Toronto and negotiated the use of a disused furniture store as a youth centre for all. All of this fell flat when the recently graduated Ken alluded to a fellow volunteer that his love for his fellow man was twofold.

He had never had any intimate relationship with anyone, but he was no longer welcomed by the charities, churches and community-minded donors he had previously charmed into working together for the benefit of those in need. Even many of the youngsters he had worked so hard for showed him that there were limits to the extent of their gratitude. His widowed father could not come to terms with Ken's life-choice, leaving Ken friendless in a place where he had felt such warmth.

Ken's religious affiliations diminished but he had never been particularly devout. His view of the world, his energy and his burgeoning optimism remained intact and pushed him to find a fresh avenue in which to express them. His old college tutor made a suggestion that enthused Ken. Realising that his corner of Toronto would no longer welcome and accommodate him, he introduced Ken to the work of the Combined Universities of Canada Overseas Service.

In its many decades of operating, CUCOS had arranged placements for students at Canadian Universities to volunteer for one year in under-developed countries across the world. Although Ken had officially left his alma mater, he had left such good will that the offer of the opportunity was agreed upon by the organisation's entire governing panel. This decision coincided with a new initiative on the CUCOS agenda. Rather than send their students to remote communities in Africa and beyond, tasking them to dig wells and inoculate villagers, there emerged an initiative to deploy the bright and enthusiastic young minds of Canadian Academia in more cerebral endeavours. Locations were identified which required CUCOS volunteers to demonstrate their skills in communication, tact and diplomacy. To bring together divided communities and hold the olive branch from an impartial standpoint for others to reach out and take. It was a bold plan but it was the way forward for CUCOS. It was the way forward for Ken too.

He was selected to be the first CUCOS overseas worker to be sent off to Belfast.

Ken was provided with accommodation at the home of a friend of a friend in Toronto. It was the granny flat of a relative who had died and the flat was lying empty. A brief period of homesickness was cured by Ken's optimism, work-ethic and, when alone, his passion for Victorian literature. He also read the CUCOS briefing document, pointing out the dos and don'ts of life in Northern Ireland as the academics of Canada had understood them to be. He went to every youth centre, church hall, college social room, University bar and music venue. He also introduced himself to the police who viewed him with some suspicion, as police officers are inclined to do.

A letter of introduction from the University of Toronto allowed him access to University libraries and social venues on campus. Ken acted upon most of the advice he was offered and took every opportunity to research the history of conflict in the province. He marvelled at the wall murals which adorned the buildings and tried to appreciate what drove the citizens to express such pride and anger in their art.

It was when Ken observed his first march that he realised the extent of the divisions between the communities. From a safe distance, he watched stern-faced marchers, adorned in colours denoting battles of centuries before and those lost in such conflicts. He also witnessed the fierce, shouting fury of those whose neighbourhoods played host to the marching routes. Young people, who had been more strongly influenced by their parents and grandparents than by history books and the teachings of their churches, carried the hatred on and preserved it for future generations.

Ken was acutely aware that he had been sent to Belfast as an initiator, to lay the turf for potential future visitors to facilitate healing in the torn estates of the city. His actions could be the beginning of an initiative for peace among the youth of Belfast, or he could fail and return to Canada as the only CUCOS volunteer ever to visit the damaged city. Alone, he was not likely to change anything substantially, but he could achieve something on a small scale. From little acorns mighty oaks will grow. This became one of the little mantras with which he focussed himself when motivational questions arose.

Ken noticed that there were parts of the city where the visible signs of division were prevalent, yet in other areas there were no such indications. Two people could pass in the street without either knowing what faith or politics the other lived by. An accidental exchange between strangers, such as bumping into each other, trying to enter a shop doorway at the same moment or struggling with shopping bags frequently resulted in gestures of kindness and concern. Ken thought long and hard about this. He came up with a simple conclusion. If he was to get the young people of Belfast to talk to each other, it had to take place in an area that did not bear the insignia of sectarianism. He also had to create an environment whereby the topic of one's origins and affiliations did not arise.

Remembering his old furniture store coup back in Toronto, Ken sought a venue which fitted the requirements. Within walking distance of his accommodation, he was unable to find any suitable place. Any room or facility large enough was either already in use or controlled by one side of the divide or the other. To look further afield, Ken borrowed a bicycle from his host and took off on a cloudy but fresh morning to find a place. Within the city there was little to stir his interest. He progressed out across the residential sprawls of blocks of flats and council houses, past industrial estates in varying degrees of under-investment, beyond the towering cranes of the docks and the shipyards, then he kept going out on the Bangor Road and eventually into the greenery of the countryside.

A brief rain-shower failed to dampen Ken's spirits. He found the contrasting environment charming and he stayed out far longer than he had intended to. Narrow lanes and ripe green hedgerows in need of cutting, birdsong and butterflies and a warm breeze, the combination of which he had not experienced back home, all combined to fill Ken's heart. He wondered at the difference in emotion this place evoked to that of the shouting and hatred he had witnessed in the city. There was none of the territorial symbolism that seemed to be everywhere in Belfast, no flags or murals, no painted kerbstones. At the end of a narrow lane around a pristine golf course he cast his eyes on a tiny, deserted sandy beach. A plain wooden sign informed Ken that he had reached Helen's Bay. He was mesmerised. The wide expanse, the lazy lapping waterline, the solitude, but most of all he felt how peaceful it was. He placed the bicycle against a larch gate and walked along the shore, greedily inhaling the damp air. He felt taller, at one with the world.

Having lost all sense of time and distance, he was reminded of the modern world by the distant peal of a church bell. He set off with a strong will to return and enjoy this place again. Mentally noting the road signs and memorable features and junctions, he rode back toward the city. As he did, an idea hatched in his mind, an idea which would solve a problem whilst allowing his return to the beach. He would organise a trip and persuade as many young people as he could to come out to Helen's Bay and share the wonderful feelings from which he was still tingling.

Publicity could be achieved by a poster campaign. Printing would mean calling on the good will of those who could provide such facilities and if he couldn't get that, he would write them out himself. Transport was another consideration, how to get people from the city to the bay and back. A coach would be prohibitively expensive and he had no budget for such things. It had to be accessible for people with little or no money. It dawned on Ken that it had cost him nothing to visit the bay. The trip would be billed as a cycle ride. Anybody who did not have a bike could borrow one as he had done. It was beginning to take shape in his mind.

What took longer to address was the method of engaging young people across the sectarian divide. If it was perceived by one side as favouring the other, it would achieve nothing. He hit on the idea of imposing a single rule, easily observed and aimed at eliminating the one issue of identity that would inevitably create a social barrier. Nobody must say who they were or where they came from. That way, people could converse and interact without the prejudice of sectarianism.

In his bedroom at a small desk, Ken drafted and redrafted until he was happy with his poster. It seemed to Ken to be the easiest way to get his message out to the young people, who he believed held the key to the peace in Belfast and become a model for the world.

It was a simple, black letters on a white background with a nice neat border, design on white foolscap. There were twenty-five made on a Roneo printing skin supplied by the college print shop which had become his unofficial headquarters. It read,

A cycle ride for peace

11am 15th of May

Setting off from Candle Park Gates

Are you aged 18 to 22?

No names and no talk of where you are from.

Meet people, talk and listen.

Reluctant as he was to impose restrictions, Ken had set a minimum age for the trip to avoid those participating requiring parental consent and risking parental interference with all of its cultural influences. He personally visited all of the places he believed could display his posters, without people asking awkward questions as to his motives and affiliations. Once the posters were posted, all Ken could do was wait and hope.

CHAPTER SEVEN

The boy in a blue, nylon anorak, whizzed along the flagged walkway on his adult-sized, gleaming, new bike, narrowly missing the feet of the University campus security guard. The bike had five gears and he was determined to use as many of them as he could, as often as he could.

"Stop there!" called the guard, fully expecting the teenager to ignore his demand and ride off as though he had heard nothing.

To his surprise, the boy applied the brakes, turned in a wide arc and slowly rode toward him. The security guard, who was in his late 50s and of questionable physical health, anticipated some confrontation and braced himself to be able to deal with such an exchange within his limited capabilities. The lad was clearly trespassing which gave the security guard the upper hand and he did have his walkie-talkie which could be used to summon help from colleagues. Usually, he had found that the threat of calling for help over the radio carried sufficient menace for most juvenile delinquents to choose to leave. Occasionally, he came across a tough-nut who wanted to challenge his authority, prematurely claiming the position of strength through aggression so prevalent in the adult Ulster male.

The boy stopped and pulled down his hood. He smiled in a manner that not only diffused any perceived confrontation but invited conversation.

33

"Hiya!" he said, regaining his breath from cycling at speed, "Sorry, I nearly knocked into you then."

The security guard tried to rationalise whether the lad was genuine or playing games with him. Eventually, he erred on the side of formality.

"You should watch where you're going lad. You could cause injuries to people, you know. What're you doing on here anyway? You're not a student, not at your age."

"No, but my brother is. He lives here. I've come to see him."

"What's your brother's name?" asked the guard, who was highly unlikely to know the names of many of the students but was merely testing the story of the young intruder.

"James Patrick Coleman," said the boy with confidence and an open and non-threatening manner which served to put the guard at increased ease each time he spoke.

"And who are you, lad?" he asked.

"Philip Magnus Coleman," announced the boy, believing that full names were appropriate when addressing any authority figure. "My brother lives in that building over there." He pointed to a beige, brick structure of four floors some hundred yards away through an avenue of willow trees. "He won't be there now," he explained, "He'll be in there, studying."

Philip pointed to the main library building, a slate-grey edifice of Norman-arched windows and low, green-painted, metal railed balconies rising up to a fifth floor of castle-turrets that dated back nearly ten years.

The guard was finally convinced that Philip was genuine. He knew that people visited students on campus all the time and for many different reasons. A member of a student's family had as strong a claim on being there as anybody.

"Alright," he declared. "but walk with your bike on here, too many pedestrians for racing bikes, eh?"

"Okay!" said Philip and he swung a leg off the bike and walked with it to the cycle rack outside the main entrance to the library building.

He entered the building unchallenged by staff or students and ascended the stairs to the reference section and through a glass panelled double door beneath a sign saying Political Studies. He passed row after row of book shelves, each stretching from the ground to top shelves that required a stepped stool to access. In the middle of the room was a clearing which was filled with individual desks and chairs, assembled in six huddles of eight desks each. There were five people all sitting silently and crouched over reading matter. Philip was about to give up and go to the accommodation block to find James, but he was stopped by the barely audible sound of a voice.

"Phil!"

Philip looked around and recognised nobody. Perhaps he heard it wrongly. He turned again to go.

"Phil!" came the voice again, slightly louder and risking the disapproval of the assembled scholars.

Philip saw James with his head raised above the others. He did not recognise him. He had only seen him two weeks previously and James had his hair to shoulder-length and his natural shade of light auburn. To Philip, James looked like Alice Cooper without the mascara. The out-sized motorcycle jacket added to the mirth. He hurried to James' desk and pulled up a chair.

"What happen to you?" he said trying hard not to laugh. "Have you been on fire or something?"

James grabbed Philip by the neck and jovially rubbed a fist into his ear.

"Cheeky little sod. I'm having a new look," he explained.

"What's it called, Dracula on a Kawasaki?"

"If you like." He allowed his brother his moment of amusement. "Anyway, what do you want? I'm a very busy and important post-graduate student now, so I am."

"Nothin'," said Phil, not really meaning it. James had a feeling he knew what was on Philip's mind.

"How's Dad?" he asked, getting straight to the point.

"Well . . . he's alright most of the time," began Philip as his eyes wandered around the table and nearby bookshelves. "When he's had his pill he's better, but it's hard for Mam. She follows him about. It's like she's waiting for him to have an 'episode' as she calls it."

"What does she mean, an 'episode' Phil?"

"He can't breathe sometimes and he gets pain in his chest. He holds himself like this."

Philip clutched his own chest with crossed arms and pulled a contorted face. "He's okay after a few minutes, but it's scary when it happens."

James considered the dynamics of his family home. It had always been the centre of their little universe and after he had moved to the other side of the city and his visits there had become less frequent, he thought that things would continue that way ad infinitum. His father Magnus had been a steel welder in the building trade until his health had prevented him from working. He was a big man whose presence had been enough to command respect from his family and his neighbourhood. He was a proud Catholic and he held his own views on the Republican movement. He did not involve himself in politics and he believed that those who engage in political violence did so because they lacked the ability to think and rationalise. Magnus believed that the future of Northern Ireland lay in negotiation and he lent his unspoken support to those who he believed were capable of achieving that.

If Magnus was in a weakened condition and their mother Clare worried and anxious, that left Philip to be the stabilising presence in the house. That was a big responsibility for a boy of fifteen.

"Shall I come up on the bus tonight?" he suggested. Philip looked relieved.

"Yeah, that'd be cool."

James considered the time and suggested,

"Have you had any dinner?" Philip shook his head and grinned in anticipation. "I could maybe stretch to a bag of chips. Come on."

He put away the books he had been reading and repacked his papers in a bag. He was proud of Philip. He had done his best to support his parents in ways that James had never had to do. Riding his bike to the University to speak to him about it showed care and initiative. In the troubled and tense climate that affected everybody in their tiny country, James had chosen to immerse himself in the safer and less-challenging world of study, exploring theories and the words of luminaries past rather than try to deal with the very real issues of the present.

They descended the concrete stairs to the ground-floor foyer and were about to step outside when James noticed a poster on the public notice board. It was for the cycle ride event that was to take place the following weekend. Pedro had been so enthusiastic about it. The notion was beginning to appeal. Phil saw that he had been distracted and he came over to the notice board to see what it was that was holding up the offer of chips. He read the poster and leapt at the chance to contribute.

"Are you going on it?" he asked.

"Erm, I don't know," said James in a state of lethargic indecision.

"You can borrow my bike," offered Philip. "It's full size and it's got lights."

"I might. I've got no excuse not to now, right enough." He accepted the inevitable. "I'll come for the bike on Saturday, if you're not using it."

"No, I won't need it. Now if you don't mind, I'm hungr

CHAPTER EIGHT

Ken luxuriated in the warm breeze, glorious sunshine and a growing assembly of young people on bicycles heralded the culmination of his preparative efforts and the start of Ken's Ride for Peace. Ken was hopping from one foot to the other at the main gate entrance to Candle Park.

'Perfect!' he thought as he marvelled through squinting eyes at the clear blue sky.

Twenty-seven people turned up, each with a bicycle in working order. There were ten girls including Lizzie Cullen and her friends Carol Jones, Ann Clough and Sheena King. Among the seventeen boys were James and Pedro. It was, unusually appropriate for James' sunglasses to be worn. Ken wore a bright yellow baseball cap bearing the logo of a Canadian ice hockey team he had heard of but never seen. He took out a referee's whistle to gain everybody's attention. After a brief road safety announcement, of which few took any notice, Ken offered the use of puncture repair equipment and spare inner tubes if required. He mentioned the three scheduled stops he intended to make, each containing a feature such as a public toilet. A village hall was also mentioned. His tone altered when he reminded everyone of the only rule in place for this event.

"Now, coming here from Canada, I don't know anybody but that doesn't matter to me. I've just met a whole lot of people I like and it feels pretty good. I know how this beautiful city can be. I have had a great welcome here from everybody I've met and we can do that for each other here today. I ask you not to mention your family names or where in the city you come from. Just keep an open mind and enjoy the sunshine. Try to stay in a group and look out for each other, okay?"

A stifled murmur of acknowledgement was drowned out by the sounds of positional adjustments of bicycles, the tings of cycle bells and high-spirits. Ken had to shout over the noise and passing traffic.

"Listen up everyone, I will take the front, look out for the hat." He pointed to his headwear quite unnecessarily. It was difficult to assess James' age but Ken spotted that Pedro was probably the oldest, he therefore entrusted him with the role of rear marker. "Can you take the back for the first part, huh buddy?"

"Er, alright," answered Pedro, effectively placing James at the rear with him.

"Well played Pedro," said James in disappointment, "There are a load of girls up there and we are stuck down here. Have you forgotten why we came here?"

"It'll be alright," assured Pedro. "We can't see any of them from in front, can we?"

James had to accede to his logic, although he still wasn't happy. He was even less thrilled when Ken handed him the bag containing the puncture repair kit.

"Brilliant. I'm on the maintenance staff now."

Pedro ignored him and waited for the snake of young cyclists to embark. They negotiated first the main roads, then minor ones and finally country lanes through fields of tall grass. Hawthorns lined the route and afforded intermittent glimpses of woodland and distant church spires. At any given time, somebody was laughing.

Ken's overriding fear was that the one rule would be broken and the divisions of the community would come spilling through the resultant chasm. The laughter confirmed that the defences were still intact. For all Ken knew, everybody there could have been from one side or the other. He hoped that there was a cross-section of the communities of Belfast, otherwise there would have been little point in arranging the trip. Short of breaking the rule himself, he had no way of telling. All he could do was try to ensure that the day went as smoothly as possible. So far it was going well.

Lizzie and Carol pedalled along in fourth and fifth places. Carried along on the good weather and team spirit, they hardly felt the strains of unfamiliar exercise. Sixth-form study carried no compulsory P.E. so they had grown used to a more sedentary life. A fact pointed out with such care by Lizzie's father.

"This is more fun than I thought it would be Lizzie," said Carol through deep breaths.

"Yeah, I agree," answered Lizzie. "I've had an idea. D'you want to hear it?"

"Sure, go on." Carol listened intently.

"You know how we aren't supposed to tell anyone where we come from and whether we're Protestant or Catholic?"

"Oh," said Carol who was experiencing some confusion. "Is that what this is about?"

"Sure it is, what else would this fellow be trying to do here?" said Lizzie in mild exasperation at her friend's lack of awareness.

41

"I hadn't thought of that but it does make sense, I suppose. Anyway what's your idea?"

"Well," began Lizzie between breaths, "nobody here knows us so we can have any names we want."

Carol's face lit up at the thought. She had never liked her name and saw an opportunity to do something about it, albeit temporarily. She embraced the suggestion without hesitation.

"Lulu!" she announced.

"What?" said Lizzie, unsure if Carol was experiencing one of her mad moments.

"I've always liked the name Lulu. If the situation arises I'm going to say that I'm called Lulu."

"Good for you, Lulu. I haven't thought that far ahead yet." Worryingly, Lizzie's train of thought was being influenced by Carol's. She had undoubtedly got her idea for a pseudonym from watching Top of the Pops. Lizzie chose the same method of selection.

"I'm going to be Kiki," which brought instant laughter to both of them, the sound of which rang like church bells in Ken's ears ten yards ahead of them.

Meanwhile at the rear of the weaving line of wheels, a similar yet more cerebral conversation was taking place.

"You know how nobody knows who we are?" asked James.

"I suppose so, what of it?"

"Well, we don't know who anybody else is either." surmised James to Pedro's bewilderment.

42

"What are you getting at, man?" asked Pedro sucking in air in gulps.

"I wonder how many here are Protestants and how many are Catholics?" suggested James. A period of silence ensued to allow Pedro to take this in. He replied with.

"Who cares? There are about twelve girls up there and they could be from bloody China for all I know. I haven't had the opportunity to chat up any bird who doesn't know me, ever – and there's twelve of them to choose from. They can all ride a bike, which means they each have a pulse, which, in case you've forgotten, is the minimum and only requirement for my undivided attention."

Pedro changed gear on the bike, rose up in the saddle and sped forward to keep up with the line leaving James no option but to do the same.

Pedro was right. It wasn't about Catholics and Protestants, Loyalists and Republicans, whereas everything else in his existence had been. Even in his studies, he had explored politics, conflicts and divisions from history and from other continents. He had begun to think that there was no way for all of that to be put aside. He could try to think of the people in front as friends and not have his thoughts dominated by cultural categorisations. It was for one day, he had to go with Pedro's logic. He caught up with him and said.

"You're right Pedro. I'll go along with that."

"Good. What are we going to call ourselves?" asked Pedro, straight-faced.

"We haven't started a pop group."

"Not telling people who we are or where we're from means we have to use other names. It makes logical sense."

"Alright, but we're not spies. Pedro and Sid will do."

"Ah! Right enough. At least we can't forget them."

At the front of the peloton a minor calamity occurred. A thorn briar had offered its barb up to greet the next soft target. It was the front tyre of Lizzie's bike. Instant deflation of both tyre and rider ensued. Lizzie stopped and Carol narrowly avoided a rear-end shunt.

"Go on, I'll be fine. I'll catch up," she called as Carol was swept off in the line of cyclists. Lizzie pulled her damaged bike to the grass verge beneath the hedgerow and leaned over the handlebars to examine the front wheel from above. The line in the cycling party went by until James and Pedro brought up the rear. James' first impression of Lizzie was of her bottom in blue jeans. He applied his brakes instinctively whereas Pedro didn't and carried on.

"I'll catch you up, puncture duties," he called.

Pedro glanced back and caught a glimpse of the girl.

"Shit!" he spat out at the missed opportunity to rescue the damsel in distress.

James spun around and rode slowly up to where Lizzie stood astride her bike, her head down and long brown hair falling over her face.

"Need some help?" he said, trying not to sound like Pedro would have done.

"I heard it pop," she said without looking up.

Lizzie stood up straight and flicked the locks of wavy hair away from her face revealing the eye-mask of black make-up. As the mess of mane settled in place, she focussed on the provider of assistance. From behind the sunglasses, he focussed on her too. Her strikingly adorned yet pretty blue eyes, filled with wide black irises lit by the sunshine had him mesmerised. A jolt of electricity went through him bringing a shiver that belied the sunshine.

Lizzie was surprised to see this tall, lean young man wearing a heavy leather jacket in the summertime and hiding his pale complexion behind sunglasses. The obviously dyed shock of black spikes exploding from his head would have looked comical, but for the smile that was his most striking feature. He was not like the boys in her college class. This guy had something to say and she wanted to hear it. Whatever it was, she was going to like it.

Neither spoke for a few seconds. Neither felt it urgent to do so. Lizzie broke the silence with humour.

"Are you going to stare at me all day, sunglasses man?"

They both smiled, they liked the situation they were in. He got her joke and offered one of his own in return.

"I'll stare for a little longer if you don't mind."

She laughed and so did he. He placed his bike against the hedge then took out the repair kit entrusted by Ken.

"Are you going to rescue me like the AA man?"

"Better than that," he assured her. "You don't have to phone and wait, I'm here already – and it is free membership."

She stepped off the bike and held it up for him to take. He gripped the frame and flipped it over.

"I'm Sid," he said as though he had always done so. He had only had that nickname for a few weeks and this was the first time he had used it himself.

"Like Sid James?" she said.

It appeared that Pedro wasn't so far wide of the mark with that one after all. James found the offending thorn and removed it, noting where the hole was in relation to the position of the valve.

"Yes, just like Sid James. What's your name?"

"You're very forward for an AA man, aren't you Sid?"

"Call it personal service. I still don't know your name."

He removed the front wheel and began pulling off one side of the tyre to get the inner tube out.

"Kiki," she declared.

"Kiki?" appealed James.

"Yes, Kiki."

"After the pop star or the frog puppet?"

"The pop star, naturally," she laughed. "Frog puppet indeed."

He was sure that she had made up the name and was using it in the spirit of the rules of the trip. He was doing the same and went along with it. She too was less than convinced by the name Sid, but he made her laugh and he was, in an odd way, quite handsome. She particularly liked how clean his fingernails had been, but the work on her tyre had ended that attractive feature. He applied the pump and put enough air into the tyre for him to feel the tiny jet of air on his cheek.

"Well Kiki, I'm delighted to be of service."

"You haven't finished yet. I've yet to see if you're any good at this . . . Sid." The hesitation before the name confirmed that she hadn't fallen for it either, but she was prepared to play along.

She sat down on the grass verge and looked up to soak up the sun like a lady of leisure.

"Oh sunbathing is it? You make yourself comfy while I graft away here."

She stood up but remained focussed on soaking up the sun's rays. He noticed that she crossed her ankles when standing still. He noticed a lot of things about her.

"You look like you don't do a lot of sunbathing," she said looking at his lilywhite complexion, but admiring the intensity of his pursed lips as he foraged in the bag for a tyre patch.

"I go pink and then burnt, it's the curse of the Celts."

"Steady now, we're not supposed to mention where we come from, even in ancient history."

"Right enough," conceded James, "I'll play by the rules."

She was under bright sunshine illuminating her slim frame. She rocked from side to side still with her crossed ankles. He found that habit, and everything else about her, instantly appealing.

He pressed on a sticky patch and put the tube back on the bike. He pressed the tyre into the rim and put it back in the front forks. As he re-inflated the tyre Lizzie felt a mischievous curiosity about him. She thought of something that would reveal at least two things about him at once.

"That sun is too bright today, it's hurting my eyes."

Without a moment's hesitation, he stopped pumping the tyre and took off his sunglasses to offer them to her. At that moment, she learned that he was naturally generous and caring as well as having the kindest and most inviting eyes she had ever seen. She slipped the sunglasses on and then handed them back straight away. She had seen what she had wanted to see. Now he had to put them back on before Carol got a look at his uncovered eyes. Competition was to be avoided. She had not, up to that point, felt proprietorial over any boy.

Roadworthy once again, she set off and was followed on by her new . . . what was he to her? He was her friend, a fellow cycle-tripper, if there was such a word. He was different from other boys she knew. A bit older but not by much, self-assured but still insecure enough to have to resort to a leather jacket and black hair spikes. He made her feel different too – tingly, excited.

James set off behind her. Admiring her bottom momentarily he thought that she looked great from any angle and it would be remiss of him to overlook any of the visual possibilities. She was fun, she made him feel as though he had been missing out on something before and she was the key to him catching up with what the world had been doing without him.

They rode alongside each other where the width of the lanes allowed and talked about nothing in particular. They were in no hurry to catch up to the main group. When they reached the beach, the air felt fresher and the atmosphere of peace that Ken had found so uplifting was again evident. Even though many of the group had visited the area several times before, almost all of them saw it in a new light, unencumbered by memories of family picnics and other visits. It had a freedom of early adulthood that pervaded the consciousness.

They parked the bikes and walked along the waters-edge. Hearts beat like ticking clocks but time stood still.

"Well, Kiki, shall we take a stroll?"

"How old fashioned are you?" she laughed but stepped forward alongside him and began strolling on the path to the water's edge.

The rippling waves scurried along the surface, tamely crashing in near silence on the sand before disappearing to make room for the next. James and Lizzie walked on the smoothed sand, away from the laughing voices of the main group where Pedro was trying in vain to impress the girls with his wit and charm. Ken spotted the punk boy and wild-eyed girl and considered for a moment going to enquire that they were okay. Their body language toward each other told Ken that they were fine, they were better than fine. The afternoon passed with no more significant incident than Pedro paddling knee-deep and failing to persuade anyone else to join him. James and Lizzie were lost in a tiny world of conversation, passing under occasional tree branches they ambled along in the warmth of the day.

The journey back to the city again found them riding side-by-side and engrossed in each other. Dispersing at Candle Park after a big and emotional 'thank you' from Ken to everybody, James was reluctant to let the afternoon end.

"Can we meet up again soon, Kiki?"

He was unconcerned about being seen to be coming on strong or playing hard-to-get. She felt the same.

"Yes please." She was also in too good a mood for games.

They arranged the time and place. The proximity of their friends and other cyclists prevented any physical gesture of affection, although it was in both of their minds. Lizzie joined the three girls she had arrived with and they all rode away through the gates and out of sight. James watched her as though he had seen his first sunset and the sky was still inexplicably lit up from it. Pedro had not had such a fulfilling experience.

"Well I'm glad you pulled, James," he said. "At least one of us enjoyed the day."

James just smiled and climbed onto Philip's bike. "Pedro, sometimes you've just got to go with the flow, you know?"

"I'm trying too hard aren't I?"

"Yes Pedro, you're trying too hard."

CHAPTER NINE

Darry McTandlyn had never had a job, at least not one that could be spoken of. He went from care home to juvenile offender's training then to unemployment, but he was very busy for an idle man. His ability to inflict violence on anyone without scruple gave him a reputation that allowed only a narrow range of social interaction, but within that range he led a fully occupied and, for him, a fulfilling role.

His manner never varied from confrontational. He was of average height yet powerfully built and had a gravelly deep voice that could be heard through walls at normal volume. He knew that he made people uncomfortable by his presence and he seldom passed up an opportunity to use that.

He took his leisure in the less desirable pubs of Belfast, drinking excessively but never losing control of his senses. He was constantly aware of who was near him and what level of threat they posed to him. Pre-emptive strikes were a speciality, although it was only McTandlyn's judgement that determined the timing and extent of the violence to be applied. His responsibilities upon taking the position began as the eyes and ears of the local brigade, answerable only to the next in line and not being allowed to have any conversation with those placed higher in that structure. When allowed to inflict low-level corrective beatings to minor transgressors such as loyalist trespassers or those who said too much whilst in drink, McTandlyn's only identifiable area for development was that he did not know when to stop. The truth was that he was enjoying himself and did not have anyone near him to tell him enough was enough. The answer was to elevate him in status and carry out the work that suited his talents. Suspected informants to the security forces were worthy of a higher degree of physicality which McTandlyn supplied with ease. Whereas some may have allowed the practice of tarring and feathering to become obsolete, there remained a significant number who believed that it was to be persevered with. Killings and disappearances required a team; a recce man, car thief, driver, lookout, clean-up and body disposal, as well as the individual who pulled the trigger.

Darry McTandlyn's voracious sexual appetite was well known among the streetwalkers of Belfast. Their collusions produced an exchange of information about him and agreement was established that he was not to be taken anywhere away from some back-up. Quite what they expected him to do to the girls was only guessed at. But he was capable of doing something and the girls had to rally to protect their own. Without any conversation on the subject, many girls did not ask for money from him. Not wishing to provoke this man was the main aim and concluding their business without sparking off some aggression or angry exchange was the best they could hope for. His connections were well known and no amount of security help that could be mustered by the working girls was prepared to cross swords with the likes of Darry McTandlyn. The result was that he took what he wanted when he wanted it and paid for very little. He knew that people feared him and he took full advantage of that. Even those higher in his own chain of command kept a weather eye for signs of discord because normal rules were difficult to apply to somebody like him.

Darry had grown used to taking pleasure in exercising power over other people and had resented anyone with power over him, although, in adulthood, he had learned to manage the latter. He had a thick neck, dark, untidy hair and stunted fingernails. When the streetwalkers stopped requesting payment for their services, Darry realised that he could intimidate without actually threatening anyone, clear evidence of his notoriety and status in certain neighbourhoods of the city. This made such exchanges easier, initially, but rendered the exerting of his will on others to be less of a challenge and consequently less satisfying. He turned his sexual attention on other men's wives, several of which acceded to his demands on the grounds that the consequences of not doing so were too dire to contemplate. It gave Darry a bigger buzz to know that their husbands knew about his activities with their wives. If they didn't know, he told them.

As well as his personal demeanour, the mere suggestion from him that any individual had collaborated with the security services was followed by extreme violence, whether proven or not. McTandlyn's allegation was enough to bring about a sanctioned, corrective measure. He became judge, jury and executioner, unchallenged and largely unaccountable.

CHAPTER TEN

The University had been James' home for four years. He remained as a resident on the campus after being accepted on a post-graduate paid internship in the Faculty of Political Sciences. The learning environment suited him. He liked the collective quest for knowledge, the variety of subjects and the colourful and unpredictable behaviour of those participating in University life. He liked to see group tutorials being conducted on the grass outside, impromptu musical and dramatic performances around every corner and every available space on the hundreds of notice-boards was filled with bright and optimistic messages about events to come. For James, one particular facility commanded large amounts of his time, attention and efforts.

James could find his way through the Political History section of the University library in partial light. Many of the books had become like old friends, always available to confirm and challenge in equal measure, imparting their knowledge freely and honestly. The library staff had not been asked to render assistance to James since his first semester, in fact at times when they were short staffed, the librarians had called upon James to render assistance to less familiar library users. It was therefore a surprise to Bill Mabben, the senior library assistant, when James approached his desk and asked for some help to find some literature.

As a young man, Bill had travelled the globe as a merchant seaman and had amassed a broad range of knowledge by seeing it unfold before his eyes. After twenty years, he had returned to his home city and whilst his travelling had been curtailed, his thirst for knowledge had not. The combination of travel and reading had given Bill an awareness of the world that went beyond most people's and, only when asked, he cheerfully pointed students and lecturers alike in the right direction to find what it was they were seeking.

"What are you after?" said Bill, "I can guess that it isn't to do with politics or history. You don't need any help with that."

"No Bill, it's something else."

James moved to the side of the desk out of earshot of Bill's female colleague. In a whisper he said.

"It's poetry I'm interested in."

"Good. It's nothing to be embarrassed about son. What's brought on this new interest?"

"Two things really, there was that poet at the Student's Union, the fellow from Manchester. I hadn't thought about poetry until then but I was impressed. Poetry can be quite cool."

"Cool! Why not? What's the other thing, you said there were two," asked Bill.

"Ah, well, I'm looking for some poetry of a particular type, so to speak."

"Don't tell me," interrupted Bill, "you've met a girl and you want to impress her with some poetry. Is that right?"

"How could you tell?" asked James who had hoped to have expressed himself more subtly.

"Whenever any student who isn't studying poetry asks what you're asking, that is usually the reason." Bill rose from his seat and walked around James. "Come with me son," he said and James followed obediently.

Through many rows of shelves bearing innumerable tomes from floor to ceiling, James was led to an aisle selected by Bill as having the answer to his problem.

"Have you any idea what sort of thing you want?" said Bill, trying to narrow the field of search.

"Not really," said James. "Just something that captures the mood, if you know what I mean."

"Oh I know what you mean," Bill assured him before turning to examine the contents of the shelves. "You can't go wrong with Shakespeare."

"Okay, I'll go with that. What have you got in mind, Bill?"

Bill selected a book and flipped over several pages. He found what he was looking for within seconds.

"Shakespeare wrote many sonnets, short poems of love. Here's the best known one, Have a look at that."

James took the open book and read aloud.

"Shall I compare thee to a summer's day?"

"Read it all and come and tell me what you think. There are lots of others to choose from if that isn't to your liking." Bill headed back toward his desk.

"Are you sure this is going to, you know, work?" asked James sheepishly. Bill came back to his side and leaned to whisper in his ear.

"This poem has been loosening the corsets of women for nigh on four hundred years!"

"Thanks Bill," offered James without looking up from the book. He hungrily took in the words and felt increasingly confident that it was exactly what he wanted. He imagined the girl he knew as Kiki melting in his arms upon hearing these beautiful words of love. That was it - that was what he was feeling, she had stirred something in him that he had not felt before.

CHAPTER ELEVEN

Gary McCabb lived within a two-minute walk of the house he was born in and may have appeared at first glance to be an under achiever. Having never travelled far, even on holiday, and mixing mainly with people who were equally static, it could be perceived that he lacked a sense of adventure. Ambition may well have been absent in his working life, but there burned within Gary a desire to change the world and his chosen method was music. A cheap, acoustic guitar and a Bert Weedon manual were the fuel on the first spark of his musical journey. Hours spent learning chords in the shed behind his parents' house resulted only in a barely recognisable rendition of Johnny B. Goode. He recruited two mates to form a group. They were selected, not because they had any talent, but because they owned a drum-kit and a bass guitar respectively, although the bassist did not own any form of electric amplification. He improvised by humming the bass line along with his guitar work. The group tried to gel, nurture, develop, create in the hope that sweet, up-to-date and danceable music would flow, but it never did. The trio went their separate ways, not because of musical differences, but because of musical similarities – they were all hopeless at playing music.

Gary opted for the next best thing. He became a disc-jockey. Early steps on the road to Top of the Pops included volunteering to read the news and make event announcements on a hospital radio station. What cash he earned had enabled him to acquire a twin record deck and some records that had waned in popularity over the years that had passed since their issue. His first engagement was for a school leavers' party in a community centre. He had borrowed a light stack, bigger speakers and a microphone and the new career was launched. Several similar gigs ensued before he was asked to officiate at the engagement party of a couple who both looked about twelve. Gary happily accepted the cash and promptly spent it on more records. A loan from the bank allowed his burgeoning entertainment empire to include a pale blue, thirteen-year-old Hillman Husky van that used to belong to the Gas Board.

Although the adulation he had envisaged as a rock star had failed to materialise, Gary did generate some increased female interest at the disco events he appeared at. On more than one occasion he had failed to notice a girl or girls hanging around during and after the disco, but he did acknowledge that he was getting more attention than he had before. He did let it go to his head and he did become largely insufferable, but it did not matter. Despite having no discernible talent, he was on the first step of the show business ladder and nothing else mattered.

All was going swimmingly until a skinny yet pretty girl in a white dress with red flowers printed on it came to a disco that Gary was running. She was about eighteen and had long, wavy, white-blonde hair, like 'ABBA –the early years.' Young men tried in their clumsy ways to get the blonde to dance with them or otherwise entertain some conversation of acknowledgement, but all attempts fell on stony ground. Gary utilised a trick he had learned, to invent an award for the best dancer of the night and bestow it upon the blonde with the Swedish looks. As it always worked out, the recipient had to come to speak to the

D.J. in order to collect the prize, which was nothing more than a record he was unlikely to play or tickets to a later disco. In that conversation he could legitimately ascertain the name and some detail about her with which he could grow a dialogue and pour his learned charm into the mix. When the Village People's high energy offering subsided, Gary announced the winner and invited her into his spider's web of bird-pulling, a poor and undefended fly about to be devoured. She announced in a local accent that her name was Theresa and that she liked Boney M. Gary obliged by rapidly digging out Rivers of Babylon and spinning it on the No. 2 turntable.

"See me at the end for your tickets, Theresa," he said without the microphone, as she re-joined the whooping throng of dancing oestrogen she had arrived with.

As he had planned it, Theresa duly lingered after the house lights had come on and the cloakroom queue had magnetically drawn all from the dance floor. In the relative calm after the noisy storm, they chatted easily and without any great effort on either's part. Theresa had waved off her girlfriends and was happy to be escorted home by Gary the D.J.

Their trysts became a regular thing and, although she made him wait for longer than he thought he could for a girl to succumb to his irresistible charm, they became exclusively bound and unmistakably in love. The Hillman van was put to a use that neither Hillman nor the Gas Board had intended. It was the mobile venue for romance and to Gary and Theresa, nothing else in the world mattered, until the week before Christmas when she told him that she was pregnant.

By Easter, Gary had sold his twin record deck, all of his records, the light stacks, amplifiers and the Hillman van. He used the cash to rent and furnish a small terraced house and took a job working shifts on a production line in a factory that assembled car exhausts. His dream of a showbiz life was over, but Theresa made it a painless transition. Family life became the norm and Gary accepted it with an enforced maturity that surprised even him. He doted on their daughter and built his world on her and Theresa. Immersed in the routine and seeming mundaneness of family living, Gary seemed not to notice that his wife had blossomed into an even more striking young woman than she had been as a teenaged girl.

The picture of domestic bliss that the McCabb family had become was shattered when, on her way home from her part-time job in a city centre café, she was seen and admired by Darry McTandlyn. He followed her home and watched the house until he had gathered that her husband was of no status or importance. It would have made little difference to McTandlyn if he had been. He stopped Gary on his way home from work one evening and told him with alarming bluntness that he was going to have his wife.

Fear and anger gripped Gary, the fear eclipsed the anger. He had heard of McTandlyn, his reputation had been carefully crafted in that neighbourhood. He tried to reason with him but that got him nowhere. Gary went home and told Theresa what had happened. They contemplated telling the police, then running away, but neither option was realistic. There was no other presence in their part of the city that could do anything to help them to get out of that situation. Only compliance remained.

There were tears in abundance in the McCabb household. Selflessly, Theresa accepted the inevitability of it and Gary had to do the same. The alternatives ranged from being tarred and feathered to being shot. When McTandlyn arrived at the house and wordlessly disappeared up the stairs with Theresa, Gary sat at the kitchen table spooning stewed apple into his daughter's mouth, trying to shut out the abject horror of his situation.

"Mumma?" said the child.

"Mumma's fine, sweetheart." Gary could barely contain the sobs as tears ran down his cheeks. "Mumma's going to be okay, we will all be okay."

CHAPTER TWELVE

James and Lizzie had arranged to meet at a duck pond in Victory Park on the next Saturday at 11am. The park was quiet, peaceful and adorned with over-run shrubs and hanging willow trees. It was not considered to be in an area belonging to any side of the community division. The plain fact that both of them had been there before and therefore knew where it was, served to assure them that their backgrounds would not be relevant to their presence there. Both had taken a bus to the park but from different embarkation spots. James had arrived first and had already walked around the pond three times when Lizzie appeared from beneath a weeping willow. He had been nervous and so had she. Upon seeing her, he felt as though he had won a prize for something against the odds. He felt elated, tingly in his fingers and toes. He had to make a deliberate effort to settle his breathing before he was next to her.

Lizzie had got off the bus and waited at the edge of the park for two minutes before approaching the pond. She had begun to doubt everything in her memory of the cycle ride to Helen's Bay. Had it happened at all? She had been distracted from all unrelated activity since then. Sid had made her feel different, happier, energetic but not for any study or other useful purpose. She had taken time to examine her appearance with a greater attention to detail than she would normally have the time or patience for. She had, momentarily, considered applying different make-up, but she had talked herself out of that idea with the logic that he might not be able to recognise her. The concession was to let her hair down untethered by any accessories and to wear flared jeans and a jacket normally reserved for best.

As she approached, James started to break into a run but checked himself and opted for a brisk walk. They stopped three feet from each other and looked into each other's faces. James removed his dark glasses and Lizzie flicked a strand of hair aside with her little finger.

"Hi," she said, smiling.

"Hi," he returned, also smiling. "You got here okay then?"

"I did. I'm glad you did too. Shall we take a stroll?" she said.

He smiled a silent acknowledgement that she was teasing him with the old-fashioned suggestion he had used when they had first met.

They walked around the pond slowly, not touching each other at any point. The weather was discussed adequately as were the lives and habits of the ducks who were hosting the liaison. They gave several of them names and invented conversation topics that were not at all duck-relevant. The sun rose higher and the temperature rose with it. James took off his leather jacket and carried it over his forearm. Lizzie took off her jacket and James carried that too. She thanked him and said.

"I did feel some relief when I saw you here today. I would have felt a bit of a fool standing here by myself, so I would."

"I couldn't imagine anybody in their right mind standing you up. I wouldn't do that. I've been looking forward to seeing you, a lot."

"That's very nice of you to say. What a charmer. Do all the girls get such compliments?"

"It's not something I've practiced. There is something else that I have been practicing."

"Am I going to like it or should I slap your face?" she joked through avid curiosity.

"I read a poem. It made me think of you."

Lizzie could not have dreamt that she would inspire someone to resort to poetry to impress her. The boys in her college class were still climbing trees and playing football. Sid was different. Mature but not over-confident. Assured enough to pass compliments but still a little nervous about it falling flat. The removal of the outsized jacket presented a lean but muscular frame beneath a Ramones T shirt.

"Nobody's ever told me that before. Are you having me on?"

"No, it's true. It's by Shakespeare."

"Shakespeare is it now? Are you going to give up a line of it then?"

"Alright." He took a deep breath and hoped it didn't appear too unnatural. "Shall I compare thee to a Summer's day?"

Lizzie was trying hard to avoid laughing, but it seemed to be the most readily available safety valve for a situation as unfamiliar as this.

"What? What are you talking about, compare thee to what?" she laughed in mock confusion. James pressed on.

"Thou art more lovely and more temperate."

"Who are you calling temperate? The cheek of the man."

"Rough winds do shake the darling buds of May."

"One minute he's calling me lovely, the next he's calling me rough." By then they were both fighting the urge to laugh.

"And Summer's lease hath all too short a date."

"This date's gonna be all too short if you carry on throwing insults about like that, poetry man."

James felt the need to add perspective, not because he was in any way uncomfortable, but because he was enjoying talking to Lizzie and it might make her laugh some more.

"It means that he finds her beautiful and uplifting, like you feel when the Sun's shining," he explained, knowing well enough that he was being teased. "He's saying that she makes him feel good. It's not an insult at all, quite the opposite in fact."

"Why doesn't he just tell her? Why use words she has to work out the meaning for?" she demanded to know in the pursuit of reason.

"I don't know much about poetry. It's just a nicer way of saying ordinary things. It makes them less ordinary, more special."

"Oh, special is it now? Who is it about anyway?"

"I don't know. The woman he loves, I suppose."

"Why can't he take a deep breath, have some guts and tell her that he loves her, instead of dressing it up as a weather forecast?"

"You have no soul and I pity you," he declared with offended piety.

"No soul! How dare you? I have enough soul to say what I think and to whoever I choose to say it, which is more than your Shakespeare man had," said Lizzie in full righteous flow.

"What 'do' you think?" he asked her.

"What do I think about what?" she answered with a delaying tactic, a ploy to buy time to think before answering the question.

"About love, how would you tell somebody that you loved them?"

"Oh no, you're not putting me on the spot like that. You're the one who started this love business."

"Shakespeare is a good enough way of getting that message across, that's my suggestion. It's yours I haven't heard yet."

"I just think you should say what you feel, not what somebody else felt years ago. Say it in your own words."

They walked on in silence for a minute, a yard apart but getting closer in every other way. He decided that it was time for a leap of faith. What could go wrong? She could scream? run away? slap his face? Or what if he didn't do anything? Would she? No, nice girls don't do that sort of thing, at least he didn't think that happened. Faint heart never achieved anything, he had heard, so it had to be done.

67

She thought that it should be up to him to make the first gesture, but what? Would he put his arm around her waist as they walked? Should she do the same? Would he kiss her, on the cheek or the lips? Would he know that she was a novice kisser? How could she appear to know these things when she plainly did not? Should she make the first move? Take the lead and do something? He wasn't doing anything so it could be up to her. Did he not like her in that way? Was he crazy about her but was just being a gentleman? He did start talking about love, surely that should mean something.

He drew a deep breath which made her respond in the same way. Without breaking stride, he reached out and took her hand, clumsily at first, holding only her fingers. She responded by adjusting the grip herself, connecting the hands with precision and silently showing that she wanted to hold his hand too. After three or four steps, the breath held in by both in tense anticipation was exhaled and they relaxed into the role of a hand-holding couple, finding their way along a road that made them both fizz all over.

In the shade of a row of trees in full leaf, he stopped and guided her around in front of him. She looked down but was smiling. He touched her chin, lifting her face up to his. Her eyes rolled upwards until she looked into his. The time for playing games was past.

They kissed in a lingering, fully-committed and passionate exploration of each other. For both of them, everything in the rest of the world ceased to be. The trees, the ground, all of history vanished to them. Their thoughts, no longer guessing the pattern of the other, were together and soaring higher than either had previously known. Nothing would ever be the same again. Time stood still and the Earth stopped spinning. When their lips separated, they held that moment, in each other's arms, joined at the heart and feeling more alive than they could ever believe possible. A tear appeared in Lizzie's eye. As it ran over onto her cheek, James caught it with his finger and held the tiny drop for a moment. He knew that it was a tear of unbridled happiness and he wanted her to know that he was determined to share each twist of emotion with her. This was no give-and-take union, no power contest, no mind game. It was so much better than all of that.

CHAPTER THIRTEEN

With the hood raised on his blue nylon anorak, Philip Coleman rode his bike across the grass beneath a mural painting of a giant flag of green, white and gold, which matched the kerbstones along the streets nearby. An undulating, warm breeze blew tree-blossom into his face making his eyes crease to being nearly closed. He swung a left turn, raising an outstretched leg to maintain balance. He freewheeled along the wide alley sloping down between the backs of three-storey, Edwardian, terraced houses toward the river path. Five houses from the end, he reached the family home of his schoolmate Graham O'Meara. Philip stepped off the bike and used the front wheel to push open the unlocked gate and enter the back yard. He leaned the bike against the side wall of an outbuilding that had once been the household toilet but lately had provided storage for tools and fishing tackle. Through the window he saw Graham standing at the kitchen sink. Upon seeing Philip, Graham stepped to the door and opened it to allow him to enter without having to knock and wait.

A back bedroom window of the eighth house from the end of the terrace behind the O'Meara house had a black cloth draped across it. It concealed the activity inside that room and rendered the temporary occupants invisible to the outside world. Two men in non-descript, black clothing sat at the window. One was looking into binoculars whilst the other held a radio the size of a house-brick with an aerial like a rat's tail. Philip's arrival at the house across the alley roused both men from bored stupor to a state of alertness and intensity. The transmit button on the side of the huge radio was pressed in by the thumb of a gloved hand.

"Delta 8 to AB. Over."

"AB receiving you Delta 8. Over," came the disembodied and robotic reply.

"Male person, 5'9'' or 10'', blue coat, hood up, arrived by bicycle to the rear of target house. Went straight inside. Can't see his face but it could be our man. Over."

"Roger Delta 8, AB to all units, all units stand by. Over."

In the street at the front of the O'Meara house sat an old van with nothing in it. The rear windows afforded a view right through to the front windscreen. Concealed inside the dirty and ragged head restraint above the driver's seat was a camera. It provided a live feed to a monitor screen in the back of a fully blacked out furniture van parked on the river path out of sight, but only eighty yards from the house. Huddled on benches around the edges of the inside of the van were six more men. Each wearing black, military combat uniforms with balaclava helmets and each holding assault rifles.

Philip and Graham prepared glasses of blackcurrant cordial for themselves and went up to Graham's bedroom on the top floor of the house, overlooking the street at the front.

"It's brilliant, my brother got it last year, he wouldn't let me play it until now, says I'd damage it, like I'm eight or something," complained Graham through his evident enthusiasm.

"We've had it for a while, but our James took it with him when he moved out to the University. He doesn't even like it now, he's into Punk." explained Philip between gulps of blackcurrant liquid that left a red stain on his upper lip.

They entered the bedroom and whilst Philip went straight for the record player in the recess by the chimney breast, Graham headed for the window. Pulling the curtain across he said.

"It's better in the dark, you could be anywhere if it's dark."

Daylight reduced to the minimum level required to be able to play records. Philip took off his damp coat and hung it on the door handle. He spotted a cassette recorder next to the box containing the L.P.s.

"Has this got a microphone?" he asked hopefully.

"Yeah," Graham rummaged behind the record player, "There are some headphones too. What're you thinking?"

Philip took the first record from the front of the box. Pink Floyd, Dark Side of the Moon.

"Here it is," he announced. "Why don't we take turns to listen to it on the headphones and use this to record ourselves singing?"

"That's a mad idea," said Graham in protest, before immediately warming to the suggestion. "but I like it. You go first."

The top floor bedroom was far enough away to not disturb the other people in the O'Meara household, not that Philip had given a thought as to who else was present in the house. They played the music, sang along and played back the results which produced great amusement. Unknown to them, two floors below, another person arrived at the house and unheard by them, a voice with a Birmingham accent transmitted from the concealed rear of the furniture van.

"Delta 4 to AB, over."

"AB receiving, go ahead Delta 4, over."

"Remote eye picked up a male entering front of target house. 5'8'' maybe, brown jacket, black pants, over."

"Can you identify? Over."

"No clear view of his face but it's the target alright. He had a key, let himself in. Over."

"AB to all units, target is in the house, ready weapons, at least one other person inside. Firearms and resistance expected. Await the command to strike."

"Delta 8 ready."

"Delta 4 ready."

"R.U.C. cordon unit ready," came the only Irish accent in the conversation.

Liam O'Meara arrived home and let himself in at the front door with his own key. Liam was nineteen and worked in a small ice-cream factory on the edge of the city. He was a bored and restless youth who had become disillusioned with the lack of excitement in his life. His education and intelligence were wholly insufficient for him to have any prospect of achieving the high life he aspired to live. He revelled instead in a fantasy world where he could be celebrated as an achiever. He had unwisely bragged of his involvement in the theft of a lorry load of cigarettes worth half a million pounds. It was largely ignored because of the flaws in his claim, but an opportunity was spotted for him to be recruited for very low-level involvement in paramilitary activity.

Whilst Liam could not be trusted with any real responsibility, he was directed to secrete a small cache of weapons and ammunition at the O'Meara family home for future use when required. The reasoning of the higher ranks being that Liam was expendable and would reduce the risk of a valuable field asset being caught by the security services.

Liam was thrilled to have been given a real task by real people who were deadly serious and therefore so was he. Unfortunately, Liam's excitement at the appointment as low-level quartermaster was too much for him and he virtually broadcast the details to the neighbourhood. Walls have ears, as it was said in WW2, and the security services found little difficulty obtaining a search warrant for the O'Meara family home.

"AB to all units, move into strike positions now."

A Royal Ulster Constabulary operations unit vehicle sped to the Irish flag mural on the gable end at the top of the street. Eight police officers clambered out and ran into positions preventing anyone from entering the street or the alley behind.

"R.U.C. unit to AB, cordon set."

"AB to all Delta units, strike, strike, strike!"

On the river path at the other end of the street, the rear of the furniture van sprang open and six masked, helmeted and heavily armed soldiers ran from the darkness of the van into the overcast daylight beyond. Three ran to the front of the house and, avoiding the

74

windows, pressed their backs against the outer walls of the house next to the O'Meara home. A sledgehammer was in the hands of the front man. The second team of three ran to the rear of the house and assumed similar positions by the gate to the yard. Again, the front man wielded a sledgehammer.

Liam took off his coat and hung it on one of a row of hooks in the hall. He went upstairs to use the toilet. The frosted glass in the window prevented him from seeing any of the movement in the back alley. Liam flushed the toilet handle at the moment the first blow of the hammer connected with the locking mechanism of the front door. The three at the front were inside the house and kicking open interior doors before the back door team smashed it the shreds and stormed into the kitchen.

"Ground floor, clear," called one soldier. The back door team ran to the stairs.

Although barely unable to take in air, Liam had the presence of mind to run up to the second floor. The cache of illicit weapons and ammunition was in the loft, which could be accessed by a narrow and steep stairway behind a crudely made door of tongue and groove pine on the second-floor landing. Liam pulled open the door and closed it behind him. He scrambled on all fours up the steps and into the loft space that was not high enough to stand up in. He pulled up the insulation and looked for the guns.

Three soldiers reached the first floor and carried out a search of the rooms, the toilet cistern was still refilling with water indicating that whoever had been in there must be in a room that had not yet been searched. The ground floor search over, two remained on the doors whilst the last man went upstairs to assist with the search there. With rifles raised, two soldiers went up to the second floor.

Philip was in full flow. With the headphones drowning out the sound of the raid, he performed with rock star abandon. Graham heard the sound of rapid footsteps and went out onto the second-floor landing, leaving Philip to pause his aria for the duration of an instrumental interlude. As he stepped out of the room he was greeted by the barrel of a rifle in his face. At the butt end of it was a figure in black with his face concealed. Graham froze.

"Get down on the floor! Get down on the floor!" shouted the soldier through the muffling balaclava.

Graham did not, could not move, nor could he speak. There was no window on that landing and the only light came from the stairway below. The second soldier grabbed Graham's shirt at the shoulder and pushed him down onto the floor. The tip of the gun barrel hovered menacingly, inches from the side of his head.

"Where are the guns?" demanded the soldier. "Answer me!"

Seven feet above them, Liam had found the canvas bag containing the contraband weapons. He stood up as far as he could and shuffled to the edge of the loft where there was a gap in the brickwork, allowing access to the loft of the house next door. This feature ran for every loft in the terrace and Liam set off to get to the last house at the river end of the street.

The second soldier stepped over Graham's motionless form, face-down on the carpet. He raised his gun again and pushed open the door from which suppressed music could be heard. Kneeling in front of the record player, Philip had his back to the bedroom door. Oblivious and lost in the prolonged, cosmic journey of the electric guitar solo, he held the microphone on his knee to await the resumption of the song lyrics. The soldier was barely used to the absence of daylight. His eyes adjusted to it and he saw the kneeling figure across the room.

"Put your hand above your head, now!" he ordered.

Philip heard nothing of that command. Gripping the gun with greater intensity and eager to complete the operation without firing a shot, the soldier repeated the order.

"I said put your hands up now!" A note of desperation could be heard in his voice.

Graham had recovered sufficient awareness to hear it.

"Do it Phil, for God's sake do it." Tears welled in Graham's eyes.

Philip anticipated the change of key that announced that the guitar solo was complete. The soldier edged forward with three-inch steps, his mouth dry and skin cold. In the limited light from around the edge of the curtain, he saw that there was something in the hand of the kneeling figure who would not adhere to his authority. The item had a protruding line from the hand of the person in his sights, a line that looked to be four or five inches long and cylindrical. The soldier jerked his already tensed body upright at the realisation of what the person was holding in his hand. It was what they had come to the house to find but he had not expected to find it in somebody's possession.

"Drop the weapon!" he called, in a higher pitch than before, "Drop it or I will shoot you."

Graham buried his face in the carpet and wept.

77

"Phil, what are you doing?" he whispered in a barely audible voice, "Do what he says, do what he says."

The lyrics of the Pink Floyd track almost took Philip by surprise. It had been months since he had heard it but he had remembered how it went. He raised the microphone to his mouth and opened his eyes. Aware that the bedroom door was open he turned his head to look toward it.

The soldier had never shot anybody before. It was a text-book double-tap to the largest target, the torso. Philip flopped over onto his side next to the record player. Pink Floyd played on.

The soldier on the landing with his gun trained on the prostrate Graham realised that something had gone terribly wrong.

"Oh shit!" he uttered, "What's happened?" he shouted.

"He had a handgun, he wouldn't drop it." He struggled to speak.

Two more soldiers reached the second floor. They stepped over Graham and entered the bedroom with guns raised. Upon seeing the darkness, one soldier switched on the light. He swung his gun aside and went to the prone figure as the others maintained armed cover.

He removed a glove and looked for vital signs.

"There's something," he said without looking up, "Ambulance, now!" The others remained still, unable to take in the situation. "Now, I said!"

From the loft of the house at the river end of the terrace, Liam had tumbled through a hatch on to the landing still holding the canvas bag. He ran down the stairs giving no thought as to whether the occupants were at home. He unbolted the kitchen door and leaving it wide open he set off through the back yard. He peered left and right at the gate.

"Delta 8 to AB, target is in the back yard of Number One."

"R.U.C. cordon unit, we will deal."

"Delta 4, urgent, shots fired inside, civilian down, ambulance needed!"

Liam emerged into the alley and walked with haste to the riverside path. Sweat ran into his eyes and his fingers trembled as he gripped the canvas bag. As he turned the corner, he walked into the arms of two police officers who hacked him to the ground, knocking what breath he had left out of his lungs.

Inside Graham O'Meara's bedroom, the soldiers awaited the emergency medical help that they hoped would save the life of the gunman on the bedroom floor. CPR and mouth-to-mouth were utilised. As the first-aider reeled back to inhale, the others saw Philip's face.

"Oh bollocks, it's a kid. What is he, fourteen? fifteen?" said one soldier.

The colleague who had fired the shots felt the need to justify his actions. He knew that he would be doing that officially soon enough.

"He had a gun, he raised it at me, I shouted at him to drop it, I did, I told him. Didn't I Keith?"

Keith had taken Graham O'Meara down the stairs in handcuffs.

"Do you mean this?" said the first-aider between attempts to inflate the boy's chest. He pointed to the microphone lying on the carpet. The realisation of what had happened hit all three of them at the same moment.

"There's going to be some serious trouble on the back of this!"

CHAPTER FOURTEEN

The day got warmer as did the feelings that James and Lizzie had for each other. They left the park and went toward the city centre, stopping to eat in a café neither of them had been to before. They held hands under the table as they waited to be served. They had eyes and everything else only for each other. Neither had experienced anything so thrilling before and they revelled in it. Chatting about their favourite things: films, food, music, it didn't really matter. Losing track of time, the daytime date became an evening date too. James was eager to keep Lizzie with him and he came up with a suggestion to ensure that.

"If you have no plans for later, we could go to see a group."

"I'd like that. This is turning out to be a really good date. You are one clever fellow," she laughed excitedly in anticipation of the prolonging of their liaison. He laughed with her.

"Have you been to the Student's Union at the University?"

"No, but I'd like to."

Lizzie had only recently turned eighteen and as the daughter of a police superintendent she had been less able to get away with frequenting pubs and clubs underage. Consequently, she had little experience of licenced premises.

"We can walk there if you like. It's only half an hour away," suggested James.

"Alright, but I'd better phone my folks and tell them I'll be late back."

She rummaged in her bag and found the coins to make a call, then headed off to the payphone on the wall near the toilets at the back of the café. She returned to report that she was ready to go to the University to learn about rock 'n' roll.

They ambled along, stopping to kiss in shop doorways and bus shelters. The University security guard gave nothing more than an approving glance as the young man with the explosion of black spikes on his head and the out-sized leather jacket walked by with his arm around a slim girl with an equally avant-garde appearance, particularly in relation to the 'robber's mask' eye make-up.

The group was a regulation four-piece and they played loud and lively American pop standards. For Lizzie it was a life-affirming place to be. She had considered the possibility of going to University, but she had thought that it would mean leaving Belfast. That place with all of its colour, energy and freedom of expression made her head spin. That day just kept on getting better. People danced without inhibition. They drank lager from plastic glasses and the aroma of non-tobacco substances being smoked permeated the air. Lizzie and James spent most of the night locked in an embrace, neither one thinking of anything else in the world. She unlocked the hold and held him at arm's length gazing at him with passion and longing in her eyes.

"Can we go somewhere? Be on our own?" she said surprising herself with her audacity. James kissed her with even more vigour and answered.

"Yes we can. Come on."

He led her out of the concert room and through the entrance to the S.U. They crossed the grass to the post-graduate block and up to James' floor where he took out a key and unlocked the door. Keeping only the desk light on, they fell onto the bed, fully engrossed in each other. Jackets fell on the floor and buttons began to leave buttonholes. James stopped and said.

"I want you to know, now, that this is real for me. I want to see you, keep seeing you, properly I mean. Not just for, you know?"

She kissed him again.

"I know, I feel it too. This is the start of something. I can't get enough of you either. Now kiss me again."

More clothing landed on the carpet and time stood still for two lovers who, at that magical moment, owned the world and everything in it.

The distant sound of moving traffic and the muffled, thumping, rock 'n' roll beat from the S.U. bar could be heard through the open window of James' room in the post-graduate block. They lay in each other's arms, kissing and caressing whilst silently celebrating what they had found together.

"You've made it difficult for me to concentrate on anything else recently," he declared.

"Well, is that right, poetry man?" she nestled her shoulder deeper under his arm and kissed his chest.

"You're kind of tricky to overlook yourself. Do you want to see me again or is this it?" He moved away from her suddenly to be able to look at her face.

"Isn't it obvious? I want us to be, you know, proper. Just you and me, if you want that too."

She pulled him back closer to her. "I want that too. When can we see each other again?"

"Tomorrow?" he suggested.

"I'd love to but I have to do family things tomorrow. Monday would be great. We can meet at the park again," said Lizzie hopefully.

"Okay, half past two?" he said.

"Yes, half past two. I'll bring bread for the ducks."

As the time crept toward midnight, she told him that she had asked her father to collect her at the main gates to the campus. They got dressed and walked back with their arms around waists, finding joy and humour in everything they saw and heard. They waited just inside the gate and planned their next meeting.

"We have to tell each other about ourselves, whatever that reveals?" said James, knowing that the community divisions in Belfast could be challenging for them.

"I know," she answered, fully aware that the families of police officers could be difficult for some people to come to terms with regardless of other factors. "I'm a little nervous about that but we have to, I know."

As they kissed with closed eyes, a Royal Ulster Constabulary patrol car entered through the campus gates and drove by them. It disappeared beyond the buildings. Lizzie and James stepped forward to peer through the gates. She spotted the family Morris Marina being driven by her father. It stopped across the street and remained with the engine running. After one last kiss, she dashed across the street and around to the passenger side. James lingered in the gateway. Arnie had not seen them together.

"Alright love, a good night, was it?" he enquired.

"Yes, Daddy, there was a group on, lots of dancing. I think I might like the University thing if I get the chance."

"Well it's certainly flushed some colour into your cheeks, not so pale and unhealthy tonight my girl."

As the red rear car-lights went from his view, James wandered back to the Post-Graduate accommodation block, playfully flicking tree branches as he went. He stepped up onto a wooden bench and simulated tight-rope walking before jumping down off the other end. He wanted it to be Monday at half past two.

Outside his block the police car sat empty. He walked past the back of it and headed for the double glass panelled doors. They opened and two stern-faced officers stepped out.

"Are you James Patrick Coleman?" said one in an accusatorial manner. James' first thought was that he was sure that Kiki had been over the age of consent, a cold shiver ran through him anyway, he had had very few encounters with the police in his life.

"Erm yes, that's me," he mumbled.

85

"We have some bad news to tell you, it's about your brother."

CHAPTER FIFTEEN

A black Ford Escort RS2000, flagship of the 'boy racer' fleet, sat on rough ground behind a late-night convenience store on the edge of a council housing estate. Behind that was a colony of old peoples' bungalows with faded cream pebbledash walls from where nobody emerged after dark. Four teenagers with bottles of cider lingered on a fire-escape leading from the flat above the store. They admired the RS2000 from afar but did not approach for a closer inspection. The figure sitting in the driver's seat, whose face was concealed in shadow, sent out a silent message instructing others to steer clear of him. All that could be seen were the gloved hands gripping the tiny steering wheel and periodically peeling back the left glove in order to inspect the wristwatch behind it.

At 7.40pm a well-built man wearing a green Parka coat with the hood raised emerged from the edge of the building. He was carrying a bag over his shoulder with a cord-string tie. He went to the car and without speaking to the driver he took things from the bag then dipped down behind the car and out of sight. A minute later he carried the bag to the front and squatted to fix a different number plate to the car. He got into the passenger seat of the car. The engine fired up and the Escort moved off with the low hum of a high-performance engine that was capable of screaming when required. The car had been stolen to order that morning and the number plates had been stolen the night before from a Ford Cortina in a scrap yard at Dunmurry.

At 7.55pm the black car slowed and pulled off the road onto a poorly-maintained council play area with two rusty football goal posts but no pitch markings. After cutting the lights, the passenger alighted and went to an open gate, halfway along a row of twenty houses in a terrace. A knock on the rear door brought on a light inside and the door was opened by Magnus Coleman. Although he had not met the visitor before, he was expecting him. The visitor stepped into the kitchen and closed the outer door himself.

"Who is it Magnus?" called Clare from the sitting room at the front of the house.

"It's nobody, to speak of love. I'll be through in a minute," he reassured her without addressing her curiosity. She got up and went to the door to listen. Although they were speaking in hushed tones, she was able to make out the gist of the conversation.

"So it will be tonight," said the stranger, whose accent was local and his voice gratingly deep.

"Right enough," said Magnus with a tone of sad resignation.

"Somebody from the family should be present, it's just the way, you know."

He sounded to Clare like a funeral director making arrangements, but they were to be discussed the following morning and could not be done without her and James. Something else was being planned, something she was not a party to.

"I will come tonight. We . . . I, have to do something about my boy. It can't be left like this," said Magnus, fighting the choking in his chest and throat. The visitor remained unmoved.

"Be ready at nine. Wear dark clothes, nothing noticeable, understand?"

Magnus answered in a clearer, stronger voice. "Aye, I get it, don't you worry, I get it, right enough."

He opened the back door and let the man out. By the time he returned to the sitting room, Clare was back in her armchair. He flopped backwards into his old, worn chair and let out a long and laboured sigh. Clare left it a minute before asking.

"What was all that about?"

"I told you, nothing," he snapped without looking at her. She gave it another minute.

"This is no time to be keeping things from me Magnus."

He said nothing in return. Instead he picked up a newspaper and pretended to read it, knowing all along that Clare would never let the matter drop.

"I've got all night, if you like," she began, "You'll tell me what your plotting and who with or so help me I'll – "

"I don't want you involved, can't you see? If you don't know, they can't do anything to you. I'm protecting you. Can't you leave it at that?"

"And who's protecting you, and from what?" she spat out the words, releasing a tiny morsel of the anger she held within. "Tell me that, Magnus." He paused to allow the tension to abate slightly before answering.

"Think about it love, a Catholic boy gets killed by the security forces, you work out what's going to happen next. It can't be ignored. An eye for an eye, you know." He had moved to the edge of his seat.

"How does you involving yourself in some act of revenge achieve anything for our son, for our family? This is not a bloody cowboy film and you're not John Bloody Wayne."

"I know that, I know that," said Magnus who was closer to tears than he let on, "They are going to do it anyway. I can't do anything about that even if I wanted to. I just, I just . . ."

"Just what?" she said in a calmer, more supportive tone of voice.

"I have to do something! This is killing me. How can I let 'them' avenge the death of our boy? I have to at least be there."

"You are in no condition to do anything, you're not a well man. It could be the death of you."

"I won't be 'doing' anything, I just have to be there. Sitting here doing nothing about it, that will be the death of me!"

Clare stood up and walked to the door. He followed her.

"Where are you going? What are you doing now?" he demanded without conviction. She continued out into the hallway and picked up the phone.

"What . . . who are you calling?" Desperation and fear had crept into his voice. They both knew the consequences of a word in the ear of the wrong party in such matters. Clare dialled the number from memory and waited with the handset to her head. Magnus considered snatching it from her but he had never raised a hand to her in twenty-five years of marriage and he was not going to now. The lull in the conversation between them was accompanied by the sound of ringing at the other end of the line.

"Hello?" came the voice. Magnus heaved a sigh of relief, relief he would not have felt had she called anybody else in the world. He sloped back to his chair and sunk into it, rubbing his temples with his thumbs whilst covering his eyes with his fingers.

"James, it's your mother."

James was surprised to hear from her so soon. He had spent the previous night and most of that day at the family home before returning to the University to collect clothes and arrange his leave of absence from his internship duties.

"Oh, hi Mam. I'm coming tomorrow to sort out the funeral, is that still alright?"

"I need you to come home now," she stated coldly.

"Now, what's happened?"

"I can't say, not on the phone."

"Okay, I'm coming now."

Clare replaced the handset and sat down to wait. Magnus lowered his hands and looked at her.

"I know what you're trying to do. James won't change my mind. He has his head in books at that University. He doesn't get how the world really is, not in this city."

Neither spoke again until James' arrival forty minutes later reignited the topic in hand.

"Are you going to tell him or am I?" said Clare being deliberately dramatic.

"Tell me what?" asked James, looking at each of his parents in turn.

Magnus looked down at the newspaper again. Clare grasped James' forearm.

"You father is going with the Brigade, tonight. They're going to do something, something to get revenge for our Philip's death." Whilst still speaking to James she turned to face Magnus. "An eye for an eye, he says. What do you think of that?"

James looked at his father for acceptance or denial. He hoped for the latter.

"What sort of a man does nothing when his son is murdered, eh? You tell me that."

"Dad, it's not going to bring Phil back, let them play out their tribal games. You don't have to involve yourself in all that."

"Philip is dead, from a British soldier's bullet!" Magnus lingered on that word then added with simmering menace. "That changes everything. We are in it up to our necks now. We, his family, must be a part of what's to happen. I'm not asking you to go, I'll do it myself. I have to be there. It's important."

"What good will you be to this family when you're in the Maze, Dad? Tell us that, now. You remember what the doctor told you. You remember that, Dad."

Magnus stood up and walked into the back kitchen. He chose to conclude the discussion by leaving the room. Clare whispered to James.

"They're coming to get him at nine. He's determined to go through with it. When I think of the years he's supported the cause without resorting to violence, it makes me so mad."

"I'll try again Mam, you wait here."

As James stood up they heard a loud thud and a crash of plates come from the kitchen.

"Oh my God!" shrieked Clare as she dashed after James to the kitchen door. They found Magnus lying on the lino. Rolling onto his side and buckling into a foetal curl, a low groan grated from his lips. They helped him to his feet and back into the sitting room. Eased into his chair, his breathing rate increased as he squeezed his eyes closed.

James knew that his father was being treated for a heart condition, but he had not witnessed an attack of any sort. It came as a shock. This man who he had always considered to be strong in heart and body was unravelling before his eyes. Magnus was advocating criminal acts of revenge. This was not the father he had known. But James had not been there to see the deterioration in Magnus' health. His visits home had been the times when Magnus had purposefully rallied to put on a brave face, sparing his eldest son from seeing him weaken.

"I'll get his tablet," announced Clare as she returned to the kitchen.

"Dad, Dad, speak to me, what happened. Do you need to go to the hospital?"

"No!" wheezed Magnus, "I'm going out . . . when I've had the tablet . . . I'll be fine."

Clare returned with a tablet, a glass of water and a well-built man in a green Parka coat with the hood up concealing his face. The Coleman family had not had any previous encounter with Darry McTandlyn. He scanned the scene and settled his gaze on James.

"Who are you?" he demanded, as though it had been James who had entered his house.

James had guessed why the man was there and what he represented. Paramilitary actions had been discussed many times in the Coleman house, but he had not known of any direct involvement. He looked at the visitor and tried to imagine what was going through his mind. About to commit an act of extreme violence, the man showed no hint of nerves or apprehension. He seemed composed and focussed, in charge of the situation and in a position to impose demands on a family weakened by grief. Through laboured breathing, Magnus answered the man's question.

"He's family, our eldest son."

McTandlyn quickly assessed the situation and made a judgement on James. He had not been told that there was an elder son in the family and he had learned not to trust anyone. It was known that the security forces would place their own undercover operatives and recruited informants into Republican communities using cover stories such as this one.

"Prove it," he ordered.

"What?" exclaimed James, "How are we expected to prove that?"

"Photograph album, birth certificate, whatever does the job." he said coldly as though he did it every day.

Clare went to the mahogany sideboard and knelt down to search in the lower cupboards. She returned with a family album and an old, tartan biscuit tin. She handed over the album and began rifling through to paper contents of the tin. The man flicked through the pictures and glanced at James as he did so. Clare found James' birth certificate and handed that over for inspection. In silence, the photographs were viewed, pictorially summarising the childhood of James Patrick Coleman. The last photograph was a graduation portrait taken one year before. Although James had altered his appearance drastically since then, he could still be recognised.

"Alright University boy, that will do."

His new name for James was scornful and dismissive. He showed clear contempt for education and the educated. He threw the album down onto the coffee table and dropped the birth certificate on the top of it. He turned to look at Magnus.

"Are you coming?" he said, ignoring the evident symptoms of his poor health.

"He's in no condition," replied Clare. "He won't be going anywhere tonight."

"Somebody from the family is supposed to be there, that's the way. Now, what's it to be? What about you, University boy?"

Before James had the chance to speak, his father gripped his coat sleeve and pulled his son close to him.

95

"There'll be no peace for me if you don't. I need you to do it for us, for Philip."

Thoughts flew around inside James' head like a fireworks display. He had no wish to be a party to whatever it was that this man was going to do, but his father was pained and desperate. Losing one family member had been traumatic but prolonging the anguish of another was too much to bear.

"Okay, I'll go Dad, I'll go."

Magnus loosened his grip on James' sleeve. He slipped back in the chair and seemed to breathe with less difficulty. James experienced a moment of relief, of acceptance that he had made the right decision but the reality of what he was going to be involved in dawned on him moments after.

"Dark clothing, a hat, scarf. Now!" said their visitor impatiently, untouched by the moral dilemma being played out before him.

James went into the hall to select clothing from the rail. He experienced second thoughts about going on the revenge mission. It had never been something he had imagined being a part of. His was a family that believed in peaceful means and his University experiences had also followed that model. What had he become? What had his family become? He was on the brink of changing his decision, telling his father and the Brigade man that he was not going to have anything to do with this organised chaos. He was about to go back into the sitting room when his hand fell upon Philip's tracksuit top, red with white stripes on the sleeves. It still had mud on the elbows. He had to go, if only to prevent his father risking his own life, he had to go for his mother and for Philip. James took an old dark grey mackintosh and a black, woollen hat and scarf. He put them on and re-entered the sitting room.

"Okay," he said. "Let's go."

They left by the back door. Magnus and Clare sat together in silence.

CHAPTER SIXTEEN

The black RS2000 was parked at the junction of
Sycamore Avenue and Beech Close. James was in the
back. The driver had not spoken since they had left
James' parents' home. In the passenger seat,
McTandlyn was humming a tune that James did not
recognise. The tension built as James desperately
wanted to know what was planned. He also wanted to
be able to say that he didn't know. The conflict within
was making him chew his lip whilst his stomach felt
as though it was chewing itself.

"What are you going to do?" he finally blabbed,
instantly regretting having done so.

Driver and passenger looked at each other briefly
then faced forward again. The passenger spoke
without looking at James.

"This is a military operation. Do you need to
know that?"

He was enjoying the power he held over the
situation. He wound down the passenger side window
and began pushing a large cobweb that had been spun
across the wing mirror. He gently tapped the glass of
the mirror with his dirty fingernails. From the back
seat, James could not bear the silence.

"My fifteen-year-old brother was killed by the
security forces. I know that is going to be followed by
a strike-back but I don't know the details. I'm

assuming that the British soldiers will be on alert for reprisals. There are hundreds of them and only two of you. You must have a plan, right? I mean, they're armed to the teeth."

A short-legged spider emerged from under the edge of the mirror. McTandlyn had teased it out then he snatched it between his thumb and forefinger and brought it toward his face to inspect it.

"Don't you worry, University boy. We have a plan alright. There's another member of this team. He'll be along any minute now."

The car fell silent once again. A few minutes later a pair of dimmed headlights approached slowly along Sycamore Avenue.

"Right on time, so he is," said McTandlyn.

Nobody moved as the vehicle stopped along the street. A figure got out and went into the driveway of a house. A minute later he went to another house, then another before returning to the vehicle. It moved nearer without the accompanying sound of a car engine. The vehicle stopped again in front of the black Ford. It was an electric milk-float.

James thought it odd for a milkman to be out in the evening. He had been living in the cosseted world of the University campus for too long and had forgotten that the practice of collecting the money had to be done when people were at home.

The milkman wore a tweed, flat cap and a short, work coat. Over his shoulder hung a brown leather bag from which he drew a tally-book and pencil. He went to three of the six houses in Beech Close, paying no attention to the car or its three occupants. Back in the milk-float he steered it away to the end of Sycamore Avenue and onto Pine Avenue. They gave it five minutes before starting the engine of the Ford and humming along to follow the milkman.

The passenger swiftly and mercilessly squeezed the remaining life out of the spider and wiped its liquefied carcass on the mirror glass.

The milkman's first stop took in four houses. He moved along the avenue and stopped. The passenger from the Ford pulled a scarf up to cover his mouth and nose, got out and hurried to the side of the milk-float, pulling out a handgun with a silencer screwed to the barrel. Before he had chance to get out of the driver's seat, the milkman turned his head to look into the business end of the gun. His mouth dropped open and he froze.

"Out!" order the gunman.

The milkman snapped out of his suspended state and leapt out to stand still on the road. James clasped his hands over his mouth on seeing the gun.

"Oh shit!" he exclaimed. The driver said nothing. He simply straightened his gloved fingers then curled them around the tiny steering wheel once again.

"Do as I tell you and you will live through this, milkman. Take off your hat, coat and bag, put it on the seat." The directions were clear and unmistakable.

With trembling fingers, the milkman unbuttoned his coat and tried taking it off before removing the shoulder bag. The resultant mess lay on the driver's seat. He hurriedly added the hat to the pile. The gunman placed the weapon in the waistband of his trousers and quickly put on the milkman's clothes and bag.

"Sit back there," he ordered, pointing at the driver's seat. The milkman did as he was told.

"Stay there and don't move. My mate in that car over there has another gun on you. If you move or do anything he doesn't like the look of, he's going to shoot you in the head. Nod if you understand that."

He nodded once, slowly, then four times quickly.

The gunman took out the handgun again and placed it in the shoulder bag. He walked casually along the street and pushed open the gate of No. 21.

The driver moved the Ford past the milk-float and stopped outside No. 17, concealed from view from anybody at No. 21. He wound down the window to listen.

The gunman's footsteps could be heard on the concrete driveway. He passed the Brown Morris Marina parked facing the gate. As he reached the front door, he checked his watch. The recce man had reported that the milkman had called there for payment at the same time and on the same day of the week with admirable punctuality for several weeks. Each time, the milkman had knocked on the frosted glass of the door with a four-beat rhythm before calling out 'Milk' to reassure the householder.

Arnie and Jennifer were watching a television documentary summarising the Queen's Silver Jubilee year. Arnie knew that his English wife appreciated that sort of programme. Lizzie was upstairs having a bath at the back of the house. The bathroom light could not be seen from the front. The whole scene was a snapshot of domestic peace and tranquillity.

On the driveway, McTandlyn scanned the front and side of the house. The sitting room curtains were drawn, a light was on behind them and the muffled sound of a television could be heard. Upstairs, all rooms were in darkness. He knocked four times on the front door.

"Milk."

The hall light came on and the outsized figure of Arnie Cullen approached the door.

The real milkman had worked out what was going to happen, but he was only able to think about keeping himself alive by staying where he was, covered by the unseen occupants of the black car. The fate of the people in that house was beyond anything he could do. The Cullens had always been civil toward him and had been regular payers. They had tipped well at Christmas. That was all he knew about them.

In the back seat of the Ford, James' entire body shook uncontrollably. His breathing shortened and he tried to shut out the image of that gun in the hand of the man who had been sent to avenge the killing of his brother. In the relative safety of self-distraction, he pictured Philip as a small child, playing behind their house with a plastic gun, pretending to be a cowboy or a spy. It was preferable to linger in that harmless memory than to accept the horrific reality of what was unfolding before him.

The driver said nothing.

The door opened and Arnie Cullen peered out momentarily, distracted by the dual action of picking up the ready-counted and exact money from the side table by the door, he did not properly focus on confirming the authenticity of the caller. Guiding the loose change into his cupped hand he allowed the door to open by a soft push with his foot. He turned to pass the money over and looked up for the first time into the fierce, staring eyes of the man who had been sent to kill him.

The gun emerged from the brown, leather bag and pointed at his chest. From a range of four feet, he had no hope of diving clear. At fifty-five there were no athletic heroics to be called upon. His mind was alert but the body's responses were less so. His only real option was to prepare for his death and the inevitable investigation that would follow. Crime scenes, exchanges of fibres and blood, he had to get hold of this bastard and give his colleagues a fighting chance to catch him. He lunged at the gunman who responded by stepping back and squeezing the trigger. He launched the .22 calibre bullet through the suppressor and across four feet of fresh air into Arnie Cullen's chest. The bulk of the policeman was not to be stopped in motion by such a small bullet. His body's trajectory continued, though most of the air in his lungs burst out as the slug hit him. Despite stepping back, the gunman could not fully get out of the way and the second bullet was fired as Cullen stretched out his arms to aim a rugby tackle around his attacker's legs. The bullet entered Cullen's torso through the top of his left shoulder, by the neck.

It was not as the gunman had imagined it to have been. In his mind he was to inflict a clean 'double-tap' to the chest of a stunned and motionless victim before walking away, unruffled and masterful. In reality, he had been attacked by a man who was much larger than him and despite firing two well-aimed shots at his core, that man's arms were wrapped around his legs, forcing him backwards onto the ground, and he could not be shaken off.

Cullen gathered sufficient breath to call out wordlessly.

"Ahhh! Ahhh!"

"Get the fuck off me you bastard!" growled the hapless assassin.

The driver of the black Ford heard the voices and sensed the urgency. Something had gone wrong and it was up to him as the back-up man to act. He hurriedly let out the clutch and made the car lunge forward then sharply stop outside the open gate of No. 21. He saw the wrestling scene taking place on the ground in the light from the hallway behind. He got out and stood next to the open door. He was unsure what to do. Did he go to his partner's aid or let him deal with it?

Although the life was ebbing away from Cullen, he managed to roll to the side onto the gun-arm of his attacker, preventing him from aiming a third at him. The third bullet did get fired but it missed Cullen and went through the sitting room window, lodging in the plasterwork above Jennifer's head. She screamed and dived to the carpet.

"Arnie, Arnie get down. Lizzie stay upstairs, stay upstairs!"

James saw the struggle of bodies on the ground and the getaway driver dithering by the open car door. It was time for the driver to speak.

"Darry, Darry, finish this, come on!"

McTandlyn rolled the weakening Cullen away from his gun arm. He turned the barrel inwards and put it to Cullen's temple. It was the fourth shot that ended the life of Arnold Worsley Cullen.

Even in death he held onto his man, the man who had to wriggle and wrestle the dead man's bulk and grip away before he could get to his feet to stagger, gasping and shattered, out of the driveway and round to the passenger side of the waiting car.

Through gaps in his fingers, James looked up at the scene. The man, who he did not know anything about, lay dead on the ground. A woman screeched from inside the house and, in the unlit bedroom above the front door, a slim young woman in a dressing gown stood motionless with her hand raised to hold open the curtain.

That closing scene, etched in his mind like a slave's brand, made tears fill his eyes, tears for the dead man, for the screaming woman, for the young woman in the window, for Philip, for the whole unfathomable mess that he was in, up to his neck.

Distant sirens could be heard, getting louder. The Ford screamed through the gears and away from Pine Avenue, away from Lodale, away from the human carnage. Slowing to cross a main road onto another anonymous neighbourhood then picking up speed once it was not likely to attract much attention. It stopped on waste ground a mile from James' parents' house. He was ushered out.

"Leave the coat and hat, they'll burn with the car," ordered McTandlyn who was still breathing heavily. James did as he was told and watched the car speed away. He set off to walk across the common land, shivering. He stopped, felt the cool night air clash with the burning of the skin on his face. He crouched down, vomited on the grass and cried.

CHAPTER SEVENTEEN

It was nearly one in the morning when James returned to his family home. He entered by the back door into the dark of the kitchen and saw light from beneath the door to the lounge. There was no sound, not simply the quiet of a home where the occupants had retired to bed, there was a deeper quiet, a disconcerting, ugly quiet. He pushed open the door and saw the room lit by a small lamp on a table between the settee and the ceramic fireplace he had so mischievously drawn on in pencil as a small child. The television screen was grey and silent. His mother's usual chair was empty as was his father's. The high back of the old settee concealed the cushions and it struck James that one of them had stayed up to await his return and had fallen asleep on the settee. He edged around and saw his mother sitting on the settee staring forward. His father was next to her with his head on her lap. She stroked his grey hair across the side of his head whilst cupping a hand under his chin.

"Mam," said James in a whisper. She turned her head and looked at him with desperately tired eyes, devoid of the zest she had always had.

"She looked down at Magnus again and continued to stroke his hair. She looked forward at nothing and said.

"What brought all this to us? What did we do to deserve this?"

She took in a full breath of air and let it out slowly. James became aware of how shallow his own breathing had become. He looked at his father and saw that his chest was not rising. He showed no movement. His normally ruddy and weathered complexion had given way to a colourless hue. A tear dripped from Clare's nose and landed on his forehead. She wiped it away with her thumb.

"He wasn't in pain, not at the end."

James was hit with the realisation of what had happened. Moments from his childhood struck like lightning through his mind. His memories of that big, vital man, always keeping the family safe from a hostile world, wrestling with him on the rug and being allowed to win, watching him take the stabilisers off James' bike but still holding on to the seat, taking and posing for photographs at James' graduation. Now he was gone.

"Oh God, Mam." He fought the choking shock of grief sufficiently to say. "I'll call the priest or something."

Clare stared at the wall and softly said. "There'll be no rush for that. There's no rush for anything now."

*

The Royal Ulster Constabulary were well used to going to great lengths to protect witnesses, but when those witnesses were the wife and daughter of a slain colleague, an increased degree of urgency became evident. With little more than the clothes they had been able to throw on in the aftermath of the murder, Jennifer and Lizzie were whisked away to a safe-house on the coast where they made detailed statements about the killing whilst being treated for shock. When they could offer no more information, the decision was made to relocate them to a place considered to be out of reach of those who would benefit most from their inability to testify.

Jennifer's origins came into play and they were flown to England. Placed in a police-owned house in a cul-de-sac in a quiet, residential area of South Manchester, they had to build lives from the devastation that had befallen them. After three days a telecom engineer connected a phone in the house. The police liaison officer issued clear warnings that any calls made or received must not mention their location. In effect, they were only to make calls that were absolutely necessary.

Jennifer and Lizzie provided what comfort they could to each other, finding strength when needed to be able to function as people. A cycle of hugging, weeping and recovering only to go through it all again perpetuated their first few days of life in England. The designated officers from Belfast provided what practical support they could, and a bereavement councillor was arranged.

The focal point of the process was Arnie's funeral, which was a source of dread for them both. They were flown by charter plane to attend the funeral and were staggered by the turnout. Countless dress uniforms of police, military, fire and ambulance staff together with countless lines of people along the route and filling the streets around Belfast Cathedral. For security reasons, the Cullens were whisked in and out of the service with clinical efficiency.

Although Lizzie felt a pang of guilt at the distraction to her grief, she allowed herself to hope to catch a glimpse of Sid amongst the crowd. It didn't happen. She did, however, see her friend Carol Jones. A loose plan formed in her mind. Upon returning to

Manchester, she called Carol at home, exercising all prescribed caution in what she said. After apologising for not getting in touch, for which Carol issued a rebuke, Lizzie asked her to try to trace Sid for her. Carol had seen Lizzie with him on the bike ride to Helen's Bay but not since. Lizzie gave all of the information she could and explained that she wanted him to know why she had to leave and that she would see him when she was allowed to.

By arrangement, Lizzie called Carol back the following day. Carol had no news. She had visited the University and had asked the reception staff to find Sid. They had scanned the student records and found only one person called Sidney who was Hong Kong Chinese. Carol had also traced and spoken to Ken Hoggard who was unable to identify any of the participants of his organised bike ride.

A dark and colourless surge of loss overcame Lizzie. It had been left on hold until feelings of bereavement had subsided sufficiently for her to experience it. She pictured Sid waiting for her at the park, walking around the duck pond alone.

CHAPTER EIGHTEEN

The body of Magnus Coleman had been taken by the funeral directors. The police had made a cursory visit to the Coleman home and had been assured by the family doctor that Magnus' death had not come as a surprise, given his chronic health difficulties. The death of his younger son was also considered to have been a contributory factor. The doctor had given Clare a sedative, not the first she had been prescribed.

At 5.45am she went up to the marital bed, alone and drained, trying to muster the resolve to face life without her husband and her son. James had tried to sleep on the old bed which had been Philip's before he had moved into the larger bedroom that had previously belonged to James. The bed was devoid of any bedding. He did sleep but not restfully. At 8.20am there was a knock on the back door. Clare's medication had maintained her sleeping state but James heard it and, still clothed, he answered the door. Two men he had not met before entered the kitchen without being asked. James did not have to ask what body they represented.

"Are you Coleman?" asked one man as though he was accusing him of something.

"I'm the only man left called Coleman in this house," said James offended at having had the grief of his family interrupted as well as his shortened night's rest. "What do you want?"

"You! Get your coat. There's somebody who needs to talk to you."

"What now? Who? My father has just died and I —"

"Now," said the man doing the talking.

James had neither the will nor the words to contest. He picked his leather jacket from the hooks in the hall and headed off through the back door. He hoped to be back before his mother awoke. He was led to a rough-looking, beige Austin Allegro with one door that did not match the others. He sat in the back, a now-familiar position, and was driven for ten minutes in what seemed to be no particular direction. The car stopped near to the block of flats. Up the stinking stairwell and across the landings apparently at random they finally stopped at the intended flat. There was the musical knock then a pause and a cough. The door was unbolted and they entered.

James was steered into the darkened room where a tall man in his late fifties sat in an armchair.

"Sit down lad." It was more of an order than a gesture of hospitality. James sat. His two escorts stood back and leaned on the wall.

"You're James Patrick Coleman. I'm saddened to hear about your brother and your father, my condolences to you and your mother. Do you know who I am?" James shook his head. "My name is Niall Mahon. I hold a position of some seniority in the Republican movement. I know where you were last night. One of the men you were with has been arrested."

James had an instant dread that the man had told the police that he had been involved in the murder at

Lodale. Mahon had the look of a man who could read minds.

"Was it the man called Darry?" asked James, trying to understand what he was being told.

"That's right lad," said Mahon gravely. "Don't worry, there's no way he'll be talking to the police about you. But we do have a problem. If the police manage to link you to that operation, it's going to be difficult, very difficult for you. You're not saying anything, is this sinking in with you?"

"Erm yes, I understand. What do I have to do?"

James' hands were beginning to tremble involuntarily, and his mouth was unusually dry.

"We need to get you away from here, right now. You've got a passport?" said Mahon.

"Yes but my mother, I can't just leave her like that, the funeral, both funerals."

"We will take care of everything here. You're no good to anyone in jail now, are you?"

"In jail?" His skin ran cold all over. "I didn't kill anybody Mr Mahon."

"I know lad, I know, but we have to send you away for a wee while, to protect you. It's all been thought through. You have a job to go to that is right up your street, using your brain, you're a clever lad, I know that. You'll be working for a man called Cooke. You are to be his apprentice, so you are."

He allowed a moment for James to take in what was being said before continuing.

"These gentlemen will take you to get your passport and a bag of clothes then to the airport. You're booked on a flight at half past eleven. Any questions?"

James had too many questions to be able to get them out. His mother would be feeling so alone, his life as he knew it was to change unrecognisably and he thought about Kiki. He was to meet her that afternoon, they were going to tell each other all about themselves and be together as a real couple.

Flying out of the country was so wrong but he could not take the threat of going to jail lightly. Mahon was right when he had said that he was no good to anybody in jail. The harsh realisation made him feel sick, only the absence of any food prevented that. He thought about Kiki, how she would think that he was a bastard, having his way with her and dropping her from his mind so selfishly. He could not bear so many things at that moment, but avoiding jail was the priority.

"Okay, I get it, Mr Mahon. Please look after my mother."

"We will lad, don't worry about that. She'll understand that you had to go and that you had no choice. You can call her when you get there."

"Where am I going?"

"America!"

*

The turnout for the double funeral of Magnus and Philip Magnus Coleman was high. The circumstances of the death of Philip, together with the additional tragic element of his youth, had made it a political event. Hooded men with handguns stepped from the crowd at the graveside and fired a volley into the air. That defiant and dramatic gesture gripped all present, provoking protest and discomfort, all unspoken. The absence of James Patrick Coleman went almost unnoticed

CHAPTER NINETEEN

Airports have long been portrayed in the movies as the scenes of tearful reunions and last-minute reconciliations between lovers who had thought all was lost. Without those highly emotive additions, airports are simply functional buildings designed to facilitate short-term use by travellers. In the event that unforeseen delays force any person to spend any more than the minimum amount of time there, the inevitable result is the sapping of all optimism and good will, the slow erosion of whatever feelings of anticipation which had been held before.

The delay of Aer Lingus flight DY4555A was, according to the mechanically motivated and monotone female announcer through the whining and tinny speakers, due to a weather front off the coast of Nova Scotia. Benny Henslow slumped onto the end seat of one of the rows of poorly upholstered short term seating. In the two years since his graduation, Benny had worked as a faculty researcher at the West Boston University. His boss was Professor Gerard Cooke, an emeritus head of the faculty of political sciences who worked Benny like a galley slave, paid him peanuts and never showed one iota of appreciation of his efforts. Benny tolerated this oppression because he had the spine of an earthworm and his life ambition was no more impressive. The thought of trying to make his way in the big, bad world sent shivers through Benny and brought out his eczema. The safe and cosseted world of West Boston

University was his home and had to be preserved at all costs. His parents' disappointment in him was, to some extent, assuaged by their ability to tell their friends that 'Benjamin was doing very well in the world of academia' - a topic so dull it was guaranteed to end any probing questions about what he actually did, or how low down the academic pecking order Benny actually was, whilst remaining respectable in their social circle.

Benny was twenty-four with the paunchy stomach of a man twice his age. His round shoulders appeared incapable of raising his arms above his head and the matching luggage beneath his eyes was clear evidence of a long-term, sleep disorder. He managed to keep his eyes open and his wits about him sufficiently to be able to identify the young punk-rocker in the black, leather jacket as the person he had been sent to collect.

The University campus was modern, clean and vast. A tree-lined perimeter road gave access on the inside to a jumble of five-storey, residential blocks of pale brick and white weatherboard. On the outside was vehicular activity on sprawling, colour-coded, parking lots with numbered rows and lettered spaces like the seating in a theatre. The sun shone with an optimism rarely experienced by James Patrick Coleman back home in Northern Ireland, a home he had no prospect of returning to in the near future.

Benny spun the Toyota off the perimeter road and onto one of the car parks on the south of the buildings. The car radio played some Paul McCartney tune, the words of which James had barely noticed before, although the tune was familiar. He had, on the journey over the pond, momentarily hoped that the American punk groups he had struggled to find in the record shops and radio stations at home would be more easily accessed in the land of opportunity, but instead of the

Ramones and New York Dolls he was being served schmaltzy love ballads by Wings. On a musical level at least, the United States was losing 1-0 to the old country.

The music fell silent when Benny pulled out the ignition key and stepped out. James followed him to the back of the car and opened the tailgate.

"I'll get that for you, Mr Coleman," said Benny reaching in and pulling the case out and onto the tarmacked ground.

"It's fine Benny, you don't need to carry it for me."

Benny closed the tailgate but didn't bother to lock the car. The case was old and had little in it due to the hurried nature of James' departure from Belfast. Benny still found carrying it demanding.

"No, I've got it Mr Coleman, Sir," he said trying to carry the case first with one hand, then the other and finally with both.

"People call - used to call - my Dad Mr Coleman. I'm James or any name derived from it, I don't much care."

Benny laboured with the case across the parking lot across the perimeter road and onto a cement footpath between the buildings. They crossed a quadrangle and under a canopy, through another quadrangle and up to a glass fronted reception. It was like a large hotel, but it was more quaint than it was corporate. The reception was staffed by two smiling women, one thin and the other enormous.

"Welcome to Boston, Mr Coleman. I hope you get to like it here," said the larger woman.

"I'm sure I will, thank you. What are your names please?"

Both receptionists seemed pleasantly surprised to have been asked. The obligation had always been on them to remember the names of people who came to their reception desk. It made a change for both of them to be acknowledged as having names of their own.

"I'm Melissa," said the thin woman, "and this is Jeanie." Jeanie smiled up at him from the seat behind the desk.

"Can I just say," added Jeanie, "your accent is adorable. Where do you come from?"

"I'm from Belfast in Northern Ireland," he said.

"Is that in England?" asked Melissa.

Rather than get embroiled in a geographic or historical discussion as to the merits of what was plainly a harmless suggestion based on insufficient knowledge, James opted to leave that conversation where it was and with dignity intact all round.

"It's near England, yes."

Benny saved James from more testing questions by guiding him to the elevator, having left his suitcase with Melissa and Jeanie. Up at the seventh floor they navigated a corridor of equally spaced white plant-pots bearing hosta plants and mini box-bushes. Closed, white doors each bore a card in a frame displaying the names, titles, qualifications and subjects of expertise of the occupant or occupants of the room beyond. At the end of the corridor by the stairway fire-door Benny stopped at a door with a sign that read:

Professor Gerard Cooke. PhD, MSc, BA. Head of Faculty of Political History.

Benny paused to gather his composure before knocking and entering.

"Come in," bellowed a bass-baritone voice that could probably be heard in Canada.

Inside, the eight metre square office was like the library of a madman. A disorganised eruption of books, which could not have been assembled in any discernible order, lay on and off shelves from floor to ceiling along every available stretch of wall and across much of the floor-space. A slalom around three uncoordinated stacks of bookshelves revealed natural light permeating from the metal-framed window, which should have taken the entire width of the room but had to concede half of the potential light to house even more books. From behind the final stack of mid-floor bookshelves came that voice again.

"Henslow, is that yourself now?"

James found it to be an odd blend of harsh Irish and smooth American, but at a volume that was neither.

"Yes Professor, I've brought Mr Coleman from the airport, Sir," answered Benny who was evidently nervous in the Professor's presence.

"Good, good," declared the voice, as its owner stood up from behind the stack to guide James around it.

Professor Gerard Cooke was a red-faced, strawberry-nosed man in late middle-age. He had an unruly spray of thick, grey, wavy hair and a matching shaggy beard with the yellowing of tobacco smoke at its lighter tips. His eyes broadcast a benign intensity from behind plastic-framed spectacles, but there was a hospitable air about him, nevertheless. He looked as though he didn't smell very pleasant and close up that was true. James detected pipe-tobacco and musty, unaired clothing.

"Welcome to Boston my boy," he said with a gap-toothed smile. "Has this clot sorted out your luggage?"

He could only have been referring to Benny, who was trying to look occupied when there was nothing that he could have been doing at that moment. James felt obliged to lessen Benny's stress.

"Benny has been very obliging, Professor. I'm grateful."

"Anyway, it's about that time, don't you think? Let's go and have a drink."

The professor led James out into the corridor leaving Benny alone in the office. There was no suggestion that Benny was invited to join them. They chatted cordially about the journey and the old country. They descended seven flights of stairs and sprang out through a fire escape door, the sunshine brought warmth to the skin and pain to the eyes. Once out of the building and away from any people, the Professor's tone changed. His voice dropped to a conspiratorial whisper.

"I have been briefed as to what brought you here, boy. Those calling the shots have plans for you. They expect great things."

"I thought I was coming here to get out of the way for a while, to take a junior academic post at the University, to study under your guidance. What other plans are there for me?"

"Well, boy, the first plan is for you to look like a bloody academic, not something to scare children away from the orchard!" He made himself laugh.

James managed to stifle his urge to laugh. What gave this scruffy, unkempt, old buffer the right to criticise his appearance? He looked and smelled like a tramp.

"Does it matter what I look like Professor?" said James, trying to keep the mood light.

"Oh yes!" The old man assured him. "What you are here to do depends a lot on giving certain people what they want."

"The students?" asked James, barely concealing his confusion.

"Bollocks to the students, they're the least of your challenges. They'll eat whatever crap you feed them. You'll see precious few of them anyway. No, you are being groomed for better things, so get yourself groomed, okay?"

"Professor, what exactly is it I am her to do?"

"You are to be my apprentice. It will be a long process but, eventually, you will take over what I do."

"Wow! I don't know how, or who thinks, but, well, thank you anyway, for this opportunity. To aim to be the head of the faculty would be a privilege."

"Oh but that's just half the job, boy."

"Half the job, Sir?"

"Oh yes!"

The professor made himself laugh again. That habit was beginning to unnerve James. He was anxious to know what he was getting involved with. Conversation was suspended as they reached the side door of a large refectory. They passed through a sea of chattering students carrying book-bags and trays of food and paper cups, all dressed as they wished to, a freedom he was soon to be denied. The professor led him through the clamour to a double door through which was a smaller, quieter bar with comfortable upholstery, low tables and velvet drapes. The bar stocked a bewildering range of drinks, but the professor steered him to one in particular.

"Will you have a Guinness, boy? I had to move Heaven and Earth to get them to stock the black stuff."

James was by then convinced that he was being referred to as 'boy' because the professor could not yet remember his name. As for the choice of beer, James had never been a willing consumer of the Irish favourite, but he did know not to appear rude in a new environment.

"Yes, thank you," he said with feigned enthusiasm.

No money changed hands and James got the impression that there was a 'pay later' arrangement in place. They sat at a table near to a window at the farthest end of the room. There were only five or six other people there and all of them remained near to the bar. The professor appeared to be trying to avoid being overheard.

"Cheers!"

"Cheers!"

They sipped through the white foam tops. The professor followed this by wiping his beard with his jacket sleeve. James pulled a face at the bitterness of the beer. The professor noticed.

"You don't normally have this do you?" he said.

"Rarely," admitted James, "I'd usually have a lager."

"Well," deliberated the old lecturer, "You're going to have to rethink a few things here. You have been, I understand, a highly rated student at the University of Belfast. A first class degree with honours, political history was it?"

James nodded with misplaced modesty.

"And your Master's degree . . ."

"I'm waiting for the final grades for that Professor."

"Well wait no longer, I know the grades, I was the external marker. You broke the bank with that one too. I think it's only a matter of time before you embark on a doctorate."

"Thank you, I hope not to disappoint."

"Academic matters are not the challenge. You'll skip through all that, I'm sure. Soon you'll find out why you were really sent here."

CHAPTER TWENTY

James was given an apartment in the staff accommodation block on the University campus. It had four times the floor-space of his room in Belfast University. With the room came the use of a small but good quality kitchen, a refrigerator, a television and a desk and chair. The shower room was in a separate bedroom.

He sat on the bed and looked around. The conflicting strands of thought that had been swimming in circles in his head were unable to find any straws at which to clutch. Memories and vivid snapshots of his life flashed by, the ones with Philip and their Dad began with high reality, but their faces faded until he could not summon them when he tried. He laid back in the bed and closed his eyes. He imagined Kiki lying on the bed next to him. They were in his old room on the campus in Belfast. He squeezed the bed covers tightly in his hand and felt the warmth of the naked body of the girl he had left behind, along with everything of his past life. Exile from his home city, his University and his mother was hard. Pedro too was also noticeably absent. But the emptiness he felt without those people was deepened to the point of desperation when combined with the sense of loss he felt when he thought of her.

He turned on his side as though to face her, to feel her light, silent breath on his neck. The overwhelming joy at being alive that he had experienced with her made the pain all the more agonising. He had no way of finding her, of getting a message to her, telling her that he would be back with her when he could and to not forget him. He could not envisage ever feeling fully alive again. His dreams had become turgid and fearful. He wasn't living, he was merely surviving. His remaining purpose was to honour Philip's memory and protect what was left of his family with whatever abilities he had. Knowing that he had no choice but to accept the challenge placed before him, he resolved to make it work and reconcile himself with what it was he was called upon to do.

CHAPTER TWENTY-ONE

Criminal trials at Belfast Crown Court were, in the main, the same as at any other crown court in the United Kingdom, a model of justice administration admired and emulated the world over. The usual ingredients of defendants, witnesses, lawyers, judges, jurors and excessive quantities of paper were universally present, but when a murder trial was convened, the court building took on a new and compelling intensity. It was invisible to the naked eye, but unmistakable to all. When the divisive complexity of terrorism is added, together with the fact that the victim was a prominent officer of the Royal Ulster Constabulary, the tension during the trial reaches a peak previously unfound.

An unprecedented security operation was in place with all police reservists called upon to participate. Army resources were put on stand-by to lend support as part of a contingency plan. Protection normally reserved for witnesses and judges was also arranged for the lawyers and jurors. By the time any individual entered the courtroom, it could reasonably be anticipated that they were already traumatised and scared out of their wits.

The case of R. v. McTandlyn had stalled several times before finally hearing some witness evidence. Allegations of witness intimidation and jury fixing were raised, investigated and dealt with without delay, the trial had to go ahead. The morale within and the confidence of the community were at stake. Belfast justice was also on trial. Five months after the death of Arnold Cullen, the first witness took the stand.

The court heard from character witnesses who told them about Cullen, some testimonies resulted in tears from both the witness and those listening. As a persuasive exercise, this had no value. Those who liked him or his profession, and those who did not, kept the same views that they had arrived with. The senior investigator, a Detective Chief Superintendent with a face like an unmade bed who looked as though he had been hewn from granite and a voice that sounded like a saw trying to cut down oak trees, outlined the initial management of the scene and explained how the evidence was to be presented to the court.

The Lodale milkman, gave evidence from behind a screen, although he was no longer the Lodale milkman. His account was most convincing. He trembled and stuttered as a hushed court room lived the experience through him. He provided clear continuity of the unfolding horror up to the point when Jennifer Cullen took to the witness box. She gave her account with comparative coolness, although she was overcome and tearful several times. McTandlyn's defence barrister's team made only token efforts at cross-examination of the prosecution witnesses, until eighteen-year-old Elizabeth Cullen took the stand.

Lizzie was initially too quiet for the judge to be able to absorb her testimony and he therefore decided that the jury could not hear her either. In the kindly fashion of a formal yet caring uncle, he asked her to speak up and she did. It had the effect of improving her confidence and she spoke with increased fluency and clarity. She was led through her evidence as it had been recorded in writing at the time. The prosecutor read each passage of the typed version of the witness statement and invited Lizzie to confirm that it was true. With minimal additional words, she repeatedly confirmed that the content of the statement was correct, prompting the prosecutor to move on. The story built up by degrees and at the point where she recounted going to the bedroom window above the front door of their home on Pine Avenue, all present were gripped and soaking up every word she said. When the prosecutor finished leading Lizzie through her main evidence and sat down, a collective sigh of relief was followed by previously held back coughing and adjustment of seating. The hush returned when the defending Q.C. took to his feet.

The barrister wasted no time in trying to introduce doubt into the evidence given by Lizzie.

"I put it to you, Miss Cullen, that you did not see the defendant Mr McTandlyn that night, did you?"

"I saw that man shoot my father," she said with unwavering conviction. The lawyer was not to be put off.

"I suggest," he said whilst not looking at her, "that this is a fabrication. You did not see any such thing. You were told by the police what to say."

Lizzie silently refused to answer until the lawyer was looking at her. At the moment he did so she replied.

"This is the truth. I saw that man kill my father." The lawyer read from his notes then said.

"You say that you saw a man standing at the gate."

"That is correct."

"Can you describe that man?"

"No," she said abruptly.

"Why not?" he said with incredulity.

"Because my attention was on the man with a gun who my father was fighting with."

"But you claim to have heard that man say the name Darry? Twice?"

"That is correct, that's what he said."

"Are you trying to convince this court that whilst a man with a gun was in mortal combat with your father beneath the window, you had the presence of mind to take in one word spoken by another man, a man you did not look at?"

"I heard the man at the gate shout Darry, twice." she replied calmly.

"He could have said Gerry or Larry or Terry or Harry, in the heat of that moment you could have heard any name. How can you be so certain?"

"After the shots were fired, only my mother spoke. She was inside the house. It was a man's voice. The bedroom window was open, there was no other sound. He called Darry, Darry."

"Come come, Miss Cullen, there was too much happening for you to have heard it so clearly. What you are telling the court is the result of coaching and coercion by the investigating police officers, isn't it?"

"I took an oath to tell the truth when I entered this witness box. I didn't hear you take one."

This brought a sharp intake of breath amongst the assembled listeners. It served to ease some of the tension and inhibit the train of thought of the barrister. The Judge intervened to put the cross-examination back on track.

"Answer the question only Miss Cullen," he said without any hint of chastisement. He noticed that the colour had drained from her cheeks. She had taken on the pallor of the anaemic. He put this down to the stress of the confrontational exchange she had risen to so impressively.

Lizzie nodded at him and turned back to receive the next question but it didn't come. The defending Q.C. indicated that the cross examination was over and sat down. The judge turned to the witness box and said.

"You may stand down now, Miss Cullen. Thank you."

Lizzie turned to descend the four wooden steps. She made it to the second one before collapsing, bouncing off the side-rail before landing on her side on the floor of the courtroom.

An usher and the court clerk went to her aid. Jennifer, having finished giving her evidence and taken a seat in the public seating area, dashed past the lawyers and their piles of paper to her daughter's aid. All other people in the room suspended their interest in the progress of the trial. After attending to Lizzie for a minute, the clerk stood and said to the judge.

"She's fainted, she'll be fine."

The judge ordered an adjournment. When the trial resumed, the remaining witnesses for the prosecution were heard. The case for the defence went ahead without the drama experienced during the earlier testimonies. McTandlyn went into the witness box on the advice of the defence team who would otherwise have virtually no witnesses to call. He gave an uncorroborated account of his movements on the evening of the Cullen murder which, if believed, painted a picture of a church volunteer who had prayed particularly hard that day. He claimed that the identification made by Lizzie Cullen was a mistake and probably engineered by the security forces who were desperate to pin the Cullen murder on somebody and they were not choosy who it was.

The jury, who were not told anything of the criminal and terrorist antecedents of the accused, believed Lizzie Cullen and returned a guilty verdict. The judge not only knew of McTandlyn's previous convictions, but he was also aware that the driver of the Ford had been a police informant. After passing information on McTandlyn within minutes of leaving the scene of the murder, he had been identified by the I.R.A. as being the source of a leak. His body was found floating in the Lagan with a single bullet wound to the back of his head.

The judge handed down a sentence of thirty-five years imprisonment.

Darry McTandlyn was taken by maximum security transport to the Maze Prison.

CHAPTER TWENTY-TWO

Three weeks after the trial and back in England, Lizzie collapsed again. She was taken by ambulance to hospital but remained unconscious. Transferred to the Intensive Care Unit, she underwent a thorough medical examination. The diagnosis was that she had contracted a virus of indeterminate origin. The virus had attacked her cardio-vascular system and her body reacted to it by closing down certain functions.

"Your daughter has slipped into a coma, Mrs Cullen – and she's pregnant." There was no spare capacity for softening such news for that overworked and under-rested casualty doctor. He may have lacked a delicate bedside manner, but he got things done without delay. Jennifer could not take in what she was hearing. Outside, the siren of an ambulance wailed its droning notes across Manchester.

"Did you hear me Mrs Cullen? I said your daughter is expecting a baby, no, it's more advanced than that. She is in labour right now. I think she's about seven and a half months gone. Mrs Cullen?" Jennifer still looked bewildered. The doctor did not have time for that. He turned to a passing staff nurse and said. "Can you do something with this lady please?"

The nurse took Jennifer into a relative's room and tried to explain the situation in more tender tones. Gradually, Jennifer absorbed the revelation along with the prognosis for Lizzie's condition. The coma could last a day, a year or she could never come out of it. Jennifer had no time to prepare herself for this news. Her strength, her rock was dead and her only child was hanging onto life by a thread. She could not take on the responsibility of a baby. She had to concentrate on doing what she could for Lizzie.

The child was delivered by caesarean section whilst Lizzie lay comatose, attached to a dozen wires, tubes and monitors. Jennifer stood by the bedside in the Intensive Care Unit. She had been to the Special Care Baby Unit in an adjoining building to see the child, but she had been unable to feel anything for the baby when her own daughter was in such a state. The doctors had told her that the virus, the pregnancy, the delayed shock of seeing her father's murder and subsequent bereavement, giving evidence at the trial and an iron deficiency had combined to bring on the coma.

The hospital chaplain and a clinical director of the hospital advised Jennifer of the options open to her. Several times she had broken down and cried as they tried to speak to her. Eventually, she understood the situation and found a lucid moment to decide. She looked at Lizzie and remembered when she had been a tiny infant. Along with Arnie, she had declared that she should want for nothing and have every good thing they could give her. At that moment, all that could be done was to hold her hand, talk to her and wait for some sign of recovery. After a week without any sign, Jennifer made the decision to make the baby available for fostering. After three weeks, she authorised that the child was to be adopted.

A tear fell on the form that Jennifer had to sign. She hoped that it was what Lizzie would have wanted for the baby or if it wasn't, she hoped that Lizzie would understand. Above all, she hoped that Lizzie would get the chance to say what she wanted. On the sixth week, there was some movement of fingers and a flick of an eyelid. Lizzie stirred and Jennifer wailed like an amplified banshee in joy and relief.

Over four days, Lizzie's ability to function and communicate returned. Her speech was at first slurred and breathless but, with her mother's help and patience, she grasped each point of progress, each modicum of development, until she felt that she was no longer a patient but was a human being in recovery. On the fifth day of her consciousness, Lizzie began to ask challenging questions.

"I have stitches here." She ran a finger across her lower abdomen. "What happened to me, Mammy?"

Jennifer closed her eyes and turned to look out of the window. She swallowed hard and turned back to face Lizzie.

"Did you know you were anaemic?" she said with surprising levity.

"Is that what caused the coma?" she asked with caution, noticing that her mother was finding it difficult to speak of it.

"It was one of the things, Lizzie. There were a few others. You had a virus of some sort then there was the trial and your Dad's death. It all put a strain on you." She evidently had not finished.

"What else Mammy? Tell me."

"You didn't know, did you?" She smoothed Lizzie's hair down to her shoulder.

"Know what?" Lizzie braced herself for some additional medical condition, one that would affect her permanently.

"That you were pregnant."

There were no words for this news. After twenty seconds Lizzie covered her face with her hands and sobbed uncontrollably. Hugged by her mother, she regained sufficient composure to say.

"I didn't know Mammy, I'm sorry, I'm sorry."

"You have nothing to be sorry about. You are my daughter and I am proud of you no matter what."

Nothing was said for a minute until, without looking up, Lizzie asked.

"The baby, did it . . . ?"

"The child was early but fine. Lizzie, I had to decide what should happen, what to do for the best. You were in a coma, neither you nor I could look after an infant. I had to do it. I said that the child could be adopted. I hope you understand why I did it and you don't hate me for it. You had a boy. It will be up to the folks who are adopting him to give him a name."

Lizzie curled her arms around her raised knees and rocked in a ball on the hospital bed. So much was darting around in her head she was unable to make sense of it. She knew that she was lucky to be alive and she also knew that her mother had been there with her, willing her to regain consciousness and live again. She did not know what to feel about a baby she didn't know she was having, a tiny person she had never seen or known. She reassured her mother that she supported her decision and that, under the circumstances, it was the right one. She was to rethink that many times after.

For weeks Jennifer had been sleeping on a foldaway bed in Lizzie's hospital room. She could, having witnessed Lizzie regain her faculties, have gone home at night but she didn't want to. When Jennifer was asleep, Lizzie allowed herself to recall the intimacy that she had shared with Sid. She felt that it had all been a dream but was painfully reminded by the stitches across her abdomen that it was all real. That reality made her realise that the love she had shared with Sid had also been real. She shared another thing with him - neither of them had known the child they had conceived. Would he have wanted to know? Would he have dropped her at the news of an unplanned child? He wasn't like that. He was a caring and gentle soul who saw beauty in things. He would have seen the beauty in that child too. After all, the child was created by two people who loved each other. How he would have resented that the baby had been given up for adoption. He would not have seen anything beautiful in that. She could not go through life carrying such gloomy thoughts. Sid was in another country now and she had to let go. She had her life to lead, a life that she had nearly lost.

CHAPTER TWENTY-THREE

Having had seven months to prepare, the Governor of the Maze Prison only needed two days to carry out all necessary assessment procedures before Darry McTandlyn was moved onto 'B' wing.

His previous experiences in the Maze, for offences of violence and theft, had afforded him a familiarisation and the prospect of a further stay in jail did not bother him very much. He had once spent three weeks on remand on a charge of rape but had been released when the victim had unexpectedly retracted her complaint.

Like the borstal training he had undergone in his formative years, there was a strictly regimented structure in the Maze. It was, as far as the prisoners were concerned, run on a basis of military seniority and each man was expected to know their place in the pecking order. Appointments were made according to status earned before conviction and imprisonment. The combined purpose created an atmosphere befitting a prisoner-of-war establishment, for the inmates were in the unshakable belief that their actions which landed them in the Maze were acts of war rather than acts of criminality.

The daily routine made little provision for the motivation of the inmates' crimes. Bells rang with precise timings, lights came on and off, cell doors opened and closed when scheduled and the usual rituals of slopping-out, sending and receiving letters, which were all read by the staff before being passed on to the named recipient, and the distribution of meals. Later in the day saw association periods, work details, which were only carried out with the approval of the highest ranking I.R.A. man on the wing. They were accepted only in the cause of improving the living standards of the prisoners. There were visits from families and on occasion, legal representatives. The searching of prisoners and cells was carried out relentlessly and was the most clearly demonstrated act to remind everyone that the security categorisation was Maximum.

On the first few association periods, McTandlyn was received by most of the prisoners as a war hero. In Belfast, the killing of a policeman was a divisive act. Whilst some considered it to be a major strike back against an oppressive attacker and some were more concerned about the victim's membership of a rival community, there existed, even among the committed Republican prison population of the Maze, a school of thought that the shooting of an unarmed man was not the act of a true soldier and should not be celebrated, nor should the perpetrator.

These differences of opinion in the ranks had the potential to cause infighting and the senior men were keen to keep order. Dissent had to be put down at the earliest possible stage. McTandlyn had all of the necessary credentials to act as enforcer. The previous incumbent was over sixty and whilst he had commanded the requisite respect, it had been noticed that some of the younger inmates were less than reverential. McTandlyn's reputation was more than enough to bring order to the wing. He rarely had to impose himself on anyone, a word or even a look carried sufficient menace to effect compliance.

After a month, McTandlyn requested a private audience with the senior ranking man, Kevin

Harraley. An intense and hawk-like man in his late thirties with an unexplained four-inch scar across his nose and left cheek, Harraley had been sentenced to seven years for being a member of an illegal organisation, which was legal jargon for being in the I.R.A. Although he had been involved in a range of attacks on the security forces, he had not been convicted of any of them. The sentence handed down to him was seen as a form of internment, even though there was no doubt as to his membership and status within.

McTandlyn laid out his plans for his period of residence, knowing that he needed Harraley's approval to do anything. Enforcer he may have been but alone and unsupported he could expect life to become difficult. Harraley listened to McTandlyn's declaration, exuding an air of scepticism throughout. When the plan was delivered, Harraley paused for a moment then said.

"So tell me if I've understood this right. You are going to escape?"

"Yes, that's right, but not yet. I have things to do here before I leave. The British have sent me on a training course and all my teachers are in this place."

Harraley was not used to, nor was he in the mood for jokes. He would have expected to have been consulted on such an audacious plan, but it appeared that not only was he hearing of it from a subordinate, the subordinate had already been assured of outside help when the time came to abscond.

"Explain," demanded the senior man.

"I have been briefed to raise my field skills, so I have," began McTandlyn, showing a degree less reverence than was usual. "There are men in here who

139

know things and they're gonna teach me what they know."

"What, exactly?"

"Ah, you know, picking locks, disabling security cameras, ringing cars that will pass for real, things that go tick, tick, tick, bang! Skills I need to have to be able to do what's needed."

"You've got a fucking nerve telling this to me." Harraley's tone changed gear and the lines in his face created shadows. "I decide if anybody attempts to go over the wall and there are about a hundred blokes I'd give that chance to before you'd get a look in. You've only been here five minutes, for fuck's sake."

McTandlyn was not intimidated at all. He barely reacted to the attempt to put him in his place.

"It's a pity you see it that way." He rocked backwards on his chair then stood upright. "There are people higher up the tree than you or I that want me out and operating again, but, like I said, I have things to do here first. Meanwhile, I'll do what you want me to do, lean on anybody who needs it, and we'll all get along just lovely. Cheerio now!"

Harraley let McTandlyn get out of the association area before kicking his vacated chair over with the heel of his shoe, sending it skidding across the floor and into another stack of chairs. He was being undermined and kept out of the loop by the senior command and there wasn't a damned thing he could do about it.

CHAPTER TWENTY-FOUR

"Mammy?" Lizzie called out from the front doorway as she hung her coat on the hook.

As no reply was forthcoming, she wrestled the key out of the lock and closed the door with purposeful volume. There was still no response. She peered into each of the three downstairs rooms before running up the carpeted stairs to her mother's bedroom. The bedroom door was closed whilst the other two and the bathroom door remained open. Lizzie stopped herself from barging in and took a deep breath before letting it out slowly. She turned the old, plastic handle and opened the door an inch. The room inside was dark. In her haste, she hadn't noticed that the curtains were closed.

Jennifer Cullen was prone to suffering migraines, but they had occurred more frequently since her return to living in England. The loss of her husband and the trauma of Lizzie's coma combined with her confinement had reduced her normally robust resolve to a state that made it impossible for her to fight the onset of that debilitating malady. A life-long reluctance to take medication gave way to a dependency that only she knew of. Her doctor was partially aware, but Lizzie was kept ignorant for fear that it might affect her recovery.

Lizzie had recovered very well, physically. She jogged or went swimming nearly every day and enrolled on a self-defence course on Tuesday evenings. Jennifer was more concerned with her daughter's inner health. She had heard Lizzie talking in her sleep, most of which did not form recognisable words or phrases, but occasionally she could make out some words that could only have been spoken to an infant. Jennifer was no psychologist, but she knew that her daughter had not uttered such things before the birth of the child.

Jennifer was not strong enough to have been able to look after both the child and Lizzie who had been a 50/50 prospect for a recovery. By the time Lizzie had regained consciousness the deal had been done and the baby was gone. There was no choice but to put it behind her and get on with her life.

Lizzie pulled the door closed again but was pleasantly interrupted by a croaky voice from within.

"It alright Lizzie," said Jennifer pushing herself up into a seated position against the headboard, "I'm feeling a little better now."

Lizzie opened the door to let light in, but she didn't switch on the light or open the curtains. She went slowly into the bedroom and sat on the side of her mother's bed. Jennifer was fully clothed including her slippers.

"Did you have another migraine Mammy?"

"Yes Lizzie, but it was only a little one this time. You know, I do wish you wouldn't call me Mammy anymore."

"But why Ma'," she stopped herself from her habit. "I've always called you that."

"It's the word that needs changing, not the sentiment."

"What's wrong with it?

"It's too Irish."

"I'm not ashamed of being Irish," said Lizzie indignantly, "Daddy would have been hurt if I was."

"He would, Lizzie, he would. But we are living in England now and we have to find ways to fit in here. It shouldn't come as any surprise that there's a war going on between England and Ireland."

"But it's not with us. We're British. We shouldn't be seen as anybody's enemy here."

"We shouldn't, you're right. But you have to realise that the average Englishman reading his newspaper and watching his television won't be able to tell the difference between Catholics and Protestants or Republicans and Loyalists. All he'll see is that Irish people put bombs under cars and kill people."

"We don't deserve to be treated as terrorists. What can we do to show people that we are on their side?"

"One way is to speak English, Lizzie, as the English do. I know that's easy for me to say. As you know I was born and raised here. I only moved to Belfast when I married your father. Speaking with an English accent is natural for me, but with me not going out very much, the situation is more serious for you."

"Serious? Am I in danger here, is that what you're telling me?"

"Calm down Lizzie, we're a lot safer here than we were in Belfast. All I'm saying is that it will be easier for you to get along with people if they see you as one of their own and with me being English born you actually are one of their own. Now I can tell by that look on your face that you're not convinced, but it doesn't mean that you're showing any disrespect to your father's memory or your birthplace. We want to live in peace, don't we?"

Lizzie nodded.

"Well this is a small price to pay to have that."

"Okay, I think I understand."

"Good," said Jennifer as she swung her feet over the side of the bed, losing one slipper to fall to the floor as she moved. "I'll help you to change your way of speaking. Don't get cross with me when I correct what you say, I'm only doing it to help."

"I know Mam'. Oh! What am I going to call you now?"

They both laughed at the preposterousness of their situation.

"What about Mama, like the Royal family do?" suggested Jennifer with a mischievous air.

"What, are you the Queen now? Behold Queen Jennifer the First."

"Now, that has a nice ring to it."

"Mommie Dearest?"

"I saw that film. How dare you?" said Jennifer in mock offence.

"Mother, how about Mother?" offered Lizzie.

"No, that makes me sound like the old nun from The Sound of Music."

Lizzie reached behind her mother and deftly pulled the pillowcase off the pillow, shaking it open and placing it on her mother's head. Jennifer pulled the front corners down around her chin and began warbling.

"Climb ev'ry mountain, ford ev'ry stream . . ."

Lizzie laughed out loud and rolled on her back on the bed. Jennifer stood up and with exaggerated majestic poise began.

"The hills are alive, with the sound of music . . ."

Mother and daughter laughed uncontrollably for the first time in many months. When it abated and the customary yet irrational moment of 'should we be doing this?' arrived, the undeserved guilt of the bereaved came on suddenly and drifted away slowly. Jennifer hugged her daughter.

"We live in the north of England. So it's going to have to be Mum."

"Agreed," said Lizzie.

"But we'll both know what we really mean, won't we?"

CHAPTER TWENTY-FIVE

Kevin Harraley watched the new prisoner on the wing as
though he was the cuckoo preparing to steal his nest and all
that was kept in it. McTandlyn's manner was nothing like
any man's he had seen before. Fearless, unconcerned with
the incarceration imposed on him and capable of exerting
immediate compliance with such ease, Harraley had to
afford a grudging respect at the way he conducted himself.
An inmate who had temporarily forgotten his place in the
grand scheme was steered back on to the acceptable path by
a short exchange with McTandlyn, resulting in a broken rib
for the man who had strayed and an apology from him to
Harraley for his conduct. Throughout this corrective
exercise, McTandlyn needed no preparation to psyche
himself up before or compose himself after. It was just
something he did without too much thinking about it.

Over the first few weeks, many inmates were spoken to
and assessed by the new man who wanted to know what
skills he could learn from them. Swiftly dismissing the
small-fry or those with a tendency to exaggerate, McTandlyn
homed-in on the men who had the proven skills and
knowledge that he sought to gain. The prison staff, aware of
McTandlyn's past record for violence were, to some degree,
relieved that his daily custom of spending association
periods in deep and quiet conversation caused far less work
for them than the violent alternatives. They kept
conversations with him to a minimum and his contempt for
the screws was never concealed or tempered. The older

officers left it at that but some of the younger ones submitted intelligence reports pointing out who McTandlyn had been talking to and for how long. Much of this intelligence became 'lost in the system' as the reason for its relevance was yet to become clear.

Whilst Harraley had largely accepted the situation and how it was going to develop, he maintained a weather eye for the moment his new enforcer would choose to usurp his authority. This position softened as the months progressed. McTandlyn did not put a foot out of line as far as the paramilitary hierarchy were concerned. Instead he placed his foot precisely where he was asked to, usually applied with force to the ribs of anyone who was deemed to deserve it. Harraley had to accept that discipline on the wing had never been so easy to maintain. If and when McTandlyn did manage to pull off the escape he was planning, he would be difficult to replace in that role. What he was going to be capable of on the outside could only be guessed. What was clear was that he would be a very bad man to get on the wrong side of. Harraley wanted to be the man giving direction to McTandlyn's activities, not mopping up after them. He needed to form a workable alliance.

CHAPTER TWENTY-SIX

"Mum, I've got something to tell you," declared Lizzie as she swung open the front door of the house. In her free hand she was clutching an A5 sized letter with a formal headed emblem in the top corner and the torn envelope she had taken it from. She had been handed it by the postman on the path between the door and the gate at ten minutes to eight that morning on her way to work in an insurance claims office. Being preoccupied with catching the bus, she had forgotten to look at the letter until she was on the return bus journey home.

Jennifer was in the kitchen cooking their dinner. She wiped her hands on a tea-towel and beckoned Lizzie forward with the letter. Lizzie passed it to her before standing back to wait for its content to sink in. Jennifer read aloud.

"Dear Miss Cullen. With regard to your recent medical examination I am pleased to inform you that there is no further need for you to attend the Outpatients Dept. Mr Sullivan feels that you have made a full recovery from your recent health issues and confirms that your treatment is complete. Please consult your G.P. if there are any recurrences."

Jennifer folded the letter and stepped forward to hug her daughter. She had been through so much and had remained positive.

"That is great news Lizzie. Well done."

"Thanks Mum."

"You've worked hard to get yourself well again." She unfurled her arms and returned to the cooker to stir the contents of a steaming pan. Lizzie took the letter from the table and put it into the outer pocket of her shoulder bag, taking another out and holding it up in the air.

"What's that? Another letter, you are in demand Lizzie. Who's it from?"

"I don't know. It looks official." Lizzie opened it. She read it to herself then announced its contents.

"Mr Sullivan has already told the Police Recruiting Office that I'm fully fit and they want me to come for interview. I'd better get myself prepared."

"You are prepared, you've been getting ready for this since you were born."

*

Three months later, a tear spilled over the lower left eyelid of Jennifer Cullen and threatened to undermine her foundation make-up. With a slightly tremulous echo, the tripod mounted outdoor speakers surrounding the parade square broadcast the clipped tones of the senior police chief, who was delivering his words of wisdom to the hundred and forty police recruits They were standing at ease yet still upright, in military squad formations before him. Training centre staff and dignitaries formed the south edge whilst the north, east and half of the west sides housed the families, friends and sweethearts of those graduating. The remaining space allowed the drill sergeant room to marshal the graduands onto the square and be shown off to maximum effect. Jennifer had been present at a similar event many years before. Whilst her late husband's passing out ceremony had been a proud moment for her, it brought back more recent and painful emotions to be present at another one.

To the slight but unspoken annoyance of other guests, Jennifer had to change her position in the audience to be able to see Lizzie, sporting boyish, short hair dyed the darkest shade of brunette possible before it could be called black, standing tall, erect and full of purpose at the end of the third column of E Class. Jennifer commenced taking the photographs she sought. The distraction of the sighing and tutting from the mildly inconvenienced fellow guests served to return Jennifer to the moment and abate the welling of water in her eyes. She knew that if she had allowed herself to dwell on all of her memories, she would weep and wail unmercifully, ruining the occasion for Lizzie and everyone else there. She was not so in control of her thoughts that she was able to completely suspend them from her mind. Accepting this, she tried hard to concentrate on the happy memories, so often eclipsed by the tragic.

How handsome Arnie had looked in his uniform when he was a police recruit - confident, upright and fearless. She saw all of that in Lizzie, who, although in many ways different in character than her father, exuded the same determination to stand up for those who needed her to. Despite what her daughter had been through, she still displayed an optimistic energy to do some good. Arnie would have been the proudest parent, had he lived to be there. To Jennifer, he was there, and he too had a tear in the corner of his eye.

CHAPTER TWENTY-SEVEN

James spent his first few weeks getting used to life in America. He found it very different to life in Northern Ireland. Some things he liked and some he didn't. He liked the range of foreign food and the basketball facilities, but he did not like the commercial insincerity that was being waved like a flag by all new faces.

In the University environment, he felt at home. The switch from post-graduate student to junior lecturer went smoothly. He was allowed to settle into his new role at his own speed. Nobody made any suggestion that he did anything at all. On the rare occasion that he was asked to do anything, the request was accompanied by an 'if you get the chance to' or an 'if you don't mind.'

James occupied himself by reading new reference books from cover to cover and familiarising himself with the department, its syllabus range and its non-lecturing functions. It transpired that the faculty generated more revenue from carrying out research than it did from educating students. James found the file containing piles of letters requesting that the University carry out various projects to paying customers the world over, such was the reputation of the department. Having no teaching experience or qualifications, James worked out that it was the researching function that he was to be carrying out. Domestically, his staff accommodation and the first proper salary he had earned was to his liking. After three weeks, Melissa asked him to call on Professor Cooke, when he had the time.

Cooke's office was a constant home to a cloud of pipe tobacco. Only the freshness of the smell of the cloud indicated that he was there or recently had been. On that Monday afternoon, the professor was in and generating smoke like there was a new pope. Even the man himself had to wave a hole in the smoke to be able to see his new member of staff.

"Ah!" he said, grabbing at the burning bowl of the pipe. "Come in, lad. Have a seat."

James lifted a pile of papers from the only unoccupied chair and looked around for a space in which to put them. Cooke didn't seem to notice. James saw a large textbook on the edge of Cooke's cluttered desk and placed the papers on it reckoning that it would not cover something up that could not be found again. The rest of the room was beyond such care.

"How are you settling in?" he said earnestly.

"Everything is grand, thank you Professor," said James who saw no reason to burden his host and boss with his homesickness blues.

"Good, good. It's not like the old country, eh?" cajoled the old don.

"No, it's a little warmer."

Both laughed at the tame meteorological observation. The professor reached to turn on a small transistor radio on the shelf above the desk. Bluegrass Country and Western music twanged from the single speaker. He turned the dial to the volume he sought and sat back down in his chair. He was no longer laughing. He leaned over to speak to James as though it were in confidence and not to be overheard.

"There are important matters to discuss. Any jackbuck with half a brain can do what you are here to do. On the face of things, you are a junior lecturer and researcher. That's a

152

fairly standard career path for a fellow with your academic grades. There's a more important role that I have to prepare you for. One which will require skills you must acquire."

James listened intently without interrupting. Cooke puffed on his pipe and continued.

"We may be far across the ocean but our hearts belong in Ireland. The Republican movement has a mammoth task and we can't be there to help. That doesn't mean we do nothing, right?"

James shook his head cautiously. He still didn't know where he stood with Cooke. He had the manner of a man with a tendency toward anger, although he had not displayed any of that in James' presence.

"There are things we can do on this side of the water, things that can't be done over there. We provide a vital service, one that our comrades back home can't function without."

Unsure what Cooke meant by 'we' James tentatively asked,

"What is it that we provide Professor?"

"Money!" snapped Cooke and he puffed on his pipe again. "There are a great many people in this part of the world who have sympathy for the cause. They want to do something to help, get involved a little, contribute. Of course they don't want to be seen to be doing so, no public acknowledgments, you know how this is. Our job is to tap into those resources, take the money that the American sympathisers are willing to cough up and then make it available for our people back home."

"What is the money spent on?"

"That's not your concern or mine, lad. The senior command needs it and that's that."

"I don't think that is that Professor."

"Oh you don't?" Cooke's tone became intolerant and bordered on hostile. "Is that not enough for you?"

"I support the cause of Republicanism, Professor, and I know that it doesn't come cheap. The British have infinitely superior resources and we have to make the most of ours. I am not convinced that the armed struggle is the way to get to where we want to be."

"Don't think that's the only thing that costs money, lad. There are people, good people, who have been interned and can't support their families. Lawyers representing our operatives need paying too. Not to mention the expense of trying to get our voice heard in the council chambers of the city. The money we raise here goes toward all of that."

James thought about what Cooke had said. He looked at the radio which was by then playing a Tammy Wynette number. He looked back at Cooke who was busily trying to suck new life into the fire in his pipe.

"I have no reservations with raising money for peaceful causes, but I am not willing to put bullets in the guns."

His memory flashed back to the doorstep murder of the man at Lodale, the frozen terror that had gripped him, the screams from inside the house and the girl in the window above the scene of slaughter. Cooke brought him back to the present.

"I admire your sentiments, lad. I'm with you all the way. The fundraising we do here is entirely for non-aggressive causes."

"Thank you Professor. I feel a lot better about it now."

"There are some practices that you have to learn and stick to. The British wouldn't hesitate to misinterpret our fundraising as terrorist-related. They have enough pull with the U.S. Government to bring a sharp halt to what we do – and we'd probably end up in jail too. I'm giving you two international numbers. You have to memorise them. They must not be called from a phone on this campus. No phone is to be used twice in a row or in any pattern. Always have some background noise and never use your name or that of anyone on the line."

"This sounds like a spy movie," laughed James – alone.

"It's no joke lad, this is too important for you to take it lightly." The professor went pink in his cheeks and his eyes took on a wide and menacing outlook. He suddenly resumed his earlier moderate mood.

"Good, good. That's the spirit. Now, there's something else I've been meaning to say to you."

"What is it Professor?"

"Your erm, appearance, it makes me uncomfortable."

"I certainly don't intend to make you uncomfortable," James reassured him.

"It's not important what I feel, but it is when you will be meeting those who we seek to get donations from. Let's face it lad, this get-up was alright when you were a student, but you're on the staff now, time to look like it."

James looked at the hairy-headed old man in the cloud of tobacco smoke. His musty suit of worsted wool had been in dire need of vigorous cleaning for some time, and the collar of his shirt would never be white again, nor any shade near to white. Even his shoes, scuffed at all sides, were barely serviceable. The suggestion that he should aim to emulate his new mentor generated some gloom in him, but he accepted that he should make some effort to conform to his new surroundings. After all, it wasn't the first time the professor had mentioned it. He left the office as Cooke

155

turned off the radio and resumed examining the contents of his desk.

James was stunned and amused in equal measure, but Cooke had been deadly serious. He was in a spy movie and there was nothing he could do but accept his role in its complex plot.

CHAPTER TWENTY-EIGHT

Arnie Cullen had always arrived for duty thirty minutes
before the allotted hour of commencement for his shift. It
was a practice the young Lizzie Cullen had been brought up
to believe was the norm. Dressed in her white shirt, black
skirt to below the knee, thick tights, leather shoes polished to
mirror-like proportions, tunic with chrome buttons and
numbers, black leather shoulder bag and curved 'patroller'
hat. She looked brand new and should have expected to be
treated as such. In a sharp deviation from the ceremony of
the training centre passing out parade, she was
unceremoniously deployed to guard, nurse and otherwise
care for a teenaged girl. She was being housed in a less
intrusive, yet similarly claustrophobic, detention room in the
cell block in the basement of a Salford police station. Old
and weathered ceramics in cream and green clad the walls of
what could pass for a Victorian public toilet facility. The
lack of natural light and the resultant disorientation of not
knowing night from day added to the gloom. The regular
shouts of orders being issued and reports of those orders
having been carried out served to disperse the invisible fug
of stale air.

An old and balding constable with bandy legs and a
belly overhanging his belt, jangled a set of keys on an old
toilet chain as he lumbered from behind a high, oak desk,
fixed as a fortress of authority for whoever was positioned in
the elevated dais behind it. A handful of uniformed and
suited police officers, all men, peppered the space, each with

their own reasons for being there. Some were obvious, like the ones who were escorting detainees to and from cells and others who seemed to be waiting or simply under-deployed.

A stern-faced sergeant wrote in chalk on an aged blackboard on the wall behind. He glanced at the people who appeared to be intruding on his tiny empire. Lizzie followed the old guy along a corridor past cells with small windows in the doors. This, she had gleaned, was the area for juveniles to be incarcerated. At the end of the corridor sat a police woman writing in a pocket notebook. Upon hearing some movement, she stood up, smiled, and started packing away her belongings into her shoulder bag. She was tall and lean with auburn hair in a pony-tail and a fringe to near-white eyebrows over bright blue eyes and freckled cheeks.

"Your relief has arrived, Sylvia," announced the old cop. He turned to Lizzie. "What's your name lovey?"

"Lizzie," she said, "Lizzie Cullen." He turned toward the entrance.

"I'll leave it with you," he said, somewhat absent-mindedly. As he neared the open gate, the police woman slipped her bag strap over her shoulder and said,

"Geraldine is asleep in here." She pointed to a door with the number six on it. "She was up shouting her mouth off most of the night, so I expect she'll need waking and taking over to court about nine-thirty." Sylvia eventually looked Lizzie in the face. She smiled benignly, ready for home and sleep.

"Are you here for the day Lizzie, or have you been posted here?" Sylvia's accent suggested she had not travelled far.

"I'm working here now, my first day."

"Sylvia Wright," she announced and she shook Lizzie's hand.

"Is this your first station?" she asked with a previously absent expression of concern.

"Yes. I'm keen to learn all I can. I'm told this is a good place to do that." It must have sounded like a mindless saying adopted by all recruits, but Lizzie believed it.

"Hmmm," pondered the more experienced officer, "You'll learn the job alright, there's no doubt about that, but there are some other things you should know about this place, things they didn't teach you at Training School."

"Can you give me any advice?" asked Lizzie, trying to show respect for Sylvia's seniority.

"Hmmm," said Sylvia again. She held up a flat hand to indicate that Lizzie should remain where she was. With a conspiratorial air, Sylvia walked to the opened gate and looked out into the main cell block. After checking that the coast was clear, she returned and spoke to Lizzie in a whisper.

"They have a custom here with new female police officers, goes back decades, kind of an initiation ritual. I had it done to me seven years ago. It doesn't hurt if you don't fight back. Try and see it as a bit of fun. They'll accept you as one of the boys afterwards, well as far as they do accept P.W.s anyway."

Lizzie was confused and a little annoyed. Whilst she was curious about what it took to be accepted into this closed world and how much she should be prepared to acquiesce to, the details of the proposed initiation became the issue of greatest urgency.

"What do they do . . . to new recruits I mean?"

"Tights or stockings?" asked Sylvia.

"Pardon?"

159

"Are you wearing tights or stockings?"

"Tights," answered Lizzie cautiously.

"It will make it a bit harder for them, but it won't make a lot of difference in the end."

"To who and what?" said Lizzie who was beginning to work it out for herself but required confirmation.

"You see the high desk in the main charge office? On it is a date stamp on an ink pad. At some stage on your first day you will be grabbed in a bear hug, turned upside-down, your skirt hem will fall around your shoulders and you will have your arse stamped with today's date in black ink."

Lizzie felt a moment of open-mouthed shock, followed by a tight-lipped determination to resist when the time came, however futile that may have turned out to be.

"Who's going to do that date-stamp thing?" she asked.

"Oh they all will, all the blokes on the shift you're working with this morning. They wouldn't miss it. It's the highlight of their year when a new girl arrives. You can tell when it's going to happen when they all arrive in the charge office at once."

"Won't the sergeant object?" appealed Lizzie.

"Oh good heavens no, he'll have organised it."

Lizzie had not anticipated that she was to be initiated. It was a new concept for her but, it seemed, an old one for her colleagues. She wanted to fit in and be accepted just as she had done when she had first arrived in England and, by adjusting her accent, she had shown that she was capable of compromise in order to achieve that. 'When in Rome . . .' had been a saying used by her father to offer advice for such a dilemma.

160

"Good luck," whispered Sylvia as she stepped toward the gate.

"Just a second, Sylvia, I'll be back."

Lizzie dashed to the high oak desk where the stern-faced sergeant was still writing on the blackboard with white chalk. Whilst occasionally peering down through his spectacles, perched at the tip of his nose, at the contents of a sheet of paper on a clipboard. He had his back to her and, if he was aware of her presence, he was determined not to acknowledge it if it meant interrupting what he was doing. Lizzie skipped up the step onto the raised area behind the oak desk. The sergeant did not finish the word he was writing once he had realised that his sacred space had been invaded.

He spun around and barked at her.

"Don't come back here without my permission!"

Lizzie stood with her shoulder bag held across her stomach with her left hand.

"What do you want?" he rasped impatiently.

"Sorry sergeant, I'm new here. I didn't know. That first-aid box," she said pointing to a white metal case. "Can I have a plaster please?"

He gestured by briefly leaning his head toward the case. She turned her back to him and opened the case then closed it again before slipping back around to the acceptable side of the desk. She stood close to it, allowing the sergeant to look down at her but unable to see any lower than her head and shoulders.

"What time do you want me to get Geraldine up and ready for Juvenile Court?" she asked, already knowing the answer.

"Be back here for half nine," he said, still gruff but this time without shouting.

Sylvia walked out with her and up the stairs to the first floor. She showed Lizzie to the General Office where two civilian clerks and a uniformed P.C. sat at desks. Sylvia headed off to the women's locker room and then home.

Lizzie completed an abundance of largely replicated forms covering, next-of-kin, annual leave rotas and reading, at least in part, documents covering fire drills and car park usage. The clerk who was conducting the lengthy administrative exercise made them both a cup of tea and let on that she too had been a police officer until leaving to start a family, which had, for many like her, been the end of her police career. The woman, whose name Lizzie had initially missed but she later learned was called Sue, was good-natured, helpful and welcoming. Lizzie was happy to hear Sue talk about the two children whose school had photographed together, smiling out from the tilted rectangular frame adorned with dried pasta apparently painted sky-blue by the two subjects depicted therein. It claimed pride-of-place next to the enamelled, metal typewriter on her desk. Lizzie was reminded at such moments of the child she had borne and never known, the boy that she could not have a picture of, nor speak of to anyone. She hoped that he had been adopted by a loving family and she briefly thought that the normality that Sue's life appeared to represent would be the life that she would want for him. He was the son who she had purposefully avoided giving a name to in the interests of preserving her own sanity and managing her continuing sense of loss.

Lizzie took the advice offered by Sue and went to the second-floor canteen for tea and toast. At 9.25am she headed back to the charge office in the basement of Salford Police Station, mentally steeling herself against the hilarity ahead. She paused at the heavy panelled door before pushing it open with her shoulder. As she entered the area in front of the oak desk, the sergeant turned and slipped the spectacles

162

from the edge of his nose and indicated that Lizzie had work to do. She took Geraldine out of the cell and supervised her as she washed and made herself as near as was practicable to presentable. Lizzie worked out that the date-stamp threat was unlikely to be perpetrated whilst she was standing next to a prisoner. This theory proved accurate and at 9.45am she handcuffed Geraldine to herself and was escorted to a windowless Transit van in the police station yard. The old, bald constable had donned hat and tunic and was driving the van. Lizzie took this to mean that the activity in the police cells was no longer sufficient to require his presence there.

A great deal of sitting around, pacing and unstimulating conversation took place as the Juvenile Court dealt with cases from other police stations and some involving defendants who had not arrived in custody. By the lunchtime adjournment, Geraldine's case had still not been heard. Re-handcuffed, they were transported back to the police station. At 1.50pm Geraldine was given a colourless but steaming hot meal in her detention room. Lizzie returned to the charge office and was greeted by what must have been the entire early turn workforce, all male, all smiling. Three suited detectives added to the camaraderie. Even the previously stern-faced sergeant curled his lip with malicious mischief.

"Alright boys, over she goes," he ordered as though he was ordering that a heavy mattress be flipped.

Amid deep and throaty laughter and cheering, three uniformed cops stepped forward. Lizzie was determined to offer what resistance she could. It began in a defensive stance with one foot forward and her arms raised. The man to her right walked into an elbow brought up sharply to the underside of his nose. He reeled backwards holding his face, but meanwhile, from the left and rear she had been caught. She tried to wriggle but she was being held by men who had restrained struggling prisoners many times and she was unable to make any difference. She was steered into a horizontal position and her patroller hat went astray. The grip was loosened by one of the men, only to get a better one

163

to turn her fully upside-down. Lizzie's ankles were held and the moment came when she considered what underwear she was sporting beneath the uniform issue, 20 denier tights. When she was fully upturned, the shoulder bag fell toward the ground, but her skirt fell only slightly, remaining miraculously intact along with a surprising amount of her dignity. Her tights-covered knees were on display but little more.

The high spirits and boisterous laughter came to an abrupt halt at the sound of the shouting sergeant.

"Wait!" he bellowed, "Who's got the stamp?"

He scanned the oak desk, above and beneath it. The men near it looked too. In the near-silence, the assembled group of initiators seemed not to know what to do in light of this unexpected development.

"We can't do it without the stamp," declared one luminary of police custom.

"I know that," said the sergeant impatiently, "so where is it?"

Shrugs and denials of any knowledge on the issue emanated from several of the men. Lizzie felt the red rush of blood to her face. She could only see trouser-covered legs in any direction she looked. The confusion had lowered the previously high spirits. The unified will to carry out the time-honoured custom had abated. It ended when the sergeant announced.

"It's not here . . . put her down."

Lizzie was returned to the ground, shoes first and released. The shoulder bag fell back to her side. Still flushed, she smoothed her hair and clothing. Somebody handed her the missing hat and she was back to normal. Everybody who belonged elsewhere shuffled out of the charge office and prepared to end the shift and go home. The unfortunate individual with blood running from his nose cut a sad figure. His eyes set in a futile expression of appeal. He received no gesture of sympathy from any quarter. Only the sergeant and the old constable remained.

"You got off lightly there, girl. I've never known a new P.W. get away without having the date-stamp before. That must be a first," declared the sergeant, shaking his head. "With luck like that you'll go far."

There was a barely-recognisable hint of approval in his voice as he replaced the spectacles in their rightful position on his nose. Lizzie looked at him, staring into his eyes, fearless. She stepped backwards away from the oak desk maintaining that fixed stare. Reaching both hands behind her and to the back of her thighs, she leaned back and lowered one shoulder. He wondered what this staring young woman was doing. She returned to standing upright and moved forward to the white first-aid case. Without speaking, she held up a large safety pin which she replaced in the case and closed it.

"Ah," he said, "so that's how you did it." A whiff of respect hung in the air. Lizzie stepped down to the front of the desk and reached into her shoulder bag pulling out first the ink pad then the date-stamp. She placed them on the desk from where she had taken them earlier that morning.

The sergeant's mouth fell open. He erupted in laughter, as did the old cop.

"Luck has nothing to do with it, sergeant," she said.

She swung open the heavy panelled door and headed out.

CHAPTER TWENTY-NINE

The leather jacket had been consigned to the back of the wardrobe. James could not bring himself to discard it, despite its poor condition. The spikes of dyed, black hair were unceremoniously lopped off to reveal a crew-cut of a military standard and back to his natural colour, similar in shade to golden sand. He took his first pay-cheque and invested in some clothes that were more appropriate for his new role. His Ramones T shirt and others like it were relegated in status and used for basketball training only. He had joined a club of University staffers and had embraced the transition from it being a minority sport in his home country to a big deal in his new one. It was after a demanding session of basketball training that Professor Cooke called him and announced that there was somebody he wanted James to meet.

Benny drove them to a sumptuous, white house on the edge of the city. It was on a hill with views of the ocean beyond a vast, sweeping, manicured lawn. The gates were opened electronically and the curved approach road allowed glimpses through trees of the mansion at the top. It had three floors and each floor had ten windows across the front façade. A Cuban manservant in a beige tunic and pressed black trousers came out to escort the guests into the house. Benny was left to wait in the car.

The owner of the house was a Connor O'Leary. When introducing James, Cooke emphasised that his middle name was Patrick. O'Leary was a self-made millionaire in the transport and construction industries. A direct and plain-speaking man, he was a second generation Irish-American and had more disposable income than his leisure needs could make use of. Sixty-five, overweight and dressed for golf, although he didn't actually play golf, O'Leary had become fascinated with the troubled history of the land of his forefathers. He had met Cooke twice before and they had talked at length about politics and how Ireland should be in the future. On this visit, James observed as Professor Cooke outlined the republican message for the North and how the struggle, armed or otherwise, could only succeed with the support of ex-pats such as Connor O'Leary.

It was agreed that the professor would arrange for research to be carried out by his faculty at the University of West Boston. It would explore the possible political routes to the unification of Ireland. The project would be funded entirely by Connor O'Leary, who was to pay the professor directly for the work. Payment would be made in two parts. Half of the quarter of a million dollars that O'Leary was paying would actually go into the University research grants fund. This was so that if an investigation into the money was carried out by the C.I.A. or the I.R.S. it could be simply explained away as a payment duplicated by administrative error and it would be returned. After a suitable period of time, the remainder was to be remitted into a Swiss bank for later distribution to Republican causes in Ireland.

On the journey back to the campus, Professor Cooke said nothing of the conversation with O'Leary. It was clear that Benny was not a party to the fund-raising practices that James was being schooled in. Once back in the staff bar at the University, Cooke sat with James away from anyone who could have overheard. Benny was sent to park the car.

Cooke explained that the earlier visits he had made to O'Leary's house had been partly to convince him of the need and the value of his contribution, but also to satisfy himself that O'Leary was on the level. The C.I.A. targeted all criminal activity that involved Non-Americans. It was well within their remit and capabilities to set up a sting operation. It was important that they were alert to that possibility. O'Leary was also connected to many other like-minded ex-pats. There was a great deal of work to do.

Eight months later, it was Connor O'Leary who put up a substantial amount of cash to fund James Patrick Coleman's doctorate. Such sponsorship was commonplace. However, in this instance, the money would not be heading into the University coffers. The subsequent visits to O'Leary's house that James made were to be explained as updates for his sponsor, although he was never asked about it. They also allowed him to meet, ingratiate and negotiate donations from many other well-placed Massachusetts benefactors. This practice ran for several years. James became a part of that Irish-American community, although he remained realistic that his place in it was conditional and specific.

In his University role, he carried out research projects to order and gave lectures to under-graduate, and later when he had completed his doctorate, post-graduate students. Doctor Coleman developed a liking for debating in the American way, which was more vocal and entertaining than his experiences at Belfast University had been. Each time a student introduced a literary contribution to the debate, James rose to the challenge of knowing the work mentioned and comparing contrasting viewpoints from other works.

Guided by Professor Cooke, he became an authority on the Sixth-century B.C. Chinese text: 'The Art of War' and many of the views and interpretations of commentators and luminaries on that work since then. He also explored in depth, the processes and examples of how peace after war had been negotiated and how war had been averted by shrewd communication. In the style attributed to the young Abraham Lincoln, he could argue for one side in the morning and the opposite side in the afternoon. Many of the debating sessions became quite heated which, for James, meant that people were taking them seriously and were learning. As his past students moved on to have careers elsewhere, he began to get invited to spice-up debates in other Universities across the United States and beyond. Each time it entailed a payment for his expertise. Any money due to James for these services was channelled to Switzerland for onward use in Ireland.

James kept in shape by training and playing basketball. By American standards he was not very good, but he could command a place in the staff team in the faculty. Post training socialising brought James into contact with a wider range of people. The tall, fit Irishman with the fierce intellect and unassuming manner was not lacking female attention, although he needed it to be spelled out to him by intermediary friends as had happened so often in his teens. Set up on blind dates by well-meaning colleagues, James invariably avoided the obligation to be optimistic. The dates he did go on were stymied by his own inability to see the girlfriend potential in each of the ladies he found himself with. He had enjoyed some of them and did acknowledge that he found many of his dates attractive. However, at the moment of realisation that an atmosphere of intimacy was on the cards, James invariably got cold feet rendering the romance null and void. There emerged a pattern of doomed liaisons. The memory of the girl who had stolen his heart back in Belfast remained too strong to be overlooked.

CHAPTER THIRTY

WPC Cullen was expected to follow the time-honoured pattern laid out for new police constables since time began.

To patrol with male colleagues until the end of her two-year probationary period, then seek a post with better hours dealing with women and children. Remain there until being rescued by a future husband, usually another police officer, then to get pregnant and leave, never to return. Sue the admin clerk had been fairly typical of that pattern, but times had changed. The law effectively banned discrimination of women and whilst it was far from being an instant cure, it did set off a chain of developments.

Lizzie was determined to pursue a career and had no desire to follow the old pattern. It was influenced by many factors. Her upbringing had instilled a positive attitude toward motherhood, but that role had been taken away from her. To Lizzie, there was something improper about contemplating being a mother to future kids when she could not be a mother to her first born. She also had, probably as a result of the previous issue, a will to determine her own course. Never again would decisions be made for her and the acceptance of a sedentary police role, caring and comforting the vulnerable, would have put her in a position whereby she had to follow the decisions of others permanently. Her aim was to match and exceed the roles of the men with whom she served.

Throughout her first two years and unbeknown to her peers, Lizzie bought the manuals and spent her free time studying for the Sergeant's exam. She maintained the thirty minutes early practice which gave her two distinct advantages; she became known to people on other shift teams and she used the resultant time to learn more about recent crime and criminal activity in the area. These assets, her 'volunteer for everything' attitude and the fact that she only needed to be told something once, made her a favourite amongst her colleagues and supervisors. Never in a hurry to leave, she completed paperwork after her peers had gone home and so appeared to never have any to do.

On a Thursday at 4am, an alarm was tripped at a warehouse which was used to store goods to be distributed through vending machines. Whilst the crisps, drinks and confectionery were of limited appeal for thieves, the sack-loads of cigarettes stored there represented a contraband commodity too good to miss. Untraceable, non-perishable and portable in large amounts, the cigarette warehouse management had fitted a good quality silent alarm system. Once activated, it was up to the police to get there before the burglars had finished their work and departed.

Lizzie was teamed up with Dave Shawcross, a constable of four years' experience and a regular panda car driver. He sped to the warehouse with rally-driver skill, but he had the presence of mind to resist activating the siren and to slow down as they approached the building so as not to alert the intruders to their attendance. Radio transmissions informed them that other colleagues were approaching from other directions. Once at the scene, the next challenge was to cover all avenues of escape, but this posed a problem in that the warehouse was in a block of other buildings, several of which had connecting rooftops.

An inspection of the outer walls of the block revealed no apparent point of entry. This was not unusual because, statistically, for every ten night-time alarm activations, nine proved to have been caused by factors other than burglary. The main entrance at one side, the loading bay at the other and the fire escape at the rear were all covered, so Lizzie Cullen and Dave Shawcross took torches and looked at the neighbouring premises. One was a wholesaler of bathroom tiles and was behind a tall gate of wooden laths with mustard coloured paintwork peeling off in neglect. Between the laths were two-inch gaps showing high stacks of empty wooden pallets on either side of a path from the gate to the building entrance within. They lingered momentarily until Dave had seen enough to satisfy himself that there was nothing in it.

"Come on," he said in little more than a whisper, "It'll be now't. Their cat will have set it off."

He set off to walk and Lizzie was about to follow until she saw something move beyond the gate. It was no more than a shadow but it was something.

"Dave!" she whispered with urgency.

Dave turned to see her beckoning him back to the gate. Her expression was serious enough for him to return and acquiesce to her wish.

"What is it?" he said.

"I saw something move," she said.

"Like I said, the cat." He breathed out heavily and hoped that she would accept his rationale, but she was not going to leave it.

"It was too big a shadow to be a cat," she explained. "Help me over this gate."

"What? Are you mad? If there is an intruder in there what good are you going to do on your own?"

"More good than I am by standing here talking about it," she told him. "Now lift me up."

He stood motionless, trying to think of an alternative. It was still very much the custom that female officers had to be protected by the male of the species. If she were to get injured, he would be pilloried at the station for letting it happen. She was, however, hard to argue with."

"I can hardly lift you up, can I?" she offered by way of reasoning. He had to accept it.

"Okay. I'm going to regret doing this but okay."

He bound his fingers together to make a stirrup, straightened his back and dipped his knees. Lizzie placed a foot on his hands and straightened herself upright. Dave expected to lift her higher with his hands but she had a better idea. She lifted her other foot onto his shoulder and graced Dave with a face-full of skirt, knocking his cap onto the ground. She drove down hard on his shoulder with her foot, stabbing his un-cushioned skin with the sharp, metal numbers of his jacket. He closed his eyes in pain but managed to stifle the urge to cry out. Lizzie could reach the top of the gate. She hauled herself over it and hung from the top until she could drop to the ground inside the tiler's yard. Although Dave was only a few feet away, she felt alone and isolated, but she had to follow up on what she had seen.

The stack of wooden pallets curved to the left and as she walked by it she saw that there was an equally high stack on the right lining the other side of the path. She walked with her torch up to the locked loading platform and back to the gate.

"It was up there."

She pointed it out to Dave who was feeling somewhat inadequate. She began to climb up the stacked pallets which moved worryingly as she ascended. On the top of the stack she stood eight feet from the ground with the ill-fitting pile of wood wobbling underfoot. There was a gap between the back of the pallets and the wall of the building. She peered over and pointed her torch to search. She moved along gradually until she saw the top of a head, next to another one.

"Dave, there's somebody here behind the pallets, two of them," she announced.

"Bloody hell!" exclaimed Dave. He called on the radio for the other nearby patrols to divert to the tiler's yard gate.

Lizzie ordered the intruders to climb out slowly and carefully, giving no thought to how vulnerable to attack she would be when they joined her on the top of the pallets. The two hapless burglars were not in any frame of mind for fighting. They knew that there was no way of getting out of there and that assaulting a policewoman was going to get them a good hiding from her male colleagues. That was just the way things were. They brought up two cement bags each, all full of packs of cigarettes ready for installation in vending machines.

Lizzie completed the formalities by telling them that they were under arrest and cautioned them. A Ford Transit police van was manoeuvred to the gate and Lizzie steered each detainee to the edge of the pallets from which they climbed over and descended to the ground outside via the roof of the van.

Once the other officers carried out searches of the men and placed them inside the van, they awaited Lizzie's return, but she remained on the pallet stack.

"Come on girl," urged Dave, "job done, let's go."

"Not yet," she said. Dave looked confused.

"The shadow I saw before I climbed in, it was cast on that wall, the one on the right of the path. Those two couldn't have got from there to here in the time it took for me to get in."

"What are you saying?"

"I'm saying they didn't make that shadow, there must be another."

"Jesus, you don't let up do you?" said Dave. "Wait, I'm coming too."

He ascended the gate with help from colleagues. As he dropped into the yard Lizzie, had already climbed down the left stack, crossed the path and was climbing up the one on the right. She positioned herself near the farthest edge and commenced phase two of the search. Dave scrambled up and balanced on the top like a surfer bracing himself for the unpredictable movement beneath. It took only seconds for Lizzie to find what she was looking for.

The third man was pressed up against the stack hoping to be obscured from view above but he had failed.

"Okay, climb up here slowly and pass up anything you've got there with you," she ordered with calm authority despite her racing heart-rate.

She was joined by Dave. The third man looked up at the two officers and he knew that his night's venture was over and unsuccessful.

Forty-five minutes later at Salford's main police station, the last of the burglars was being escorted from the charge desk toward the male cell block. He turned to the sergeant and said.

"That bird, the one that found us, she's got some nerve, that one."

"She has," he acknowledged as he turned to write the new entries on the blackboard behind the desk. "She certainly has."

CHAPTER THIRTY-ONE

Brian McSwail had been a prison officer for eighteen months. Before that he had driven a bus, processed raw chicken carcasses and had a brief spell as a bingo caller. Marriage and fatherhood had altered his priorities and led him to apply to join the Prison Service, lured by the job security and pension prospects. His wife, Catherine and infant daughter Daisie were the centre of his universe and it was the thought of being welcomed home by them that got him through some of the more challenging elements of his working day. When a prisoner presented a situation that was aimed at testing the inexperienced screw, Brian silently reminded himself that he was going home that night or morning and the individual who sought to torment him was not.

Brian had always been a churchgoer and he involved himself in the community activities that the congregation generated. He took the collection plate round at Sunday services whilst Daisie, supervised by the Mums, played with her peers in the adjoining portakabin. On Tuesdays, Brian helped out with cubs and scouts in that same portakabin, having recognised the value of the institutions from his own childhood.

On a Thursday in April, Brian left the church scout group at 7.45pm allowing just enough time to walk home, put his uniform clothing in a holdall to be donned once inside the prison staff area, kiss his girls and head off to the Maze for the night shift. He arrived at his semi-detached, two-bedroomed house just before 8pm. The lounge curtains were drawn and a light was on inside. He passed his VW Polo on the flagged drive and entered by the side door to the kitchen.

"I'm home," he said without shouting, "Is she still awake, Cath?"

He closed the door and awaited either a reply, or for his wife to come into the kitchen to tell him that the little girl was asleep, so he was not to make so much noise, neither happened. He walked into the open-plan lounge and dining room, expecting the usual quietened television and one or both of his family sitting on the velour settee. The settee was occupied but by a man in blue jeans, a black waxed-cotton jacket and a black ski-mask with a line of yellow wool around the eyes and mouth. In his hand was an old revolver with a four-inch barrel which he was pointing directly at Brian.

"Looks like it's not your fucking day, McSwail."

Brian had heard stories from his colleagues about the attempts made by convicts and their associates to victimise prison officers away from their work. The stories were usually concluded with an account of how they had successfully dealt with those threats. At that moment, Brian could think of nothing to abate the threat in front of him. All he could think of was his wife and daughter, who he pictured as being upstairs. At first, he envisaged them tied up and terrified, then he thought that they were already dead. He began to shiver and sweat.

"My f-f-family, what, where?" He could barely speak.

"Got a stammer now, have you McSwail?" teased the man, "I'll help you there, right enough."

He adjusted his position on the settee as though to make himself more comfortable. The gun remained trained immovably on Brian.

"You've got a nice little family there, haven't you? Lucky man, so you are. It would be such a shame to go and make a mess of that, wouldn't it now?"

Brian managed to utter a coherent sentence.

"What have you done with my family?" His breathing was stunted and wheezy.

"Don't interrupt me, McSwail. What I have to say is more important than what you have to say. Now, your little family are safe and sound, for now. Whether they remain that way is up to you. We have a little job to do and providing you do your part of it well, your family life can continue as though none of this happened."

The soft tone of the man's voice carried a threat greater than that of an angry man. The gun ceased to be the main focus, it was what the intruder was saying that carried the greatest menace.

Brian knew that compliance was his only option. Once that had become clear in his mind, his ability to breathe and speak showed instant improvement.

"What do I have to do?" he asked in supplicant obedience.

"That's better McSwail. You catch yourself on like that and everything will be lovely." He paused before issuing Brian's instructions to him. "Your family are safe and well somewhere else. You'll get them back when you have done what I tell you. You will go to work tonight as usual. You are going to be on 'B' Wing."

Brian interrupted with barely concealed panic in his voice.

"I don't know what wing I'll be put on until I get there."

"You will be on 'B' Wing." repeated his tormentor, "Don't question how I know, I have made arrangements for you to be on 'B' Wing, let's just leave it at that shall we? If you're late for work tonight it's going to cost you more than your job, know what I mean?"

Brian nodded.

"You will become aware that a prisoner is experiencing acute abdominal pain. His cell mate will tell you that he has been retching blood and that he thinks he has eaten light bulbs. You are going to make sure that man goes to the City Hospital, Accident and Emergency. You know what you have to say and do to make that happen. He will appear too ill to be treated in the hospital wing of the prison and you have to convince whoever is in charge of that. If you fail . . . well, I don't have to spell that out for you, do I McSwail?"

Brian shook his head in acceptance. The criminal in front of him, sitting on his settee and talking to him as one would talk to a naughty child, had correctly identified his weakness and had flicked that switch with remarkable ease. Now he had to be complicit in the springing of a convict for reasons that he could not contemplate.

"I need to get my bag, some things for work," he said, trying to compose himself for what he was going to do.

"Hurry up then, McSwail. You don't want to be late for work, tonight of all nights."

Brian went upstairs and gathered his kit from the bedroom wardrobe. He peered into his daughter's bedroom in one last forlorn hope that it had all been a hoax or a dream, or anything but what it was. Daisie's bedroom, normally such a joyful place, lay cold on his skin. The pink and white box-bed was unmade, the flower-patterned quilt lying ragged at the base. Had she been removed from the bed whilst asleep? Did she know that she was in danger? It was his job to protect her and he felt like his whole life had

179

been a failure. His thoughts turned to his wife. She definitely knew that she was in danger even if she had managed to keep that fear from their daughter. What torture she must be enduring as the prisoner of masked men. The thought of what they could have been doing to her brought bile to his throat. He dropped the holdall and squatted to his knees holding his head in his hands in acute anguish.

He shook his head free and stood up, sucked in a huge lungful of air and stretched his jaw to awaken his contorted face. Brian returned to the lounge to find that the masked man had gone. He darted outside and looked along the street but there was nobody to be seen.

He returned to pick up his keys. Somewhat irrationally, or simply hopefully, he considered leaving the house unlocked in case Cath and Daisie needed to get in whilst he was at work. He knew that everything had to appear normal, he had to avoid raising suspicion, firstly in his neighbours then his work colleagues. He locked the house, got in the VW Polo and drove away.

When the night's duty roster was read out in the briefing, Brian McSwail knew that although there was a one-in-six chance of him being deployed on B Wing, it was, in reality, a foregone conclusion. He booked out keys and a radio and reported to the Wing office where a second and more prisoner-centred briefing took place. The usual exchange of current and recent intelligence was aired. A scuffle between two inmates earlier that day over ownership of a pencil had been resolved with minimal intervention. There was a list of those requiring medication and those whose behaviour had become a cause for concern because it could lead to self-harm or violence. Brian had to steel himself to resist shouting out loud that it was all nonsense and could not be compared in importance to the kidnap and threat of death that was being faced by his family at that moment.

At 11.10pm the wing fell quiet. The cameras on the landings showed no movement and it seemed that the staff were in for an undemanding tour of duty, but it was folly to make such assumptions. McSwail had been alert to the possibility that the task he had been directed to carry out would not be possible if he were to allow a colleague to attend and deal with it. He had to be the one to go, but that meant that he had to go to every call. He stood up and watched the monitor screens intently. At 11.40pm, a red light came on above the door of cell B121.

"I'll go," he said with abrupt haste.

His peers were content to let him. He took his bunch of keys and let himself onto the landing. He peered into the fish-eye viewer of B121 and saw one of the two occupants pacing up and down. The other was in his bed raised up on an elbow and looking at his promenading cellmate. In accordance with approved procedure, Brian radioed in to the control room with an account of what he had seen. Having assessed the threat level as low, he opened the hatch which was designed to allow the passage of nothing larger than a dinner plate and a cup for those confined within.

"Jessop!" he addressed the pacing man. "What's up with you?"

He looked for signs that he was going to feign internal injury but instead he was greeted with Jessop's less pressing complaint.

"I haven't had my pill, Mr McSwail."

Brian tried to take in what Jessop was saying. Was it a part of the plan? If it was, he didn't look very convincing. Why would anybody go to such lengths to get Jessop to the hospital? He wasn't anybody of value. He had supplied vehicles for the use of the Provos and had not been called upon to do anything more demanding than drive them. There were a hundred of him available at any time. McSwail began

181

to think that this was not the call he was to deal with. Over the radio, he checked Jessop's meds records.

"You've had what the doctor said you could have," he told him.

"Ah no, Mr McSwail, that's not right, see. I've had no pink pill, just the white one. I should have a pink one too. That's the one Mr McSwail, that's it, pink pill, pink pill."

McSwail closed the hatch and ended the conversation. Jessop reacted by dropping his earlier politeness and shouting about McSwail having the devil in him and that he should burn in hell. His recumbent cellmate laughed heartily at him and the noise from inside the cell abated in seconds. The jailer turned to head off back to the control room. At the end of the landing he turned and saw another red light come on. He went to cell B128 and peered through the lens. Both top and bottom bunks were empty and the bedding messed up. On the floor was an inmate, curled up in a ball and holding his knees to his chest. The other man was crouching over him, trying to tend to his ailment. He looked up at the door.

"He's in trouble here," he declared, "He needs help, an ambulance, now! For fuck's sake man!"

This was it. Brian tried to compose himself to be able to appear to be doing what was expected. He made a quick radio call which summoned colleagues from the control room to the cell. He put the heavy brass key in the lock and opened the cell door outwards.

"Step away." he told the uninjured man, "Go to your bed." The cellmate did as he was told.

The officer crouched to examine the pained inmate, shaking and murmuring in agony on the hard floor. He pulled the man's shoulder and saw who it was. McSwail grabbed his radio.

182

"Control, he's in a bad way, it's McTandlyn."

CHAPTER THIRTY-TWO

This made more sense. Darry McTandlyn was viewed by the prison staff as the hardest of hard-liners. Assessed in his psychiatric evaluation as a sociopath, there was no conversation between McTandlyn and the prison staff that was less than hostile. If Brian didn't know better, he could believe that somebody, an inmate with a grudge after having been tormented by him, had finally given this madman what he deserved, a taste of his own medicine. That momentary thought held an air of justice about it, but it inevitably gave way to the brutal reality that this prisoner's injuries were being faked. The truth was far more compelling and harder to grasp. He had to concentrate on saving the lives of his wife and daughter and that meant suspending his beliefs in all other aspects.

McTandlyn appeared barely conscious. He moaned in tense agony. Brian McSwail went through the motions.

"What happened to you?" he demanded whilst squatting next to the foetally curled-up prisoner.

McTandlyn didn't respond but his cellmate did.

"He's eaten glass from light bulbs. He's trying to kill himself and it's fucking obvious, you prick!"

He was speaking in a manner that would not be tolerated in normal circumstances, but these were far from normal circumstances. Brian understood that the man had the upper hand. He knew that the officer attending the cell was to facilitate the removal of McTandlyn and was not in a position to impose minor corrective measures imposed for disrespecting an officer.

Two other prison officers attended the cell confirming that an ambulance was on its way. The cellmate was temporarily moved to an isolation cell to allow for the medics to attend to the suffering inmate. The ambulance crew were escorted to the wing. They examined McTandlyn but could get no words from him. They had to rely on other information. Brian McSwail was the only one with an opinion.

"He's got to go to casualty," he declared, "If he's got glass inside him we can't handle that on the hospital wing."

The ambulance crew prepared to lift McTandlyn and place him on the folding wheelchair they had brought with them. Brian's colleagues knew that taking a prisoner to hospital at short notice was an undesirable event, taking up staff from other duties and presenting a security risk. They would always opt for the patient to be treated in the prison hospital wing. Brian could not allow that decision to be contemplated.

"We have no choice," he said, "If this bastard dies, we're all in the shit. It has to be the Casualty." Despite being the junior man of the three, his plea had convinced his colleagues. One went back to the control room to arrange for staff from other wings to cover for the absence of the escorting team. Brian was one of the two deployed to go in the ambulance. The other was Mark Whitby, a former Royal Navy stoker who ran marathons for his fun.

In the sterile area between the inner and outer gates, the ambulance, which already displayed flashing, blue lights on its roof, was kept waiting until the armed police escort vehicle was in position outside. Once radio confirmation came through, the electric gate slid open and the ambulance rolled out. Onto the dual-carriageway and away toward City

Hospital which was the only facility considered to be secure enough for high-risk detainees to be admitted.

On the journey, Brian McSwail acted the part of the impassive and detached prison guard whilst Darry McTandlyn acted the part of agonised, self-harming patient. Brian hoped that his performance was as convincing as McTandlyn's. Thoughts that he had postponed from entertaining began to creep into Brian's mind. It was clear that the aim was to spring the lifer from jail but he did not know how it was going to happen. He had already seen for himself the lengths they were prepared to go to in order to get this man out, but there was an armed police escort in attendance and that would have to be overcome. He could not see how without somebody getting hurt. He hoped it would not be him then instantly checked himself with guilt at having contemplated that. He was effectively wishing it on somebody else; the police? his colleague Mark Whitby? Only by focussing on his own family could he finish what he had set out to do.

The police escort, an elongated Land Rover, swung into the drop-off area of the Casualty Department. Four armed officers got out leaving the driver alone at the wheel. They positioned themselves at all corners of the tarmac to seal off the area. The ambulance was allowed to reach the glass doors, and the crew began to deliver the patient along with the two prison officers into the building. Two of the policemen remained outside whilst the other two accompanied the party into the hospital. All of this was being watched by unseen observers. Two in a Ford Transit van, positioned away from streetlamps, on the car park at the end of the building and two more on the roof above the Casualty building. Time had not allowed for a thorough sweep of the building and grounds. The prescribed security arrangements had to be adapted to make the best of what could be done at such short notice.

Inside Casualty they were led to a secure room set aside for this purpose. The hospital staff entered and left only when the door was unlocked and locked again from inside. The door could be seen from the public waiting room forty yards away, where a sixty-six-year-old man was being monitored having been admitted forty minutes earlier with pains in his chest. His condition was also a fabrication.

The door to the secure room came open and McTandlyn was wheeled out on a gurney being pushed by a porter and surrounded by uniforms. It trundled along a corridor to the X-Ray Department at the back of the building. As soon as this happened, the man with the chest pain announced his intention to go outside for a cigarette and he detached himself from the wires placed in his chest and arm. Once in the chill, night air he went to the Transit van on the car park and informed the occupants that their target had been taken for X-ray. He returned to the building and when he was sure that he was not being watched, he activated the fire alarm by breaking the glass panel with his elbow.

Instant, amplified ringing of bells filled the department and all wards in that block. A nightmare scenario ensued with staff darting in all directions. Those who could walk were guided, by shouting and hand gestures, to leave and go to the assembly point outside. Others less mobile were steered to acceptable locations and extra blankets were liberally distributed to keep out the cold.

Meanwhile, in the X-ray department, the radiographer called a halt to the quest to examine the internal organs of the man in custody. The escorting police and prison staff began to suspect that their task was not what it had seemed. One of them was sure it wasn't.

A double door marked 'In case of fire' and held shut by a metal bar on a hinge, was flung open and a policeman with a carbine rifle stepped out first to check the area. It was a square with ten parking spaces and the only light came from the windows of the floor above. Whitby had begun to apply handcuffs to McTandlyn, but McSwail convinced him that it was not worth doing as they would be back inside soon. The gurney was wheeled outside into near darkness. A man in a black mask with yellow wool around the mouth and nose holes stepped out of the shadow behind the door and put a short-barrelled Webley revolver to the neck of the leading policeman. He turned him and held him around his chest.

"Drop it!" he said with surprising composure. The gun fell to the ground.

The second police firearms officer raised his weapon and trained it on the masked man. He knew that he had no choice. Much as it pained him to accept it, he could not risk his colleague's life. The barrel of the masked man's handgun was in the crease behind his colleague's ear. That faceless criminal held all the cards and everyone knew it.

"Put that down, now!" he demanded, and the weapon was lowered all the way to the ground.

McTandlyn rose from the gurney like Lazarus. He swung his legs to the side and stepped barefoot onto the cold concrete. He snatched both police guns and, with one hung behind his back by its shoulder strap, he trained the other on the frozen party in the doorway.

"Nice work, son," he complimented his rescuer who nodded acknowledgement then concentrated on the now unarmed and unprotected group.

"Get down on the floor, all of you!"

They laid down, including the hapless hospital porter and the radiographer. The Transit van spun into the little car park and reversed up to the doorway. The passenger, also masked, got out and opened the back doors. The policeman being held at gunpoint was lowered to the ground and left face down. His attacker got into the back of the van, still training his gun on the group lying prone on the ground. The engine of the van revved impatiently. McTandlyn was in no hurry.

He raised the carbine to shoulder height and edged backwards to the open van.

"Come on," said a voice from within the van, "job's done, let's go."

"Nah," said the newly liberated man, "I haven't finished. I owe these fuckers, big time."

He stepped forward as a stalking predator with his long-detested quarry at his mercy, of which he had none.

"Leave it, there are others at the front," said the now plaintive voice of reason from the van.

Thoughts raced through Whitby's head like a wild storm before giving way to the clearest decision there was to make. This psycho was a convicted cop-killer and he had two cops and two prison officers lying down waiting for him to shoot them. Whitby leapt to his feet and like a sprinter out of the blocks he took off from a crouching angle to straighten up. He hit McTandlyn, but he was alive to the threat. He stepped backwards and as his shoulder blade touched the open door of the van, he fired three rapid shots into the head and torso of the prison officer. His rescuers grabbed him and pulled him and the two stolen guns into the back of the van. The doors were clanged shut and the van sped off across the car park and out of sight behind the hospital.

Brian McSwail looked at the lifeless body of his colleague. The two police firearms men and the radiographer ran to try to give first aid to the man who had undoubtedly sacrificed himself to save them, but there was nothing they could do. McSwail buried his head in his folded arms on the hard ground. His nightmare just got ten times worse.

When the detective team arrived at the hospital he was unable or unwilling to speak other than to say that he needed to go home. In order to seize McSwail's clothing for forensic, the officer in charge authorised that two officers take him home in order for him to get changed. The house was empty but the sound of McSwail and the police officers talking caused a reaction from within the garden shed at the back. Alerted to the sound of banging on wood, they opened it to find Cath and Daisie McSwail tied up, terrified but alive. Retrieved and untied, the reunited family sobbed and shook in trauma and relief. Brian McSwail managed to blurt out the story of his night. Cath and Daisie were taken to hospital and Brian was arrested and held for questioning.

CHAPTER THIRTY-THREE

If it meant that she could take part in something new, Lizzie volunteered to work on her days off. Her enthusiasm was recognised when the shift Inspector nominated her for driver training, which included the passing of the state driving test. Still only twenty, she was the youngest panda car driver in the city. Faster attendance meant that Lizzie got to deal with more demanding incidents: More burglaries in progress, shop and building society robberies and violent crime. Taking care to avoid confrontation with colleagues where it was likely, she managed to win the approval of people in other departments and on the day of the results for the annual Sergeant's exam, she was called into the office of the Superintendent, congratulated on passing and given a three-month secondment to the Criminal Investigation Department.

After being given the cases that her more experienced peers thought were beneath them, she applied herself to all opportunities that came her way, turning up previously overlooked lines of enquiry and often escalating little jobs into big ones. Trust was built up gradually and her meticulous attention to detail, combined with a fearlessness in moments of confrontation that made some of her colleagues nervous for her safety, earned her the freedom to generate her own caseload, a status rarely afforded to a seconded officer. Not relying on others to allocate work for her, she gathered what proved to be reliable intelligence from many sources, including several of those who she had arrested and charged. By offering to carry out unpopular tasks she got to work on teams investigating three murders, a protracted multiple-mortgage fraud and a night-time stranger rape. Having made herself indispensable, on the conclusion of the agreed three-month posting, she was confirmed as a substantive detective constable. She was twenty-one.

Her mother wanted Lizzie to have as full a life as possible. She held the view that her daughter had endured more unhappiness than most people had in a lifetime, and Jennifer encouraged Lizzie to get out and be sociable. She wasn't going to lead a full and contented life by working and staying home. To placate her mother, Lizzie did attend selected social events and was introduced to a number of suitable young men. Each had to overcome the professional suspicion she activated and skilfully operated like a built-in radar system. There were four separate occasions that could be called dates. They ended early and were not revisited. She could not resist the compulsion to make adverse comparisons to the boy she had known as Sid. After a while, Jennifer stopped offering her suggestions and Lizzie settled into a life without such pressures.

CHAPTER THIRTY-FOUR

"You're looking a little pale lad. Some sunshine might do you good," suggested Professor Cooke over morning coffee in the University staff café. Cooke's health was a more pressing issue. His previously ruddy complexion had taken on an insipid pallor and his deeply embedded coughing seemed to provide less relief from congestion and make a more disturbingly grating sound for those nearby. He looked older and weaker. He was not the sort of person to accept the observations or concerns of others on matters relating to his perceived health.

"I can't see that being a holiday, Professor," answered James, who had long before realised that Cooke's work ethic did not allow for such time wasting.

"Well, no, it has a purpose, this trip that I want you to go on, but it will certainly be sunny." He rasped out a long and pained coughing aria. "You can call it a holiday if it makes you feel better," said the old man in a gesture of compromise he rarely demonstrated.

"I can guess at the purpose of the trip but I'd like to know where, California?"

"Florida," announced the Professor as he filled his pipe with his preferred blend of tobacco. "We have a useful contact there who can engineer certain introductions. You can take it from there. Officially, you are discussing political research contracts. When you get back you will have to document that, or we'll have the I.R.S. as well as the C.I.A. all over us like a snowdrift." He returned the old and discoloured tobacco pouch to his coat pocket and slipped the chewed end of his pipe into the corner of his mouth. Once lit, the smoke seemed to still the coughing.

James paused to await more information but it was not forthcoming. Eventually, when the old man was content that his pipe was adequately ignited, he puffed intensely on it, making exhaling sounds of satisfaction before continuing with his briefing.

"You'll be there a year, initially. You'll be collected at the airport and taken to meet a realty agent called Johnny Callick. He will arrange all of the introductions. There will be some deep pockets to work on lad and remember that you can't be too careful with your security measures. It's not just us who are not what we appear to be, you know?"

"Okay, I get it," said James, finishing his coffee. "Is there anything else I should know?"

"Yes," began the Professor, pausing to pick an atom of stray tobacco from the tip of his tongue, "pack your swimming trunks, ha ha!"

James was driven as usual by Benny. On the highway approaching Logan he let on to Benny where he was headed for. Benny had prior knowledge of the south-east.

"Florida, the goddam Sunshine State? I went there once on vacation, too hot for me."

James looked at Benny's globe of a stomach squeezing under and over the steering wheel. His bulbous chin added to the side profile of neglect and over-eating. Benny sweated in a cold room. His well-meant warning about the climate in the south carried no weight, unlike Benny.

In the queue for check in, James was aware that he appeared to be the only person travelling alone. Families and couples formed the line as it zig-zagged through the cordon-taped expanse of the cavernous check-in area. Once through and into the departures zone, James knew that it was easier for the American security services to monitor passengers and spot unusual patterns of behaviour. He looked for an opportunity to blend in, and he found it with a woman in her early seventies who was walking with a surgical stick and pushing her cabin luggage on a trolley with tiny wheels. He waited until she sat down on the end seat of one of thirty rows of seating in a church-like formation. Seeing that she was glad to be seated, he chose to sit next to her. She didn't acknowledge his presence until he offered to get coffee for them both.

"I can see that you're walking with a stick Ma'am. It's easier for me to carry it so would that be okay?"

"Why sure, Honey. That is kind of you to help an old lady."

With two coffees in hand, James retook his place with his new friend, chatting harmlessly and appearing to all observers like a guy travelling with his Mother. Parting only once on the aeroplane and out of sight of the terminal and anybody in it.

At Orlando, he re-joined the old duchess at baggage reclaim and accompanied her through arrivals, seeing her safely into a cab before returning to meet his driver who had been holding a home-made card sign bearing his surname.

Once aboard a blue Ford Taunus sedan, James took in the Florida mood, marvelling at the blaze of colour lit up by the white sunlight. Professor Cooke had not been exaggerating when he had promised sunshine. After ninety minutes, the car swung onto the driveway of a single storey house with white walls under a terracotta tiled roof. There were six windows across the front of the house and the garden was bordered by green and yellow high hedges. The Ford came to a stop alongside an eye-catching, yellow Corvette Stingray with black windows. As James stepped out into the baking heat, not tempered by any breeze, he felt instantly dizzy before composing himself to approach the front door of the house. It was opened from inside by a twenty-stone man in a light-blue and white, short-sleeved, formal shirt, cream trousers and brown, leather sandals. A pair of mirrored sunglasses hung from the first fastened button of the shirt. The glare of light from the sunglasses was matched by the gleaming white teeth of his richly suntanned host.

"Hi, welcome to Florida." He sounded like a television advert for beach condos. "James Patrick Coleman, I guess. Sure is great to make your acquaintance. Shall I call you James or Patrick?" Professor Cooke's insistence that the 'Patrick' should be emphasised at every hint of an opportunity was evident in Johnny's prior briefing.

"It's James, but I don't mind, anything goes. You must be Mr Callick, am I right?"

"You sure are. Johnny Callick at your service, come on in."

The driver left James' suitcase by the front door and left. Johnny Callick took in the case and closed the door, continually talking in excited and welcoming tones.

The interior was all light, pastel colours. It was as though the intended occupant had expressed an aversion to any colour that could be seen as bold or substantial. Everything was long and wide; the furniture, the doorways, the windows, even the rugs on the floor and the pictures on the walls. It was all high-quality merchandise and Johnny Callick wasted no time or effort in pointing out how dreamy this property was for the discerning tenant.

Callick proved to be affable company. In the impressively equipped kitchen the size of a squash court, he fixed two long, iced concoctions of indeterminate content. He led James out of the French windows at the back of the house, where a raised concrete area contained a blue-tiled swimming pool surrounded by six padded loungers of polished wood and accompanying low tables.

"You' been to the Sunshine State before, James?"

"No this is my first visit. It's certainly warmer than Massachusetts."

"It sure is, you're gonna love it here. Oh, just a minute."

Johnny Callick went into the house and emerged with a portable radio/cassette player. He reeled out a cable and plugged it into a power stand at the edge of the raised concrete dais. He switched it on and moved the dial until he was happy with the station. He sat down heavily on one of the loungers. James thought how tough it must be for a guy who was carrying so much weight around in heat like that. Callick appeared to have grown accustomed to it. James, who was little more than half of Callick's weight, was buckling under the grill of the Florida afternoon. He sipped the cool, sweet drink, which had some element of whisky in it, and sat on a lounger with a raised back.

"This is going to be your home, at least for a little while anyways." said Johnny.

"That's very good of you to put me up Johnny, most hospitable."

"Aw, think nothing of it. I'm only sorry that you're gonna be here on your own most of the time."

"On my own? All this is just for me?"

"Why sure it is. We have to create the right atmosphere for the business you're gonna be conducting, don't we? It 'aint no problem, the owner is sympathetic to the cause. He's a substantial donor himself and he wants you to meet some of his friends. There's a lot of dough in this part of the country and much of it belongs to ex-pats who want to contribute in their own small way, well not so small, huh?"

197

James enjoyed the Florida sunshine and laid-back attitude of the people. He suffered with sunburn in the first week but that settled and became less painful as he became accustomed to it. At the poolside and accompanied by a soundtrack of American background music, he met and took payments from sixteen different people, all introduced and transported to the villa by Callick. Negotiations usually took place in the swimming pool. The holiday atmosphere pervaded and it proved to be a most enjoyable and productive secondment.

CHAPTER THIRTY-FIVE

Three weeks after James had returned from his year-long stay in Florida, it was Benny who first mentioned the discoloured spots on the side of James' neck. Unencumbered by any social graces, Benny had the naïve but occasionally valuable ability to cut through tricky social situations others may have seen fit to shy away from. Benny had not noticed the abrasions before and had simply verbalised his thoughts.

"What are you talking about Benny?" asked James as they walked between buildings on the University campus.

"On your neck, two brown spots. Maybe you had them all along, but I just noticed them."

James felt with his fingertips. There was some raising of the skin, but it was barely present. He would look in a mirror later. More pressing matters awaited them in the offices of the senior management of the University. The 'Ivory Tower' as Professor Cooke had habitually called it.

Once received by a secretary in an office suite of considerably greater opulence than in their own faculty, James and Benny stood when called and progressed into the office of Senior Vice-Chancellor, Professor Warren Isherwood. Benny was stopped at the door by the secretary who clinically and dispassionately pointed out that it was only Doctor Coleman who was to see the boss. Benny retreated back to the guest seating and picked up a Home and Style magazine.

"Ah, Dr Coleman, please come in, take a seat," said Isherwood rising from behind a presidential desk to shake James' hand. All that sprawling office lacked was the Stars and Stripes tilted across the wall behind the desk.

"Thank you Professor," said James and he took his position on a black leather chair that was not casual enough for a lounge but too informal for an office. Isherwood returned to his seat. He was not a man to waste time or mince words.

"I understand you have been in Florida."

"Yes, that's right," answered James.

"Productive trip?"

James considered whether Professor Isherwood was a party to the real reason for the secondment. He erred on the side of caution.

"Yes, I think so. I'm confident that I've managed to secure some research business for the faculty."

Isherwood seemed to accept that and progressed on to what he wanted to talk about.

"You are aware that Professor Cooke has been unwell whilst you have been away?"

"I understand that he has had some time off, yes," said James.

"His health has taken a downturn, Emphysema, condition of the lungs. I am a medical man myself, had my own practice before I came into Academia, and I know that it's not a condition to be taken lightly. Professor Cooke has been taken to a health facility that I recommended in Vermont."

James momentarily pictured Gerard Cooke in an institution dedicated to the pursuit of health. He was probably banned from drinking Guinness or smoking his pipe and was berating the staff with every laboured breath simply for trying to care for him.

"I'm sorry to hear that. He could be away for some time then," he said in genuine concern adding "I must go and see him, take some grapes."

"Sure, good idea, give him my best," said Isherwood without showing any genuine concern. "Meanwhile, the Political Sciences Faculty has got a little neglected and I'm keen that it gets back on track. Professor Cooke may not return at all. We must prepare for that. It's an opportunity for you Dr Coleman to take his post on a temporary basis, but I realistically anticipate that we can make that permanent later this year. Even if Professor Cooke is well enough to return, I want him in a position of less day-to-day responsibility, a consulting role, perhaps. So how do you feel about running the department, Professor?"

"Well, I appreciate the situation and I'm ready to take it on. Thank you."

Isherwood rose from his seat and shook James' hand again but this time with more congratulatory vigour. He guided James to the door, silently declaring that the audience was over. He opened the door and James passed him but Isherwood surprised him by placing a hand on his upper arm.

"Hold on a minute," he said in a sombre tone. "How long have you had those spots on your neck?"

"I became aware of them today," said James.

"Since you came back from Florida?"

"Yes."

"Would you let me arrange for this to be checked out? I have a former colleague at City General, expert in the field."

"If you think it necessary, Professor."

Isherwood went to the secretary's desk and spoke to her.

"Mrs Deraulle, would you contact Harry Braschert's office at City General Hospital, make an appointment for him to examine Professor Coleman?"

"I'll do that right away," she said, picking up the phone whilst writing on a pad of paper.

James expressed his gratitude and nodded to Benny that they should go. Benny hurried along through the door onto the corridor.

"Did he call you Professor? I heard him call you Professor."

"He's just given me a temporary promotion, Cooke's going to be ill for a long time and I'm going to be doing his job on an acting basis. It's no big deal."

"Yes it is, we should celebrate."

James knew that in Benny's limited imagination, celebration meant beer, hot dogs and basketball - watching basketball not playing it. He had a point. It was worth a little celebration and Benny's way was as good as any.

"What was he saying about City General Hospital, was that about Professor Cooke?"

James was about to explain that Cooke was being treated in Vermont and that the conversation about City General was about him and his unexplained new spots, but he checked himself and left Benny to believe that he was right. It was easier than engaging in further debate about it.

"Yeah, Professor Cooke's getting the best treatment. Come on, let's get a beer."

CHAPTER THIRTY-SIX

The following morning began with a telephone ringing. At that moment, it was the second loudest ringing sound in James' head. He reached for the phone and answered it without opening his eyes.

"Hello," he croaked.

"Good morning, this is the office of Doctor Braschert. Am I speaking to Professor Coleman?"

It hadn't been a dream. He really was now called Professor Coleman.

"Yes, I am Professor Coleman." He tried to sound awake but probably didn't.

"Are you available to attend the Hospital this afternoon at three o'clock to see Doctor Braschert?"

The conversation with Isherwood came flooding back to him.

"Erm, yes. I'll be there. Thank you."

He put down the phone and tried to sit up in bed, but his head was too heavy. After several deep breaths he stood up and went to the kitchen where he commenced rehydrating his body with what amounted to about a litre of water. He hoped that Benny was somewhere feeling equally rough.

After an unproductive morning mainly centred on recovering his cerebral and physical capabilities, he took a sauna and carbohydrate-based lunch before driving to the City General.

On the ninth floor he found Dr Braschert's office. A brief flick through a magazine about sail boats ended when the consulting room door opened and a chubby-faced bald man with a thick moustache and wearing a white, buttoned-up, surgeon's tunic came into view.

"Professor Coleman?" he asked.

"Yes. Dr Braschert?"

James stood and replaced the magazine on the low table. He entered the clinical whiteness of the room. A view across the vast complex of hospital buildings and parking lots spread across the full-width expanse of the windows. Everything in the room was white. It was like living through a 1930s Hollywood representation of Heaven, but without the choir of angels or the sound of harps.

Braschert was the sort of chap who was instantly trusted. He had a bedside manner that had been honed over decades of breaking good and bad news to people and lessening the agony of the processes in between. He had James remove his shirt and trousers before conducting a thorough examination. Under a bright UV light, he scanned his entire body, tested reflexes, hearing, vision and through detailed conversation, explored his diet, lifestyle, exercise and pressures of work. Blood samples were taken along with a biopsy of the skin on his neck. When James was dressed he sat on the table and waited for the doctor to finish writing in a notebook.

"Well, Doctor. Any early diagnosis?"

Braschert put down his pen and turned to look at James.

"I have to test these samples, but I think I know what I'm going to find."

"You do?"

"Hmmm. I can be direct with you about this, Professor Coleman. I am sure you can take it. The marks on your neck are cancerous. Urgent surgery will be in order."

"What! I've got cancer?"

"Yes," said Braschert with neither relish nor empathy.

"How?"

"The power of the Sun is not to be underestimated. Your skin pigmentation, largely determined by your genetic background, is particularly susceptible to certain skin problems. This is one of them. Thankfully, up until recently, you have not been exposed to intense sunlight over a prolonged period."

"Urgent surgery, you said?"

"Yes. You have several instances of malignant melanoma. The encouraging facts are that you have only had them for a few weeks and you are young and otherwise healthy. I can remove them and arrange a course of follow-up treatment. The possibility that this could happen again remains but, now that you know what you are up against you can do something about it."

James sat quietly for a few minutes as Braschert finished his notes.

"Doctor Braschert, when can this surgery be done and how long will I be laid up?"

"I can do it two days from now, right here. You'll be a day patient, home in time for dinner. A couple of days' rest and you'll be back at work and fully able by next week. We'll keep regular checks after that, look for any recurrence."

"That's encouraging, thank you."

"Good. Hold that thought because what I am about to tell you will be the bit that might be harder for you to get used to."

"Go on."

"The melanomas aren't just on your neck. There are four more on your face and forehead. They're just under the skin at present but they are there alright, and they have to come out too. This will inevitably result in some facial scarring. I will try to limit that, but you may want to consider some corrective cosmetic surgery afterwards. I can recommend someone if you wish."

James stared open-mouthed, firstly at Braschert then out of the wide window. The doctor gave him a minute to think then added.

"You would not be the first to feel that the Earth has been pulled from under you today, but just get this into some shape. You've got to have an operation, maybe a couple of operations, and you'll look a little different, but you are highly likely to live through this. Not everybody gets that break."

"Thanks Doctor. I'm beginning to get it clear in my head."

"Good. I'll do the tests right away. I need you here at ten-thirty in the morning the day after tomorrow. Don't eat or drink anything before coming and arrange for somebody to collect you in the late afternoon. Is that okay with you?"

James took a deep breath and let it out slowly. He stood and shook Braschert's hand.

"I'm in the picture now. I get it."

The surgery was carried out under local anaesthetic but James slept through much of it anyway. Benny collected him and took him back to his apartment at the University. The bandages covered his head and much of his face. He managed to make a joke about being a Mummy from an old horror movie. It made Benny more relaxed about it all. A side-effect of the cancer surgery was that James' tolerance to light was lessened. His occasional wearing of spectacles became permanent and they were fitted with tinted lenses to diffuse light.

The resultant scarring was extensive. It bore the hallmarks of ritual torture. Dr Braschert's colleague in the cosmetic surgery department performed three operations. When the final, miniature stitches were removed, James looked and felt human again. The skin across his cheeks was stretched and the surgery on his forehead had lifted his eyebrows a few millimetres. His mouth remained the same but his entire upper face was reshaped. He could not readily picture how he had looked before the diagnosis, but when comparing his passport photograph, it became clear that he would require a new one.

CHAPTER THIRTY-SEVEN

As one of only three female detective constables in the department, Lizzie divided opinion amongst her colleagues. She was the youngest and a degree of animosity and envy was to be expected from those who believed her career elevation to be undeserved. She was also better looking and although the switch from uniform to a suit seemed a minor one, it added to the divisive nature of her presence.

Several male colleagues noticed that the new girl represented a change in female influence. 'A runner where they used to have shot-putters,' was how one office wit put it in the after-work drinking arena. Would-be suitors were effectively put off coming forward and asking her out on a date by the plain fact that she did not engage in even the merest of flirting, saving her personal warmth for the vulnerable victims of crime that she seemed to have endless patience for. At the first hint of any amorous behaviour, she began typing or reading something intently, shutting out the interloper until he got the hint and left her to it. Most of the time, she didn't notice at all.

Whilst Lizzie may have appeared aloof and beyond the reach of her admirers, the suggestion that she was a machine was unfounded. Her demeanour belied a deep longing for the things that she had lost, things she did not speak of other than to her mother. In a short space of time she had lost her father, the child she had never seen and the young man who had made her feel so alive. What her C.I.D. colleagues had mistaken for unbridled ambition was really a self-imposed mechanism for coping with loss. The more time she spent doing the job, and in her off-duty time studying it, the less time remained for contemplating sadness. She had no wish to discuss it with them.

After two years of revisiting burglary scenes and coaxing useful conversations out of victims, witnesses and suspects, Lizzie once again usurped more senior peers to be given a period as Acting Detective Sergeant in charge of a team of five D.C.s.

"Don't take any shit off those clowns, love." was the extent of the helpful advice offered by Detective Chief Inspector Bert Malcolm who, by the standards of Salford C.I.D. was considered to be a forward-thinking liberal. He waddled around the ancient desk in his third floor office, pulling his overworked belt and trouser waistband up to cover at least the lower half of the ample belly he carried around. He tended to play with his tie, which gave him an Oliver Hardy air. Lizzie had been present in the main office when impersonations of Malcolm had been performed to wide amusement. She had the ability to distance herself from that bloke humour.

It had been Bert Malcolm's decision to give Lizzie the acting role over at least three other credible and more experienced candidates. Malcolm was a shrewd manager of people. He recognised the problems created by having too many old and immovable detectives in his department and knew that it was equally problematic to have a team with insufficient experience. He sought to strike a balance and achieve an efficient mix of both. Looking at it clinically, he chose Lizzie because he could not identify anything she had done that he could have improved upon. By then she had passed both the sergeant's and inspector's promotion exams and it was clear that she was 'going places.'

"There's no doubt that you are going to be offered promotion before too long," he said to her whilst staring out of the window at the movement of a yellow crane lowering a girder in the distance. "I want that to happen here, not in A

Division and not in H.Q. There'll be time for that later, I'm sure. You need a backer to get anywhere in this job, love. Right now the only one you've got is me. This is still a new organisation. Amalgamation is in the past now, the old ways of doing things belong in the past too. But there are some who still want to bounce people around cells to get a cough and they moan 'cause they're not allowed to. I want this department bringing up to date. No dinosaur mentality, know what I'm talking about?"

"Yes Sir, I think I do," she said, trying not to offend but feeling uneasy about trying to turn the oil tanker that was C.I.D. canteen culture. "You want your officers to be more professional, to get evidence and convictions without cutting corners."

"Exactly, I couldn't have put it better myself," he said turning to look at her. "So, if anybody on your team wants to dig their heels in and pretend it's the Sixties, you refer them to me, okay?"

"Yes Sir, thank you."

Lizzie left the office with the clear intention of not referring anybody on her staff to Bert Malcolm unless they had actually committed a crime, in which case she would arrest them herself. Low-level misdemeanours had to be dealt with at a low-level.

After some initial sluggish reluctance from the five constables in her charge, she gradually wore them down by working in a pair with each of them herself over the first few weeks. On a one-to-one basis, each one saw that she was doing the job of a sergeant as well as that of a constable, a skill not often seen in that department. One-by-one they accepted that Lizzie was worthy of their loyalty and a new sense of comradeship and combined purpose was born. Sniping comments from colleagues on other teams within the department were taken as insults to the team and were defended vigorously. One such exchange resulted in an altercation outside the George and Dragon one Friday night. A torn shirt, a broken tooth and a black eye ensued which were all forgotten by Monday morning. Lizzie was oblivious to the fact that her team had been defending her reputation to the point of violence.

CHAPTER THIRTY-EIGHT

On an old and sprawling farm in rural County Mayo, seven miles from the nearest substantial settlement, the late-summer harvest attracted seasonal workers from other Irish counties. Every year brought a new batch of men, usually unknown to each other. Accommodated in sparse and basic conditions, mainly in the barns they were filling with crops, they either saved their earnings to take home to their families or they found their way into the pubs of nearby villages to blow the lot on beer and whisky. Only one itinerant farm labourer did not follow that pattern. He was known to his colleagues as Padraig. To Interpol he was known as Darry McTandlyn.

He barely spoke to his fellow workers, preferring instead to shut himself off in a den of his own construction in the barn's rafters. On three evenings a week, he walked to a crossroads half a mile from the farmhouse, where he was collected by any one of a variety of vehicles. He was returned to that point two hours later. During those missing hours, he was driven thirty miles to an old mill building where he was being trained in the use of high-powered firearms and plastic explosives. At the end of the Summer, when the temporary workforce dispersed and returned to where they had come from, McTandlyn was taken to a private clinic in the city of Cork. He underwent surgery to alter the shape of his nose, jaw and eye-sockets. A four-week period of convalescence ensued. Although he had spent the season doing hard and constant physical labour, he embarked on a punishing fitness regime, honing his destructive skills. By December, there was little visual similarity between the man who called himself Padraig and the fugitive he had been before.

Incarceration followed by life on the run had made Darry McTandlyn re-evaluate his priorities. His status in the I.R.A. had been confirmed by the efforts made to free him from the Maze, authorised at the highest level. Denied his earlier lifestyle choices, he considered what he had missed most and had found that excessive drinking and abusing women ranked lowly on his programme of pleasures. What had become clear to him was that it had been the power that he had held in his hands, the power of life or death over other people that had given him the greatest buzz.

Many times, he had relived and reviewed the two most recent killings he had carried out. He was angry at how clumsily he had performed in the shooting of Arnie Cullen, how he had nearly failed and been tackled to the ground by a wounded, unarmed, middle-aged man. The composure and clinical execution of the prison officer that he had displayed during his escape gave him greater satisfaction. He wanted more feelings like that. Little victories he had taken pleasure from had slipped into obscurity to be replaced by the absolute will to be the best at what he did.

CHAPTER THIRTY-NINE

The tone of Melissa's voice over the phone was different, uneasy, joyless. James detected some reluctance where there was usually an upbeat air.

"James, there's a telegram for you at the reception desk."

"Okay, thanks. I'll come down."

He took the elevator to the ground floor and found Melissa on the phone behind the desk. She looked up and saw him then adopted the creased-eyebrows of someone unsuccessfully trying to perform two methods of communication at the same time. Whilst still on the line and listening to the caller, she picked up a paper and handed it to James. Her head was uncharacteristically tipped to one side.

The telegram came from Western Union. It had been initiated by the parish priest of James' old neighbourhood in Belfast. Below his name it read;

'Your mother died peacefully, stop.'

'Funeral 11am Thursday 24th, stop.'

'Contact St Patrick's, stop.'

After reading it twice, James continued to look at it but his eyes no longer focussed on its content.

"James, I'm so sorry," said Melissa when she had finally managed to end the call.

James let out a long slow breath of air and stood up straight before acknowledging that Melissa had spoken.

"It's okay. She hadn't been well for a while but . . ."

Melissa came around the desk and took his free hand in both of hers.

"I know it's not worth much at such a time but if there's anything I can do."

This brought him back to the here-and-now, at least momentarily. He turned his head to look at Melissa.

"There is something, if you can."

"Sure, what do you need?"

"The international phone number for St. Patrick's Catholic Church on Milderby Street in Belfast."

"I'll get it right away," said Melissa who was relieved at the chance to change the atmosphere from tragic and hopeless to occupied and useful.

"And Melissa . . ." he added.

"Yes James?"

". . . can you get me on a flight from Logan to Belfast please, the sooner the better, eh?"

She smiled benevolently and began flicking through a card index.

James summoned the elevator and once inside he recalled the last time he had spoken to his Mother. It had been on the previous Friday, as had been his custom since his arrival in Boston. She had complained of being tired but it was, as she had put it, nothing to bother the doctor about. The doctor would be busy with people who were really ill, she said.

Back up to his office he closed the door and locked it. He sat down and looked again at the telegram. His breathing became shallow and his shoulders sank away from the inside of his coat. His head tipped forward until it touched the blotter on his desk. Silently, he rehydrated the long-dried ink making blurred blue clouds on the paper.

A call was made from James' desk phone to Father McGorn at St Patrick's. James thanked him for his message and authorised him to nominate the appropriate people to administer the arrangements. It was to be low key and the plot containing the graves of Magnus and Philip was to be Clare's final resting place too.

Another call was made but this one was from a phone off the University campus.

"I've had a death in the family."

"Sorry to hear that lad, my condolences to you."

"It's my Mother. The funeral is on Thursday and I have to go."

This was the first time the issue of breaking his exile had arisen. There was no plan in place to address it.

"That might cause a problem," said Mahon with a clear lack of sensitivity under the circumstances.

"Are you telling me I can't go to my own Mother's funeral?"

"Now hold on a minute. No, I'm not saying that. I'm saying that you are an important asset where you are and I don't want anything over here to jeopardise that. This is how it has to be. You come to the funeral and you don't see or speak to anybody else. You have to keep your distance from anything to do with the cause."

James agreed and hung up. He had no intention of doing or saying anything to anybody about the role he carried out in America for the cause of Irish Republicanism. He had other things on his mind. Principally, the girl he had left behind in Belfast so suddenly, so foolishly. He had to try to find her. He had to explain, as far as he was able to do so, and apologise. He knew without any doubt that she had felt for him the same fully immersed love that he had had for her, still had for her. A visit to the old city could not miss an opportunity to at least try to find her.

CHAPTER FORTY

In the early hours of a Thursday in March, a car collided with a container wagon as it tried to enter Salford Docks. The wagon lost its cargo and the metal container had landed on its side. Damage to the hinges allowed the contents to be seen. It was a Porsche 917 Touring car, one of only 200 ever made. Only minor injuries were sustained by the driver of the car. The driver of the wagon was not injured at all. Although the wagon driver was not to blame for the collision he tried to run away, but he was easily caught and detained by the traffic cops. They would otherwise have seen it as a routine bump resulting in minimal paperwork followed by a civil insurance claim. The wagon driver proved uncommunicative, refusing to give his name or any information about who he worked for or what was planned for the rare car. He was taken in for questioning.

A fingerprint search revealed him to be Jonathan Charles Newhart, from Belfast. Newhart had criminal convictions dating back thirty years. He was an old lag and he knew what not to say. He also knew that there really is no honour among thieves. When questioned at Salford Police Station by the C.I.D. he said nothing for hours. A change of approach brought Det. Sgt Elizabeth Cullen into the hot seat. Tired, isolated and feeling sorry for himself, Newhart began to realise that he would be kept there for days if he kept up his siege mentality. Lizzie slipped into the dialect of her home city and Newhart felt the warmth of a familiar accent. He told her everything.

Newhart did all he could to implicate his paymasters in the thefts and illicit exporting of the Porsche and dozens of other high value motor vehicles. As he had done many times before, he was to collect the container from a given location and drive it to a dock; Holyhead, Salford, Liverpool, Stranraer, Heysham or Fleetwood for transporting usually to Warrenpoint in Northern Ireland. What happened after that, he did not know, but the cars were never seen driving around Ulster.

Newhart's account indicated that over a hundred stolen cars had been moved in this way. Some had been stolen to order, whilst some had been the subject of fraudulent insurance claims. All of the evidence pointed to Northern Ireland. Lizzie and three of her team boarded a plane to Belfast.

She said nothing of it to her colleagues but she spent the journey thinking about returning to her birthplace. She held no rosy nostalgia for the city or the places in which she had grown up. She had decided to place flowers on her father's grave, but the trip had evoked many other stimulating memories; the racing heartbeat, the warmth of the night, the breathless and overpowering passion of the only love she had known, a love that could not since be matched because she would not allow anyone else to try.

Tempering the thrill of those memories was the guilt, guilt at having accepted the giving up of her child, although she had not consented to that at the time, guilt at the resentment she had felt for her Mother's decision to approve the adoption, but overriding all of that was the guilt she felt for leaving so suddenly. The young man she had fallen so intensely in love with, the poetry man in the leather jacket who had awakened so many uplifting emotions in her, the father of her child, albeit in ignorance. Would she ever feel anything like that again? What must he have thought? She had simply disappeared from his life without an explanation or a goodbye. Their brief time together had brought tears of joy to both of them, it had been no passing fancy. Going back to Belfast presented an opportunity for Lizzie. The prospect excited her and caused a tingling in her skin. She had to at least try to find him, the young man she had known as Sid. She knew that it could be a disaster and all end in embarrassment and disappointment. He could, and probably was, married, possibly with a family. He could have got over it better than she had. She couldn't find any reason not to do it. Even if it all collapsed around her, she could not progress with her life not knowing.

Three days of taking statements and questioning suspects for the large scale movement of high value stolen cars resulted in five people charged with conspiracy offences. The day before they were due to fly home to Manchester, Lizzie's team were invited to join their R.U.C. hosts for a drink, which invariably meant a prolonged drinking session, starting at 10.30am. Lizzie, who had only ever made brief, token appearances at such social events in Salford, said that she would join them later and set off in a hired car to visit Belfast City Cemetery, calling at a florist shop for a small wreath.

The sun shone with a vengeance, causing squinting eyes and hands cupped over brows. In the Protestant area of the cemetery, Lizzie reached the grave of Arnold Worsley Cullen. She knelt to tidy up the weather-beaten plot and wiped the headstone with a tissue, making little difference. She wasn't as sad as she had expected to be. She remembered the big, powerful yet gentle soul her father had been in her eyes. She thought that, if there was a Heaven where people get what they deserve from their lives on Earth, then her father would be driving a campervan across America, like in the movies. She found a bench near a sunken wall and sat on it to let the hot sun soothe her face.

Thirty-five yards away, beyond the sunken wall and in the Catholic area of Belfast City Cemetery, a casket was being lowered. A grey marbled headstone lay on its back, temporarily removed to allow the new addition to the plot and to be replaced once the name of Clare Coleman, beloved

221

wife and mother, had been added. Four men from the funeral directors, a handful of elderly folk from the church and some close neighbours stood in silence as Father McGorn eulogised with practiced fluency about the cycles of ashes and dust and the rooms in God's house. James Patrick Coleman stood in a brown corduroy suit and brown tie under a borrowed, black twill coat. He thought of the life his mother had lived and try as he did to stay positive and look for the joy, he could not see past the tragic - the loss of her husband and son so closely together. He felt acutely guilty about leaving for America straight after. A weekly phone call did not seem nearly enough. As the graveside ceremony ended and the people drifted away, James remained alone to commence the post-funeral ascent back to emotional normality.

When he reached the gate and set off toward the city and the hotel he was staying in, he tried to form a plan to trace Kiki. With no other ideas in his head, he headed for a taxi rank and was driven out of the city on a road which suited bicycles rather than cars.

All Lizzie knew about Sid was that he had been a student at Belfast University and that he could quote poetry. She headed for the English Department on the University campus and appealed to the administration officer who, although sympathetic and willing to help, could not find any student record of anyone called Sid, apart from the Hong Kong student, around the relevant time. She tried to think of the things he had said to her when they had first met. They had not been allowed to talk about who they were or where they came from which, at the time, was liberating but she now found it frustrating. The only course of action she could think of was to revisit the place where they first met. Back in the hire car, she replaced her sunglasses and set off along Bangor Road to Helen's Bay.

James got out of the taxi and asked the driver to wait for a few minutes. The driver had experienced many bizarre requests in his time and had long since ceased to find anything a surprise. He left the meter running and waited as asked.

James walked on the sand and hoped for a miracle. It didn't show any sign of happening so he ambled back to the cab, got in and asked to be driven back to his hotel in the city. This place was just a memory now, it was no longer real. The girl who continued to pull his thoughts back to here was probably enjoying a full life somewhere and wouldn't be giving him more than a passing wisp of a thought. It had been life-affirming and was still real to him. He had read a poem to her, at least a part of one. It was the only poem he had ever learned.

The taxi swung around and headed back along the uneven road, slowing to pass a hire car being driven by a lone young woman in sunglasses. From the passenger seat James turned his head to the left to take one final look at the beach. He didn't see the hire car, nor did Lizzie see him. She nodded an acknowledgement to the taxi driver for slowing to allow her to pass on the narrow lane. Lizzie stopped and walked to the water's edge. The taxi headed off to the city.

CHAPTER FORTY-ONE

Three days after Lizzie had returned from Belfast, the lawyer representing Jonathan Charles Newhart made a request for Lizzie to go to Risley Remand Centre in Cheshire to see his client. The request was made over the phone and gave no indication as to what Newhart wanted to talk to her about. Lizzie reckoned that he wanted to know how the information he had supplied about the stolen car scam had affected his case and would not normally give such a request any urgency. However, it had proved to be a good job and whilst gratitude was not the best word to describe it, she did feel that Newhart had entrusted her and letting him know of the developments would be the civil thing to do.

Whilst Newhart was undoubtedly guilty of his part in the conspiracy, he was merely a bit-player and the key men would not have been caught without his contribution. Another thing sparked Lizzie's curiosity: the lawyer had asked for Lizzie to initiate the prison visit and not Newhart. That indicated that Newhart could later deny making any contact with the police of his own doing. He could, if challenged by a fellow criminal, claim that the police wanted to speak to him, which was less troublesome to explain in prison culture.

Lizzie arrangements the visit herself and made the thirty-five minute journey alone in an unmarked police car. After observing the standard security checks and searches, she was shown to the visits block which was otherwise unused as it took place in the morning whereas family visits tended to be afternoon practices.

Wearing a bright-yellow tabard over his own clothes, as prisoners on remand were allowed to do, Newhart was brought into the tiny, sparsely-furnished room by a young, male prison officer with short sleeves and oversized muscles. Newhart seemed pleased to see her, but he had probably had no other visits.

"Hello Miss Cullen," he said in the manner of a schoolboy who had chanced upon his teacher in the supermarket.

Lizzie nodded in acknowledgement then indicated to him to sit opposite her at the graffiti-covered table that had once been of white Formica over plywood. Before the officer left, Lizzie asked him if Newhart could be given a pack of cigarettes that she had brought for him. The officer checked that the pack had an unbroken wrapping and approved the gift. Newhart already had safety matches so he lit up and puffed away in the comparative paradise of real fags and not the hand-rolled alternative.

"Your lawyer said you wanted a visit, Jonathan. Here I am!" she opened the discussion.

"Yeah, good, yeah. Did that turn out good, what I told ya, Eh?" He said between cheek-altering sucks on the cigarette.

"It turned out pretty well. Thankfully for you, the people who were charged are all on remand over the water."

"That's good, yeah. I told the truth to you, I want you to know that because . . ." he paused to strain at the cigarette again, twice. Lizzie anticipated that a request for the trial judge to be made aware of Newhart's co-operation when considering his sentence would follow, but that was not the purpose of the visit.

"You see, there's something else, something I know, I'll tell you about."

"Go on Jonathan, I'm listening," she said, intrigued but not building up her hopes.

"There's a container, not like the one I had the car in, a smaller one, came into Manchester by air cargo on Monday last week."

"Where from?" asked Lizzie, still unconvinced.

"Belgium, but it came from somewhere else before, further away. Anyway, it's what's in it that bothers me."

"What bothers you Jonathan?"

"Well, you see, it's like, the fella I got the wagon from, the one I got caught in with the car?"

"Yes, I know the wagon, carry on, what about this fella?"

"He said that he'd taken it from the airport to a bonded yard near Wythenshawe, Sharkey Estate, near the main road."

"That's not unusual, it happens all the time," she said.

"Ah! but there's something else," said Jonathan moving his chair an inch nearer. "He said that if I got the job of moving it on I had to be really careful with it, really careful. He said if I went over a bump in the road too fast I might be up with the angels."

Lizzie paused to take in what he was saying. She was trying to keep the conversation in perspective. It was in a remand prison and coming from a career criminal, but he had proved that he could come up with reliable information.

"What else did he say?"

"Don't you get it Miss Cullen? That container, it's got stuff in it that's a million miles away from knock-off cars and you know that I got all my jobs from over the water, so that fella probably did too. You know what that means?"

"Yes Jonathan, I know what that means. Can you tell me anything about this container?"

"Only what that fella told me. I didn't see it myself. He said it was red with a white base and it said something about a dog on it."

"How big is it, this container?"

"Only small, six-foot square, he only told me to warn me I had to be extra careful with it. I only know him from changing wagons sometimes. It was good of him to say what he said, really."

Lizzie led Newhart through the whole story again. It didn't change. They discussed the letter to the judge that Lizzie had expected him to mention from the outset, but she gathered that Jonathan was more bothered about avoiding the death of the friend who had tried to prevent his. Perhaps there was some honour among thieves after all.

Back at Salford, Lizzie went to see Bert Malcolm. Behind closed doors, she unfurled the intelligence as she had heard it. Malcolm chewed his lip as she spoke and continued to do so after she had finished. When he had thought in silence for long enough he said.

"We have to get the Special Branch involved and maybe the Military if there's explosives to be found. We don't even know if the container is still there, they've had over a week to move it on. Bonded warehouses are tricky, we can't just walk into those places and start searching. Getting a warrant is a minefield too. Any ideas, Elizabeth?"

"Yes Sir, I have an idea."

CHAPTER FORTY-TWO

Lizzie had sent for two uniformed constables, paired on patrol in a standard panda car and a dog handler with his own van. She briefed them alone in her office before deploying them. Their task was to attend the bonded yard when summoned and search for the container described by Jonathan Newhart. Once they had left the police station, she too left the building and headed for a phone box. She dialled 999 and reported that she had seen a hooded figure inside the bonded yard, trying to prize open the containers with a jemmy. She listened to her radio and heard the briefed pair of officers respond to the call followed by the dog handler offering to back them up. They arrived at the secure yard and commenced a search of the outer perimeter. The control room operator added that the key-holder had been called and was on his way.

After ten minutes the patrols confirmed that he had arrived. The key-holder was the manager of the yard named Frank Clark, a man of sixty who wore his blood-pressure like sunburn. Although he had reservations about allowing unauthorised personnel, including the police, into the premises, the thought of tackling a hooded man armed with a jemmy by himself was enough to make him ask them to search the yard with him. He did not notice that the dog-handler had left his standard use German shepherd in the van and commenced the search with a Cocker Spaniel instead.

In fine Manchester drizzle and in failing evening light, the three cops and one manager made a search of the yard, examining all of the hundreds of containers of different sizes and colours. Eventually, the uniformed constables found a container that matched the description they had been given. Red with a white base and Dogger Bank Freight painted in stencil across all four sides. Without alerting Clark, they told the dog handler who took a look at it. The Spaniel sniffed energetically at the edges of the container before yelping in celebratory anguish, flicking its head from one side to the other repeatedly and narrowly missing the hard metal of the red cube.

A uniformed cop went with Frank Clark to check inside the warehouse and adjoining office, whilst the dog handler and the other cop radioed for C.I.D to attend but did not, as instructed, say why.

Lizzie arrived at the yard accompanied by Bert Malcolm. Once the dog handler had pointed out the container and assured them that his well-trained dog was a reliable expert witness, they went to speak to the manager.

"Mr Clark, I am D.S. Cullen and this is D.C.I. Malcolm."

"Oh, alright. This looks serious, the plain clothes lot coming here," remarked Clark.

"Well Mr Clark, there is something you should know and I must warn you that it is serious," she said with an intensity to her voice that could not be mistaken. "The good news is that no intruder has been found on your premises, nor is there any sign of a break-in."

"What's serious about that?" asked Clark.

"Nothing," said Lizzie. "The serious part is that our sniffer dog has identified a container that may contain live explosives."

"Explosives! Bloody hell," exclaimed Clark, going an even deeper shade of unhealthy. Lizzie pressed on.

"We have to seal off this yard and prevent anyone getting in until we have made it safe."

"What? How long is that going to take? I've got a business to run here." Bert Malcolm stepped into the conversation.

"No my friend, you've got a crime scene that's soon to become an ugly crater where your 'business' used to be. You need to get a little perspective now. This is how it's going to go. We're getting the experts in straight away to sort this out. You can tell people that there's been a gas leak or something and that it's not safe for anyone to enter."

Frank Clark realised that he was powerless to prevent the ensuing disruption.

"Okay, what do you want me to do?"

His office was commandeered as incident HQ. Roads around the yard were subject of diversion signs intended to inhibit prying eyes, although a local newspaper hack called Sean Nicholson, using a monitor tuned to pick up police radio frequencies, arrived in the hope of getting a lead story or at least making one out of a minor event. Prevented from getting too near, Nicholson tried to engage in conversation with some of the uniformed cops guarding the perimeter. Getting nowhere, he waited outside the sanitised zone with an eye on the yard entrance. In the early hours, he saw Frank Clark emerge and go to his car outside the gate. Recognising that he was not a police officer, Nicholson approached Clark and brusquely asked him.

"Hey, who are you?"

Tired, flustered and thinking that Nicholson was one of the cops, Clark answered.

"I'm the manager here, I've spent the last five hours talking to your bosses about all this explosives business. I've given them all the paperwork, now I'm going home if you don't mind. I'll be back in the morning."

Nicholson was quick to take in what Clark had said and equally quick to seize an opportunity.

"Have you worked out who planted these explosives?"

"Have I? That's not for me to work out, all I know is that it supposed to be in one of the containers. I can't be expected to search them all, for Christ's sake. Now if you don't mind." He got into his car and left for home.

Nicholson went straight to a phone and called his night editor.

CHAPTER FORTY-THREE

An Army Bomb Disposal team was deployed from the Royal Ordnance Unit at Haydock some twenty miles away. Once inside the bonded yard and fully briefed, a series of lights were erected and the remote controlled bomb disposal robot was deployed. Cameras fitted to it relayed live picture footage of the inside of the container once the locks had been cut off and the doors had been pulled open manually using ropes. The Captain in charge of the ordnance team viewed the footage which was merely a series of blurry images to any untrained eye. He turned to Bert Malcolm and said.

"The markings will need to be verified but I am sure that the flat crates inside the container do have plastic explosives inside. It's still in the crates the manufacturer put it in."

"Is that Semtex?" asked Malcolm. The Captain smiled as though trying to find words that were simple enough for a child to understand.

"That's one of the possibilities, yes. The good news is that nobody is going to transport this stuff along with the necessary primer or anything else that will initiate an explosion. If they did, it would never get to its destination. In its present state it's quite harmless. You can't smoke a cigar without a match, so to speak."

Photographs were taken of the crates in the container before the Army took them away. The remaining container was given a thorough overhaul by police fingerprint and forensic officers under the watchful eyes of both senior police officers. Aided by binoculars, Sean Nicholson did the same from the top of a warehouse fire-escape two hundred yards away.

The night editor of the Manchester Telegraph did not get home that morning. A bedraggled yet excited Sean Nicholson arrived back in the newsroom bearing celluloid film stills of the bomb disposal team at work in the bonded yard. Together with the quote from Frank Clark, they went with the story splashing it across the front page in the largest headline lettering they had used since the Falklands War. The press pack from London arrived in droves within hours.

A strategy meeting involving Bert Malcolm, the head of G.M.P. Special Branch and a man from M.I.5 concluded that enquiries should be concentrated on where the container had come from. As Lizzie had initiated the enquiry, it was decided that she should continue with it and be transferred to a currently vacant post with the Special Branch at Manchester Airport. She was temporarily promoted to Detective Inspector.

CHAPTER FORTY-FOUR

The newsroom of the Daily Tribune was a sea of cigarette-burned, beige, nylon carpet that sent electric shocks through the handshakes of about half the people who shook hands or touched anything metal and all of the desk and chair frames were made of metal. The room formed virtually all of the second of twelve floors and contained islands of four to six desks, some with partitions to conceal the seated and expose the standing. Cigarette smoke had hung in the air until the new health obsessed owner insisted on banning smoking in the building. The nicotine stains remained on the off-white walls and false ceiling.

Like most of the exodus from Fleet Street to Wapping, it relied on old journalistic glories whilst modern economics and irrational public consumption of celebrity inanity actually generated the money. An advertising contract with a high street retail chain, or better still a multi-national, was prized far more highly than a Pulitzer winning story generated solely by a member of the paper's features team.

One of the rising stars of the team was Damian Alty. Twenty-nine, single and a workaholic, Alty had charmed, fought and outshone all before him to reach special assignment status and the expense account that came with it. The management, with the notable exception of the finance director, were happy to allow Damian his freedom, because it made them feel as though they were running the newspaper they always wanted to run. In return he came up with printable stories that sold copy whilst remaining within the acceptable parameters of legal complaint. Unencumbered by anything so staid as a journalism degree, Alty had strutted into the building as a sixteen-year-old with the attitude of an old pro with all the answers and talked his way into a job as a runner. Self-taught speed-typing and a finger on the pulse of Reuters and the predictable and generic Press Association releases, were stepping stones into the confidence of the news editorial strata. Stories that were deemed to be a waste of the valuable time of more senior reporters were picked out of the waste paper basket and turned into printable stories. As his skills improved, so did the proximity of Alty's work to the front of the newspaper.

When given a chance he took it with both hands. A wafer thin allegation of improper electoral practices in the West Midlands was transformed into a national scandal resulting in the resignation of a junior government minister with responsibility for local government. Alty had arrived.

Political intrigue was his forte but there was nobody above being targeted by the new broom of newsprint. Corruption at any level or walk of life held a fascination for Damian Alty. There was little he liked more than toppling an individual or an entire corporation and he did not spare a thought for who may get caught up in the misery. He would have moved onto the next challenge and forgotten the names of the people on whose lives he had inflicted such devastation.

Damian Alty had three attributes that made him a successful reporter; he was prepared to work eighteen hour days relentlessly, he knew instinctively what would sell newspapers and what would not and he was the most sociopathic liar in the history of journalism. He cared not whose trust he had to betray in order to get people to open up. The final submission had to be near enough to the truth to be accepted by his editor, but his words were written for a purpose and had to be published.

He gave away leads to his grateful colleagues, many of whom were older and had been on the staff longer than he had, often convincing them he was doing them a favour. He always called in a bigger favour in return.

When the Manchester explosives find came to the notice of the Daily Tribune, the editor could have given the job to anyone. He gave it to Alty partly because he knew that he would return with something printable, but also because he was sick of the sight of him and wanted him to go away for a few days. Alty took a train from Euston, chain-smoking and reading the early editions on the way. The story had already broken and was, as his trained eye had detected, about twenty percent fact, thirty percent guesswork (ten percent of that being accurate guesswork) and fifty percent padding out. He had worked with lower margins than that and come out of it smelling of roses.

There was no point in regurgitating the same story from the same questionable sources. He was more than just a 'turn up at the scene' hack, jostling for a mis-quote or a photograph along with those from rival newspapers. Alty felt that he had status, special-assignment status, and he had earned that by dogged and imaginative investigative practice. He got stories by using his brain, not by elbowing people out of his way in a free-for-all at a police cordon. This Manchester job required a different approach, less speculation and more innovation. He liked that phrase, he would put it in an article someday.

Arriving in the city, he headed straight for the offices of the Telegraph and introduced himself to the editor. As Alty's paper was under the same ownership as the Manchester Telegraph, the editor had to show a willingness to cooperate, although his opinion of Alty was the same at that of Alty's boss. He introduced Alty to Sean Nicholson who was in big demand and revelling in it. Alty recognised this and sought to make use of it.

"Hi Sean, Damian Alty."

"Yeah, I've heard of you from that Birmingham Council job a while back." Alty was in no mood to relive old glories.

"Listen Sean, great job on the foiled bombing plot, I can lend you a bow-tie for the press awards if you want. 'Got a minute? I'd like to get an angle on this story and you're the man in the know."

Nicholson was flattered and off-balance. He acquiesced to everything Alty suggested.

"How did you get onto this in the first place, Sean?"

Nicholson relayed the series of events, emphasising the elements that he knew to be true and skimming over the parts that were supposition.

"So, there was an Army team there to deal with the dynamite?" said Alty, who already knew that but was feeding Nicholson with more of what he wanted.

"Yeah, we didn't get any footage but we got some pics. There's going to be another batch in tomorrow's first edition."

"How did the cops perform, at the time and afterwards on the record?" asked Alty, beginning to resent the centre-stage revelling that Nicholson was displaying.

"Well, they tried to keep things hush-hush and they managed it until the manager let slip to me about the explosives. Everything they have said in press release confirms what he said, but they are still playing the 'it's early days yet' game. Some Chief said about how they've prevented widespread destruction and saved lives, blah blah blah!"

"Who's the lead cop on this, do we have a quote?" pressed Alty.

"The main guy at the container yard was a bloke called Bert Malcolm, old sweat, been around for decades. He won't tell us the fuckin' time. There was this young C.I.D. cop, a girl, cold as ice but quite fit, she was pulling the strings, her name's Cullen. We didn't get jack-shit out of her either."

"What do you know about her?"

"Not much, came from Salford, bit of a high-flyer by all accounts. I've covered a couple of Crown Court cases she's given evidence in. Efficient, nice talker, she's on some of the pictures, here."

Nicholson produced some prints of the images he had obtained from his fire-escape vantage point. Alty was forming a picture in his mind, it looked a lot like a newspaper headline. He had spent the morning trying to find an angle on this story, something that the others wouldn't think of. He knew that the readership wanted people to identify with, clearly defined heroes and villains. A tin box with a crate in it and a load of 'what might have been' rhetoric had no resonance in the readers' minds. They wanted personalities they could relate to. He concluded the conversation with Nicholson with clinical abruptness and picked up a nearby desk phone. He gained a line to the switchboard and turned away from several people who could have overheard. Treating the receptionist as his own unofficial secretary, he demanded,

"This is Damian Alty, get me Greater Manchester Police HQ, now!" He paused as the connection was being made. He looked at his watch. After a minute the call was answered.

"I am trying to speak to one of your officers, a detective called Cullen, a woman detective. It is rather urgent." More waiting ensued until the phone was answered by one of Lizzie's team.

"Salford C.I.D. Office. John Banks."

"Hello, I'm trying to get in touch with Detective Cullen."

"She's the D.S. and she's not here right now, who's calling?" asked Banks.

"Mike Benson, Press Liaison at HQ," lied Alty with practiced ease. "I'm fending off the hounds about this Airport job with the explosives. Can I confirm that her first name is Ann?"

"It's Elizabeth," said Banks, despairing at how ill-informed the force's own staff were.

"Elizabeth, yes of course. Do you know where she is today? I could do to speak to her, get our facts straight with the press, you know."

"You'll find her at the Airport, S.B. Office. She'll be working from there for quite a while we're told."

"Thank you John, much obliged for your help."

"You're welcome, bye."

Alty replaced the receiver and instantly picked it up again, demanding a connection to Manchester Airport. He did not have to wait as long as he had with the police. The airport switchboard connected him to the Special Branch office and the person answering the call was more careful than the earlier one.

"Hello?" said a man's voice.

"Er Hello, is that the Airport Police Special Branch office?"

"Who's calling?" asked the receiving but not receptive voice.

"I'm Mike Benson, Press Liaison at HQ."

"Never heard of you." The staff in the Airport SB office felt no obligation toward politeness.

"Oh, well, I'm trying to speak to Detective Sergeant Elizabeth Cullen, I understand that she is working from there."

"She's busy, try later," and the call was ended.

Alty was surprised and slightly impressed that he had spoken to somebody who was ruder than he was. What had been established was that D.S. Cullen was working from that office. He took another look at the grainy photograph before giving it back to Nicholson.

"Sean I need to get to the Airport. I'll need a cab."

"The desk will call one for you," said Nicholson. "Have you got a lead on the explosives job?"

"No nothing so juicy," he said playing down his idea. "I'm going to do a bit of background, how safe is our air freight? That sort of thing. I'll see you later, Press Club still good for a drink, is it?"

Alty was driven to the entrance to the terminal. With no idea where the Special Branch office actually was, he opted to ask an elderly man who was operating a shaggy mop and a warning triangle on the polished floor near to the check-in desks.

"Are you Police?" said the cleaner.

"There's no getting past you, is there?" said Alty, carefully avoiding actually saying that he was a police officer, but allowing such assumptions to be made.

"Far end mate, door on the far left wall of check-in, you'll have to knock. It'll be locked."

Alty thanked the old cleaner and headed on foot to where he had been directed. He stood as though reading the information screens but was instead watching the three doors at the edge of the vast room. Neither of them opened so he went back outside and around the side of the building where there was a small car park beyond a barrier-controlled entrance. Ignoring the 'No Unauthorised Personnel' sign he went into the car park to see five cars, two of which were marked police Land Rovers. The cops had to use these doors so he waited for them to open.

Two cigarettes later, a green Vauxhall Cavalier drove under the raised barrier. A thick-set man in in his fifties and wearing a padded anorak over a grey suit stepped out and headed for the door. He stopped upon seeing Alty leaning on another car.

"Can I help you?" he asked.

"I've an appointment to see Elizabeth Cullen. I knocked but there was no answer," said Alty trying to sound disappointed.

"Wait here," said the man who had worn, old cop written all over him. "What's your name?"

"Alty."

The old cop knew better than to ask what Alty's visit was about. Such things were not asked nor given in his working environment. He punched numbers into a pad on the door-lock. It clicked open and he disappeared within. After two minutes the door opened again. Recalling the photographs that Nicholson had shown him, he recognised Elizabeth Cullen stepping out into the bright outdoors. As she walked toward him he found himself agreeing with Nicholson's visual assessment. Although there was evidence of fatigue in and around her eyes, she was upright and confident with a good figure and appealing face. The boyish haircut simply gave her gravitas without skimping on sex-appeal.

She was not quite sure what to make of him. He wasn't a lawyer, not a criminal either. He wasn't a cop nor in the military. Witnesses and informants took many forms. She was leaning toward those possibilities.

"Miss Cullen?" he said.

"Mr Alty? I understand you believe that we have an appointment. I was not aware. What do you want to talk to me about?"

"About the superb example of police work you pulled off last night, Sergeant. Well done."

Lizzie instantly added another suggestion to her list of possibilities: Audacity plus flattery equals reporter.

"Which newspaper do you write for Mr Alty?"

"There's no getting by you is there Elizabeth. I'm with the Daily Tribune."

"Well you've come along way for nothing Mr Alty. I have nothing to say to you. Go and speak to the Press Office at HQ."

"Now, Elizabeth, there's no need to be so frosty. This could be to our mutual advantage. I could write a piece about the new face of the fight against terrorism. That could make your career, what do you say to that?"

"Go and speak to the Press Office at HQ," she repeated.

"Has anybody ever told you you're even more attractive when you're annoyed?"

She said nothing.

"Okay, I got this wrong. Let's start again. How about letting me take you out for a drink? You might get to like me if you give me a chance."

"No Mr Alty, that is not going to happen."

He wrestled a camera from his coat pocket and flicked open the lens cap. "How about a picture then, a smile never hurts?" He raised the camera and pointed it at her.

"I do not want my picture taking, stop that please," she demanded with unmistakable irritation.

"Just one snapshot, make a star of you."

"Don't!"

He clicked the shutter, allowed the self-wind to end then took another one. Lizzie had tolerated enough. She grabbed his hand, still holding the camera, and turned it inwards at the wrist causing him sharp pain and gaining instant compliance. Alty let out a high-pitched,

"Ahhh!"

She steered his arm up his back, turned him around and spread him over the bonnet of the car he had been leaning on. His hand and arm were in a wholly unnatural position.

"Ahhhhhh!"

"I said no pictures and I meant no pictures."

She took the camera from his hand and slipped it into her pocket. She let go of him and allowed him to stand up.

"My camera, I need that, you can't take it," he said as he tried to shake his aching arm back to full use.

"An expensive camera, found in the possession of a person of your social status Mr Alty? I find that suspicious and I think you might have stolen it. I take it you haven't got

243

a receipt with you? No, I didn't think so. I'm going to check the stolen property register and with you being from out-of-town, that means the whole country, so that's going to take some time. Leave your name and address at the desk at Salford Police Station. Meanwhile, if I see you again I will arrest you for obstructing me in my duty or perverting the course of justice. I trust I have made our respective positions clear?" She didn't wait for him to answer. "Goodbye Mr Alty."

In the middle of the afternoon in the Press Club in Manchester City Centre, Damian Alty was buying drinks for Sean Nicholson and several others on his expense account. Encouraging others to talk more than he did whilst still steering the conversation in the direction he wanted, he listened to Nicholson's false modesty in respect of the best day of his professional life. Nicholson turned the topic around.

"Did you get what you wanted at the airport, about the safety angle?"

"Oh yeah, I have to do more work on that but it went okay. I'm more interested in that Cullen bird you mentioned."

"Oh you are, are you?" said Nicholson in conspiratorially 'blokey' fashion. "She's fit isn't she? I wouldn't say no to a pop at that myself."

"She's a flirt too," said Alty. "She wanted to meet me for a drink."

"You old rascal, I didn't think she was the type."

"They're all the type if you know how to charm them. Anyway I need to find out a bit more about her. Do you have any contacts in the police? I could do to have a butcher's at her personal file."

Nicholson was excited at the prospect. This was how things were done in London and he liked it. He saw himself as the next Damian Alty. "I know a fella who can do that, he works in police HQ. I could give him a call."

"Brilliant. I'll build her up with a public image then I'll pull the rug from under her and see how far she can fall. All I need is the dirt on her, everybody has a skeleton in a cupboard. You just have to find the cupboard. Right Sean?"

"Right, yeah." Nicholson was eager to please his new best friend.

"Good man, you do that and let me know A.S.A.P." He handed Nicholson a business card and left for his train.

CHAPTER FORTY-FIVE

The following Sunday brought bad news for Lizzie. She was in Belgium following the trail of the semtex container. She was in her hotel room awaiting her Interpol contact who had been facilitating her enquiries. The phone rang, it was Bert Malcolm.

"You won't have seen the newspapers today, will you Elizabeth?"

"I wouldn't have time to read them if I was in the U.K. Sir. What's in them that I should know about?"

"Did you give an interview with a hack called Damian Alty?"

"An interview, no, but I did speak to him. He came to the S.B. office at the airport looking for a story after the semtex find. I didn't tell him anything."

"He thinks you did. He's written a feature all about you. It's in the Tribune, photograph too."

Lizzie recalled the confiscated camera which was still in the store at Salford Police Station marked 'Do not return to owner without permission from D.I. Cullen.'

"What picture and what does the article say?"

"It looks like your original warrant card photo, you're in uniform. I'll read you a bit of it. 'GIRL COP WON'T STOP.' The woman detective leading the hunt for the gang responsible for planning a blitz of terror across the U.K. has pledged to track down every last one of them. Det. Insp. Elizabeth Cullen, 27, of the Greater Manchester Police announced in an exclusive interview for the Tribune: There will be no place for these criminals to hide, I will find them and keep the country safe."

"That's ridiculous, Sir, he's made all that up," protested Lizzie as she punched the pillow imagining it to be Damian Alty's head.

"He doesn't stop there. You're going to love this next bit. I certainly do." Malcolm read on. "Elizabeth represents a new wave of go-getting, female, police officers, taking advantage of recent sex discrimination laws to carve careers for themselves in the previously male-dominated police force. 'Why can't a police officer be a woman too?' she said."

"The lying bastard!"

"There's nothing you can do about it Elizabeth. We will make a formal complaint to the newspaper and the Press Council, but they won't achieve anything. It's probably a good thing that you are out of the country. How are you getting on there?"

"Some progress. The container arrived in Belgium from Egypt although the explosives were manufactured in the Ukraine. Interpol are helpful but there's a lot of red tape."

"Okay, keep on it and update me when you can. The top brass are asking every half hour."

Lizzie hung up, collected her bag and headed down to the hotel lobby where British newspapers were on sale. She bought a Tribune and found the article. Bert Malcolm was right about the photograph. It was the one taken when she was first appointed as a constable. That picture was, as far as she knew, only held by the police personnel dept. Alty was a devious and ruthless operator. She had to be very careful about such things in the future.

247

CHAPTER FORTY-SIX

With Alty's business card in his hand, Sean Nicholson dialled the number on it. The phone rang on Alty's desk.

"Alty!" he barked.

"Hi Damian, it's erm, Sean Nicholson."

"Who?"

"Sean Nicholson from the Manchester Telegraph?"

"Oh yeah, of course, how're you doing?" Alty did not think he would hear from Nicholson again and had effectively forgotten about him.

"Fine ta. I got some more info about our favourite girl cop."

"Ah! the delightful Miss Cullen. Go on, I'm listening."

"She's not as delightful as you'd think. She might appear to be all squeaky clean but I've found the cupboard she keeps her skeletons in. I got a look at her police personnel records as you know, that's where I got the photo of the photo from, remember?"

Alty was getting irritated and wanted Nicholson to get to the point.

"Yeah, I get it, carry on."

"Well, there was a letter from a doctor going back to when she first applied to join the police. It said that her previous medical issues were all clear and she was okay to join. I followed up the doctor who had written the letter and traced him to a hospital here in Manchester. The doc had moved on but a word in the right ear and a few quid in the right pocket and I got a peep at Elizabeth Cullen's medical records. It turns out that she had a baby when she was eighteen and had the kid adopted. I thought there might be a good angle in this, you know, 'Woman cop abandons her kid to put career first.' What do you think, Damian?"

"I think you're a fucking genius, mate. Have you still got the medical stuff?"

"I took photographs of the relevant pages. It includes the adoption forms. Do you want them too?"

"You're damn right I do! Brilliant job Sean. Can you fax them to me?"

"Sure, I've still got your card," said Nicholson wallowing in newly-found esteem. He was up there with the big-boys in the Smoke now.

"I owe you for this, mate. I'll put some decent work your way, don't worry."

Alty prepared his piece on the heartless, career-obsessed she-devil turned terrorist-catcher. His editor had strong reservations about publication. Alty argued that the public had a right to know about the character of their police officers, whereas the editor felt that the complaint made to the Press Council by Bert Malcolm on Lizzie's behalf had made further such stories harder to approve. The editor also knew when a story was largely true and when it was embellished to unacceptable proportions. Alty showed him the copy photographs of the medical records and adoption papers. The editor accepted that there was a basis of truth in the story. He agreed to publish it but refused to allow the illicitly-obtained medical and adoption papers to be shown with the article.

CHAPTER FORTY-SEVEN

"Elizabeth, can you hear me?" asked Bert Malcolm who was convinced that international phone calls and the slight delay in hearing the distant voice was a form of witchcraft that could not be understood.

"Yes Sir, I can hear you fine," she answered. "I'm in Tangiers, but it's all pointing at Libya. I know I can't go there, officially."

"Or unofficially, so you put that thought out of your mind right now. Libya is off limits and has been since that Yvonne Fletcher murder. Understood?"

"Yes Sir. I have some enquiries to do here and back in Egypt, but I expect to be home early next week. Am I missing anything back there?"

Bert Malcolm heaved a big sigh and said. "I have some good news and some bad news, love. The good news is that your temporary post has been made permanent so you are a full D. I. now."

"Thank you, what's the bad news?"

"That arsehole of a reporter has put out another article about you, this time not so complimentary. He's saying that you had a child then gave it up for adoption because you put your career first."

Lizzie's heart sank and her skin felt cold. Many emotions fought for her attention: anger bordering on hatred toward Damian Alty, renewed resentment at her mother's decision to have the child adopted and an upsurge in the ever-present sense of loss that had dogged her for years.

"Don't worry Elizabeth, everyone here knows that the first piece was made-up so nobody believes this one either. By the time you get back it will have all blown over."

Malcolm was probably right. It probably would blow over, for everybody else. It was not going to pass her by so easily.

When she did come back to work, nobody mentioned either of Alty's articles.

CHAPTER FORTY-EIGHT

On a country lane in North Yorkshire on a Monday afternoon in March, an Irishman watched another Irishman planting out onion bulbs. The man doing the planting was unaware that he was being watched, although he usually felt that he was. That day, his watcher was in the driver's seat of an old, brown, Leyland van, parked in a lay-by on an elevated stretch of road. A radio, turned down low, played the number one tune in the country at the time. It was a Whitney Houston number, 'One Moment in Time,' which he found appropriate.

Across a field of thistle and dandelion and edged with low hawthorn, he observed, through binoculars, the man he had come to find. An hour earlier, when he had arrived and taken up his position, there had been four men, all of them working on the cultivation of vegetables. He had spotted the man he wanted and had waited until the other three had left and only his quarry remained. Once he was satisfied that nobody could see either of them, he reached into the back of the van and took a rifle out of an already opened case. A sound-suppressor was fitted to the rifle. The other Irishman worked busily with a trowel, only another ten bulbs to plant before he could return to the storage building and put everything away for the day. The sights on the rifle were adjusted as the gun was raised and pointed out of the open window. The planting of bulbs was paused as he stood upright to stretch his back. The bullet passed through the top of his ear and continued through his skull and into his brain causing instant paralysis, and death soon after.

The rifle went back into the case and the engine of the van started up. The driver steered it along the lane to a junction notable only for the red telephone box which had not been used for some time. He turned right and accelerated past the entrance to the open prison which was to have one less prisoner to feed that evening.

The dead man was Jonathan Charles Newhart, formerly of Belfast. He had been serving two years for handling stolen goods, a sentence that had been reduced in light of his co-operation with the police. It was that communication that had resulted in his murder. His killer was also a convict, although he had escaped some years before. His face no longer resembled the one shown in all of the newspapers in the U.K. and Ireland. He still had dark hair, a thick neck and barely any fingernails.

CHAPTER FORTY-NINE

A telegram was received which contained encoded information. It came by Western Union and was from a Carlos Rodriguez, who did not exist. When decoded, it contained instructions for James to go to South America. His journey had to be untraceable and avoid any questions as to the real reason for undertaking it.

"I have to go to Recife in Brazil," he mentioned to Benny and Melissa one afternoon. "There is a college there and they want us to validate some of their under-graduate courses. I should be gone for a few days, a week at the most."

"Sure, I can do that," offered Benny, whose weight was getting out of control again, "I did it for the Canadians last fall, it's not difficult." Benny was trying hard to please.

"I know you can do it Benny, but I think I should take this one."

"Are you sure that's a good idea? Remember what happened to you when you went to Florida?"

James was touched that his colleagues were so keen to protect him, but they did not appreciate the real reason for the trip. The melanomas he had suffered during his stay in the Sunshine State had taken their toll on him and Melissa was worried about a reoccurrence in the baking sun of Brazil.

"I have learned my lesson," he reassured them both. "No more reckless sun worshipping, I promise." He raised a hand in mock solemnity.

James' lesson was revised every day. The scars had healed on the outside but he had paid a price. The cancerous tumours that had been removed from his face had required corrective cosmetic surgery, stretching the skin on his forehead and both cheeks. He had called it the world's cheapest facelift due to the bill being picked up by his health insurance company. He had taken to wearing tinted spectacles, even in the Winter. The Florida sunshine had preyed on his 'Celtic curse' and the thought of travelling to Brazil for a week gave him similar concerns as those expressed by Melissa.

James had effectively promoted Melissa from the Reception Desk to his Administrator. She did all of the tasks that were not done by either James or Benny, who had been given the title senior researcher but generally did the things he had always done. His family were happy and showed it by continuing to make a generous donation to the University research fund which paid Benny's salary and still turned a profit.

Once packed, James was taken to Logan to catch a flight to Recife. An Irish-American University don attending another seat of learning, it happened all of the time and would raise no suspicion. The instructions he had been given said that he would be met at the Arrivals gate by Carlos Rodriguez, who he knew did not exist. His movements after that were yet to be disclosed to him. All he could do was make himself comfortable, sit back and enjoy the journey. In the back of his mind, however, he knew that he would be doing something that was going to make high demands of him.

Recife International Airport was clean, new and only slightly smaller than Logan. The arrivals gate was the same but it smelled fresher. The Brazilian sun warmed the glass-

covered cathedral and all of its luggage-dragging faithful
within. James passed a line of people pressed against a rail
and carrying name cards across their chests like mugshots,
but the names referred to their visitors. James looked for his
own name but couldn't see it. What he did see was a short,
fat man with rubbery, olive skin and a neat black moustache.
He wore a pale blue casual shirt and white trousers. He
dressed like a man on a holiday but the serious expression on
his face told another story. He flicked his head to the right to
indicate that he wanted James to follow him. James
complied with the man's directions. At the point where the
arriving travellers were no longer corralled by rails. The
little fat man came close enough to speak. To James, his
accent was Spanish, although he knew that he was in a
country that primarily spoke Portuguese.

"Senor Professor, hallo, welcome. Please, a meeting has
been arranged at your hotel. This way, thank you."

James was not invited to engage in conversation. He
followed his contact through the exit doors and along the
sidewalk lined with service buses and luxury coaches.
Across the four lanes of noisy traffic was a taxi lot with row
after row of identical white, Mercedes sedans. Expecting to
be steered to one of the taxis, James awaited the chance to
cross to the lot but it did not arrive. They kept walking and
followed another path down a subway lined with artistic
ceramics. It ascended into the lobby of a stylish hotel. It had
quality stamped right through it.

Across the floor of orange-peel effect tiles, James
followed the uncommunicative man to a recess which
contained six elevators. Fifteen people in differing sized
groups awaited the opening of the elevator doors. A man and
woman in holiday garb joined the queue behind them. When
the chance came for James and his new friend to take the
elevator, he stepped back to allow the couple to take it
before them. Only when there was nobody behind them, did
the man move forward to enter the elevator and when he did

go inside, he took them up to the eighth floor then back down to the fifth.

James would have thought it strange behaviour but for the warnings he had been given by Professor Cooke shortly after arriving at Boston. 'Remember lad, everything is being recorded until you have established that it isn't' he had told him. The same principal applied to being followed in foreign airports. He was to assume that he was being followed until he was sure that he was not. He waited at the end of a corridor of identical doors interspersed with wall mounted paintings of flowers and pots of real or imitation flowers on narrow tables. After a final look at each end of the deserted corridor, the little man knocked on the door of room 529.

Fascinated by the cloak-and-dagger activities of his host, James held onto the handle of his suitcase, remembering that he had not yet checked in. He erred on the side of being polite and decided to wait and see what was in store for him. The door was opened and a familiar face appeared. Without stepping out, Niall Mahon stood back and allowed James to enter. The guide was not invited in.

"Well I wasn't expecting to -" began James before he was interrupted by a raised hand.

Mahon walked past James and led him into a lounge with two doors at either side of it and a window overlooking the airport's long-term parking lot. James put down his case as Niall Mahon rolled down the mink coloured blind and switched on a table lamp. He also turned on a radio set which was playing trumpet-based, samba music at low volume. Only then was he ready to engage in a conversation.

"Welcome to Brazil, lad," said Mahon.

"Thank you," said James as he slipped into one of two single-seat, upholstered chairs.

He noticed that Mahon was looking old. The skin on his neck and forehead had taken on a papery dryness and his eyes seemed to be set further back in his head and bloodshot. His neck dipped forward which made him look like a tortoise emerging from a jacket shell. His voice was croaky but he maintained the disconcerting presence he had always carried.

"How are things in the academic world?" asked Mahon, who was unlikely to have been making small talk or otherwise offering platitudes. James assumed that he was asking about the unofficial role he had been carrying out for several years.

"The people whose opinions count for most seem to approve of our efforts," he said, intending to be vague until it was the time for specifics.

"Good, good, the rewards are well worth your efforts."

Mahon reached out and turned up the volume on the radio set. Only then was he confident that their conversation could not be overheard. James anticipated being told of the real reason for his being summoned to South America. He was right on the money.

"An unfortunate situation has arisen which has given us a problem. I want you to go and put it right."

James nodded his understanding and awaited more information. Mahon paused and looked indirectly at him.

"You're booked to fly out in two hours," said Mahon.

"Fly out? So it's not here in Recife then?" asked James in bewilderment.

"No, no. The money you have been raising for our cause has to be spent with a degree of caution that equals that which has been exercised by you in acquiring it. It is the person who deals with that next phase who is indisposed at present. You are to fulfil that role on this occasion before you return to the asset collecting role you normally do for the cause."

"Where am I flying out to, am I allowed to know that?"

"Sure, sure. You're going to Africa. We have a business arrangement with some people there. They prefer to deal in person, face-to-face, so to speak. Once they know you, the business can go ahead. We're looking for a longer term replacement for the previous representative. You are more valuable to us where you are in the United States, that's where the money is, of course."

Whilst James was reassured that the authority Niall Mahon carried gave him confidence in the task he was to perform, he could not eliminate some doubt in his mind. What was he going there for and who was it he had to see? He hoped that whoever it was spoke English because, apart from a little French, he spoke none of the languages in common use on the African continent.

"I've never been to Africa. I'm interested to learn what there is there to further the cause," he suggested.

"All will fall into place there, my boy. You simply have to meet some people, drink tea with them, or whatever it is they do, and maintain the current cordial relationship. In their culture they won't deal or trade unless they trust you. You'll be back here in a couple of days then back home to Boston where everybody will accept that you have been on one of those damned business trips that later turns out to have been a bit of a waste of time. Hopefully, you'll get some sleep on your flight to Banjoul, Gambia."

"Gambia? So I'm meeting the contacts there?"

"Ah! no, no, you'll fly on from there, up-country. It's a bit remote, away from prying eyes, that's the best way I think."

James had been putting two and two together.

"So I'm flying from Brazil so that there's no connection between the Africans and Boston, right?"

Mahon nodded.

"Therefore, I'm not going to use my own name, am I?" he suggested.

"Correct, you're not."

Mahon reached down the side of his chair and produced a buff envelope. He passed it to James who opened it and found some documents purporting to be from an international children's charity requesting free and unencumbered passage for the bearer, repeated in several languages. A smaller envelope contained some money in at least three identifiable yet unfamiliar currencies. Behind that was a Canadian passport containing his photograph, one of the unused ones taken for his own passport, and his temporary name, Ian Henry Dalmain.

"Canadian? Mr Mahon, why Canadian?"

"Your accent has become somewhat diluted. Nobody really knows what a Canadian accent is, so you'll be fine being Canadian for a few days," explained the old man with amusement.

It took James a few minutes to rationalise his situation. He was to cross the ocean to an unfamiliar continent and visit a country he knew nothing about in order to maintain a trading alliance with unnamed people for a commodity he was not aware of. All of that was to be carried out in an assumed identity and nationality. He was also in the dark about how much his intended contacts knew about him.

He had become used to certain measures and practices aimed at preserving the security and anonymity of his fundraising, but this task seemed to include a series of leaps of faith beyond his experience. It was a prospect he found unsettling. He listened intently as Mahon filled in some of the missing details, but at the end he was still trying to understand it.

CHAPTER FIFTY

After a shower, a change of clothes and a meal, during which he practiced saying his new name and date of birth aloud, James found himself back in the airport, albeit in Departures. He slept fitfully throughout the flight. Too many unknown factors swam around in his thoughts. Why was he going to Africa? Who was he supposed to be meeting and what was it for? Reaching for an anchor in that maelstrom of confusion, he delved back in his own history. He was a University academic, which was all he had ever excelled at. Precisely how he had gone from researching endless data and teaching barely-conscious students to crossing the ocean pretending to be someone else at first bewildered him. More rational analysis produced thoughts of his distant past: of the death of Philip and the devastation of his parents, the doorstep execution of the man in Lodale, both events proved to be a painful challenge for him to recall. It was, without doubt, a mad world, a world that would drown him, should he stop treading water.

His memory allowed him to return to that summer before his world collapsed and everything changed, the one that had been the best time of his life. Changing a tyre on a girl's bike and being unable to concentrate on anything but her. How her hair smelled clean and how it fell across her wildly-decorated eyes when she hadn't tied it back. Where was she now? Married with kids, probably. Did she ever think of him as he thought of her? She had not just been his first love, he had been unable to commit to a relationship ever since. Constantly trying to recapture the magic, he baulked at the prospect of accepting second-best. Many times, he had considered trying again to find her, but the unofficial exile he had been made to endure rendered this unrealistic.

He thought about asking Pedro again to find out about her, ask more questions as he would have done, had he been there. Pedro had met her on the bike ride, he knew what she looked like. But he then remembered how he had all but abandoned his old friend when he had left in the hurried circumstances that had developed. Only when the madness he had become embroiled in was over could he return to Belfast and find that girl again. It was a powerful ambition which could fall at many hurdles, but he had to believe it. What they had briefly shared had held so much promise, so many possibilities for joy. It had been so much more than a summer romance, a youthful and passing liaison, it was stronger. He could not control how he had felt about her, not at the time they were together or at any time since. It was the war in his homeland that was keeping them apart. That divided city had divided him from the girl he knew as Kiki. She was rarely far from his thoughts.

Banjoul International airport was little more than a series of hastily erected warehouse buildings made of pre-fabricated aluminium and painted pale green. People stood in queues in searing heat whilst barely trained or literate border guards and passport inspectors pored over documents and luggage. James tried to shelter from the scorching sun, aware that his skin's tolerance to exposure was weaker than most. By leaving the line of tourists and other charity workers and sheltering against the wall of the arrivals building, he aroused the suspicion of the gun carrying uniformed airport guards. They ushered him back into the line and in the hundred-degree West African sun. An hour and a half in that barbecue turned his skin bright red and tender. With some relief he reached the front of the line and was officially received as a guest in Gambia.

"Mister . . . ?" started the senior guard from within a pointless glass panelled kiosk, pointless because the door at the side of it was wide open.

"Dalmain, Ian Dalmain," said James with practiced but cautious confidence.

"Yeah, yeah, what are you in Gambia for, huh?" asked the guard.

"Charity work," began James who had overheard several people in the line who had spoken of their charitable intentions, which he had hoped were more beneficial to the poor and unfortunate of Africa than his fictitious claims were. Perhaps they were spies too? The guard looked at him with what James detected as contempt. In an attempt to win some approval, he added "It's a children's charity, I have letters of introduction." He offered the documents but the guard showed no interest.

"Go, go!"

He waved James on then lit a cigarette and kept the next person waiting as he smoked it. James made a mental note not to complain about airports in the developed world that he existed in. Soulless they may be but they had many redeeming qualities.

Outside and again in the furnace, he headed for a taxi rank, mobbed by volunteers, all eager to carry his case for reward. There were at least eight people fighting each other for his custom. James would have been happy to carry his own case and end the bickering, but he was playing the part of a charity worker and should therefore behave charitably. He tried to give his custom to one of the unwashed and barefoot kids that stared up at him with outsized, jaundiced eyes, but equally desperate but more forceful young adults elbowed the little ones aside to claim the job and its pittance of reward.

Amongst the incomprehensible collective of syllables being exchanged, James heard the word 'Dalasi' repeatedly. He worked out that it meant money. He waved away all but one willing porter, a girl of about eleven with gaps in her teeth and a withered left arm.

"You!" he said firmly enough for the others to accept it, "You can help me with my bag."

The little girl took the case and nearly dragged it along with her only functioning arm. James watched her and had to resist the urge to help her. The unsuccessful candidates followed in a group fifteen yards behind, staring but not speaking. When they reached the taxi stand, the driver of the Renault at the front got out and relieved the child of her burden, placing the case in the boot of the car. James had no idea of the exchange value of the currency in his possession. He gave her a banknote not knowing if he had issued an insult or endowed her with a fortune. The widening of her eyes and smile showed that he had erred on the side of generous.

He got in the taxi and handed the driver a slip of paper bearing the next stop on his trip. The driver nodded and set off. James watched as the girl was readmitted into the throng of unwashed youth, likely as she was to be relieved of her earnings, he felt that at least for a minute she had enjoyed a good bit of her day. He looked with pity on the African kids 'the tired, the poor, the huddled masses' as he recalled the inscription on the Statue of Liberty. He thought how the developed world should be able to share their good fortune. He felt a little ashamed that he had long considered the lives of the people of Belfast to be intolerable.

A taxi ride of two hours on roads that became increasingly challenging ended at an airstrip which was little more than a field. A light aircraft sat at the end of the tyre-worn track. It had seen better days which filled James with a sense of dread. Three African men, one of slightly lighter colouring, sat beneath the plane, sheltering from the baking sun. Upon seeing the car approach, the three rose and stepped forward making gestures of self-grooming for a good first impression.

The taxi stopped at the rear of the plane and it was then that James hoped that he had sufficient currency to cover the journey. He chided himself for not raising that from the outset. He got out and went to his case to retrieve the money. The lighter skinned man crossed and uncrossed his flattened hands vigorously whilst shaking his head. He walked by James and spoke to the driver who was half-in and half-out of the car. The driver accepted without protest what he was told. He got back in and drove away, kicking up more dust as he disappeared.

Some muted greeting took place as James' luggage was placed aboard. He took his place and fitted his headphones when the pilot gesticulated for him to do so. With only two of them in the cabin and after an inordinately long period of stationary engine activity, the plane finally taxied across the field and limped into the air with a discouraging whine.

The temperature soared higher and faster than the plane. James was handed a bottle of water by the pilot who had taken it from a cool-box behind the seat without looking. His English was limited but he did manage to say enough to reassure James that he was capable of getting him to their destination, although he did not know the name of the place.

Reaching heights insufficient to allow for any error, the tiny plane hummed along over trees, then crossed barren land then featureless desert. The occasional railway line or unmade road broke the monotony of the landscape. After two and a half hours, the aircraft rose higher and the pilot explained in badly damaged English that he was looking for the landing strip and could see better from higher up. James could see nothing but desert in all directions. This did not inspire confidence in the competence of the pilot.

Having circled in a figure-of-eight twice, the pilot finally spotted what he had been looking for and began their descent. What came into view was a collective of canvas-covered structures amongst dirty sand and sparse vegetation. The landing involved a diminishing and disconcerting series of bounces before the engine sound lowered and the aeroplane taxied toward the tiny, temporary hamlet in the wilderness.

James could see four men of North African appearance and wearing patterned, Bedouin robes, emerge from under the shelters to face the plane. As it came to a rest they approached and waited for the door to open. James climbed out, leaving his case inside. There was a 'temporary' atmosphere about his visit. The pilot stayed with his plane, kicking the tyres in a gesture of concerned and conscientious, aeronautical maintenance. James was escorted under the shelter where a cloth-sided chamber came into view. All four men slipped off their shoes before entering. James did the same.

Inside the tent were two anterooms. One was occupied by a large and fierce-looking African man who had 'tribal warrior' written all over him. He spoke English in such short sentences it remained doubtful that he was fluent. He made himself very clear.

"Mista Dalmain?"

"Yes, I am," answered James, feeling that he was playing a game, the rules of which everyone knew better than he did.

Some silent nodding took place between his hosts then the large man told him.

"Lift arms."

James complied.

Except for the absence of a metal detector, he was searched more thoroughly than he had been at any of the airports he had passed through. The warrior leaned unceremoniously into James' neck as he ran his hands across his back, chest, arms and legs. He smelled of body odour, musk oil and spiced food. The musk oil was losing that contest. When they were satisfied, he was escorted through another draped canvas of rough weave and into a comparatively sumptuous chamber of high cushions and low tables. There was a dizzying smell of some additive-infused tobacco creating a hanging fug. Ornate and intricately woven tapestries draped the walls and four blue gas flames burned in glass lanterns on what looked like horse saddles with gold horns.

Seated regally on a throne-like bean bag was a lean, bearded man in preposterously clean white. He looked like a pre-Raphaelite representation of God. This was the man who Niall Mahon had sent him to meet. James felt hopelessly out of place and was desperate not to look so. There was nothing he could do to manage that situation. The scene did not lend itself to levity. He did not need telling that offence could be taken easily. He was urged forward by the large man and directed to sit on a mound of cloth. His corduroy suit made him look like a colonial official. The main difference was that a colonial official would have known what it was he had gone there for. Seated but far from comfortable, James waited for the conversation to begin. Several minutes later, it did.

"Mr Dalamin," opened his host in error. It had to have been erroneous because his accent was as English as a Duke. The added spice of it being an alias made any correction quite unnecessary.

"Thank you for agreeing to see me, Sir," said James, playing safe.

"I trust that your journey here was . . . comfortable?"

"Yes, thank you."

Nothing else was said for two or three minutes. James fought the urge to restart it.

"Your associate Mr Levent is unable to travel today. That is unfortunate. I have come to enjoy his company."

James decided to answer only when he was asked. He noticed that his host's fingernails were perfectly maintained, as was his beard. When he spoke, he revealed perfect teeth too. He had status and conducted himself as such.

"Tell me Mr Dalamin, do you have a wife?"

"No Sir, I am unmarried," answered James, curious as to where the conversation was going.

"A man should have a wife. I have many," he said as though he was talking about socks. "You have so many women to choose from, are you so difficult to please? Perhaps you don't like women." For the first time he looked directly at James. He smiled, beaming broadly but it was short-lived.

"I do, erm, like women Sir, but I am fully occupied with my work," said James, hoping to rule out any doubt about his sexuality and progress the meeting to a productive and satisfactory conclusion.

The host seemed to dismiss James and looked bored. His universally accepted line of patter had fallen flat with this guest and he appeared to dislike him because of it. James felt the need to rescue the situation and the only topic that had caused his host any interest was that of women.

"I did have a woman," His host looked back at him with renewed interest. "but I had to leave her behind when I went overseas. That was fourteen years ago. I have not found any woman who made me feel like that. I went to find her but I couldn't."

"How could one woman have that power over you?"

"I did not see it as power over me, in fact, I found it empowering. I felt alive with her. I had power."

"Power to do what?"

"To see beauty and appreciate the world."

"Interesting. You are a man of art and culture, Mr Dalamin?"

"A little, Sir, but I cannot appreciate those things as I once did, I have lost my inspiration."

The desert prince moved forward in his seat, clearly fascinated with James' cultural variation from his gender role customs.

"Although I have many wives, and I have a fondness for each of them, I have never been inspired by a woman to see such things. I envy that in you, but I do not envy your solitary life. The beautiful things in the world and the love of a woman to share them with can be a cause worth dedicating one's self to. Don't you agree?"

"I do agree. Thank you for your wisdom, Sir."

"Mr Dalamin, I hope you find the inspiration to see beauty once again."

Another silent period ensued, until.

"Our previous arrangement will be renewed," said the host. "The consignment will be delivered to Tangiers as before."

"The consignment, Sir?" asked James, unable to contain his curiosity.

"I have no wish to discuss your cause or your intentions with the merchandise. I just don't want to be on the same continent when you use it. Goodbye Mr Dalamin."

The warrior stepped in front of James and silently communicated that it was appropriate for him to leave. Once outside, he was escorted to the aircraft. The afternoon sun baked the dusty red earth and the air was too humid to take in without straining.

Once in the air and skimming over the harsh terrain, he was given more water. He rehydrated his body and allowed his mind to rationalise the content of that bizarre exchange. Who was that man and what was his connection to the cause of Republicanism in Northern Ireland? A well-spoken, desert prince with many wives could not be further removed from any element of his world. Although he had met several students who may have had similar backgrounds, the reason for their presence was clear, not so with that man.

James' mind turned over what had been said. The prince seemed to look for something to like about him and when he had found it, he agreed to the transaction, but what had been exchanged? His parting comment came back to James, 'I just don't want to be on the same continent when you use it.' There was some hint of contempt in the way he spoke, a tone not evident in his previous words. 'Don't want to be on the same continent.'

The prince had mentioned a Mr Levent, who was he? James began to drift into semi-consciousness as the light aircraft bumbled along, nearer to the earth than to the sky. He fought fatigue and tried to recall Niall Mahon's words of instruction. One part made louder noises in his head. Mahon had spoken of 'The person who deals with that next phase' and how he was indisposed. That must be Levent, but the next phase of what? It was his role to raise money, so what did Mahon mean by 'the next phase?' The realisation hit him and caused the instant return of his fully conscious state.

The money he was sending to the Swiss bank was not being used for peaceful purposes.

CHAPTER FIFTY-ONE

There was no logical alternative. He had been taken for a fool by Mahon. James had raised a large amount of money from the Irish-American community who, through him, had been lied to as well.

At the airport in Recife, James was again collected by the man who was not really named Carlos Rodriguez. They followed an equally elaborate system of subterfuge before arriving at a different hotel from before. Once inside the room where Niall Mahon was sitting with a heavy-looking book on the arm of the chair, James was about to speak until Mahon raised the palm of his hand and turned on the radio, bringing the music up to the required volume.

"Good trip lad?" he said, missing James' mood completely.

"No, you've taken me for a mug, haven't you?" The anger was unconcealed.

"What are you talking about?" Mahon played the innocent.

"You know damn well, the fella who should have been there has been spending the cash I've raised on bomb-making equipment and you knew all along, didn't you?"

"Calm down lad, there are a great many aspects to what we're trying to do back home," said Mahon trying to keep the tone of the conversation sedate. James was not to be placated. He stood over Mahon with his finger pointing in his face.

"You and Cooke lied to me. You said the money I was raising was going to go toward peaceful measures: lawyer's fees for those interned, buying political influence, supporting the families of our people in jail, that sort of financial help and I believed you. I didn't sign up for buying bombs and bullets and neither did the people I'm taking money from. That is not the answer and it never will be."

"Let me explain," said Mahon, clearly shocked at the fierceness of James' tirade. "Like I said there are many aspects of what we are doing and I have, in the main, been able to use the money you have generated for the purposes you and Cooke agreed upon. Unfortunately, the armed element of our movement has had a setback. A certain consignment was intercepted and some reorganisation was necessary."

"Who is Levent?" asked James.

"Shhh, no names," answered Mahon.

"They're not real anyway, who is he?"

"He maintains certain foreign links, as you have learned, but he has had to relocate for the time being. The intercepted consignment is likely to lead straight to him, so he's out of the picture."

James sat down and put his head in his hands. The pain and heat of sunburn on his stretched and repaired forehead repelled the skin on his palms.

"What sort of madness have you got me mixed up in? What's going to happen next?"

CHAPTER FIFTY-TWO

Having returned from an early morning appointment at the hospital where he had undergone the latest of many check-ups carried out by Dr Braschert or a member of his department, James was in his apartment on the University Campus eating a breakfast of toast and coffee. The television was on nearby but he wasn't paying much attention to it. Midweek morning television was invariably delivered from an over-lit studio furnished in pastel shades and made to look like a magazine version of a New England mansion. The resultant, sanitised product then being forced upon the public by a cheesy pair of ill-matched presenters failing to convince the viewers that they liked each other.

James' commitments meant a leisurely start to the day. He had a tutorial group of post-graduates to listen to but not until 1pm. The T.V. scene switched with some haste to a newsroom where a silver-haired anchor man was pushing a finger into his ear in the hope of taking in the raw and unredacted message, the revelation he was supposed to impart into the camera. No autocue or pre-read, just a piece of paper and a man reading from it.

"Some breaking news from overseas now, we are receiving reports of two explosions in the town of Warrington in the north of England. Eye witnesses describe what they believe to be a double bomb attack in a crowded shopping area. Many people are injured, but it is not yet known if any fatalities have occurred. We'll have more on this in our regular bulletin at eleven. Back to Mike and Jan in the Daytime Live studio."

A sinking, cold knot formed in James' stomach. He knew that multiple explosions in commercial areas on the U.K. mainland carried the hallmark of the paramilitary arm of the Republican movement in Northern Ireland. He didn't need CNN to tell him that.

He went to the faculty building but was unable to concentrate on anything else. He tuned the staff room television onto the 11am News. The same information as before was relayed in the preamble but this time it was accompanied by footage of police officers reeling out cordon tape and fire trucks speeding to the scene. The walking-wounded were wrapped in blankets and nursing blooded heads and limbs. Reporters were trying to thrust microphones in the faces of the bewildered. James was unable to hear the accompanying spoken bulletin as he watched the chaos unfold, but one line cut through the mists of his mind and hit him like a freight train.

"It has been confirmed that two children are amongst the dead and at least 40 people have been injured in the two bomb blasts close to the heart of a busy shopping centre. The blasts happened within a minute of each other and the second one caught people fleeing from the first." A sleeveless hand appeared in the bottom corner of the screen. In it was another bulletin paper with the latest developments. Again without pre-read, the newsman gave it out as it came. "British television news agencies now tell us that one of the children is believed to be just three-years-old."

The Anchorman slowed down the delivery of his words toward the end of the sound-bite. Even if it was not done for dramatic effect, it certainly achieved it. He paused, allowing the viewer to take in the gravity of the news and to allow him a moment to compose himself before pressing on. "We'll bring you more on this story after this." The screen cut to some unconnected item and James switched off the television. He sat on the velour chair and wrapped his hands around the back of his head.

CHAPTER FIFTY-THREE

"Yes I'm on a bloody secure line, I'm not new to this you know!"

"Calm down Lad, what's got into you?"

"What's got into me? I don't believe this. They're killing kids in the street, for Christ's sake!"

"Don't get all fucking pious on me now. In case you've forgotten, your own brother was a kid when those bastards shot him."

"I'm not likely to forget that."

A momentary flash of memory sprang forth in his head. He relived the moment he was told of Philip's death. Fleeting, misted images zipped through his mind and were lost again as quickly. He was racked with guilt because of it. That grief left his mind to make room for the juggernaut that had been built from the resentment of how he had been recruited. Put into an impossible situation, he had been exiled and effectively enslaved, albeit concealed behind a respectable façade of a University Professor. A go-between, a cashier for the relentless killing machine he had been sucked into. But none of it had been against his will, he had no grounds to be aggrieved.

He had had no choice, but how many times since then could he have distanced himself from all that madness? He had been caught up and had revelled in it: the subterfuge, the false names, the foreign travel, all of that had overtaken whatever ideological justification there may once have been. But he was hearing that bombs were being placed in litter bins miles from any legitimate military targets and killing children, small children. James felt a molten mass swelling in the pit of his gut. It was going to erupt. He swallowed hard and breathed deeply. His voice lowered to where it normally was.

"This changes things." Mahon didn't respond so James continued. "Whatever was going on before doesn't matter now, this cannot be condoned. The armed struggle, this killing, it isn't working."

"It wasn't planned that way, lad. The aim was to disrupt commercial and transport facilities on the mainland. You know that warnings are given for direct action like this, you know that."

"I know that, but it didn't work, did it?" James' words were acid-laced.

"No, something went wrong, I don't know what."

For the second time in their many conversations, the power lay with James.

"You're damn right something went wrong," he spat out.

"The warning didn't get through. We'll look into that." Mahon floundered, his confidence evaporated.

"What the hell is Warrington anyway? The gas plant blast last week was enough surely?" demanded James, referring to an earlier news report.

"Hold your horses now, lad. You're not alone in thinking what you're thinking. There is some discussion among the senior command. It's a small voice but it is a voice, at least."

Neither man spoke for twenty seconds. James used the hiatus to take in what Mahon had said. He broke the silence.

"That voice needs to get louder and I want to be a part of it. There'll be little for me to do here. Nobody wants to throw their dollars into a pot that pays to kill kids in the street."

Another long pause ended when Mahon said.

"There is a difference of opinion within the senior command, it could go either way, I don't know for certain but there could be some changes coming, significant changes. Don't talk to anyone about this."

"That's not going to be a problem now, is it?" James assured him. "I only have you to talk to anyway."

CHAPTER FIFTY-FOUR

Martha Lascelle was the daughter of George Lascelle, a former British Ambassador to China. Her mother, Barbara, as well as carrying out her duties as the diplomat's wife, was a noted linguist and translator of oriental literature. Martha's childhood was spent between an austere boarding school in Kent, the family seat, a seven bedroomed, former vicarage in Hampshire and the British Embassy in Peking. Cambridge educated, Martha followed her father into the Diplomatic Service and was appointed as an attaché in Germany, Chile and the Middle East. A spell as Deputy Ambassador to Jordan brought Martha to the realisation that an ambassadorial role was not what she wanted. Instead she took a role of Special Envoy for the Foreign and Commonwealth Office. Without the weight of unhelpful press coverage, she had successfully, and sometimes unsuccessfully, negotiated the release of British detainees held in countries outside the circle of friends of the nation.

Martha's late husband Eric Grantley had been a noted economist, working as a consultant for the European Economic Community and the International Monetary Fund. His death, some twelve years previously from Motor-neurone disease at the age of forty-eight, had left the childless Martha with no better purpose than to work harder and longer on her various diplomatic missions. An eligible and socially well-placed widow, she resolutely espoused remarrying and had remained romantically solo. At fifty-four, she still cut an impressive figure. Slim and finishing-school elegant, immaculately attired and coiffured at all times and with an intellect that was the equal of anyone, but with the common touch when that was needed too.

The only time Martha's work had failed to evade press interest had been when she had spent six weeks trying to persuade senior officials of the government of Iran that the British four-man crew of a civilian aircraft, erroneously spotted in Iranian airspace and forced to land by the Iranian Air Force, were merely poor navigators and not a threat to the Islamic way of life. They had been detained on spying charges. Despite no weaponry, surveillance equipment or any other physical evidence of espionage, they faced a farcical show trial which was televised for the world's attention. It had taken only two hours and the sentences of death had been decided in an additional twenty minutes.

Martha had requested, pleaded, promised trade deals and luxury goods not widely available in Iran, charmed and even flirted a little with the senior official of the Iranian revolutionary state who was responsible for overseeing homeland security. Realising his long-held interest but poor skills in the game of chess, Martha offered to teach him how to improve his game, which he agreed to with disproportionate enthusiasm. She attended the opulent state palace every day for a week for the purpose of playing and talking about playing chess. On the eighth day, she let him win a game. He was so delighted he immediately ordered the release and repatriation of the four hapless British aviators, and subsequently issued a proclamation that he was an international chess icon and all schoolchildren in the country should aspire to emulate his achievements.

Through several changes of government, the British stance on the Irish question remained that they were not prepared to negotiate with terrorists. Any connection, or the suggestion of any connection, to any acts of violence precluded any individual from participating in a conversation with any representative of the British Government. That made the initiation of any peace talks difficult. But what was equally challenging for the

282

Government was who to appoint as their own negotiator. A short list of candidates was mulled over at length by officials from the Foreign Office and the Northern Ireland Office. This was chaired by the cabinet secretary who kept the P.M. updated periodically. Of the seven esteemed diplomats on the list only one stood out as the first choice. Not because of any achievements or skills the others lacked, but for one simple fact. Martha Lascelle was the only Catholic.

CHAPTER FIFTY-FIVE

The executive tier of Sinn Fein together with the senior command of the I.R.A. had an equally thorny problem. The intelligence gathering machine of the security services in Northern Ireland had made links for all of them to terrorist atrocities, some dating back forty years. What was needed was a committed Republican who had nothing to do with the Republican movement. Anybody who had been in the province could in some way be linked to violence, even if it was only talking about it afterwards. Niall Mahon made a suggestion.

"There is a man who has been kept out of the picture for nigh on twenty years exactly for this eventuality." He looked at each man in turn to confirm that he was being understood. Silent approval was nodded and he carried on.

"A professor in an American University," he began but was instantly interrupted.

"What good is that to us, for fuck's sake man," spat one cynic through the cigarette smoke.

"I suppose I have to spell that out to you, don't I?" said Mahon in derision. "This man has the intellect and the credibility to carry out this task. He was born and raised here and his kid brother was shot by the security forces in the seventies. He has all of the motivation but has no known links to any violence. He'll not do anything without us knowing and approving, I'll guarantee you that."

"Will he do it, has he been approached?" asked a faceless voice from beyond the range of the light.

"He has not yet been approached, but I am confident that he will do it. I've been in contact with him ever since he went to America. I know this man. I know how he thinks."

Mahon sensed that some among that gathering were insufficiently aware of the situation. He adjusted the position in his seat, adopting a stance of a preacher delivering a sermon.

"If you want to keep up the armed struggle until we're all in our graves, let's not bother at all. Just leave things the way they are until the last man falls, so be it. Amen and goodnight. But if you want to bid for peace talks, get our people out of the tank, take on the fight with politics from now on, well, he is the best hope we've got of starting that process."

Nobody spoke for fifteen seconds. It felt like an hour for everyone. Some took the time to take in what Mahon had said whilst some did not, or could not understand what it might mean in the long term. The silence was broken by the same darkened figure.

"Will the British accept this man as our spokesman, Niall?"

"He fits the bill as far as they're concerned. They have no reason to avoid the talks, they want it to happen more than we do, but they have to insist on certain things, just as we do. It's a negotiation, we have to set the ground rules out right. If they are seen to be reasonable and we're not, that means we might lose some support, from our own people as well as from overseas."

"Overseas? What do we get from overseas?" asked a bitter voice.

"Where do you think the money has come from, eh? This war is being fought on many fronts: weapons, lawyers, influence at home and abroad - do you think that all comes for free? We rely on financial contributions from those who are sympathetic to our cause. The tide is turning now. The money will dry up unless we take some big steps. This is the time."

.

CHAPTER FIFTY-SIX

Alty was restless. He was experiencing, by his standards, a lull in the normally relentless stream of stories crying out for him to report them. His desk phone steadfastly refused to ring, and when it did the resultant content of the call contained nothing but trivia. When this happened there was only one course of action open to him, make something happen then report it. He could call upon a survey, commissioned by some unknown body, revealing disturbing facts about how the British public had been conducting themselves. They usually allowed for the flimsiest of information to be misrepresented as being of vital importance. The fake survey was the last resort. Only when all else failed should he call upon that. He had to get out of the office.

Giving the excuse 'I have to see a source' to the sub-editor, not that he felt answerable to him or anybody, Alty pulled on his coat whilst walking to the stairs. Outside in the fresh air, he passed the security booth without acknowledging the concierge, who was used to being ignored. He headed for the Golden Horse pub, known in his trade as the Hack's Hovel.

It was the sort of pub that never seemed to close. Quite when the management chose to clean and replenish their stocks was a mystery, but it was clear that it was not done frequently enough. The carpet, predominantly maroon with rectangles of assorted sizes, each resembling a stained glass window in a medieval church, had become threadbare at the point where it reached the bar. Drinking glasses hung from a frame over the bar counter. The meagre light shining from behind served only to show that the glassware was either old or poorly cleaned. The woodwork was genuinely old. Weathered and darkened mahogany formed every window sill, partition and interior door. There were four booths adjacent to the window facing the street, which formed the ideal venue for conspiratorial encounters of the clandestine kind. He passed through the lethargic assembly, made up mostly of other newspaper employees, a few from the Tribune. The snippets of chatter heard were predictably uninteresting as they contained nothing new. Name-dropping, boasting and any number of other self-congratulatory speeches filled any empty spaces.

At the bar Alty waited, with irrational irritation, for the barmaid to finish serving another customer. Her misplaced cheerfulness went unacknowledged as he ordered a pint of Guinness. As she poured, he turned and scanned the room with increased interest. He nodded a terse greeting to a couple of familiar faces who did the same to him, neither wanting that exchange to develop into a conversation. He was presented with the slowly settling brew, but he didn't wait for the perfect black and white to form. Without ceremony or dignity, he wiped the beer froth from his lip using the back of his hand.

From his jacket pocket his mobile phone let out a tinny 'ring ring.' Uttering an unfinished expletive, he reached in to retrieve it, silently reassuring himself that, if challenged, his 'seeing a source' ruse would stand up.

"Alty!" he snapped, showing that he didn't care who was calling, everyone was to be treated with similar discourtesy.

"There's a guy trying to get hold of you, says it's urgent." The caller was Mike Rouse, an old sweat journalist of the crumpled variety who occupied a desk near his, but shared little else.

"Who?"

"He won't say, he's left a number but you have to call it right now."

Alty's first thought was that a source had not received the agreed payment and was hassling for the money. He wasn't responsible for the 'bean counters' slack practices, so he didn't see it as his problem. His second thought was that a good source was worth cultivating and steps should be taken to keep them onside for future business. The second one won and he took out a pen and pad to write the number down. Rouse passed the number and hung up before Alty had the chance to check it back with him.

He looked at it for a moment before dialling in the number. Although it was unlikely to make any difference, he picked up the drink and slid into an empty booth, swapping the phone to the other ear to reduce the noise. After four rings a female voice came on the line.

"Hello, how can I help you?"

"I got a message to call this number, from a guy, didn't leave a name."

"Your name please, Sir?" she said coolly.

"Damian Alty."

"Hold the line please."

Music intended for a saxophone but played on a stylophone filled the space left on the line. After ten seconds, a man's voice took over.

"Is that Damian Alty?"

"It is, who is that?"

"That will keep for now. Listen carefully, Alty, it might be to your advantage."

Alty had been receiving calls such as this since his name started appearing on front page articles. Most of them could instantly be assessed as being of no value and didn't warrant investing any time in listening to them. Cranks, fantasists and attention-seekers in the main. The knack, as he saw it, was to categorise them early and drop them before he risked becoming one of them.

He had always enjoyed a compelling conspiracy-theory in the same way he enjoyed a movie, although it had been some years since he had been to see one. Sightings of Elvis Presley, faked moon-landings, foreign spy-rings in Whitehall, all contributed to the rich and colourful tapestry of investigative journalism and there remained, however slight, however remote, however unlikely, the possibility that a golden nugget could be found amid the detritus. All, however, were greeted with a healthy dose of sarcasm with which to preserve his sanity.

"Oooh, I can't wait," he declared.

"The British Government say that they do not negotiate with terrorists, right?" opened the anonymous source.

"So I've been led to understand," conceded Alty.

"Wrong. They are in talks with Irish Republican groups as we speak."

"And how do you know this?"

"I have Parliamentary access and I have heard it from a reliable source."

Thoughts flashed through Alty's mind. Among them were the long-term implications of this story being true and exposed in the media. A journalism award for himself was the first thought, quickly followed by the copy generated by an exclusive of that magnitude. He then contemplated who would benefit from the story being true and out there in the press. Leaks were commonplace in government matters but they were not usually offered in this way. Those involved knew who to leak to and what they were going to gain from doing so, usually political point-scoring. This offering was speculative, a guess, a shot in the dark. He considered that he might not be the only journo being dangled this particular carrot, and that he was being set up as a patsy for some game being played out in circles he didn't move in. One thing he did not feel was that it was just another crank caller with a vivid imagination. It refocused his mind on the call in hand.

"I'm going to have to see that as reliable too, my friend, so I will need to be convinced."

"I'm not giving you the whole caboodle over the phone. A senior civil servant has been briefed by Whitehall to begin the dialogue. It's a long-term plan and it's not going to be derailed by a future change of government. They've chosen someone close enough to No. 10 to have clout, but far enough away to not implicate them if it all hits the fan."

"Clever," agreed Alty. "and this is without a cease-fire over the water, huh?"

"Precisely what they said they wouldn't do. Now, are you in?" Alty had heard enough to keep his interest, at least for the time being. It was time to mention the unspeakable.

"How much are you after if I am in?" he asked.

"I want fifty thousand for the name of the British negotiator and another fifty for the name of the Irish one."

"That's up to my managing editor, but as far as I'm concerned, I'm in."

"I'll be in touch." The line went dead and Alty returned the phone to his pocket. He finished his pint and headed back to the office.

CHAPTER FIFTY-SEVEN

"Promoted? Wow, thanks."

"Congratulations, Detective Superintendent."

Lizzie had not seen that coming. Having transferred to the capital on promotion to Detective Chief Inspector, her two-year tenure had gone well enough and there had been some evidence of successful operations in counter-terrorism, but the post was largely administrative. The department was responsible for the gathering, and subsequent analysis of intelligence in relation to politically and ideologically motivated criminal activity. A minority of her detectives were deployed in recruiting and cultivating informant sources from within the communities and single issue causes with a subversive ethos. Most of her staff stared at computer screens and digested paper reports for the majority of their working day. Only when something arose that was out of the mundane did Lizzie get involved in the decision whether to take action on it. Action was something she saw little of and the absence of it was beginning to give her itchy feet.

She thought about her father. He had reached the rank of Superintendent at the age of fifty. How proud he would have been to see her with that title at the age of thirty-four.

This was the first elevation in rank since her mentor and backer Bert Malcolm who, having reached the rank of Chief Superintendent, had called it a day and taken a new position, in a high-backed leather armchair and wearing tartan trousers and a diamond-patterned jumper in the lounge bar of a nice golf club somewhere.

Lizzie was more excited at the prospect of spending more time away from a desk than she was about the title of Detective Superintendent in Counter Terrorism. Her role was to be the head of five syndicates of detectives and maintain a delicate balancing act. Each team had to know enough about what the other was doing but nobody should know too much. She had a second tier to rely on who was the D.C.I. This freed Lizzie to embark on some initiatives of her own. One such idea was to launch a campaign under the guise of disrupting organised shoplifting gangs. The campaign encouraged the owners of shops and other commercial premises to install CCTV cameras and recording equipment. Whilst there was some merit in this measure to aid the fight against thieves, the real purpose was to have a prevention and detection tool to combat terrorist activity. Shoplifting was one thing, but bombs were quite another. In the event that a bomb was placed, a huge quantity of electronically recorded footage of the relevant area was at the disposal of the Counter Terrorism Department and its partner agencies in the security world. The real coup was that the expense was borne by the private sector and not from police budgets.

Lizzie was called into the office of Deputy Assistant Commissioner Hillditch at Metropolitan Police Headquarters. She had entered that room only once before and that had been when she had first arrived in London and had to be formally welcomed. As the D.A.C. showed her to a seat at the twelve-seat conference table, she recognised only one person amongst the four others already seated at the table, he was her head of department Commander Ian Kent. The remaining three were introduced by the host after he had announced who she was.

"Superintendent Elizabeth Cullen is one of our rising stars of counter terrorism, gentlemen. This is Mr Whitlake, a government security adviser."

293

Whitlake stood and offered a hand for a token shake with minimal movement. He was about sixty, lean, silver at the temples and of military bearing. He wore a grey, high-quality suit and had at least seven pens and pencils inexplicably bulging from his left breast pocket.

"Good afternoon Mr Whitlake," she said looking into his eyes for something untrustworthy. She didn't find it.

"Delighted to meet you Ms Cullen," he said quietly. D.A.C. Hilditch pressed on with the niceties.

"This is Mr Farbarn, Permanent Secretary to the Secretary of State for Northern Ireland."

Farbarn also stood to greet her although he appeared less practiced than Whitlake had been. He was an overweight, balding, sweaty man with a worried expression. His hands were sweaty too.

"Hello Mr Farbarn," said Lizzie who knew that she was more likely to remember a name if she said it aloud. There was little else memorable about Mr Farbarn.

"Superintendent," said Farbarn, exercising an economical use of words.

"And finally," said Hillditch, "Mr McEllerd, who holds a similar position with the Home office.

"Hello Mr McEllerd," said Lizzie who was glad that the ritual was finally over. She touched fingers with him and noticed cuff-links with a naval crest that matched a tie-pin. McEllerd was forty-five, tall, tanned, athletic and had a sparkle of energy about him. He smelled of expensive cologne.

"Hello Superintendent," he purred in ill-concealed, predatory-male, ego-driven charm. She let go of his hand, hoping that it would drop to the floor. His looks may have been appealing but his manner gave her the creeps.

"Now that we all know each other," began Hillditch, "we can get to the business in hand. Perhaps you might put the Superintendent in the picture Mr Whitlake?"

"Certainly." He adjusted his seat to face Lizzie. "I understand that your roots are in Northern Ireland, is that right?"

"Yes Sir," answered Lizzie who also knew when to be economical with her words.

"I appreciate that you will have undergone suitable vetting for your deployment in the Special Branch, but it is important that we establish precisely what your position is, politically, I mean."

Lizzie was surprised and a little offended but she showed neither.

"Are you gentlemen concerned that I may hold some biased agenda that might affect my ability to carry out my duties impartially?"

"We are merely seeking to cover all bases, so to speak," said Whitlake effortlessly.

"Alright," she began. "I was born and raised in Belfast and it's true that it's rare to find someone there who doesn't have an opinion."

The men around the table appreciated her humour and smiled, all except Farbarn who still looked worried. Lizzie continued.

"Our opinions about life are invariably formed by what we have lived through. My father was a Superintendent in the R.U.C. He was shot dead on our doorstep by the I.R.A. I saw it happen. That experience tends to form strong feelings in people and I'm not immune. Any chance I get to catch a killer, or better still prevent a killing, will be taken without compromise. The motivation for killing, be it political or otherwise, merely helps me to catch who did it. It isn't as important as the lives lost or the families of the victims. If you think that I would treat a murderer with Loyalist motives any differently to those of a Republican, you would be wrong. I trust that makes my position clear."

The assembled group said nothing. Commander Kent nodded and allowed himself a slight smile. Whitlake resumed his interview.

"Thank you Superintendent. That explains the position satisfactorily."

He opened a buff card folder and slipped on a pair of gold framed spectacles to read from the paper. Lizzie noticed TOP SECRET in large letters on each page of loose leaf.

"We have a development which has created a need for a security operation. There are, in effect, two people who must meet, in private to conduct some delicate negotiations. We want you to ensure that they get to do that. There will be groups and individuals who do not want these meetings to take place and will take extreme steps to undermine this initiative."

"There is already a substantial security framework to ensure the personal security of politicians."

"There is," agreed Whitlake. "However, the people I refer to are not politicians and therefore the usual arrangements are inappropriate. They would merely draw attention precisely where we don't want it."

Lizzie collated the information in her head. Putting all of the pieces in order she came up with this equation; Top level police + Counter Terrorism Chief + Northern Ireland Office + Home Office + Government Security Adviser, asking probing questions about her impartiality and all for two non-politicians to be able to discuss something in private, something that others may want to kill them for doing. The only logical explanation was that the British Government had found an acceptable way of beginning to negotiate with the Republicans. Successive British Governments had long said publically that they were not prepared to negotiate with terrorists. This deadlock had been the obstacle to progress toward peace for years and whilst Lizzie knew that it was to be a mammoth task, she was enthused even at the possibility of it.

"I think I understand the situation, Gentlemen. I can assure you of my best efforts for a peaceful and successful operation."

Kent nodded again. It was what he was going to say. Hillditch said something even more corporate and it became clear that Lizzie's presence was no longer required. She returned to her own office to await the briefing dossier. Within an hour, two techies with steel cases full of scanning equipment arrived and began to sweep her office and those nearby for bugging devices.

CHAPTER FIFTY-EIGHT

The document arrived in the hand of Ian Kent who turned up unannounced the following morning. He closed the door and turned up the venetian blinds to make the room semi-dark. Lizzie flicked on the angle-poise desk lamp. The dossier came in a leather case which she unzipped and pulled out a buff card folder, the same as the document Whitlake had been reading from the day before. Even the TOP SECRET part was the same.

Three pages of security warnings and legal jargon preceded the actual meat of the meal. She read the brief quietly to herself as Kent hovered anxiously, first by the door then the window, although he was unable to see through either. When she sat back in her seat, Kent added his view of it.

"It has to be as low key as possible without compromising the principals involved. There must be no motorcades and sirens when they move to and from the venues. They aren't well known faces so it can be done on the hush-hush as long as they cooperate too. I don't know how much they know about it yet."

"Venues?" asked Lizzie. "Is there to be more than one?"

"Yes and it must follow no pattern when each one is to be used. You decide without notice. Oh yes, you'll want to know about your team, won't you?"

Lizzie waited for him to tell her.

"Resources are not restricted here Elizabeth, the cost of this operation is to be met by Central Government and they don't want us to keep receipts. How many staff do you need?"

Lizzie had only just read the brief but she knew what it would take.

"Twelve, all firearms and surveillance trained and I don't want any of them to know each other. I'm going to borrow them from other forces. No disrespect intended Sir but this place leaks sometimes."

Kent held up both palms in supplication. She went on.

"Three vehicles, borrowed for the duration under the Force covert policy but at different cities."

"It's your operation. Do it how you want to and speak only to me. If anybody asks any questions I want to know about it. Understood?"

"Yes Sir, thank you."

"There's something I want you to bear in mind, Elizabeth," said Kent in a lower voice. Lizzie felt something unethical coming along. "There are no guarantees that these preliminary negotiations will come to anything. This chap who's doing the talking for the Republicans may have been deemed acceptable by the Government, but he has to have links to the high-ups in the I.R.A. I want to know what he says and who he says it to. This is a unique opportunity to gather good quality intelligence about them at a strategic level."

Lizzie was shocked but didn't show it. She had correctly anticipated that Commander Kent had an agenda of his own and, although it seemed to be motivated by a desire to catch and prevent serious criminal activity, it potentially put her in an impossible position. Was she protecting that person or spying on them?

"Keep that with you at all times," Kent said, pointing at the open document case. "There's a lot riding on this and we have to do our best work."

"I understand Sir," she said. She began planning as soon as he left the room.

CHAPTER FIFTY-NINE

The Boeing 747 touched down at Heathrow Airport at 8.16pm on a cloudy Thursday. Professor James Patrick Coleman's official reason for travelling to the UK was for business. Academics criss-cross the world in the pursuit of expanding their knowledge and expertise as well as the reputations of their home Universities. However, James was probably unique in that he was accompanied by two plain-clothed British close-protection officers seconded to the Metropolitan Police Special Branch.

Usual arrival procedures were dispensed with by prior arrangement. The police bodyguards led James through a low-key variation of passport control then straight to a waiting black Range Rover with darkened windows. The journey into the heart of London afforded James his first view of the capital city of the nation that was, in his view, occupying his home country. The enmity that he felt toward his host, whilst remaining intact, was tempered by the sights and sounds of the main western access route into the city, a vibrant and colourful display of culture and commerce at every glance. Jamaican dreadlocks, musically-influenced costumes of the young, Muslim beards, far-eastern faces, each human being was an unfolding story. He revelled in the intensity and evident purpose in the movement of the population, so different from the sedate and measured pace of campus life and the narrow, neighbourhood mentality of his home city.

The sombre, hearse-like vehicle crawled and purred through the streets until it entered the barrier controlled car park of a blue-glass and beige-panelled twelve floor hotel. Flanked by his airport companions, James was guided into the hotel reception then up to his room on the ninth floor. He dropped his case on the bed and looked out of the window through chiffon inner curtains. This brought the security of his visit into the conversation.

"Lingering by the window isn't a good idea, Professor," said the older of the two bodyguards.

"I know that there is some risk with my visit here, that's why you're here of course, but I should be able to look out of the window, shouldn't I?"

James became aware that his Ulster accent, described, by Niall Mahon, as having been 'diluted', could have served to emphasise the differences between himself and the people who he had agreed to negotiate with, as well as those sent to afford him protection. It was better to avoid alienating anyone. Although he was representing a large body of people, he was alone in that place. He was also acutely aware that the main threat to his life was from a faction of his own side.

"The Superintendent wants to speak to you about the arrangements. I'll call her now," said the Special Branch man reaching for the bedside telephone. He gained an outside line and dialled a memorised number.

"Hello Boss," he began, "in position with our principal now. Do you want a word with him?"

He held up the receiver for James to take.

"Hello, this is Professor Coleman," he said.

"I am Superintendent Elizabeth Cullen of the Metropolitan Police," she announced. "I am heading the team that will be ensuring your safety during your stay in London. I hope everything is acceptable so far?"

He detected a faint North of England dialect, reinforcing the cosmopolitan vision he had experienced on the journey from the airport. He was yet to meet any native Londoners. The Superintendent seemed efficient yet personable.

"I'm not allowed to look out of windows, but I accept your reasons for that. Is this how it's going to be Superintendent, an existence in a well-furnished cell with bodyguards?"

"Try to think of it as being treated like a member of the Royal Family, Professor. V.I.P. treatment."

"I'll try," he said, finding the confident optimism of his protector-in-chief reassuring. "I hope my limited imagination is up to that."

"I will brief you fully in the morning. Meanwhile, I would appreciate that you don't leave your room without one of the protection team accompanying you. They have a mobile phone number for you to call if you need to."

"Thank you. I'm not going anywhere tonight."

"I realise you may want to call home, but I suggest that you don't call anyone to say where you are."

"That's not an issue for me. I'm a lone wolf, I have no family to call."

"Okay Professor, please be ready to go at eight o'clock. You'll be fully briefed with the arrangements on the way to the first venue."

"That's fine, thank you."

He ended the call happier than he had been before it. He also felt a pang of curiosity as to what the Superintendent looked like. Female police chiefs were rare indeed.

She replaced the receiver and let out a breath of relief at the successfully uneventful completion of the first part of the security operation. The American professor may have been representing the Republican movement in Northern Ireland, which evoked uncomfortable emotions in her, but he seemed to have an agreeable manner and appreciated her humour. She pictured him as being about sixty and wearing a thick woollen cardigan.

The bodyguards returned to the office to speak to their boss before standing down for the night. Once the door was closed, Lizzie waved the men to sit at the conference table. They had little of any consequence to say, but they did report that the principal was easy-going and no trouble to deal with.

"Is he a typical mad, old boffin?" asked Lizzie.

"No, not at all," said the S.B. man. "He's only about forty, tall, lean chap."

"Oh!" she said, re-evaluating her earlier opinion in light of this fresh information. "Married to the job, do you think?"

"Could be, he seems a sound enough bloke," said the second man. "You can hold a conversation with him alright."

"Let's hope so, that's what he is here to do," said Lizzie, adjourning the debriefing exercise for the night. She left the office in an uncharacteristic mood of personal rather than professional curiosity concerning the visitor from the U.S.A.

CHAPTER SIXTY

In the corridor on the ninth floor of the hotel, Lizzie and one of her team strode up to the door of James' room. It was 7.58am. She knocked and stood back.

At that moment her mobile phone rang. Aware of the need for fluent communication with the other members of her security team, she reached into her coat pocket and took out the phone, answering it at the moment the door was opened. James stepped out and saw Lizzie wave a silent apology toward him. She turned away and spoke quietly into the phone as he closed the door and locked it behind him. The bodyguard set off to walk with James to the lift, leaving Lizzie to catch up when she was clear. James had only seen a fleeting glimpse of her and whilst he had noticed that she was a brunette and was dressed smartly, his mind was focussed intensely on beginning the delicate and challenging negotiations on the best possible footing. James and the S.B. man reached the Range Rover which was under the canopy of the foyer of the lobby. The driver was already in the car and the engine was running. They both got into the rear seats and waited for the officer in charge. James opened his document case and removed a notebook which he opened and began reading from.

After two minutes which, to the bodyguards felt far longer, Lizzie climbed into the front passenger seat. Pulling her seatbelt across, she turned her head to the side. The bodyguard was behind the driver and James was behind Lizzie.

"Good morning Professor."

"Good morning," he said whilst maintaining his concentration on the notes on his lap. She was aware that she did not have the full attention of this particular principal.

"I'd like to run through some of the security details, if I can have your attention."

"Sure, go ahead, I'm listening."

Lizzie explained the way she intended to keep James from being assassinated. She pointed out some ground rules for him to observe and tried to explain things in language and manner befitting a university professor. He acknowledged without posing any questions.

The conversation ended, denied nourishment by James' concentration on his notes. The car was manoeuvred through the London traffic as Lizzie and her officers looked out for anybody following or otherwise paying any undue attention. The journey ended outside a triangular, grey office block at Earl's Court. The car came to a halt next to an identical Range Rover with another S.B. man standing by the driver's door.

"My team will take you inside to meet with Mrs Lascelle. They will be outside the room throughout. Tell them when you are ready to leave."

"I will, thank you."

James and his shadow got out and entered the building. Lizzie watched them walk from the front of the car. She saw that he was tall and lean as reported. He had sandy red hair and a pale complexion. The curiosity she had been feeling gained in intensity. She had not yet seen his face and he had not seen hers either.

The driver noticed her staring at him as he disappeared into the building.

"Chatty sort, don't you think?" he asked.

"It makes a welcome change," suggested Lizzie distractedly. "Some of these V.I.P.s have too much to say."

"True. Back to the shop?" asked the driver.

"Yeah, come on. There's a stage briefing with Commander Kent. Drop me there and get back here in case they take an instant dislike to each other. A fall-out at an early stage is a distinct possibility."

*

On the second-floor office of the Daily Tribune, the desk phone rang.

"Alty!"

"Have you got a decision from your editor about the negotiators yet?" said the same voice he had encountered in the previous phone conversation on this subject. Alty sat upright and moved the phone away from eavesdropping colleagues.

"I'm working on that," he said without thinking.

"Well work harder, Alty. There are other hacks I could be giving this to."

"Okay I get it," he said with undisguised irritation. "but it's not going to be easy. An anonymous source carries little weight around here. If you can give me something that I can use to argue my case, we might get somewhere."

There was a pause which was ended by the caller saying.

"The security operation for the negotiations, it's very low-key. I know who is in charge of it. The Met. won't admit it of course, but I know that it's in the hands of Superintendent Elizabeth Cullen of the Met. Special Branch."

"Superintendent?" said Alty.

"Yes," said the caller who had taken offence at Alty's tone because he had seemed to disbelieve what he had been told. "She is the officer in charge of it."

"Oh, I don't doubt that for a minute," Alty reassured him, whilst demonstrating amusement at the revelation. His next move was quickly being revised. Elizabeth Cullen was in London and that fact was going to work to his advantage.

CHAPTER SIXTY-ONE

The modern and tastefully decorated suite of rooms with connecting doors could have been utilised for any number of purposes. A commercial training course whereby the class are divided into small syndicates for later reunification, a series of differently-sized offices affording a hierarchy of visual aspiration for the ambitious or an anonymous venue for a sensitive negotiation on which the future security of Northern Ireland and beyond may depend.

Each room was adorned by pale yellow décor and magnolia furniture. Whilst most had aluminium-edged windows across an entire wall, one room had no windows. Beneath a square-framed example of modern art that required explanation was a wide table where one may have expected to see cutlery or glassware. Instead, it contained a crystal glass chess set. It was illuminated by up-lit standard lamps in each corner and housed one imposing oval table with twelve chairs. Only two of them were to be used that day.

James was escorted to the negotiating room by his police bodyguards. Martha was already sitting at the table wearing a bottle green trouser suit and a cream blouse. She stood and watched him approach. His first impression was that his adversary was a smart woman, a person of high standards of appearance which would indicate that she was not simply there as a token. Martha's first impression was that James was taller then she had imagined. His clothing, however, was precisely how she would have pictured an Irish born, Americanised academic to be, more concerned with matters of the mind and of the world than with his fashion credentials. She smelled of subtle and expensive French perfume. He smelled of supermarket-bought soap.

Each suspected the other of trying to play mind games and the early exchange was understandably cautious.

"Good morning Professor Coleman, I am Martha Lascelle."

Respectful and modest, Martha was herself no slouch in Academia, having a PhD in international studies. She could have introduced herself as Doctor Lascelle, but that wasn't in her plan. She held out a doll-like hand. James lightly took only the fingers of Martha's hand and curtly tensed his grip before releasing.

"Good morning Ms Lascelle."

Avoiding saying Miss or Mrs seemed to James to represent the least troublesome form of address to a widow who had always used her maiden name anyway. He knew that he was at a disadvantage in matters of diplomacy, but good manners could serve to narrow that chasm.

"I've been looking forward to meeting you," he said. "I hope we can find some common ground to build on."

"I hope so too," answered Martha. "The first thing to acknowledge is that we are both here. That is progress I believe."

"Yes, it's a good start." They laughed a little which reduced the tension between them.

"Shall we sit?" suggested Martha.

They took their seats at the table leaving one empty chair separating them. Harmless and topical dialogue ensued covering the weather and the suite of rooms at their disposal.

Martha steered it toward personal matters whilst avoiding anything contentious.

"I understand that you live in Boston?"

"Yes I do. Are you based in London?"

"Officially but I spend most of my time overseas. This role doesn't involve air travel for a change which I welcome. Do you travel much in your work?"

James thought about his journey to Brazil and Africa. Recalling his use of a false identity was enough to remind him that he had to be careful not to mention any connection to the Irish Republican cause. These negotiations were taking place on the basis that he had no such connections.

"I have travelled a little. One University campus looks pretty much like any other after a while. I'm out of that zone in this place."

"I have spent much of my time in embassies and consulates, too many to remember. I am also in unfamiliar territory here."

Martha was a skilled conversationalist. Her ability to find empathy and use it to bring down barriers was sublime, at least it always had been before.

"Ms Lascelle, I don't buy that."

"I don't understand, Professor."

"We are in your home city, a place I have never visited before and you want me to think that is not in some way advantageous to you and those you represent. I'm not going to suggest that this venue is inappropriate, I don't care where we are. It's what gets discussed and ultimately achieved that matters. What concerns me right now is that you and I have to find reasons to trust each other. So let's not play games. Cut out the carefully crafted empathy and soft-soap and we will both be able to recognise what we agree on and what we don't."

Martha had not seen that coming but she was determined to keep one hand on the reins during the negotiations. It was clear that Coleman was not going to roll over and accept the first thing that was put on the negotiating table.

"Okay Professor, is there anything else that you are unhappy with so far?"

"It's noticeable that you chose to wear green today. I don't know if that decision represents respect or bullshit. All I know is that I'm not going to turn up here dressed as a Beefeater."

"You have made your point. I accept that trust is important although we may disagree as to how that is going to be reached or how we will both know when we get there. I am looking for trust in you too, Professor, and straight-talking is a good start. Does anything else about my appearance offend you?"

"Offend me? No Ms Lascelle, I'm not offended, but something does stir my curiosity."

"Go right ahead and ask," she said.

"That lapel pin you're wearing. If that is supposed to evoke some reaction in me, I can't recognise what it might be, so that gesture was wasted I'm afraid."

James had inadvertently pushed a button. Martha's reaction took him by surprise. Her eyes hardened along with her previously melodic tone of voice.

"This pin represents the Motor Neurone Disease Association of which I am a patron. Don't think that my involvement with that cause is entirely charitable. My late husband suffered for several years before he died from

MND. My decision to wear the pin was not on your account."

James felt like a heel. He had suspected that everything about that meeting was planned and engineered for the playing of mind games. Perhaps he should have recognised that some things were what they appeared to be and were not set to trap him. It was no use raising the issue of trust without exercising some of it himself.

"That's a cause very close to your heart Ms Lascelle," commented James innocuously.

"Yes it is. I just didn't expect it to be discussed in this environment." Her tone was returning to her earlier conciliatory one.

James stood up and walked to the modern art masterpiece. Without really looking at it he said.

"Did your briefing notes mention my brother?"

"No. I know you have no living family, but I wasn't informed of anything else."

"He was shot by a British soldier in Belfast. He was fifteen years old."

"So I guess we all have things that we feel strongly about. Bereavement is as strong a motivator as any. That's clear at least," said Martha.

"Yes it is. I think we have made a start Ms Lascelle."

"We have," she said. "I look forward to tomorrow's meeting."

CHAPTER SIXTY-TWO

Martha spent thirty minutes on the phone to the Secretary of State for Northern Ireland. She had little to tell him, but the Minister still had a lot to ask. She reassured him that both Professor Coleman and herself had opened the discussion and were working hard to establish a solid base for negotiating. She dined on Dover Sole and dry white wine in her room whilst reading her Government authorised briefing notes. She had one request of the Secretary of State. She wanted to know about the death of a fifteen-year-old Belfast boy by the name of Coleman involving the security forces. She was assured that, once located, the file on that case would be made available to her.

James had been briefed by Niall Mahon about communicating the developments of his task. It was a mere variation on the methods he had employed for many years. Telephones could be bugged but not all of them were. As James was being transported back to his hotel, his police bodyguard was surprised to be asked to stop in the car park of a shopping complex that James had spotted that morning. Lining the wall of the building was a row of ten public phone booths. James asked the driver to wait as he had to make a call. The bodyguard was understandably uneasy about it. His principal was at his most vulnerable at such times. He reported the situation by an encrypted radio channel as James entered a phone booth and lifted the receiver. Resting it on the crook of his neck, he also took a mobile phone from his pocket, switched it on and dialled a memorised number. He conveyed a brief message confirming that negotiations had begun, and that he would call again the following evening. He told Mahon the name of the hotel and his room number. He was told that a letter would be delivered to the desk later that evening. He returned to the Range Rover and climbed into the rear seat. In his hotel room, he dined on Spanish omelette and orange juice.

The briefings he had received prior to making the journey were concise and inadequate. He felt that he had nothing to negotiate with. He had been assured that once the talks were underway, he would be briefed in more detail. Everything was on a need-to-know basis. At nine o'clock, he heard voices outside in the corridor. Through the viewer, he saw that his bodyguard was talking to a young desk clerk he had seen earlier in the lobby. James opened the door to catch the end of the conversation.

"Okay mate, I'll see that he gets it," said the plain-clothed policeman.

"But I must hand it to him, it's hotel policy to . . . . "

James cut the discussion short by asking the clerk.

"Do you have something for me?"

"Professor Coleman?"

"Yes, I'm Professor Coleman."

"This is for you, Sir."

He handed over a letter. The policeman nodded his approval. James took the letter, thanked them both and closed the door.

The letter contained a typed list of twenty names. Some he had heard of and some he had not. It was the proposed Republican negotiators that he had to convince Martha Lascelle and the British Government could participate in the peace talks that he was trying to broker. He ran through several possible disclosure options in his mind. By eleven-thirty he had decided how he was going to play it.

The following morning, Lizzie chose to accompany Martha to the venue. After establishing that Martha was happy with the arrangements, Lizzie risked upsetting that equilibrium by announcing that she was to be moved to a different hotel that evening. Martha had anticipated this and had packed her case ready to go. Lizzie also announced that the venue for the negotiations was also due to change. Martha said that it was fine too.

"All these changes," she said. "Tell me that I'm still going to be talking to the same Professor Coleman or are you going to change him too?"

Lizzie accepted Martha's humour as it had been intended.

"No, the professor remains as he is."

"I assume that you have met the visitor from the States?"

"I have, briefly," said Lizzie who had to acknowledge, if only to herself, that she found him intriguing. "He didn't say much to me."

"Let us hope I have more luck with that," concluded Martha as the car arrived at the venue in Earl's Court.

James had arrived first. He waited at the negotiating table reading his notes. Martha entered the room alone and greeted him in a business-like manner. He stood to greet her. She wore a beige, two-piece suit and black high-necked blouse.

During the morning they drained a thermal coffee pot and discussed acceptable terminology for the key parties under discussion. With minimal objection on either's part, they got through a great deal of what they had planned to talk about.

"Meanwhile, I have some things I want to ask of you."

"Go ahead and ask."

James took out the list of names that had been delivered to him the night before. He folded it in half and tore it along the crease. He placed the top half in front of Martha who slipped a pair of pink-rimmed spectacles on to read its content.

"This is the first part of the negotiating team I am proposing. I want you to take that and familiarise yourself with all intelligence, convictions, gossip, rumour and antecedents of those people. It's going to take some time to cut through to the facts regarding each one of them. When we meet again we can discuss the suitability of each individual in turn."

"The position remains that the British Government does not negotiate with terrorists." Martha chanted the mantra as a blanket reminder.

"Well, we have to determine who is and who is not a terrorist now, don't we?" he said, staring through the spectacles and into her eyes.

"Alright," she said. "I expect that you want to know who will be nominated to speak for the other side?"

"Yes I do. If anybody is suggested who is believed to have been involved in any unacceptable conduct toward civilians in Northern Ireland, it would be inappropriate to include them."

After a brief rest break, Martha returned to the table with a challenge for James.

"One important point I must raise, and I have no wish to offend you Professor, but I need confirmation that you do have the requisite authority to speak for the Republican movement. I have to be able to convince the British Government that what we agree on will carry through to the people who can call a ceasefire, should we manage to negotiate one."

James did not speak for thirty seconds. He stared intently at Martha. Nobody blinked.

"I see," he said impassively. "You have the authority of the British Government but you doubt that I have the authority of my own side. Have I got that right, Ms Lascelle?"

"I merely seek confirmation," she said in calming tones.

"Then you shall have it," said James with no idea as to how he could provide such an endorsement without involving and implicating the senior command. "I propose that we don't meet tomorrow but we do again the day after. We both have plenty to do before we discuss anything else."

"Agreed."

CHAPTER SIXTY-THREE

James followed his method of reporting back to Mahon, although on that evening he chose an alcove within a cinema foyer to make the call.

He explained the challenge to his credibility that Martha Lascelle had issued to him. Mahon pondered for a minute before asking James to call him back in five minutes. Aware that his shadows were following his every move, James went through the motions of making another call before calling the original number again.

"This is what's happening," said the old man. "Tonight there will be an event out at Strangford. It will take place in a field and nobody will be harmed. At the scene we will place an item, something old that the security services have been looking for. You can tell that woman that the event was intended for a loyalist target but we have redeployed it as a gesture of good faith in your presence at that negotiating table. She will have to accept that as an endorsement of you as the spokesman for the Republican movement."

James told Mahon that he understood and that he agreed with the plan.

He returned to his hotel room and called the number he had been given when he had arrived, explaining that he wanted to speak to Ms Lascelle with some urgency. The voice on the other end of the line assured him that he would arrange for her to call him on his phone in the hotel room.

He ended the call and took off his jacket and tie. He rubbed his temples and felt the uneven layers of cosmetic repair beneath his skin, a stark reminder of the frailties of his health and mortality. He felt an unfamiliar rise in his skin above his hairline. He recalled the scarring that his plastic surgeon had worked so hard to repair and reminded himself that it could have been much worse.

A knock on the door brought him back to the here-and-now. He peered through the viewer to see two of his protection officers outside in the corridor. He opened the door and an officer announced.

"We have to relocate you to another hotel Professor."

"Oh no, I'm waiting for an important call, I can't go anywhere until I have dealt with that."

"Sorry," said the policeman. "We have orders to move you straight away, the Super's orders."

"Then it's the Super I have to speak to, but either way I'm not ready to leave here yet."

He closed the door and left them to decide how to handle the issue. After twenty minutes the bedside phone rang.

"Hello?"

"Professor Coleman it's Martha Lascelle. You wanted to speak to me?"

"Yes, thank you for calling back Ms Lascelle. I have to tell you about something that will demonstrate my credentials. During the night, an 'event' will take place in a rural location in Northern Ireland. Nobody will be harmed. There was a target, deemed legitimate by the I.R.A., but that order has been rescinded."

"I understand Professor. I seek your assurance that this will not be an act of violence."

"I can assure you that this is an alternative to an act of violence."

"Very well, thank you. I shall await news of this 'event.' Goodnight."

James ended the call and began packing his suitcase ready for the move. Having addressed the need to speak to his British counterpart and amid the relief of having done so, he felt some regret at having snapped at his bodyguards who were carrying out orders intended for his protection. It seemed wrong that he should have shown such impatience to the team who had been so patient with him. He thought that perhaps he should speak to the lady superintendent and tell her that they had done a good job. At that moment there was another knock on the door. Observing his habit of peering through the viewer, James saw that the police pair had been joined by a woman who had her back turned. He opened the door and she spun around to speak to him.

"Professor Coleman, I understand that there is an issue with your relocation," she said.

"Come in Superintendent, please."

Lizzie stepped over the threshold and James closed the door after her. She walked to the dressing table and turned to face him. He resumed packing his case which lay open on the made bed.

"I'm sorry you have been inconvenienced. Your fellows out there were quite right and I understand the need to move now. It was important that I took a call here before I left for the new place. I've done that now and I'm ready to go. Give me a minute to finish packing."

Out of habit, she checked out of the window then she looked at him as he busied himself with shaving accessories and books. Having only seen him in outdoor clothes before, she noticed that he was quite broad across the shoulders and was in good physical shape. He was too occupied to notice. He finished by zipping up the case and slipping on his jacket.

"Right," he said, lifting the case from the bed and adding his brief case to the same hand and pulling his coat from the back of the chair. "Thanks for waiting. Shall we take a stroll?"

It was a seemingly harmless saying, a light-hearted quip, a throwaway question which would normally have passed unnoticed. Lizzie had not heard anybody say that for several years. The memory that was unearthed in her was a happy one. Her mind lingered on the memory rather than the person in front of her who had reactivated it.

She stepped out of the room and James followed, locking the door behind him. The bodyguard took possession of the room key and headed off to the reception desk to return it. Lizzie, James and the other S.B. man headed to the car park. In the Range Rover, James sat behind the driver and Lizzie rode shotgun. They crossed the evening traffic chaos without speaking until the driver broke the silence.

"Does Boston have traffic jams like this, Professor?"

"Probably," he said gazing out of the window. "I tend not to visit the city much. The University campus is much less stressful to navigate."

More silent seconds passed before James commented to nobody in particular.

"Every nation in the world appears to be represented here. I've seen nothing like it. People don't tend to gravitate in such numbers to Boston, or Belfast for that matter."

Lizzie's attention was raised at the mention of her home city. Aware of the political movement that Professor James

Patrick Coleman was representing in the negotiations, it came as no surprise that he was familiar with Belfast.

"Do you intend to visit the old city whilst you are over here?" she asked innocently.

"No, I'd better not. I don't want people thinking I'm a terrorist," he joked, knowing that a good joke has some truth to it.

Lizzie found him compelling to listen to. She detected a certain warmth to his voice, a self-deprecating charm, unforced and supported by a sharp intellect. His humour and general good manners were admirable qualities too. Any earlier hidden resentment she may have held toward the faction that had included her father's killer had begun to lighten, at least toward James Coleman. His selection as negotiator proved that he was considered by the British Government to have no links to any acts of terrorism. It further elevated him in Lizzie's esteem that he was working to build peace in Northern Ireland, a quest close to her heart. He deserved more than the protection her team was affording him, he deserved some respect.

From his seat in the back of the car, James could not see Lizzie's face. He had glanced at her and noticed that she was to his liking, though he was habitually eager to avoid prolonged focus on any female, a custom derived from maintaining a lecturer/student distance in the University environment. He found her to be agreeable in demeanour and efficient without being officious. She was also unusually young to hold such a senior position. She could only be about thirty, he thought, although in truth she was thirty-five. Career above everything, married to the job, probably a workaholic, no social life. The ironic realisation that he could have been describing himself made him smile.

"I have no meeting with Ms Lascelle tomorrow so there's no need to ferry me about, thank you," he announced. Lizzie tried to offer some hospitality.

"I expect that you will have work to do Professor, but please let me know if there is anything we can do to make your stay more comfortable. Anywhere you need to go, we should be able to help, providing that your safety isn't compromised."

"That's appreciated, Superintendent. A day in my hotel room prison or a guided tour of London, hmmm. That's a tricky one."

The car arrived at the new hotel at 8.50pm. It was different from the first one. Not a high-rise, the building was only three storeys high and was shaped around several quadrangles. Vehicular access was through a stone arch into a walled car park leading to the foyer. For James, the room was better, a separate table and chairs along with a tiny kitchen and a good quality television. For the team, security was better because the room was on the top floor and the window looked out onto a secure quadrangle. The team swept the room and cleared it for James to enter. Lizzie stayed in the car. One man remained in the hotel whilst Lizzie was taken back to her office.

"I said he was an affable bloke, didn't I, boss?" said the driver.

"Yes, he has a nice way about him," she said attempting nonchalance. "I just hope he knows what he's talking about with Mrs Lascelle. She's no fool. Made of steel, that woman."

"What are we going to do with the mad prof tomorrow?"

"Keep him alive and maybe manage a trip around the museums," she said, looking out at the light rain that had begun to fall, whilst forming a plan to keep one step ahead of the threat to her principal.

CHAPTER SIXTY-FOUR

The rain had stopped near Strangford Lough leaving broken cloud and intermittent glimpses of diffused moonlight and the occasional star. Two men, who appeared to be on a nocturnal mission to catch rabbits, left a powerful lamp and a cross-bred lurcher dog in their small, Japanese hatchback car and set out across a field of grass-stubble and molehills, devoid of livestock or crops. When they reached what they judged to be the centre of the field, with gloved hands they removed the contents of a rucksack and set to work. A small, green, angler's shelter was erected in seconds for the men to work in unnoticed by passers-by on the road or the prying eyes of the security forces using night-vision equipment. Hoods partially concealed their faces but they were not being watched by anyone. That place held little interest for either side in that war. The device was prepared but not yet primed. A timer was attached but not yet set. Under a small battery powered light, also shielded to further avoid remote detection, one of the men prepared the device as he had done several times before. When he was satisfied that it was as he had intended it to be, he stood up and said.

"Ready."

The second man said in reply.

"Here, you hold the torch, keep it pointing down."

"Got it."

Out of the rucksack came two thirds of an old but recently cleaned assault rifle. The stock was missing, the wood having rotted away from years of storage in a damp cellar. The gun was placed on the ground ten yards from the primed device.

"We've got fifteen minutes. We need to be across the other side of the lough if we want to enjoy the show. Come on."

They returned to the edge of the field, removed hoods and gloves and set off in the car without using the lights. Driving slowly and making minimal noise, they reached a point that afforded them several options of egress and a view of the field they had just left. Their instructions, whilst senseless in many respects, were clear and unequivocal. Nobody must get hurt and nothing must be damaged. A hole in an unused field in the middle of nowhere could not be considered as damage.

Once in position the men had two minutes to wait. They had never before hung around to see their work come to fruition. When it did, even though they were expecting it, they jumped involuntarily in their car seats. Every nerve was tensed, every sinew strained. The explosion took place nearly two miles away but the deep, unearthly boom filled the valley and the white flash fully illuminated the sky. A grey cloud of smoke, grass and mud floated unseen into the ether. In the isolated farmhouses and hamlets surrounding the lough, crockery clattered inside cupboards and cutlery rattled in drawers like ghostly chains in the night. Cattle lowed with distress, family pets yelped and screeched, tables, chairs and window-frames rocked, beds shook and pictures in frames fell from hooks on walls. In the interrupted darkness, people feared for their safety then feared for the safety of others.

Inside the small Japanese hatchback car, the two men said nothing. The driver put it in gear and set off to take one of the long routes back to Belfast.

CHAPTER SIXTY-FIVE

"Good morning Professor," said the Special Branch officer as James opened the hotel room door.

"Good morning yourself!" joked James. "No school for me today," he said, although he was dressed and shaved as though he was venturing out.

"The Super' thought you might like a trip to the museums. What do you think?"

"I'd like that very much. If the Super' says it will be okay, I'm in."

"She says you have to get changed," added the guard as he stepped inside and produced a carrier bag from behind his back. He laid it on the table and removed from it a black denim jacket, a maroon baseball cap, a plain grey T shirt and a pair of new blue jeans with the labels still attached.

"Good choice, give me a minute."

He took the clothes into the en suite bathroom, leaving the door slightly open and started to change. His guard inspected the facilities in the kitchen and compared them favourably to those in his own temporary accommodation. From inside the bathroom he was asked.

"The Super' is a pretty sharp operator, don't you think?"

"Yeah, she is. She's a good boss."

"She puts the hours in, huh?" asked James.

"That's right. She has no family though. That helps."

"Yes," agreed James. "I can relate to that."

"She's from your old neck of the woods, you know?"

"From Northern Ireland? You wouldn't know it from her accent would you?"

"And you can't tell from yours either, Professor."

"Ah, fair point. I've been told that my accent has become 'diluted' by living overseas."

James emerged from the bathroom a changed man. The clothing fitted reasonably well.

"So this is the new look I've been given to blend in, is it?"

James checked the safe which contained very little and took a light shoulder bag from the floor at the side of the bed. They set off to meet Lizzie in the walled car park. Upon seeing the newly casual visitor, she stepped out of the Range Rover. She too was casually attired in black jeans, brown Doc Marten shoes and a short, brown leather jacket concealing her police issue handgun, custom-made with a smaller grip. She slipped her police radio into the outer pocket of the jacket and a near-invisible, remote earpiece into her left ear.

"So, you went for the tourist option, Professor?" she greeted him. "It suits you."

James shrugged a gesture of acceptance. Lizzie announced how the day was going to go.

"The Professor and I will be on foot from here. It won't look out of place to see a male and a female together in the tourist spots. You two should be apart, remain in radio contact and at least one of you have the Professor and myself in sight at all times. Understood?"

Everyone nodded, including the principal.

"Any questions?" she demanded.

"I have one," said James. Lizzie raised an eyebrow and listened. James continued.

"If we are going to pass for an old married couple, we can't keep calling each other Professor and Superintendent, can we?"

"No, you're right." She thought for a moment then ordered. "First names are a dead giveaway. What's your middle name?"

"Patrick," he declared.

"It's not exactly anonymous, is it?" she said with an air of resignation. "With all due respect, of course, Patrick it is. You had better call me Mary."

Whilst the joke was lost on James, the two bodyguards could not contain their mirth. Cop humour is not universally appreciated. Lizzie knew it very well and knew how to deal with it.

"Any cracks from either of you two about 'virgins' and you'll be directing traffic at Scotch Corner until you die and probably after too."

"Yes Boss," they managed to utter, regaining sufficient composure to be able to get to work.

Lizzie and James set off to walk to South Kensington. Their remote shadows, bearing concealed handguns in underarm slings, split up and each kept a loose tail, testing the radio connection as they walked.

For James, the art galleries and museums were a treat for the senses. For a man with a lifelong hunger for knowledge, it was a feast for mind and soul. Any cultural discomfort he held about the presence of British troops in Northern Ireland and the perceived impediment to unification with the South, gave way to the fabulous ability the British had to celebrate its art, history and culture in surroundings of high opulence. His enthusiasm infected Lizzie too. She had, with her customary diligence, begun by watching the entrances and exits of every room they had entered, looking for any sign of a threat to the life of the principal she was tasked to protect. Occasional glimpses of their two remote bodyguards reminded her of the main task, but between them she found time to admire the unfolding and glorious exhibits and artefacts taking the visitor on a journey though the history of the world in ever-increasing depth through every door.

They stopped in front of a vast painting nearly reaching all four corners of the wall on which it was mounted. James sat on a backless viewing bench. Lizzie sat down next to him. The painting depicted a colossal battle across valleys, mountains and into the heavens in breath-taking detail.

"Are you the artistic type Mary?" asked James without looking away from the awesome picture.

"Not really. All this hidden meaning stuff does nothing for me. I prefer it when things are clear, they don't need to be explained," she said.

"Where's the fun in that? There are nicer ways of telling a story than just spelling it out. Take this painting for instance. It's telling a series of massive stories. I don't even know who or what they're all about but I feel elated from looking at it. Would you rather it read like a witness statement, all clinical and no interpretation?"

"I just appreciate it when people say what they think," explained Lizzie. James felt a memory return to him, a walk in a park by a duck pond under willow trees.

"You remind me of someone I used to know," he said. Lizzie held a momentary thought that the principal was coming on to her. It was not an entirely unpleasant thought, but it was not to be encouraged.

"Good," she snapped attempting to nip the imminent comparison in the bud. It didn't work. James was going to expand on it anyway.

"She didn't get the beauty of art either, which was mad because she had the most beautiful soul."

Lizzie could not resist engaging in the discussion.

"I was told I had no soul once."

James relived that moment in the past. The girl with the wild, black, eye make-up, the bike-ride to Helen's Bay and that warm evening that followed; the loud music, the energy, the passion. He felt her presence inside his veins and the dawning of realisation that she was back, physically present, in flesh and bone, sitting next to him. He could not catch his breath. His fingers trembled as he looked at her. The young woman who had made him feel so alive, made him a man, filled his heart and soul with the ecstasy he could not imagine ever happening to him again in his whole life. He blinked and looked away. He looked back at her side profile as she looked up at the giant painting.

"Oh Jesus Christ, it is you, it really is you! I can't believe . . . " his voice faded before his sentence ended. She turned to look at him in bewilderment and concern. He jumped up and stepped away from her staring intently at her as though she had appeared out of thin air.

"What are you doing?" she said in a corrective whisper. "Stop drawing attention to yourself."

She was beginning to regret the whole museum trip idea. The principal had no notion of what low-key activity meant. She saw that he was displaying shock and the inability to express it. She felt more protective than mere professionalism could engender. She wanted to help him, to get him calm and rational again. What had all of the hallmarks of a panic attack abated sufficiently for him to utter.

"Kiki!"

CHAPTER SIXTY-SIX

It hit her like a demolition ball. Her jaw fell and the blood drained from her head leaving her whirring and disorientated. She sucked in tiny breaths as though a lungful of air would have been painful. She remained seated on the bench, staring wide-eyed at the man who had turned everything upside-down with a single word. Her mind raced and careered around imaginary corners threatening to fall off steep cliffs at every twist. The most ecstatic and traumatic period of her life was being poured over her like an avalanche. The acute and layered sense of loss duelled with the memory of high-passion and the bizarre circumstances of once again meeting the young man who she had fallen for so completely all those years before. She raised her hand to her mouth and whispered through opened fingers.

"Sid?"

He nodded as confusion and desperation to comprehend showed in his eyes. Neither spoke for a minute. They stared at each other. One of the bodyguards passed an arched entrance at the end of the room. He saw that his boss and their principal were alone and no threat was evident so he passed by and went to the entrance to the stairway, appearing to admire a portrait of a Georgian Hussar in battle whilst really waiting for the next cue to move.

Lizzie broke the silence.

"You remember too?"

"I couldn't forget. I wanted to find you, to explain."

"I had to leave," they both said at the same moment.

"I had to come to England," she explained.

"I had to go to Boston. I didn't want to go but I had to. I tried to get a message to you, through a friend, but I didn't even know your name."

"I tried too. My friend went to the University but they couldn't find you from what we knew. I felt so bad for leaving. It was a terrible time for me. It's all coming back now."

She put her head in her hands and tried hard to compose herself. James wanted to go to her, offer comfort in her distress and embrace the woman he had wanted to hold again for so long. He sat down next to her. He reached into his pocket to find a tissue but, as he was wearing clothes that were not his own there was no tissue to give. He looked up at the ceiling and breathed deeply.

"I thought about you a great deal," he confided. "Not just at the time but ever since. I went back to Belfast when my mother died. I went back to Helen's Bay. It was silly of me to think that you might be there, but I didn't have anywhere else to start from."

"I did too," she admitted. "I went to the beach and hoped. I didn't forget you either."

A few more silent moments passed. Each gathered their thoughts, there were so many to gather. James restarted the conversation.

"In my more realistic moments I wondered what you were doing, I mean with your life. I understand you have no kids, any husband?"

"No, I didn't do anything about that. I worked a lot, no time for romance, no inclination either. Did you find someone?"

He shook his head.

"Me neither, it was painful at the time, less so once I'd built walls around myself, so to speak."

"I get that. I haven't heard it described that way before but I can understand. You're still finding nicer ways of saying things, aren't you?"

Lizzie felt a desire to embrace James. She was, for a tiny slither of time, that love-thrilled teenager she had once been, full of optimism for life and all that the world could show her. In adulthood, scarred by tragedy, cool and aloof she had undoubtedly become, that fleeting thought of happiness and abandon lifted her to where she could see and recognise the girl she had once been.

James too was transported back to the happiest time he had known. This revisited joy cut through the pain and challenges he had endured. The loss of his family, the diagnosis that had made him face-up to his own mortality, the exile from his home city. They had much trauma in common but they were remembering a moment of bliss that they had found in each other's arms.

Lizzie remembered what they had set out to do that day. Although she wanted to talk to James as the long-lost love that he was, she found the presence of mind to appear to observers, both colleagues and casual, to be a couple of tourists out admiring the sights of the city. She stood up and James did too. They both shared a second of laughter at nothing except their bewildering reunion. He looked into her eyes, savouring the story they told.

"I feel stupid now," he said, turning away to start walking. "only because it took so long for me to recognise you. You do look a little different, though. I remember the crazy eye make-up. If you had kept that look I would have spotted you right away."

"I had to tone it down. I couldn't see the police force approving of that particular fashion statement."

"I suppose they wouldn't understand why a police officer would be wearing a robber's mask."

"And a professor would be unlikely to look like you did."

Lizzie's reminder of her role brought James up-to-speed with their current purpose.

"You are my bodyguard-in-chief, I must try harder to remember that. I find myself concentrating on better memories."

"You look so different," she said, recalling the visual threat to the older generation that he must have posed back then. "I've had the sight of you in my head for so long I couldn't imagine what sort of person you would have matured into. Now you're a peace negotiator. That's a noble cause I'd say."

"And you are the keeper of the peace." He stopped and wrapped his palm around his forehead in disbelief at his own oversight, pressing hard on the uneven repairs below the skin. "Your name, it's Elizabeth isn't it? I thought about that too, convinced myself of so many names, none of them lasted in my mind. I know it wasn't Kiki, right enough."

"No, only you ever called me that. What about Sid? Where did that come from?"

"Sid Vicious, I was a fan."

They ambled through the galleries and corridors, past glass-fronted oak displays of the world's complex and colourful story. Their steps were slow and in time with each other. They chatted and edged their way to filling the gaping chasm that had existed between their different worlds, careful not to frighten each other away. Taking baby steps, not knowing where they were headed but finding the progression uplifting and exciting for them both. They spent a further hour in the museum, talking freely but not about the circumstances which had caused them to part. Neither gave much thought to the sides of the city that they had come from.

CHAPTER SIXTY-SEVEN

Outside on the street and in the brightness of daylight, they went to a café where Lizzie chose a spot with the safety of her principal in mind along with a wish to avoid being overheard by anyone, especially their remote custodians. Over lunch, they briefly summarised their career paths since leaving Belfast. The conversation between them was easy. Without delving too deeply, they both got some of the answers to questions they had asked themselves long ago. What was clearly established was that neither wanted to leave the other behind and both had felt wretched for having done so.

A mobile phone let out a tinny ring-ring imitation of a normal phone. It startled them a little. James had his phone concealed in his bag and was sure that he had switched it off before leaving the hotel. Lizzie reached into her jacket pocket and produced a phone which was the smallest version James had seen. She answered it curtly.

"Yes? . . . I see. Yes, he's here."

She handed the phone over the table to James. He put it to his ear.

"Hello."

"Hello Professor," said Martha Lascelle. "I hope I'm not disturbing anything."

"No it's alright Ms Lascelle."

"The 'event' you mentioned happened last night. It went as planned and we have received confirmation that it was authentic. It was suggested, at this end, that this indirectly links you to acts of violence, but I argued that it directly links you to an act of peace. I got my way on that score. The doubt has been eliminated and I look forward to our meeting tomorrow."

"Tomorrow then, goodbye."

He handed back the phone, lacking the knowledge of how to end a call on the unfamiliar model. They set off to walk to another of London's cathedrals of culture, passing through a small square of paths through manicured grass. Ambling tourists, skateboarders and picnicking families brought the tiny park to life. James stopped at an information sign set at head height. Lizzie saw an opportunity to check on her team. She walked on twenty yards and spotted first one then the other protection officer. She remained to await James' resumption of the journey. At that moment the professional task she and her team had been given became all too real.

A figure with a black woollen hat pulled down and a track jacket fully zipped up dashed from behind the sign that James was studying on Lizzie's blind side. He lunged at James knocking him to the ground then attacked him bodily by hunching over him to prevent him from getting up. Lizzie took in the scene and set off to assist. The fleeting thought that her principal could be attacked on a London park in broad daylight whilst she was supposed to be protecting him brought on something close to panic.

The two remote guards saw it happen too and broke cover to race to the scene. Before Lizzie reached James and his attacker, the disguised man, charged away from his victim and, luckily for Lizzie but unluckily for him, ran straight at her. Intending to side-step and make his escape, the figure went to Lizzie's right and into her outstretched leg. She had timed it to contact his trailing leg, therefore reducing the impact on her whilst still succeeding in bringing him down to the ground mainly by his own weight. He hit the tarmacked path and spilled James' shoulder bag onto the grass next to him. Lizzie dived on him like a vulture on a fresh carcass.

The attacker groaned in the pain of landing bodily on hard ground as well as having the wind knocked out of his lungs by Lizzie's knees on his torso. She pulled an already damaged arm up the man's back causing additional agony and rendering him completely under her control. She darted a glance at the two protectors and shook her head, indicating that they should not intervene further as she had the situation under control.

James had got back to his feet and, although shaken and breathing heavily, he approached the scene of the apprehension to try to make himself useful.

"Ahhh! It's just a bag, man, ahhh!" wailed the mugger.

Lizzie saw the tell-tale pallor, the gaunt, sunken cheeks and the broken teeth of the addict. This was no planned attack. It was an act of desperation and a clumsy one at that. She looked up at James.

"Are you alright?" she asked without a hint of having been in any way derailed.

"Yes, he just grabbed the bag. I don't think he wanted to do much harm. It was a bit scary though."

"Get your bag," she said whilst checking the prone man for weapons.

James quickly reclaimed the bag and gave it a cursory check. "It's fine. What are you going to do with him?"

Reluctant as she was to let a crime go unpunished, she had to prioritise the operation in hand. Lizzie kept a straight

341

face and said to James. "Do you want to give him a kicking?"

"Do I what?" said James in surprise.

"It's what happens to most muggers in the capital. The cops don't get involved. People usually break the legs of those who do this sort of thing."

It came a little late but James got the joke. It had been intended for the sole benefit of the thief.

"Let's give him ten yards' head start then we break his ribs. What do you say?"

Satisfied that the man posed no further threat and determined to avoid any distractions from the main task she let go of the man who scurried off across the grass, dragging a lame left leg, sustained on impact with the ground.

James patted dust from his jacket and trousers. Lizzie had no need of such adjustment, having landed on somebody and not the ground. The other users of the park resumed their leisure, silently consigning the experience to 'colourful city life.' Further nods from Lizzie to the team ensued and the procession resumed. Lizzie spotted a mobile phone on the ground at the point where James' bag had landed. Unseen by James, she picked it up and looked at it then at the back of James who was lifting the strap of his bag over his shoulder. The briefing she had been given by Commander Ian Kent came back to her mind. Any call made to or from that phone could contain a breakthrough in intelligence relating to the senior command of the I.R.A. That was what Kent had wanted. It would have been easy to simply slip the phone into her pocket and say nothing to James. The absence of it from the bag could easily be attributed to the thief. It was unusual for Lizzie to experience a moral dilemma but there was definitely one taking place within her. James noticed that she was slow to move. He turned to ask her.

"Shall we take a stroll?"

Lizzie was so full of happy memories of her youth, especially those with Sid in them, that the dilemma was answered in absolute clarity. Commander Kent would have to manage without his dream source of intelligence.

"Did this phone come out of your bag?"

James acknowledged ownership, effectively accepting that his covert use of the phone was at an end. He didn't care.

The remainder of the day was before them and neither knew if that would happen again. They were in no rush to draw the day of tourism to a close and the situation may have been different, had it not been for the additional pair of bodyguards. They had diligently kept their principal safe and their boss happy, but they did represent the reality of the present and James and Lizzie had to accept that.

At the hotel, they both felt like teenagers concluding a first date. She told him that she would see him at the negotiating venue the next day as she was travelling with him and Martha on alternating days.

"Thank you for today, Elizabeth. I've thought about this day for a long time, I don't mean the museums, you know."

"I have thought about it too," she said not looking directly at him. She spoke slowly and quietly. "We have jobs to do here and we should concentrate on our respective roles."

"I couldn't agree more," he said smiling at her.

"Don't look at me like that," she too cracked a smile.

"Like what?"

"You know."

"I'll be glad when we have finished what we have set out to do here. Perhaps I can look at you without restrictions."

"Is that you flirting, Professor?"

"I don't know, it's not something I've done much of."

"Goodnight, James."

"Goodnight Elizabeth."

CHAPTER SIXTY-EIGHT

The negotiations resumed and Martha was quick to afford credit for the gesture of good faith at Strangford. James was also keen to establish Martha's credentials.

"You have had your proof Ms Lascelle. Now I want some assurance that you speak with the authority of the British Government. What are you going to do about that?"

"I expected that, Professor. You are no doubt familiar with the Secretary of State for Northern Ireland?"

"I know who he is, I can't say I'm familiar with him," joked James.

"Well that is going to change. The Secretary of State has agreed to vouch for me in person. He wants to meet you."

"Does he now? That's your authority to negotiate I suppose," said James.

"And he'll be bringing the Prime Minister with him."

"The Prime Minister?"

"Yes, the Prime Minister. Be in no doubt Professor, that the British Government is fully behind this initiative."

"That's clear enough. When?" he asked whilst trying to comprehend this development.

"In a few days. It would be nice if we had some progress to report, to both of our respective authorities."

"Yes it would. I suggest that we begin with the list of names I gave you. I trust that you have had time to look into those people."

"I agree." Martha opened a file and took out several sheets of paper. "Before we discuss your proposals, I have some names for you to consider." She slipped the list across the table toward him. He looked at the list then placed it in his document case for later scrutiny.

Each name was discussed in turn. Old reasons for the non-participation in formal negotiations were aired and arguments for and against ensued. Bigger issues were thrashed out followed by lesser factors. Whether or not a person who was believed to have attended an I.R.A. funeral could be linked to acts of violence because of that alone was discussed at length.

This process continued all day and for the next five days. Meanwhile, James had revealed the nominated participants that he had been given and lengthy discussions took place in other locations.

Briefed with what was known about the people on the list, James argued against the inclusion of some whilst accepting, conditionally, some of the others. Slowly, a picture emerged. Agreement followed disagreement then more disagreement and eventually more agreement. When acceptable terms of reference were discussed in fine detail, both Martha and James knew that the end, of the preliminary negotiations anyway, was in sight.

James looked forward to being alone with Lizzie. She explained it to her team as an important part of the security operation that she held regular briefings with the principals, although the meetings with Martha were over much more swiftly. There was an unspoken understanding that their

346

conversations could reach full informality once the security operation was at an end. It came as a surprise to Lizzie and Martha when he announced that he was suspending the negotiations with immediate effect as he had to return to Boston.

He suggested that the interval be used wisely by both sides. The individuals who had been mutually agreed upon had to be confirmed as available and fully briefed to participate at short notice. Lizzie escorted James to Heathrow Airport and left him with his appointed bodyguard. At the moment of departure through the gate, he turned to look at her and swapped his bag to his left hand. He shook Lizzie's hand and appeared to be thanking her for her efforts. His words, unheard by anyone else, told of a different sentiment.

"I will be back, you know, Elizabeth. It's wrong to leave important business unfinished." He smiled. She smiled back.

"Yes, there is a lot of unfinished business here." She picked a speck of non-existent cotton from his jacket. "I'll see you when you've done what you have to do over the pond."

He stepped away and out of sight through the gate. She turned and headed to the airport police office with a spring in her step she had not felt for a long time.

CHAPTER SIXTY-NINE

James was back two days later. His shadowing protection officers escorted him to his hotel where he received a call from Lizzie.

"Welcome back, Professor." She could not disguise that she was pleased that he was back.

"Thank you Superintendent." He sounded surprisingly formal.

"Oh, I just wanted to confirm that you will be meeting Mrs Lascelle in the morning."

"Yes, of course, that's what I came back to do."

She experienced confusion and a hint of embarrassment. Had she misread what they had spoken of at Heathrow? She snapped back into formality.

"Fine. You will be collected in the morning." She ended the call.

He put down the phone and began chewing his thumb. There was work to do and he had to prepare. It was not anybody's business why he had put the talks on hold to return to America. Everybody had more than enough to be getting on with in his absence. They were down to the fine detail and had to start thinking about the next phase. He was not going to be a part of that. He was sent to conduct the initial negotiations only and that was nearly complete. He looked at his reflection in the mirror on the vanity table. He stared at himself for long enough to lose all sense of time.

*

Behind drawn curtains, in a room in an unoccupied flat above a travel agent's shop in Belfast, six men sat around a table.

"So there you have it gentlemen, our Professor Coleman has made good progress negotiating a platform from which formal talks can now take place. He will see to it that our political representatives will take over the next stage of the talks. Any historic links to alleged acts of violence have been thrashed out. A form of words has been agreed and this can no longer be used by the British as an excuse for not talking to us. We will enter into this from a position of strength. We don't have to concede anything, not at this stage. We intend to secure the release of all political prisoners in British jails and have our claim to self-government recognised in the long term. Our current operations are to continue, but we will have to call a temporary halt to direct action soon. That will be the price of our place at the table. This is your chance to speak before this gets going."

"How do we know that the British are going to follow up on these preliminary talks? It might be some game we aren't in on," asked a previously unheard voice.

"We said from the outset that we had to trust Coleman to speak for us and he has. All we know about the negotiations is what he reports to us. He told me today something that confirms that the British government are serious about this. In one week, Coleman and the woman who's been negotiating for the British are going to meet the British Prime Minister at a secret location. This means that they accept what Coleman has proposed."

"Why a secret location? You'd think they would want to mouth off to the press about it?" Mahon was asked.

"Because, officially, these preliminary talks have never taken place. They still need to be able to deny it if it goes wrong. When the time comes, the cease-fire will be announced as our initiative, nothing to do with them. That should win back some popular support we lost after the Warrington incident."

Nothing was said for a few seconds. Copious cigarette smoke hung in horizontal strata across the room. Chair legs moved on the nylon carpeted floor, people looked at each other for non-verbal signs of agreement.

"What happens now, Niall?"

"Coleman's work is not finished. He is still working with the British woman on the final details of the agenda for the formal talks. The meeting with the British P.M. will take place when that's been finalised."

Kevin Harraley remained unmoved.

"I don't like it. As soon as we stop our campaign of active resistance, as soon as we stop being a threat, we become weak and all of our years of fighting will have been for nothing."

"Aye."

"Right."

"True."

The murmuring was minimal but it did confirm that not everyone was in agreement with the proposed move toward peace. Harraley had other ideas to put to the meeting.

"I propose that we enter into these talks from the strongest position possible. We make one clinical and strategic strike, one operation that will destabilise the British in their own back yard, with minimal risk of collateral damage and maximum strength to enter negotiations. Everything is in place to make that happen. There's an active cell in England ready to act on our say-so."

"Have you been listening at all Kevin?" said an exasperated Niall Mahon. "This is an opportunity to move forward not backward. There must be no acts of aggression. We are going to enter the period of ceasefire ready and able to maintain it. The risk of retaliation is too great, and we risk that the peace talks won't take place at all."

"Yeah!"

"Aye."

The collective assent was louder and more compelling than the earlier disagreement had been.

"So are we in agreement, gentlemen?" appealed Mahon.

All concurred. Harraley said nothing.

"What about you Kevin?" asked Mahon.

"I'll go by what the committee decides," said Harraley. "But my active unit will be ready when the fucking wheel drops off, right enough."

"Meeting adjourned," declared Mahon.

Twenty-five minutes later, Kevin Harraley made a call from a payphone. It was answered by an Irishman in a boarding house on the south coast of England. He was the sole member of the active unit Harraley had suggested in the committee meeting of the senior command. Once he was satisfied that he was speaking to the correct person he wasted no time.

"The senior command has approved the action we discussed earlier. What do you need?" asked Harraley.

"I have the equipment already. I need details of the location, the transport and the timings."

"You sound like you want somebody on the inside. You'll be lucky."

"I am lucky. You should know that by now. What about your man doing the negotiating, is he a party to this?" asked the man in England.

"The negotiator's job is to set up peace talks," explained Harraley. "He has no connection to any military operations. It will be best if he doesn't know what we intend to do."

"Who is this man doing all the talking?"

"He's an ex-pat living in America, name of Coleman, James Patrick Coleman."

Harraley imparted the name as an aside only. He could not have imagined that the man he was calling remembered James from seventeen years previously.

"Is he the same man whose brother was shot by the British years ago?"

"That's right, he is," answered Harraley in surprise.

"Ha! That's brilliant, so it is. Find out where he is. I'll pay him a call. He's going to be my man on the inside."

"How are you going to get him to help you?" asked Harraley in disbelief at the audacity.

"I've got dirt on Coleman, we go back a long way. He'll do whatever I fucking say, right enough."

"There's another thing you ought to know," added Kevin Harraley. "The target is bigger than we thought, much bigger."

CHAPTER SEVENTY

James was surprised to hear the ringing tone of his mobile phone. Until then, it had been him making the calls. The voice was instantly familiar and caused a chill down his spine.

"Well well, University boy!"

Nearly twenty years had passed since the last and only time they had met, but the years fell away in an instant. James felt exposed and vulnerable. Only people within the Republican senior command had the number of his mobile phone. Someone had given it to Darry, and it could not be for any good reason.

"Nice to have a catch up, so it is," teased McTandlyn. "Cat got your tongue, eh, University boy?"

"What do you want?" asked James, who was dreading hearing the answer.

"You, ya wee shite, I want you, right enough."

"What are you talking about?"

"The policeman outside your bedroom, I either shoot him or you slip away and come and join me for a wee chat. Use the fire escape. What's it going to be, University boy?"

James' mind was a storm of conflicting thoughts. The night of the Lodale murder flashed across as did the pained face of his father, shots were fired and each one echoed as though there was a steep valley in him that would not let that sound end. When his mind finally managed to gain some semblance of order, he had to act to prevent the murder of the cop at his door.

"Okay! I'll go down the fire escape. Where are you?"

"I'll ring you when you're out of the hotel, so I will," ordered McTandlyn and he hung up.

James slid open the window making minimal noise. He stepped out onto the iron staircase and slid the window back to being almost closed. Edging sideways down to the ground he crossed the car park and left the hotel complex. As he crossed the street his phone rang again.

"Go to the junction with the betting shop on the corner. Go down there," said McTandlyn before hanging up again. James complied, knowing that he was not dealing with a reasonable person. He passed the betting shop and turned into the side street as he walked along the pavement. The bright lighting of the main road gave way to a dimly-lit, quiet avenue. As he passed a row of parked cars, a passenger door opened and a tiny light came on inside the car. James climbed into the passenger seat.

"Well now, University boy. Aren't you the big noise now?"

"You're taking a big risk being here Darry," said James trying to lessen the feeling of helplessness inside him.

James glanced at McTandlyn's face. He did not recognise him but his voice was unmistakable. He was determined to avoid being intimidated by McTandlyn, but bravado and bluff were not his natural assets. He knew that this man had a hair-trigger and was capable of killing with barely any thought for the victim or the consequences.

"I'm a free man, so I am. Not like you, shackled to the Englishman's table asking for crumbs and hand-outs."

"It's a pity you see it like that Darry."

James found that using the man's name made him less menacing. McTandlyn's contrasting refusal to address him by name was probably similarly driven.

"This is the future, political solutions, not bombs and bullets. Your methods are history. It's time you moved with the changes." James spoke with a calm that belied his inner discomfort.

"You and those other cowards are giving up!" declared McTandlyn contemptuously, "Giving up our rights to have our own country. The only thing those English bastards understand is fear."

"That's in the past now Darry, the armed struggle may have contributed to the position of strength that we – "

"Strength? Don't make me laugh, University boy. You've given away what strength there was, earned by the likes of me who had the balls to make them fear us."

Darry had opened the side window and begun tapping the wing mirror through a spider's web. James remembered seeing him do that once before. He was not to be put off.

"So that's the Irishman you want the world to know, is it Darry? No respect without fear? Well you're living in the past. You're a dinosaur and are about to become extinct."

"I don't want to hear your shite, University boy. You hear this . . . you're going to help me with a little business, so you are. We're going to reclaim the power now."

McTandlyn continued tapping the glass until the creator of the web appeared. He nipped it between his thumb and forefinger.

"I don't know what you're expecting me to do," said James. McTandlyn told him.

"You're going to put someone right where I want them to be. You, the negotiator, you can get me close enough to shove a giant rocket up the arse of the British."

"I'm conducting negotiations for peace, for Christ's sake. Why would I do anything to help you commit more murder?" James spoke with increasing confidence.

Darry did not reply straight away. He sat forward and turned his head to focus on James. In little more than a whisper, he said.

"The armed struggle goes on, University boy, and you're about to become a part of it, no wait a minute, you've already been a part of it, haven't you?" James knew where this was going but was unable to do or say anything about it. McTandlyn squeezed the last trace of life out of the spider. He closed the window, sat back in his seat and settled into a more comfortable position.

"You've got a dirty little secret. You were a member of the I.R.A. unit that rubbed out Superintendent Arnie Cullen all those years ago."

"Cullen, did you say Cullen?" asked James, his mind racing to unpleasant conclusions.

"Don't make out you don't remember, University boy."

James thought about how Lizzie had left Belfast for England at the same time he had left for America. She had spoken about it being a terrible time for her. He pictured the young woman standing at the window holding open the curtain to witness a murder, the murder of her father. His mind flashed to the girl with the wild eye make-up who he had last seen getting into her father's car to go home. The two images fused together until he could see the same car in both places, outside the University gate and in the driveway at the side of the house where McTandlyn had shot the man.

James felt the cold through his body. The blood left his cheeks and although Darry McTandlyn did not fully know why, he knew that he had James on the end of a hook. Darry pushed the cigarette lighter button in and reached inside his coat pocket for a pack of Benson and Hedges gold. The lighter clicked out and soon the inside of the car was billowing with pale grey fog. James tried to redress the imbalance with some hard truths. The blizzard of his thoughts cleared sufficiently to allow him to say,

"Who would believe you Darry? I mean, you're not exactly a star witness for the prosecution, are you? You're a fugitive. You can't walk into a police station and give a statement." McTandlyn smiled.

"That fool of a driver, remember him? He'd been grassing up his mates for years. He didn't know your name, only where we picked you up. The British soaked up everything he said – before we shot him. There's another thing you should know, University boy. That black car we used for that job, I didn't get chance to burn it. Your fingerprints were all over it. The police have been looking for the owner of those prints for near twenty years. How they'd love to put a name to them now, the other man in the hit squad who killed one of their own. You'll not just be dropped as the negotiator, like a hot turd, ha ha! You'll probably get arrested too. Peace talks? Away and bollocks."

James' mind chewed through too many possibilities for any solutions to this problem to able to take any recognisable form. There had, briefly, existed a real chance for peace and it was all hanging in the balance because of a murder nearly twenty years before, a murder that he had played no part in. Or had he?

The ramifications of that revelation catapulted in a high arc through his thoughts. The reason he had been chosen to conduct the negotiations was partly because he was pro-peace and partly because he had no connection with any terrorist activity. If that were to come to light, all of the progress made so far would be valueless. The British government would have to discontinue the talks and the violence and killing would continue as it had done for too many years.

His heart sank as he considered the human misery it would cause, but it was when he thought about Lizzie that his resolve hit its nadir. What would she think of him? She would dismiss him as just another terrorist, hell bent on killing people, but it was far worse than that. She would see him as complicit in the murder of her father, a murder she had witnessed and borne the scars ever since. McTandlyn had manipulated the situation to his advantage. Knowledge is power and he wielded it over James as an executioner would wield an axe. One swing and everything he held dear would be taken from him.

He cast himself back into his memory, to an ugly time and a painful place. He could have said 'No' on that night. He could have told them that nobody from the family of the late Philip Magnus Coleman wanted to be there to witness the avenging of his death. He should have stood up to his father, despite his evident grief. What had he really expected to happen? Had he been so naïve as to think that the mission he was going to bear witness to might involve anything less than a tit-for-tat sectarian killing? He put his head in his hands. McTandlyn knew he had James where he wanted him.

"Now, it'll be like old times for us," he said feigning nostalgic pathos. "We're going to make our mark in London and this time everybody's going to know about it."

"What are you planning to do?" he asked in quiet acceptance.

"Ah no, University boy. It's what 'we' are 'going' to do."

CHAPTER SEVENTY-ONE

Damian Alty had become all-consumed with the prospect of breaking a story which could bring down the Government. He was less concerned about spending a hundred thousand pounds for information about it. He was fully capable of finding out the names of the negotiators himself and saving his newspaper some money. It had even crossed his mind to keep the hundred grand for himself. He had a name to go on, Elizabeth Cullen. All he had to do was follow her and she would lead him straight to the nest of treachery that would be his 'holy grail.'

Employing the services of two hired hands, he maintained a primitive but committed surveillance on Lizzie. Monitoring the entrance to New Scotland Yard and the police vehicles she would ordinarily use. When this pattern changed and a new black Range Rover began collecting her from her office at set times, Alty sensed that the negotiations must have begun and the need to find out who and where became an urgent one.

When Lizzie was seen to enter a Park Lane hotel, Alty wasted no time sweeping in and gleaning as much information as he could. Photographs were taken of Lizzie and anyone she spoke to. This included several of her close-protection team and a well-dressed, middle-aged woman. A hundred pounds in cash placed in the appropriate pocket of a member of the hotel staff resulted in a name for the woman. 'Good value,' he thought. He could have paid fifty thousand of the Tribune's money for that name.

That the British had appointed a negotiator was less important than the name of the individual nominated to speak for the other side. It was that person who was the key to blowing the story wide open. The British Government, who do not negotiate with terrorists, would fall apart when that name came to light. The surveillance operation on Elizabeth Cullen had to be stepped up and become more discreet.

*

Lizzie drove to the hotel where James was staying. By using an unmarked police car, she had passed unnoticed by the people Alty had deployed to watch her. She was confused and anxious: confused about the coldness that James had shown her after returning from America, and anxious because he had demanded assurance that the present security arrangements were as effective as they could have been. He had expressed no such doubts up until then. Why, after the negotiations were complete and agreement on the structure of formal talks had been reached, was he so nervous? All that remained was for him to meet the Prime Minister and the Northern Ireland Secretary. It was to be a low-key meeting and its purpose was merely for the P.M. to thank those involved.

He wanted to know the details and, whilst he didn't need to know everything that she had arranged, she intended to tell him enough to satisfy his concerns. To do that she had the TOP SECRET file in her bag on the passenger seat of her car.

She spoke to the man she had posted outside James' hotel room before knocking on the door. He answered it and stepped back to let her in. She wore a dark-blue, two-piece, trouser suit and cream blouse, an ensemble she had habitually donned for her work. James was informal in shirt-sleeves. She had not been inside this hotel room. It was slightly larger than the earlier ones he had occupied. It had a few facilities that the others had lacked, not least a

362

typewriter and a fax machine on a desk lit by an angle-poise lamp. On another table by the wall and on it was a tall jug of water and four short glass tumblers.

"Thanks for coming Elizabeth." A hint of warmth had returned to his voice. She found this reassuring.

"That's alright. I heard you were concerned about the security arrangements for tomorrow."

"Yes, I am. Please sit down."

He pulled out a chair at the table and guided her to it. His hands were shaking and his movements were uncoordinated. She noticed that he was sweating in a room of moderate temperature. She sat at the table and he sat opposite her.

"It's this meeting tomorrow. I think somebody's going to make an attempt on my life."

"Is there some reason for thinking that? Has anybody made a threat toward you?"

"Well not directly. I can't explain it. I just feel, you know, like it's all gone so smoothly so far and now, oh! I don't know."

He put his sweat-soaked head in his hands. She wanted to reach out to touch him, to reassure and to comfort. She stopped short of doing so.

"What can I do to put your mind at ease?" she said soothingly, as she had done professionally many times with worried and traumatised victims of crime.

"Please just run me through the visit," he asked.

She took the folder from her shoulder bag and, without allowing him to see any of the documents, she referred to the sheet at the front of the file and told him the intended time of departure the following morning. He asked a series of questions that really did not need to be answered, such as what transport and who would be taking him. Each time she consulted the file and answered his questions calmly and patiently. He stood up and moved to the table behind where Lizzie was sitting.

"Excuse me, I need some water. Do you want a drink of anything, I should have offered earlier, I'm sorry." He was still visibly nervous.

"Not for me, thanks," she said, folding the file shut.

James took the jug and began pouring water into one of the tumblers. He stopped and placed the half-full jug back on the table next to the edge. He pushed the jug over toward Lizzie sending a litre of water all over her back and the left side of her leg.

"Oh shit!" he exclaimed in the instant horror of embarrassment.

She leapt to her feet and tried to shake as much of the unwelcome cascade off her clothes before it had a chance to soak in. She put the file down on the table and used both hands to wipe the water away. James swore and apologised.

"Elizabeth, I am so sorry, my fingers, they just . . . You're soaked! I'll get a towel."

"It's fine," she said, remembering her early years in uniform when she had been regularly covered with blood, spit, vomit and rain, often in the same day.

"There's a hairdryer in the bathroom," suggested James. "That might help if you want to dry off a bit."

"Yes, it might be the answer," she said, knowing that there was an officer under her command outside the door who was not to know of it at any cost. James continued to express his regret at his clumsiness as Lizzie went into the bathroom. She closed the door and the hairdryer noise started. James went to the table and opened the file. He took the first piece of paper which was marked TOP SECRET and, with trembling fingers, slotted it into the fax machine and pressed 'Copy.'

The whine of the hotel-room hairdryer went high and low as Lizzie shook it across the wet cloth of her trousers and jacket. James took another sheet of paper and hovered over the machine, willing it to process the first one through its rollers. He slotted the second sheet, pressed 'Copy' again and quickly put the first one back into the file. He took out a third sheet, glancing at the closed bathroom door as he did so. How could he possibly explain this if she emerged from the en suite and found what he was doing? The second sheet fell into the spent tray and the third went through the same slot and began to be copied. The hairdryer stopped and so did his breathing. His heart beat a rapid, pounding tattoo through his body.

He looked down at the table. The third paper was still moving through the fax machine at an unacceptably slow rate. 'Come on!" he mouthed silently at the inanimate object that was torturing him with its tardiness.

The hairdryer sound started up again allowing a modicum of reprieve to his angst. The third sheet passed through and was replaced in correct order in the file. He put the folder back in the place where Lizzie had hurriedly placed it. He snatched the three copies from the tray of the fax machine and slipped then into his own attaché case, which was at the side of an armchair by the window. He busily mopped the water off the table top and the back of Lizzie's chair with tissues. When the hairdryer sound stopped, and did not restart, Lizzie opened the bathroom door and stepped out.

"It's not perfectly dry but it will be okay," she announced.

"Good, I am relieved to hear it."

He seemed a fraction calmer than he had been when she had arrived. They stood facing each other and both appreciated the funny side of the water incident.

"I have to go," she said, slowly she turned to walk to the door.

"Elizabeth?" she turned back and smiled at him.

"Yes James."

"I am really glad I got to meet you again after all these years. The circumstances were unusual for a reunion. Don't you think?"

"Yes, I wasn't expecting this either," she said glancing briefly at the floor before looking back at him. "Do you think we could meet again, once this work is done here?"

"That sounds, well, great. I would love that," he said. "But we both have busy lives a long way from each other. I've had you in my thoughts all this time. You were always going to be there anyway, that won't change, whatever happens."

"Whatever happens? Are you still convinced that somebody's going to bump you off?" she joked about his earlier paranoia.

"It does seem somewhat irrational doesn't it?" he conceded.

"It is," she said. "and you'll be okay, I've got it covered."

"Thank you, and Elizabeth?"

"Yes?"

He took her hands in both of his. It was the first time he had touched her skin since Belfast.

"This work we're doing, it is bigger than us, both of us and it'll be worth it!"

She didn't fully understand what he was getting at. She put it down to his focus on the negotiations and his nerve-induced clumsiness. Looking at his face made her think about the time they could have spent together, how she could have witnessed the changes in him and shared them. The child they had conceived, never far from her thoughts, might have grown up in his image. He may know nothing of the boy but it was possible that he was aware of the newspaper article that Damian Alty had written about her. How would James feel about the child's existence if he were to be told? Would he blame her as she had blamed herself? This was not the time, but the end was in sight for the negotiations. She would disclose all to him when the time was appropriate. If he really was that decent, warm human-being that she had always believed him to be, he would receive the news positively and with compassion.

She smiled, let go of his hands, headed out of the room and closed the door.

James sat on the armchair and put his head in his hands again. He moved his palms away and stared into them before refocussing to look in the vanity mirror on the wall table. He let out a long breath, reached down into the attaché case and took out the three copies of documents from the security file. He read them then took out a mobile phone. He dialled the number and waited for the signal to connect. When it did there was no voice at the end of the line.

"I've got it!" he said.

CHAPTER SEVENTY-TWO

At 3.00am, as the daytime personnel of the Special Branch close protection team slept in their three-star hotel near to Hyde Park in West London, a figure in black entered the rear car park below the wall on which the two CCTV security cameras were mounted. A scan of the building showed that the electrical supply to the cameras was externally provided and had no reliance on the service inside the hotel. Where the electrical cable reached the junction box, the shadowy intruder applied a small suppressor to the cable, effectively breaking the circuit and suspending the electrical current to the cameras.

He retreated to a recess over an archaic and long-unused coal-hole. He waited in the silent darkness for fifteen minutes. When he was sure that his interference to the camera system had not been noticed by anyone inside the building, he went to a row of customer's cars and ducked down between the cars and the back wall of the compound. Taking out another electrical suppressor, he applied it to the door lock of a black Range Rover. A thin strip of metal slipped from his right sleeve and into his gloved hand. He slotted it between the side window and the rubber seal below it. He felt for the hook to grip the interior wire then pulled it up to release the door locking mechanism. The door came open and he reached in to release the rear door. He closed the driver's door and slipped into the back seat. He raised the flat base of the seat to reveal the coarsely spray-painted fuselage over the fuel tank.

From another pocket he took a small package, slowly and carefully unwrapping it from the soft linen it had been carried in. With near-surgical skill, he attached the device to a dip in the metal panel with strong tape. Having completed his installation, he replaced the seat, checking it and the features around it for any sign of interference. He slipped out and closed the door, holding down the locking mechanism by the outer handle. He used the soft linen square to wipe the doors of any evidence that they had been touched by anything. The suppressor was removed and he tried the door locks. They were secure again. The suppressor was detached from the camera cable on the wall and replaced in his pocket. At 3.24am the hotel car park was again unattended and remained so until the morning delivery vans started to arrive.

CHAPTER SEVENTY-THREE

The venue for the meeting was a Victorian mansion off Kensington High Street. Once owned and occupied by the Earl of Penrith as a second home, it had since changed hands several times and was presently owned by an old school friend of the Chancellor of the Exchequer. When the suggestion was made to find secret premises for the meeting between the P.M. and the preliminary negotiators, the house in Kensington was deemed to fit the bill.

The owner, who was overseas and unlikely to return for some months, had authorised a Knightsbridge property agent to furnish a junior official at the Foreign Office with keys and security codes. The low-key approach to security meant that the individuals involved all belonged to different government departments and were less likely to make links and therefore leaks. Whilst that method had merit, it lacked the thoroughness of a full security review. The operation was built on ignorance, the ethos being that the fewer people who knew, the safer it all was. One person who was not satisfied with this was Detective Superintendent Elizabeth Cullen.

The only avenue of protest open to her was Commander Ian Kent, who had also been the only source of updated information to enable her to co-ordinate the security operation for the meetings between the negotiators. She closed the blind in her office and turned up the radio playing old pop music.

"How are we expected to keep these people from being shot in the middle of Kensington High Street?" she asked, not expecting a straight answer to such a leading question.

"It's not in the middle of the High Street, Elizabeth," he began with a paternal air. "It is in a large house with minimal approaches and a secure rear courtyard for vehicular access. The negotiators have your team stuck to them and the P.M. doesn't go alone either. They have to meet somewhere and that somewhere has to be off the radar. I can't think of a better venue, myself."

"I can," she fired back. "The front of that house has people walking by only inches away, and the courtyard is overlooked by at least a dozen taller buildings that haven't been swept or sealed off." Realising that she was getting heated, Lizzie drew breath and her tone of voice came down a measure. "With due respect, Sir, we are underestimating the people we are trying to protect our principals from. Professor Coleman is convinced there's going to be an attempt on his life. I had to go and calm him down yesterday evening."

"I know you want this to go smoothly," he said moving away from her as he spoke before turning to face her again. "We all do. But we can only 'advise' the Prime Minister. He doesn't have to take our advice, he's the bloody Prime Minister!"

He opened his attaché case and placed in it the daily briefing sheet for the operation.

*

Training in close protection, surveillance, advanced driving and firearms along with eighteen years' experience in a variety of operational roles, mainly in plain clothes, had made Ben Wiper an ideal candidate for inclusion in Superintendent Cullen's security detail. The added bonus of him being single and able to commit to long-term operations without becoming a welfare case enhanced his suitability still further. At 5' 10" and of average build, he cut an unremarkable figure. His light brown hair was thinning, he was clean shaven and largely uncommunicative when in company. He could be alongside a target in a lift without leaving a memory of his presence. He saw a lot yet was seen a little. When he had to speak, his soft north-east accent was difficult to place, but he had the ability to recognise the origins of many accents, home and abroad. For two weeks, Ben had been one of the three possible bodyguards tasked with collecting James from one of the four hotels he had been staying in, all within three miles of Central London.

Ben arrived at the Dolphin Hotel in West London where, on the evening before, he had left James who was referred to in the secure briefing document as his 'principal.' Over the previous few days, Ben had what, for him, been long and intense conversations with James. By anybody else's standards they had spoken very little. Applying reverse psychology to his surveillance experiences, he knew that an irrational manoeuvre by a target either exposed his follower or made them believe that the target was onto them. Having driven the black Range Rover clockwise around the block containing the Dolphin Hotel, Ben deposited the car in the under-croft and set off to walk the same circuit anti-clockwise before entering the hotel. He went up the stairs to Room 414 and knocked.

James was ready to go, apart from putting on his jacket and collecting his document case and contents, which lay on a side-table near the main window alongside a clock set on a wooden plinth. Ben stood by a plain white closed door with the keys to the Range Rover dangling in his hand. James made a flustered mess of putting the papers into order whilst trying to open the document case. Ben's patience lasted until he began to doubt that he was going to arrive at the venue on time.

"Do you need a hand with that?" he offered.

"Thanks, but it's okay. Actually, I don't know why I'm struggling with this thing. There's a better case in that cupboard behind you. Could you pass it to me please?" said James without looking directly at Ben.

It briefly crossed Ben's mind to tell him to get it himself, but he had learned long before not to court confrontation with a principal.

"Sure," he said and he turned and opened the door of the full-length cupboard.

Reaching into the unlit space within, that was less than a square metre, Ben felt the ironing board and sweeping brush then he dipped his knees to find the case James had asked for. Unable to see anything like a case among the detergent bottles and cleaning equipment, he started to straighten up when he was hit with considerable force on the back of the head. He slumped in unconscious form into the cupboard, crushing and damaging most of the items in there. He came to a stop with his lower half crumpled across the carpeted floor outside. James stood over the dormant bodyguard holding the clock with the wooden plinth, trying to make his own breathing start again.

James checked that Ben was still breathing, then he took the car keys from his hand and pulled off his tan leather jacket. In a shoulder strap sat a black handgun, the sight of which made James suspend his breathing again. He replaced the clock on the side-table then, using two pairs of socks, he tied the ankles and then the wrists of the man who had been detailed to protect him from attack. Finally, he covered Ben's mouth with a sticking plaster, again checking that he could breathe, and bundled his legs into the cupboard curling him into a foetal position. The inside of the cupboard door had no handle, so James was satisfied that Ben would find it difficult to escape when he regained consciousness. He went to the phone and dialled a number. The recipient of the call answered without speaking. James said,

"It's done."

In less than a minute, there was a faint tap on the door. James peered through the spyhole before unlocking it and pulling the door open. Darry McTandlyn stepped inside.

"Where is he?" he demanded.

"Out cold, gagged and tied up," answered James. "Here's his jacket, as you wanted."

Darry snatched the jacket and searched the pockets. Not finding anything of interest he snapped.

"Show me where."

"He's in the cupboard." James nodded toward the closed door.

Darry opened it and stepped back to allow light in. He dipped and pulled the gun from the strap. He held it in the palm of his hand and examined the side view of it.

"A fucking Glock, that's shite. I thought these eejits had Smith and Wessons."

He flicked out the cylinder and saw that it was loaded before pushing it back into place. He stood up and pointed the gun at the unconscious man.

"Don't" blabbed James with low volume but clear panic in his voice. He quickly realised that he was unlikely to convince Darry that he should not kill the cop on his say-so alone. "The noise, it will bring them here to investigate the shots. We have a more important task now Darry. Keep your mind on that. You'll get your scalp soon enough."

Darry grinned. Moving the gun from one hand to the other, he slipped on Ben's jacket then placed the weapon in the inside pocket. James closed the cupboard door again, concealing the comatose but alive bodyguard inside.

"Keys, University boy, come on."

Unseen by McTandlyn, James slipped a letter addressed to Superintendent Elizabeth Cullen, and marked Private and Confidential, onto the table and at the side of the clock. He handed over the car keys and they headed out to the stairway and down to the car park. James walked behind McTandlyn. Nothing was said by either of them.

They got into the Range Rover and Darry lit a cigarette. He fired up the engine and, with a slight squeal of rubber on the shiny, concrete floor, they headed out into the London sunshine. The vehicle and its occupants looked largely the same as they had done the day before, but on that day, peace talks were not on the agenda.

CHAPTER SEVENTY-FOUR

For breakfast, Martha Lascelle had enjoyed smoked haddock with a poached egg on it, rich Columbian coffee and a flick through the complimentary broadsheets. Her Park Lane hotel claimed to be five-star and, in those lavish surroundings of chandeliers, tapestries and gold leaf, styled as a mediaeval Moorish palace, Martha would have agreed with that rating if asked. The sunlight was filtered through horizontal blinds, giving the room a timeless, colonial air.

On the brink of handing the negotiating baton on to parliamentary officials and politicians from both sides, she had the feeling of a job well done. It was tinged with the remote possibility that she had overlooked some detail that would, if not addressed, render her considerable efforts a failure. The job that she and James Patrick Coleman had taken on was merely a first step, many more stages and obstacles needed to be overcome before a lasting peace could be contemplated. But it was not yet in the public domain. That was for others to tell. All that could be done was for the planned meeting between James, herself and the Prime Minister to take place unhindered. It was for James, on behalf of the Republican movement in Northern Ireland, and herself, on behalf of the Government of the U.K. to formally acknowledge that peace talks could commence.

She had known from the outset that there were ruthless and driven individuals who would stop at nothing to scupper the preliminary talks. To kill her would be an obvious way of doing that, re-igniting their perceived war and setting peace back years. If she did not assent, no further negotiations could progress. What she had managed to agree with James had been achieved through hard-nosed yet intelligent argument and counter-argument. This had produced the best chance for peace in a generation. Martha had to get to the rendezvous point in one piece.

Henry Boult stepped up to the side of Martha's breakfast table. He was of rugby-forward build and wore a high-street bought grey suit and plain blue tie under a blue, three-quarter length anorak of lower quality. He had been acting as her daytime bodyguard throughout the negotiation period. A former paratrooper, Henry had been recruited from a Regional Crime Squad in the East Midlands and Martha had grown to enjoy his company. As was her way with all colleagues, regardless of status or longevity, she called him by his first name and insisted that he do the same. She looked up from her newspaper and peered at him from over her spectacles.

"Good morning Henry. How are you today?"

"I'm well, thank you Martha. You sound upbeat but you always do, I've found."

"I have every reason. We wouldn't be going to report no news now, would we?"

Henry nodded an acceptance of her logic. He knew where they were going, who Martha was going to meet and what it was she was going to tell him. He also knew how crucial it was that he got her there and exactly what was riding on this meeting. It was not simply the orders from Superintendent Cullen, or the pride he took in carrying out his duties, although he had been outside the door whilst the lengthy negotiations had taken place. On this job, he knew there was far more at stake. He would have preferred to have gone high-profile. Overt and rigorous security measures rather than the low-key, low-staffing option to match the level of secrecy of the negotiations that he was facilitating.

Martha folded and put down her newspaper, delicately wiped the tips of her fingers on the linen napkin and stood up to leave. She carried her own document case as she had insisted on throughout.

"Are you sure you won't change your mind about the Kevlar?"

"Quite sure, thank you Henry. What's the point of a girl trying to keep her figure just to look like the little Michelin man in one of those things? I'll be fine."

"I'll bring the car up to the front steps," he said. "Please wait for me to collect you from the lobby. Outside this building and at the venue, no more than a foot away from me, okay?"

He had a pleasant way of giving instructions that Martha found easy to comply with. She nodded her agreement and followed him to the reception desk. She took possession of some mail and opened it to read as Henry left through the revolving doors. Within a minute he returned and Martha set off to the exit. They passed through the revolving doors with Henry forming a human shield for Martha all the way to the rear door of the Range Rover. He closed her door and she disappeared behind darkened glass. Henry slipped into the driver's seat. To the eyes of the world, a middle-aged woman in a business suit being driven to an appointment just as at every hotel on Park Lane all day, every day.

Lizzie had travelled to the venue in Kensington alone in order to liaise with her colleagues in the Prime Minister's protection team. They too were less than content about the arrangements. Once she had entered the house, a call was made to the office of the Daily Tribune. Alty felt the hand of journalistic destiny on his shoulder. He headed off to Kensington to expose the lies of the British Government and make himself a star on a 'Watergate' scale. He arrived at Kensington and spoke to his man at the scene. Hearing that only Elizabeth Cullen had arrived was good news, the others were yet to make an appearance. He primed his camera, having opted not to use one of the Tribune's own photographers, on the grounds that he was not prepared to share a stage at the award ceremony with anyone. Leaving the front of the house, he walked back to Kensington High Street and along the street behind the house to assess the likelihood of his targets arriving there.

CHAPTER SEVENTY-FIVE

At 9.10am, the black Range Rover containing James and Darry entered Kensington High Street. After crawling along in nearly stationary traffic, Darry turned right and headed steadily and calmly down a side street. It was three streets away from the venue. Having read the illicitly-obtained documents, James knew the name of the place they were going to. A left turn into a wide alley which ran behind the high commercial buildings of the main road and the car slowed to walking pace. A high arch presented the entrance to a multi-storey car park, for permit holders only but there was a sign announcing that the barrier was under repair. Darry steered the huge car under the arch and up a ramp to the first level of parking directly about the shops on the High Street. Out of the sunshine but lit by slits of frosted glass and strip-lights above, the car gradually moved up and up until it reached the penultimate floor. Bright sunlight streamed in through the final access ramp illuminating another temporary sign hanging from a chain across the base of the ramp. It read 'Closed for Essential Maintenance.' Darry broke the silence.

"University boy, get out and move the chain out of the way, then get back in here when you've put it back. I want you where I can see you." He tapped the outside of the pocket containing Det. Con. Ben Wiper's Glock. James swallowed hard and climbed out. He did as he was ordered. Darry drove forward onto the ramp. James replaced the chain across the base of the ramp before getting back into the Range Rover. Darry hill-started it and slowly moved the car forward. It emerged into blinding sunlight on the rooftop. James shielded his eyes. Bright sunlight was no friend of his.

Unsurprisingly, there were no other vehicles on the exposed roof. A low wall ran along all edges of an oddly-repaired surface bearing worn, marked, parking spaces that made a Battenberg pattern on the top of the building. Darry drove slowly and with purpose to the south end of the roof. He stopped the car and looked out of the side window. In the back seat, James moved to the same side to see. Across the rooftops there were chimneys, TV aerials and telephone cables as could be expected. James lowered his vision to the millionaire's playground below. Vast, cream-fronted terraced mansions with railings lining steps up to perfectly glossed doors under Roman triangles held up by pillars. Scanning the houses in the street behind, he spotted some human activity in the wide courtyard of the end house that was double the width of the others. That house had a rear entrance every bit as classy as the fronts of its neighbours. Either side of the doorway and outside the gate were men in suits. That was the place he was supposed to be attending that morning.

"This gives us a brilliant view of proceedings. Don't you think, University boy? Just far enough away to be out of danger, but near enough to smell the fucking barbecue."

"You really are one sick bastard, you know that?" said James who no longer saw any need to tread carefully with Darry.

"You watch your lip, you wee shite. I'll fucking waste you soon as look at you, so I would."

"You're just a homicidal maniac, Darry. You kill people, that's all. You don't have a cause to kill for, nothing that you love enough. You only hate and that's out-of-date now. You're a dinosaur, you're extinct."

381

Darry turned in his seat to face James. His eyes narrowed and his voice lowered. He opened the side window and began gently tapping the glass of the wing mirror with his fingernails. There was no cobweb visible but James remembered what Darry was hoping to achieve by tapping the mirror. When no spider appeared, Darry gave up and concentrated on the task in hand.

"I have important work to do here. When I've done all my jobs, all three of them, you and me are going to be having a serious chat, so we will."

A pause ensued. James thought over what Darry had said.

"Three jobs? What three jobs and how are you going to do that from here? Fire mortars? Throw grenades?"

"What?" exclaimed Darry, whose mood suddenly seemed lighter. "The device is under the back seat of that car with the English bitch in it. When I said I was going to shove a rocket up the arse of the English, I fucking meant it literally."

"That's one job, what are the other two?" asked James trying to sound nonchalant.

"You've hear of two birds with one stone, University boy, well I want to get three with this one. In a few minutes that back yard down there will contain all of them and if I'm lucky, and I know I am, I'll get to torch all three of them. It'll make the Brighton Bomb look like a Fermanagh tea dance."

James had understood the target to be Martha Lascelle. The objective was to derail the peace negotiations to inflame and provoke the British into committing reciprocal atrocities of their own. It now became clear that the house below was to contain the Prime Minister of the United Kingdom. What had begun as a plan to assassinate a little-known diplomat, without a role in government, had become a regicidal murder plot that would change the course of everything. James sat back in his seat to contemplate the magnitude of Darry's brutal ambitions. He was about to ask him about the third and final piece of his macabre puzzle when Darry sat forward in his seat and stared intensely out of the side window.

A shiny dark green Jaguar limousine swept up to the high wooden and metal gates of the courtyard. Some urgent muttering into the cuffs and lapels of the men in suits inside and out of the courtyard resulted in the gates swinging open to allow the car to enter. It stopped outside the ornate entrance to the house. The front passenger, a personal protection cop, no doubt, got out and looked all around the yard. One of the other plain clothes cops stepped forward to stand at the back of the car. No greeting party came from the inside of the house. The bodyguard opened the rear nearside door of the Jag and, in a navy blue suit, white shirt, blue tie and parade-standard black shoes, out stepped the Prime Minister. He nodded to the man who had opened the door and went from view under the portico of the back doorway of the Victorian mansion. The Jag was moved away and parked almost out of sight under the wall nearest to where James and Darry were watching from.

"That's one piece of the jigsaw in place," said Darry with relish. His eyes widened again.

"Here we go, our goods have arrived," he declared.

The other black Range Rover with the blacked out windows came into view. It stopped outside the gates as two protection cops stepped out and spoke to D.C. Henry Boult who had wound his window down slightly to speak to them. A visual inspection of the exterior of the car was carried out swiftly and they returned to open the gates. The Range Rover crawled in and stopped in the centre of the yard. Nothing happened for several seconds. Neither James nor Darry spoke until they saw a figure standing under the portico, a female, wearing black, loose-fitting trousers and black, two inch heels. She stepped out into the light. It was Lizzie Cullen.

"Fucking bingo! A full house," declared Darry, finally revealing the identity of the third of his targets.

James looked at her. He did not see the mature, professional police chief in a business suit. He saw the girl he had fallen in love with nearly twenty years before. The girl he had been in love with ever since, the girl he would always be in love with. Her hair was different, and the eye make-up was minimal, but there she was in the same bright sunshine illuminating the same slim frame and the same habit of standing with crossed ankles.

CHAPTER SEVENTY-SIX

She spoke into a radio microphone on the inside of her left wrist.

Darry wrestled a new looking mobile phone from his trouser pocket along with a slip of paper the size of a playing card. Holding the phone in the palm of his left hand, he looked at the paper and pressed the numbers into the key pad with his right forefinger.

James had limited experience of mobile phones. The one he had been using to make contact with Mahon was a basic model.

"What are you going to do, ring them to death?"

"Your University brain doesn't know enough. This has a button that makes it vibrate instead of ring, if you want it to. So has the one that's strapped to the slab of semtex under Lascelle's arse. So in answer to your question, yeah, I'm going to ring them to death."

He stared down at the scene. James continued to gaze at Lizzie. The other movement and activity in the courtyard held no interest for him. It was as though he was reliving their first kiss, when everything else in the world had ceased to exist. She was the girl who he had favourably compared to a summer's day and there she stood in the full blaze of a summer's morning,

"Oh there's going to be a fuckin' carnival down there, University boy. It'll go with a bang! a massive bang, right enough," said Darry, "just as soon as I get all my skittles in a line here."

His finger hovered over the key pad of the mobile phone in his hand. He felt the surge of empirical power, the life-or-death of other people in his hands, waiting for his skill and timing to end it all for those who had no value to him alive.

"It's not too late you know Darry," said James, knowing that he could not persuade this man from his course of killing people. "You could switch that thing off and we just walk away. Nobody has to die."

Darry snorted through his nostrils like a bull facing a novice matador. His hungry eyes widened as he smelled blood. He did not answer James. He appeared totally focussed on the task in front of him. It had been Kevin Harraley's idea, but it had been his plan. He had worked it all out, manipulated the right people, done his homework, planted the plastic explosive in Martha's car and picked his moment with deadly precision.

Martha remained in the Range Rover parked in the middle of the courtyard of the Kensington Mansion. The cop in the driving seat and the others nearby would just be extra casualties of the main multiple assassinations.

James also looked into the courtyard but his emotions could not have been more different. He felt a bittersweet poignancy about this scene.

"You should be near those you love the most at the moment you die. You can't ask for more than that. That's what I think." It was as though he was somewhere else, adrift from the here-and-now.

"You've lost your mind, University boy," said Darry without looking at him.

The shoes of a man came into view in the doorway of the house. Shiny, black and of parade-standard.

"Come on, come on you bastard," urged Darry, almost certain that the Prime Minister was about to emerge from the house and into his view. When he appeared, Martha Lascelle would start to get out of the car and Elizabeth Cullen, the bitch who had put him in the Maze, was going to get it too.

"Come on . . . " his finger began to waver over the tiny phone keypad, " . . . Come on!"

The P.M. stepped into view and Lizzie Cullen stepped forward with him accompanied by the P.M.s own protection officer.

Darry sucked in air and pushed the final number into the keypad. The connection between the phones began. There was silence. The P.M. approached the side of the car. Henry Boult climbed out and went to the rear door to open it. The signal on the tiny screen of the phone read 'Connecting.' All three of Darry's victims closed in on each other and on the bomb hidden beneath the seat of the huge car. Henry reached for the door handle. He squeezed it and unclicked the door. It opened slightly then it stopped. Henry adjusted his position to get out of the way before opening the door fully. Martha's stiletto-heeled shoe appeared, it landed on the gravelled ground and her head emerged. With an earnest and statesman-like benignity, the Prime Minister stepped forward and offered an outstretched hand of greeting. Martha held out her hand whilst still standing by the open door of the car. Lizzie stopped three feet from the car, looking around herself with nervous vigilance.

"Connect, for fuck's sake, connect!" Darry ordered the remote and inanimate phone to receive the call he had sent.

James sat back in his seat as though none of it involved him anymore. Amid the silence came a low and barely distinct hum.

CHAPTER SEVENTY-SEVEN

Eye witnesses described the blast as being 'like an earthquake.' Others said it was 'like the Blitz.'

The destructive energy released by the detonation of a slab of semtex the size of a cigarette packet was colossal. Every window in an eighty-yard radius was shattered. Building rubble was fired into the air and landed on other buildings causing secondary devastation. The fireball scorched neighbouring buildings and the dust cloud flowed through the streets coating all before it in an unearthly layer of pale, grey building masonry. Black and grey billowing smoke, fuelled by diesel oil, repelled all but the fully committed as the emergency services tried to restore order and normality to a shocked and uncomprehending world.

At the epicentre of this chaos, among the running, screaming and desperate swathes of humanity, shrouded in all of its vulnerability, lay a mass of twisted and wildly misshapen metal, burning rubber and fuel. This object, no-longer mobile, a theatre of combat, a single rectangle of utter carnage, annihilated, a deathly effigy demonstrating man's innate ability to destroy and his unfathomable inhumanity toward his fellow man.

The breaking news on television channels kept a constantly rising tally of casualties, which was largely guesswork for the first six hours after the blast. When the fire was eventually brought under control, the task of making the buildings safe for investigation teams to approach and find the answers could begin. It was the seven o'clock television news that first delivered these statistics. They turned out to be accurate.

Injuries: Forty-seven people. Eighteen still detained in hospital. Two described as stable but poorly. Most of the injuries were sustained by smoke inhalation, falling debris and flying glass.

Fatalities: Two.

The rear courtyard of the Kensington Mansion resembled a post-apocalyptic scape of off-white, barren nothingness. A Jaguar limousine which, under the grey layer of hard-core icing was green, sat as though it had left for decades. In front of it sat a Range Rover, intact but also beneath a crust of grey. Incident preservation cordon tape flickered in the barely noticeable breeze.

Sixty-five metres away, in a wide alley sat the chassis and surrounding scorched ground of the seat of the blast. It had been a Range Rover. The emergency services together with forensic scene investigators had recovered the remains of two men, one from the driver's seat and another from the rear seat. Tests were being carried out to identify the dead men.

The Prime Minister, together with the diplomat Martha Lascelle, had been taken with rough haste into the house within seconds of the explosion. The chief security officer, Detective Superintendent Elizabeth Cullen of the Metropolitan Police Special Branch, and several members the P.M.s own protection team, had placed vehicles at the front of the house which had shielded them from the blast. The dual-positioning of the police vehicles had been detailed on page five of Lizzie Cullen's security planning document. The P.M. and Mrs Lascelle were taken straight to Downing Street. An emergency cabinet meeting was called but was poorly attended due to summer recess and difficulty in travelling to No. 10.

The question that had been asked at the first of three major incident briefings that Lizzie had attended during the day of what was being called the Kensington Bomb was; Why had James Patrick Coleman failed to attend the rendezvous, despite being transported by one of her own team? The next question concerned Ben Wiper. The immediate conclusion was that Coleman had been killed by the I.R.A. and Ben Wiper had been a collateral casualty. A pained hush fell on the assembled police officers in the briefing room. Lizzie held it together long enough to issue some sensible instructions and to delegate roles to competent subordinates. Announcing that she had top-level calls to make and that she should not be disturbed, she retired to her office, closed the blinds, locked the door and sat at her desk. She pushed back her chair and slipped to the floor on her knees. She wept without restraint.

CHAPTER SEVENTY-EIGHT

Several hours later, Elizabeth was in her office when the news broke that the missing officer, Ben Wiper, had been found bound and gagged in a broom cupboard in James Coleman's hotel room. He was shaken but otherwise unharmed. He related the story that he had been struck from behind whilst helping the professor with his luggage, left open the possibility that it had been Coleman himself who had slugged him, or he had been hit by somebody else who had then kidnapped the professor to murder him somewhere else. Ben declined hospital treatment and went instead to the Special Branch office to be debriefed.

Finding Ben Wiper alive had brought some much-welcomed relief to the Special Branch Department and all other police officers who had known that he had been missing and presumed dead. There remained a hunger for up-to-date news about the bombing. Any source was to be absorbed.

The television in the corner of the police canteen was always on. Rarely was there a time when there was nobody to watch it. The regular news bulletins did, in the main, match the facts as the police officers of London knew them to be. The newsreader broke the latest revelation.

"The Kensington Terror plot has taken a dramatic new twist. In the last few minutes, it has been revealed that one of the two men killed in the car bombing yesterday was the I.R.A. fugitive Darry McTandlyn, the convicted murderer of a police officer who escaped from the Maze Prison in Northern Ireland after killing a prison guard in 1980. The other man to die was James Patrick Coleman, a University professor from Boston, Massachusetts. It is believed that the professor, who was born in Belfast, was in London trying to broker a peace deal to end the troubles in the province. The Metropolitan Police Special Branch are pursuing the theory that the professor was murdered by a splinter group of Republican hard-liners, who had been in dispute with the majority of the Republican movement, who were open to engaging in negotiating a peace deal with the British Government. There is no official comment on this from either side this evening. Meanwhile, early analysis of the scene of the bombing would suggest that the assassination of Professor Coleman was bungled, the bomb being activated by mistake and killing the assassin as well as his target. The I.R.A. have not claimed responsibility for the bombing."

Amongst the injured was an unnamed man who had been pulled from fallen building rubble. He had remained unconscious for four days and during that time nobody had contacted the hurriedly established Family Support Line to enquire about anyone fitting his description. A police detective was tasked with ascertaining the identity of the comatose man. It was only when the film was taken from his camera and developed that it became clear that he was a member of the Press. The film and photographic prints were kept in a police store to await collection when the owner was able to do so. Enquiries made at the offices of the Daily Tribune were impeded by the decision of the Editor that nobody was available to confirm that the injured man was a member of his staff.

A knock on Lizzie's office door was followed by the appearance of a member of the team deployed to search James Coleman's hotel room. He handed her a letter with her name hand-written on it, explaining that it was found on a table in Coleman's room. Lizzie waited until the search officer had left then paused for a few more minutes before opening the letter.

Kiki,

I need you to know that I am not a man of violence, I am a man of peace and I hope that the work that you, me and Ms Lascelle have done carries on to become the platform for peace that we all sought to establish. I would like to have been a part of that but I can't. If what I expect to happen has happened, you will by now know that I was unable to stop the assassination, but I hope I was able to change the target. I am sorry for tricking you, but I copied part of your security file then I changed the car registration numbers in order to divert the attack away from the intended target.

I have to tell you something else, something that will change your opinion of me but this is not the time for holding back the truth. Your father's murder was in revenge for the killing of my brother. I was there when your father was killed. That was why I had to leave for America. I am truly sorry for what happened to your family. Too many families in Northern Ireland have had that experience. I want, more than anything, for that to end.

I know that my actions could seem unhinged, but you have to know that I did what I did in full awareness of what was going to happen to me. The killer I know as Darry could only be stopped by this extreme action. You know, better than anyone, how dangerous a man he is. Don't think that my deeds are particularly noble or what I did was any great sacrifice because that is not true. Doctor Harry Braschert at Boston City General will tell you the full story, but I know that whatever life I am giving up, it was not going to last.

I have got many things wrong but my biggest regret in life is that I didn't try hard enough to find you. Losing you again, permanently this time, has been the hardest thing, but I had to do this. I hope you can find it in you to accept, if not forgive, my motives.

With love, Sid.

A year later, Lizzie went to the Protestant part of Belfast City Cemetery to visit her father's grave. She took what was needed to clean the headstone and refresh the plot with new flowers. Once satisfied that it was as Arnie would have wanted it, she placed the unused cleaning and gardening items in her bag and left through the main gate. She walked along the road and turned into the gateway of the Catholic side of the cemetery. After searching for ten minutes, she stopped, knelt down and used the remaining items in her bag to clean and adorn the Coleman family plot.

Once completed, she again put away everything and left the cemetery. An hour later, at the pond in Victory Park, she took out a small loaf of bread and scattered it on the water for the ducks.

■■ ▪

Also available on Kindle from this author.

This City of Lies.

It is 1959 and war veteran turned San Francisco private eye Kerrigan takes on a routine matrimonial case in which those involved are not what they appear to be. Events take a dangerous turn when he finds that he too has become a target, but for who? When he witnesses a murder, his instinct to survive takes over. Alone and struggling with the memories of his war experiences, Kerrigan must find the killer before the killer finds him.

The Governor's Man.

It is in the Fall of 1959 and San Francisco Private Investigator Kerrigan is hired to find a missing person. A name from the past evokes painful memories which force him to challenge his own judgement and question his loyalties. Cast into a complex web of deceit, politics, religion, theft and murder, he has to investigate and eliminate many suspects, each with equally compelling motives, to uncover the truth, catch a killer and put right an old injustice.

By Sword and Feather.

It is 1960 and San Francisco Private Investigator Kerrigan reluctantly accepts a job as a bodyguard to foil a kidnap plot. Whilst trying to avert a diplomatic incident, he becomes involved in an investigation into a murder with a bizarre yet familiar modus operandi. Made to relive old traumas of the Burmese jungle, he is driven by the need to avenge the death of an old friend.

Wasps Among the Ivy

When a sting operation to catch Manchester's most notorious drug dealer goes wrong with fatal consequences, detective Russell Warren gets the blame and is sent back to uniform in disgrace to work a beat that nobody wants. Stretched to its limits and dangerously under resourced, Heavem Hospital is home to the mentally ill, the handicapped, the addicted, the troubled, the vulnerable, the suicidal and the criminally insane. It is described to Warren as 'a disaster waiting to happen.' When it does, and with devastating consequences, it is up to Warren to keep the innocent safe from the murderous.

Track and Eliminate

When destruction and death strike the picture-postcard village of Eckscarfe, Inspector Imran Bhatta and PC Mel Sharpe are called upon to investigate. Inexperienced, ill-prepared and poorly supported, they probe what appears to be a tragic accident, but it soon becomes a much more shocking and demanding enquiry. They must follow every lead, examine every item found and challenge every witness account to get to the truth. Many suspects, motives, alibis and half-truths come to light, and yet the question remains. Who, in that idyllic setting, could be behind that murderous act?

The Blue, the Green and the Dead.

When a company fracking for shale gas are found to have caused earthquakes, the community forms a strong objection and large-scale protests follow. Amidst the protesters, one of them has a secret. An agent of a powerful player is trying to inhibit the fracking operation, but for different reasons. Highly trained, ruthless and a seasoned killer, he will stop at nothing to achieve his aims. Among the police lines is another secret, a cop with a past and the skills to equalise this situation.

Violence and rancour grow and deaths soon follow. When the anti-fracking campaign takes a dramatic and catastrophic twist, it creates a flashpoint that really does shake the ground beneath.

barryleesauthor@gmail.com